WHITE DOVE

WHITE DOVE

Adventures of Madam Mollie Teal

Catherine L. Knowles

DEDICATION

For all the women in history and even today facing adversity of the magnitude that Mollie Teal faced and overcame, I dedicate this book to you.

AUTHOR'S NOTE

This book deals with several unsavory topics from our nation's history during the time of the Civil War—namely prostitution and sex trafficking, child prostitution, brothels, rape, murder, slavery, and all the ugly realities of a nation at war. While this work in no way romanticizes or condones the atrocities of child prostitution, history does show that Mollie Teal was forced into this role at the young age of ten.

As an author and historian, my goal is to tell Mollie's story in an engaging manner, following historical documents as evidence. While I cannot change her history, I do hope to show that she, against all odds and horrible circumstances, persevered to make a successful and happy life for herself and those she loved.

CONTENTS

PREFACE

From April 12, 1861 to April 9, 1865, the United States of America bled on herself. Four long years of combat left 750,000 dead Americans—civilians and Confederate and Union soldiers—and had destroyed most of the South's infrastructure. After the Confederacy collapsed and the slaves were freed, the Reconstruction process began restoring national unity...a process that took many years and one that many will say is still not complete.

Mollie Teal's story begins here, in the throes of civilian life in the American South during the War between the States, the likes of which Scarlett O'Hara never experienced. Mollie was born in Bedford County, Tennessee, on August 20, 1852. Documented research shows she was a child victim of the Civil War. A court witness testified that he had seen her mother, Mary Smith, take her into Union soldiers' tents at ten years old, the age of consent in the state of Tennessee at that time. In the historical fiction version of *White Dove,* Mollie is seen fibbing about her age, making her twelve when she entered the soldier's tent, but historical testimony does show that she was only ten years old.

The journey of becoming a madam begins in Nashville, Tennessee. The commanding general of the Union forces had a problem with his men and their need to consort with the local women. He first dealt with the disease issue by rounding up the most-patronized one hundred prostitutes, commandeering a steamship, and forcing the captain to take the undesirables on the Cumberland River to Louisville, Kentucky, and drop them off. Louisville would not allow the ship to dock, nor would other cities, once they learned who the passengers were on board. Eventually the captain was allowed to bring the ship and women back to Nashville.

The general decided to make all prostitutes register, pay a five-dollar fee, and be checked once a week by a doctor. The money raised was used to treat the sick at a hospital for prostitutes. Sad to say, many of the prostitutes were just young mothers trying to feed their children during this most tragic time. This was the life that Mollie Teal, at the tender age of only ten, began to experience.

Research shows that Mollie was only fifteen in 1868 when she moved to Huntsville, Alabama, and bought her first Huntsville property on January 3, 1868. She had enough money to eventually purchase five properties, despite being a female when property was not generally allowed to be purchased in a woman's name. The 1870 census shows her to have been eighteen. She was rumored to be one of the owners and founders of Dallas Mills, a cotton manufacturing plant.

During these troubled times, one man became her captor, teacher, and tormenter. That man was Ivan Vasilyevich Turchaninov. Born in Russia in 1822, he served in their military, moved to the United States, and anglicized his name as John Basil Turchin. The US Army asked him to join as the Civil War broke out. Turchin was known by many in the South, especially in Alabama and Georgia, as a villainous figure for the "rape of Athens" and being the mastermind behind William Tecumseh Sherman's "scorch-the-earth-to-the-sea" campaign, which rained down total war against the Confederacy. Thus were the times that first shaped the notorious "Madam of Huntsville," Mollie Teal.

Upon her death in Huntsville, Alabama, in 1899, she bequeathed her large home and land to the City of Huntsville for a hospital. Yet not one preacher in Huntsville would officiate her funeral. Urban legends even suggest that Jesse James became a preacher and held her funeral services.

Her will was contested, and the litigation eventually went to the Alabama Supreme Court. The City of Huntsville ultimately won the case and used Mollie Teal's home as the city hospital for over twenty years. Today it's known as Huntsville Hospital, the nation's third-largest publicly owned hospital, with more than 1,800 beds and twelve thousand employees. We have Mollie Teal to thank for saving countless lives and bringing just as many new ones into the world.

During the annual Maple Hill Cemetery Stroll, her grave is the most visited site. Some claim that for many years after her death, never a Decoration Day passed that a rose wasn't placed on her grave.

CHAPTER 1

1899 COURT: HUNTSVILLE, ALABAMA

The Huntsville Madison County Courthouse is overflowing with spectators for the trial to settle the estate of the notorious Madam Mollie Teal. Judge Stewart is presiding—a loud, boisterous gentleman in his mid-fifties who forcefully rules over his courtroom. The case is being contested by an alleged next of kin, Celia Hall, a raggedy elderly woman bent on Mollie's estate, and other fortune seekers of Nashville, Tennessee, who were found by private detectives hired by greedy Huntsville lawyers.

The will clearly bequeaths her home, an extravagant eleven-bedroom Victorian mansion sitting on fifteen acres of lavish gardens and ponds, to the City of Huntsville to be used as a hospital. One of the final two witnesses today, the plumber, Terrance O'Reilly, a twenty-two-year-old dorky individual who signed the last Will and Testament, describes, "I was working on a clogged-up drain in a big claw-foot bathtub inside Madam Teal's big ole house, and in case you didn't know, it is the only residential home in Huntsville to have indoor plumbing. As I was leaving Madam Teal's home, Sheriff Fulgham was there when she asked me to sign the last-will papers. I was glad to help a neighbor. I signed right after Madam Teal, with the same pen; then two other beautiful women of the house signed it. I will always remember that day... you know...because those fancy women began to flirt with me." The courtroom spectators burst out in a roar of laughter and snickers, given his gruffly appearance. "Really...they did," the plumber professed.

He is released from the bench and walks down the aisle. The plumber smiles and thinks, *Let them laugh,* as he chuckles to himself and remembers the best day of his life. At this point, Judge Stewart takes this opportunity to call a recess.

The tension in the courtroom is at the highest level since the trial began two long weeks ago. Many of the witnesses who claim to be relatives of Madam Teal are largely discredited, except for Celia Hall, a woman who claimed to have been Mollie's cousin and then changed her testimony and said she was Mollie's aunt on her mother's side. Many of the men in the courtroom knew Mollie on a personal or, let's say, "professional" business" level. Rumor has it that a secret diary may exist, and they want to be in the room to defend their good name should this secret diary surface.

The courtroom deputy calls for silence and requests all to please rise as the Honorable Judge Stewart comes back into the courtroom. After the short recess, the judge approaches his bench, and he's well aware of the pressure as all eyes in his courtroom are on him. He takes a large, deep breath and inhales the tobacco from his pipe, looks around the overfilled courtroom, slams down the gavel on the old oak bench, and announces, "Court is now open for the case of Celia Hall, plaintiff, versus the City of Huntsville, defendant, regarding the estate of Madam Mollie Teal." He points to the defendant's table and says, "Sir Alderman of the city, you're up next. Do you have another witness?"

"Yes, sir, Your Honor, the City of Huntsville calls to the stand Mollie 'Sissy' Greenleaf." The room goes silent except for the sound of the nervous few who are chewing on their cigars instead of smoking them. The court officer opens the enormous, squeaky pine door to a petite woman dressed in modern, plush green Edwardian attire with a hint of art nouveau influence. As her skirt swirls around her feet, forming in fans like bell flowers, she saunters toward the witness stand, only stopping once to throw a burning glare at the deceitful, lying Celia Hall.

Her green hat draws the most attention, with a swirl and swoop around her head. The lavish brim sweeps around her face, creating an illusion of a hat suspended, as if by magic, on her head. It appears as a shapeless mass swathed in tulle and smothered in flora and colorful ribbon rosettes, with large lace veils giving an impression of the hat being extravagant and outrageous...a personification of Madam Mollie Teal's apprenticeship, which was always about getting every man's attention.

The woman stands in front of the witness stand and is presented a Bible by the court deputy. He gestures for her to place her hand on the top and then says, "Repeat after me, ma'am. 'I'—state your name, age, address, and occupation—'duly swear to tell the truth, the whole truth, and nothing but the truth, so help me God.'"

The woman scans the room to see which of the vultures from Huntsville are in attendance, and not to her surprise, many were actually clients of Madam Teal's brothels. David Overton, a short, squatty, overweight, dark-haired Huntsville police officer stands alone in the back corner. She also notices the large presence of newspaper reporters, with paper pads and eager hands holding idle pens, anxious for her first public words since the trial began.

She holds her head up high, back straight, chin forward, and with a confident, strong voice says, "I, Sissy Greenleaf, forty-nine years old, reside at 111 St. Claire Avenue, Huntsville, Alabama, retired business manager, do swear to tell the truth, the whole truth, and nothing but the truth, so help me God." She then turns and finds her seat, and with much fuss she straightens her dress to settle in. Then she looks at the judge as if to defiantly say, "Let's begin already."

Besides the city alderman, the mayor, Alfred Moore, a well-groomed, medium-built individual with a quick wit, also represents the city at the defense table and is the first up to question the witness. "Miss Greenleaf, as you know, I am the president of Huntsville, Alfred Moore...you can call me mayor if you wish. I represent the City of Huntsville in the estate settlement of the home in which you reside, at 111 St. Claire Avenue, and we all agree that you have every legal right to live there, God willing and with his blessing, until your passing." The mayor turns around and nods at the jury, defense table, and courtroom as if to tell them that the city just wants to do the right thing. "We also want to prove to the court that per the will of Madam Mollie Teal—you know, the one which you witnessed as to being the last and only will of such said deceased—it was Miss Teal's lasting desire for the City of Huntsville to take such ownership and use the said house as the city's hospital."

"Objection, Your Honor. Leading the witness" is strongly heard from the plaintiff's table before the mayor has a chance to begin his questioning.

"So noted," says the judge. "Defense, continue, staying in the boundaries of questions to the witness."

The mayor, focusing on his written list of prepared questions, slowly looks up and begins to walk around his table, closer to the twelve men in the jury box. "Miss Greenleaf, will you define the meaning of a *bordello* for the jury, please?" Everyone in the whole courtroom immediately straightens up to listen carefully to every word.

The witness slides up closer to the edge of her chair, knowing she must give the performance of her life, for this will be the only chance for her to get it right and tell the entire world about her best friend, Mollie, the woman whom she loved like her sister. Boldly, she leans forward and announces, "You may refer to me as Sissy for the duration of the trial."

4

The court reporter looks at the judge and says, "Record will show the witness will be referenced as 'Sissy' in all remaining documents."

"*Bordello* is of French origin, meaning a building in which prostitutes are available. The women in Huntsville referred to it as a 'bad house.' My question to you, sir, is, why would you begin your questioning by insulting the home which all of you in this courtroom seek to possess?"

Objection shouts come first from the plaintiff's table, and, not to be outshouted, the mayor also blurts out. "Objection! Have that comment struck off the record," he barks to the court reporter. As both councils approach the bench, he says, "Your Honor, may we go ahead and stipulate that we have a strong-willed witness, and I'm asking to please direct her to answer only the questions that she is asked...nothing else." The plaintiff's lawyer agrees as he leans toward the mayor, nodding his head as though to persuade him to agree.

Sissy sits high in her chair and puts her nose in the air as if to say she doesn't have a care in the world while she looks across the crowd flippantly and then to the jury. The big hat has the focus of every man in the room, which is exactly why she wore it...anything to keep the men's attention from the two battling counselors.

The judge listens to the two men and leans back in his chair, staring up at the ceiling while blowing out a big plume of pipe smoke and contemplating his response. Without looking at them, he begins to speak, "Gentlemen, you're asking to refrain the witness because you both have been told that she has a reputation of being a 'spitfire.' What do you have to say, Miss Sissy? Are you going to cooperate and not give these two a difficult time during the questioning and cross examination?"

Sissy rolls her eyes back and then directs her attention to the judge. "Your Honor, I can read and write, so if these gentlemen would like yes or no answers, I'd be more than happy to comply with written questions if they would prefer. If they are going to try and use their trickery and say something derogatory about Mollie, I won't comply."

The judge looks at her with a stern glare. "Are you saying you want me to charge you with contempt of court, Miss Greenleaf?"

"No, sir. If I may…I would like to request a recess to meet in your private chamber with the four of us. I know this is allowed. My father is Federal Court Judge Greenleaf here in Madison County. I am quite familiar with court proceedings." A collective gasp is heard throughout the courtroom, it having heard for the first time that she is related to a well-known federal judge. It starts with whispers and then reporters scratching down the details, sending runners back to their local offices and others to the Western Union telegraph station.

Someone stands up in his seat and shouts to the judge, "Let her speak. We want to hear her side of the story!" Others cheer him on, and just as many scream no for fear of exposure, for it was rumored that Mollie Teal had kept records of all her clients, and if this were true, Sissy was most likely in possession of this information. The sound of the wooden gavel hitting the bench has a thunderous-sounding effect that echoes to the very back of the courtroom and quiets the frenzied crowd.

The crowd goes to a hushed silence as the judge takes back control. "Another outburst like that, and I'll clear the courtroom, and you'll all be charged with contempt and spend a night in jail! This court is now in recess. Counselors…to my chambers! You, too, Sissy." The four left the courtroom through a dark wooden door located to the right of the judge's bench and a few feet in front of the jury.

As soon as the door closes, the room again erupts in speculation as to whether she will testify…or more seriously on many minds…what she might tell. No one leaves the crowded courtroom for fear they won't get his or her seat back for what looks like the show of all shows in Huntsville, Alabama.

In the chamber, the judge sits behind his tidy mahogany desk, packing his pipe and striking several wooden matches before he gets it lit. The pipe fills the air with a sweet tobacco aroma of cherries, as if smoking is the only thing on his mind. He stands up and leans forward on his hands across the desk with an agitated look on his face. "Let's start with you, Sissy. You have information both of these men want to prove their side of the case, and you have just shown us you have the capability to cause havoc in my courtroom. All four of us will have to come to an agreement before we leave this room. I will not go out there and have my court turned into a three-ring circus. So the question to you, Miss Sissy: what are your intentions?"

"Your Honor, I have no intention of making your courtroom anything but civilized and respectful to you and the other officers of the court. Mollie chose you, Your Honor, and the mayor as executors to carry out the terms of her will because she trusted you both. The two opposing sides today have distain for Mollie Teal and what she did to pay for that house and the fifteen acres it sits on. They only want her remembered for being a prostitute...not for all the good, kind, and wonderful things she did for so many. She never felt sorry for herself for being forced into prostitution at such a young age, but she made the most out of what life gave her without being bitter. It seems to me, since the two are fighting like starving wolves over a carcass, the least they could do is learn something about this incredible person and the generous gift she wants to leave for this city.

"I want it recorded as a matter of public record the true story of Madam Mollie Teal's life and adventures...the good, bad, hard, fun, sad, and happy times...things I know myself to be true. Many years ago, Mollie taught me to read by sharing her diary with me, I know every word in it. I will not speak publicly or slander anyone through hearsay only. It will be the facts and truth. I don't want to be put on the stand and repeatedly interrupted with objections, overrulings, sustaineds, or deletions from the record. I can sit there and say yes or no, and you'll never get to the real truth without allowing me tell the whole story of her life. I promise you gentlemen today, you'll be enlightened when you hear her true story."

The mayor speaks up and says, "I'm reading in between the lines here—so you're basically telling us you have information that could help us all with this case, but only if you're allowed to tell Mollie's story your way. Or you're going to be an uncooperative witness and use your daddy's influence to keep yourself out of jail for contempt."

Sissy perches up on her chair, throws her shoulders back, and says a resounding yes.

The faces of the mayor, the plaintiff attorney, and the judge all contort into a surprised stare as they now realize they have been outsmarted by this tiny spitfire of a woman.

The next day, the trial resumes sharply at eight o'clock, in a tightly packed courtroom with the smells of tobacco, cologne, and man-sweat, as the mayor calls his witness back to the stand. Sissy enters with style and elegance once again, just as her mentor Mollie would have expected. Her plush blue velvet dress has a very elegant high collar and a train that flows behind, her boots have heels, and her extravagant hat is more conservative than the day before, except that today's hat has two twenty-inch feather plumes from the hat's center and a golden coin attached as a centerpiece. The court deputy swears her in as the day before, and the trial opens. Sissy looks around the courtroom and knows everything she says today will be important to the legacy of her best friend.

As Sissy sits in the witness stand, she pulls an old, tattered photo from her purse and focuses in on the Civil War–era image with young, beautiful Mollie. As she swallows hard, inhales deeply, and closes her eyes, she knows she has to take the whole courtroom with her far back in time. Her eyes open once more, and in the next breath, she begins to tell the story:

"Being from the same neighborhood on the Cumberland River, in Nashville, Tennessee, Mollie and I met before the war interfered in our lives. Things were good. We were seven and eight years old when they moved here from Virginia, and on our very first day we met, Mollie declared to me, 'We both can't have the same name if we're going to be sisters.' She took her mother's sewing needle to prick both of our thumbs, and while pressing the two blood drops together—unlike me she was a churchgoer—she began to pray: 'Dear Lord, thank you for the many blessings, mostly for answering my prayers about a sister. I will spend my life watching over her. In Jesus's precious name, we pray. Amen.' Without skipping a beat, Mollie said, 'I think since you're much smaller and younger, I'll call you Sissy from now on. Is that OK by you?'"

Sissy, with watery eyes, looks out into the many faces in the courtroom and states, "I don't know how I got so lucky to be chosen by Mollie that day, but she kept her promise to God and always took care of me. She risked her life as a young teenager to find me during that nightmare we all went through here in the South…you know…the Civil War. Even now, after she is gone, she provides me with her home until I return to my heavenly home."

Sissy is gazing into the air as if in her mind she has gone back to that very first day. She tells the court the two met and shared each other's lives from childhood up to until they had first met. "I went first, as we sat out on the beautiful porch at Mollie's house, partaking in a teacup party. I confided to her that my mother was dead from tuberculosis and I lived with my loving grandparents, who owned a butcher shop. I never knew who my daddy was until later. They lied to me and told me my daddy was a no-good scoundrel, and they blamed him for my mother's death. I told Mollie that I hated my daddy."

As Sissy closes her eyes once again to share her story, the courtroom fades away to a distant moment in time. "Mollie goes next and shares that her daddy is the best man in the whole wide world and that they share the same almost-white blond hair. He is a teacher at the University of Nashville, and both his and Mollie's passion is horses. On the weekends, all of their time is spent at their farm in Franklin, Tennessee, as racehorse breeders. Mollie and I talked all afternoon until supper.

"Mollie was the smartest person that I ever knew. Even then she had read most of the books in her daddy's library, and once she reads a book, she remembers everything in it.

"Things went along great in our friendship for a year or so, until all of the talk of the adults was about war. Life as we knew it ended when Nashville was taken over by the Union Army and used as a strategic Western headquarters. My grandfather was taken away by Confederate soldiers, never to return, and things got really bad for my grandma and me. When the mean men in blue coats took over the butcher shop, sometimes they made grandma go into rooms alone with them, and she would always come out crying.

"Mollie's dad says our neighborhood is being ruined and turned into a neighborhood of ill repute. His plans are for them to leave Nashville after his job teaching ends. Anyway, the university is now a Union hospital, and the only jobs available are producing supplies for the North. Her dad is able to secure a job at Athens University, in Athens, Alabama, in order to protect his wife and daughter by escaping the war and the ever-growing prostitution in his neighborhood. Meanwhile, Mollie's aunt on her mother's side would remain in their house. Her dad loaded up several wagons with most of their household belongings and headed to Franklin to pick up all of their highly prized racehorses and moved with them out of the dangerous fighting area to the safety of Alabama. Mollie and I hated to say goodbye, and again she promised she would always take care of me. We were little girls and had no idea the magnitude of what we were about to endure."

CHAPTER 2

RAPE OF ATHENS, ALABAMA

After the court recess, Sissy sits in the witness chair again. She dramatically draws hard on her cigarette holder, which keeps the fire twelve inches from her face, and then blows out a long plume straight up to the ceiling to join the layer of thick smoke already hanging in the hazy fog. The air is stagnant and the southern humidity is high with the distant sounds of cicadas from the open windows. Sissy begins telling Mollie's story to an eager audience as she drifts back in time, almost like she's there.

The family arrives in Athens after a fairly slow journey, due to so many horses and other livestock. Also, there were two gun battles with lawless bandits out in the wilderness between the towns of Lynchburg and Fayetteville. Fortunately, the cowboys working for the family outnumbered and outgunned the thieves.

Upon arrival at the Limestone County Courthouse in Athens, her father stops to pay their new property tax and licensing tax on breeding horses, and Mollie jumps out of the carriage with her daddy. He grabs her up and places her safely back inside the coach. Suddenly her daddy hears a ruckus of men approaching up the street and tells Mollie and her mother to lock themselves inside their carriage until he returns.

Sometimes a bit defiant and distrustful of adults, and with no one noticing her, Mollie slips outside anyway into the nearby sweetly fragrant row of Elaeagnus bushes. Angry soldiers in blue coats begin to burn buildings, including trying to torch the courthouse where her daddy is still signing tax papers. She sees the men in blue uniforms cut the ropes of her daddy's priceless horses as the hired hands try to fight them off. Other soldiers begin to set the rest of the small town on fire. Mollie's dad comes outside only to witness his carriage on fire and all their personal belongings engulfed in a fiery blaze of smoke and ash. He is close to the University of Athens. If he can get his wife and daughter there, that's where he will take them to safety.

Mollie watches in horror as her daddy is caught in the middle of the dirty street and runs for his life from a large man dressed in a blue Union uniform riding a huge white horse. The man chases him until her daddy fatally runs head-on with his own stampeding horses. She screams at the top of her lungs as she witnesses her daddy being trampled by the frightened pack of racehorses. No one hears her cries for help. Her mother is outside the carriage crying as she watches everything she owns go up in smoke. Mollie runs toward her, screaming hysterically. She is sobbing about her daddy as her mother is now desperately trying to pull anything off the carriage and wagons before they completely burn. With fire everywhere, she suddenly realizes how futile her efforts are.

Finally understanding little Mollie's cries beside her, she goes into shock and collapses in the grass near the shrubs where Mollie hid earlier. Mollie is confused and disoriented and doesn't know what to do next. The bellowing smoke from the adjacent church on fire burns her eyes to tears. People run in every direction, scared for their lives.

Mollie pulls her mother safely into the shrubs. All of the belongings her mother pulled off the carriage to save from burning, crazed soldiers begin to pick up and toss back into the burning carriage. Several German-speaking bluecoats bring out all the Bibles from another church into the middle of the street and set them ablaze.

Mollie foolishly steps out from safety into the chaos when she sees her daddy's beloved saxophone case being kicked into the street. It is the only thing left of his, and she's determined to retrieve it. As her hand grasps the handle, she begins to run for cover when all of a sudden a strong man's hand clamps down on her shoulder. With no time to think and with all her might, she slings the case in the direction of her mother, and fortunately it lands well hidden in the bushes.

The grip on her shoulder turns to pain as she turns to see it's the large, overbearing Union soldier leaning off his white stallion, who just earlier chased her daddy down the street to his death. Although debilitating fear dosed with pure hatred is about all her eyes can see, she focuses in on this evil man's face as if to burn it into her memory forever.

The soldier isn't going to let go. Mollie hears screams from a woman as a gang attacks her, ripping off the woman's clothes. Desperate and so afraid he is going to harm her in the same way, she turns around and bites him with all the might she can muster in the tender area between the boot top on his calf and below the knee until he lets go of her.

As quickly as he releases her, from the many years of being around horses, she knows exactly how to get a stir out of one and make him rear up. She pinches hard on the inside of the white stallion's back leg, and he rears up on his hind legs and nearly throws the soldier off. Mollie then runs to escape from the soldier and the fiery flames of the buildings. In the bushes she finds her conscious mother, still in shock.

"Come on, Momma. We need to move, or they'll surely find us if we stay here. We have to go—now." She pulls her mother up with one hand, holding the saxophone handle tightly in the other. Mollie wants to find her daddy but knows it's too dangerous to stay around. They find safety in an empty backyard cellar, lock themselves inside, and hope not to be found. They listen to the soldiers outside talking in English and clearly hear, "Turchin said he would close his eyes for two hours to burn, rob, pillage, and rape this town. 'Burn everything to the earth, and teach them a lesson for resisting my superior army yesterday,' he said with his Russian accent, as he bellowed orders at us."

At sunrise the next morning, the smoldering smell of burning wood lingers in the air as Mollie pokes her head up through the heavy door and looks about, making sure things are safe outside. She sees no one as far as she can see, in any direction. The only movement is a collapsing adjoining wall of the still-burning general merchandise store and a still-blazing lumberyard. Mollie ducks back into the cellar to wake her mother, and she notices a shelf of apples, picks one up, and begins to eat as she notices how hungry she has become. The apples are so delicious. She makes a knapsack out of a nearby piece of burlap to hold the apples.

Her mother begins to wake as Mollie gently presses on her shoulder. "Momma, I looked around outside, and all the soldiers seem to have gone. We need to head to the university before it becomes too dangerous again. I know that's what Daddy would want us to do." Mollie pauses as reality again sets in. *Daddy's gone*, she thinks. Fighting back the tears, and with a painful knot in her stomach, she turns to her mother and tries to continue, "They were expecting us yesterday. They'll help us know what to do next... where we need to go to be safe."

Her mother is still in a daze but slowly stands and lets little Mollie lead her up the stairs and outside to the remaining horrors of what they saw yesterday. As they travel back toward the town center, merchants are picking up what's left after the raid of their stores. They are too busy to give any notice to a young child and her distraught mother. They make their way to what Mollie thinks is the site of her daddy's gruesome murder only to find that the area is empty of humans and her daddy's body is nowhere to be found. They push onward to where the nightmare first began, with hopes to salvage anything from their wagons or carriage. No such luck—only ashes and a few metal pieces that glow a dull-orange hue and stick up out of the smoking embers.

Suddenly Mollie hears a familiar snorting sound. It's Jack, her daddy's fastest racehorse. Her little arms wrap around this big fella's neck so tightly, as if she is clinging for her very own life. The horse continues to graze on the grass as she sobs and then buries her face into his big, broad, hairy chest while she wishes she'd wake up from this nightmare, but she knows all too well it's real.

Mollie and her mother arrive at the university atop Jack, with the saxophone case and a knapsack full of apples and nothing else. They discover that the university was damaged by yesterday's mayhem also. They spend most of the morning trying to locate the person in charge. At Founders Hall, they meet a kind woman who takes them to the makeshift infirmary. On the way she tells them how she singlehandedly ran the Union soldiers off with her shotgun. "I told them this has been a fine female college since 1822, and I'm not about to let some Yankee man from Ohio burn it down. They must have thought I was crazy. Either way, they were too chicken to shoot a woman. So they turned around and went back to town."

She introduces them to the dean, who is a patient with wounds from the raid yesterday. Mollie talks because of her mother's severe case of shock. "Hello, sir." As this beautiful little girl with dirty ash on her face and disheveled, smoke-smelling dress drew closer to the man on the cot, she continues, "My name is Mollie Smith, my daddy is…"—she hesitates and bites her bottom lip as if that would make what she was about to say not so—"was," she sobs, "Professor Harrison Smith, from the University in Nashville. This is my mother, Mary Smith. She hasn't talked since we arrived yesterday as the battle broke out. That's when Daddy was chased into the stampede of horses by a large soldier on a big white horse. All of our belongings were torched right there in the street. We have nowhere to go and nothing to eat. Will you help us?" Then she breaks down. The little girl puts her face in her hands and begins to wail in sorrow for herself and her beloved daddy, whom she will never see again.

The injured dean sits up and weakly speaks. "You are a brave little girl, Mollie. You and your mother will be in grave danger if you stay here. The Yankees are mad as hell because we resisted and beat them back two days ago. They'll occupy Athens, and they'll make the townspeople pay for resisting their invasion. You're better off back in Nashville, where the Union is friendlier to its civilians. Your father wrote me that he hadn't sold your house. Go back home, precious, and take care of your mother. If you plan on living through this godforsaken war, you have to continue to be brave, Mollie."

As tears streak through the ash and char on her face, she asks him, "How will we get there? We have no money. Please let us stay; it's very dangerous out in the countryside, with bandits who tried to rob us on the way here. Our wagons and carriage are burnt; the farmhands are missing. Except for Jack, all the other horses were cut loose or taken by the bluecoat men. We have nothing," she exclaims.

The dean's eyes lift as he speaks again. "I'm too old for this war. My plans are to stay with family in Chicago as soon as I'm able to travel. All of my horses are gone. I had plans of purchasing a few from your father, and I'll pay a good price for one now."

The following day, the dean, with bandages on his shoulder and arm, stands proudly at the stagecoach station giving Mollie the tickets for two. As she buries her head in Jack's side for the last time, inhaling his scent, Mollie takes the tickets and some money from the dean as payment. She and her mother board the coach bound for Nashville, Tennessee.

The sound of the striking gavel startles Sissy and immediately brings her out of the trancelike state that she has been in for hours. "My Lord, Judge, you scared the dickens out of me," Sissy says, in a loud unsettling voice.

"Well, Miss Sissy, I'm sorry about that, but it's time for me to go to supper. You can continue your story in the morning." The judge calls for the court to reconvene the next morning. Before she gets up to leave, Sissy looks around the full courtroom that's been in complete silence to find not a single dry eye and knows they'll all be back in the morning.

CHAPTER 3

BACK TO NASHVILLE

In February 1862, Nashville, Tennessee, becomes the first state capital to fall to Union forces, and it becomes headquarters for the Union Army's western theater. There are problems with the large population of prostitutes and disease. Refugees have been pouring into Nashville during the war because jobs are plentiful in the depots, warehouses, and hospitals, serving the war effort. The city is a much safer place than the countryside.

Nashville, with its very large transient population, has a flourishing red-light district. The most famous is Smokey Row, the neighborhood on the riverfront near lower Broad on Front Street. It is also the site of the home of the deceased Professor Harrison Smith; his wife, Mary, and his daughter, Mollie. Nashville becomes the first city in the nation to legalize prostitution. Memphis is second. Nashville's nickname is "City of Whores."

In the short time the Smiths were away in Alabama, Mary's sister and another woman moved into the Smith home. Starving, the sister and the other woman were reduced to prostitution. Mary, disgusted by her sister's behavior, says in a condescending voice, "You must leave. No kin of my mine will behave this way. My husband, God rest his soul, would never allow such filth under his roof. This is exactly why he took us away. Leave, all of you."

Her sister quickly packs up her belongings and yells back, "How dare you look down your nose at me! We women here in Nashville are starving, and they won't let us work in the factories or depots for money. What else were we supposed to do, precious Mary? The war has now taken your husband, like mine. You'll be in my shoes before you know it. You'll see soon enough." As she closes the front door behind her, Mary runs and locks it as quickly as she can. Leaning against the door, she notices the frightened look on Mollie's face.

Mary realizes it was her daughter's strength and bravery that got them back home, and now it's time for her to protect Mollie. "Now that we are back home, pretty baby, let's get cleaned up and see if we can find some of our old clothes that we left behind." She looks around at the mess of used bedding. "Then we've got some washing to do."

Shocked by what she just witnessed happening in her home, Mollie replies, "OK, momma, after the chores, can we do some baking? The house smells so good and makes me feel safe when you bake. Remember, I bought supplies when the stagecoach stopped in Franklin yesterday with the money from…Jack." Her voice fades as she thinks about her daddy and his favorite horse.

Mary sees the sadness in her daughter's face and says, "Mollie, we just might do that. The smell of baking just might bring this old house back to life. But for now, go get the washing bin. I'll pump the water and boil it on the stove. We must be aware of everything around us outside. We are in dangerous times."

Later that afternoon, after they pinned sheets, blankets and clothes on a line, Mary looks at the root cellar and gets a sinking feeling in her stomach. What if her husband's plan to hide some of the stores of food had been discovered? Finally she and Mollie venture into their old root cellar to see if the secret wall was discovered. With lantern in hand, they go down to find the cellar totally empty…not a morsel of food in sight. With her heart racing, Mary goes to the end wall and puts her fingers under the bottom of one side, lifts it slightly, and slides a pin sideways…then the same for the other side. The wall drops down and lightly falls forward. She and Mollie easily move it to the side, exposing the food they had left behind during their hasty departure for Athens. There are some canned fruits and vegetables. One bin has quite a few sweet potatoes, and there is a partial bin of onions and red potatoes. Over in the corner is a small barrel of apples.

Although elated at the find, Mary is somewhat disappointed. It is not nearly the amount of food she thought was there. She has to admit that she really didn't know what was there. She was always afraid to go down in the cellar and always sent her husband.

Well, it is what it is, thinks Mary. She picks out some food for supper and lays it aside. After what seems like hours, Mary realizes that she cannot get the secret door back in place. The pins just won't go in, and the hidden wall is obvious. Anyone trying to rob the cellar would notice it. She turns to Mollie and tells her that they must carry everything into the house.

"Momma, do you really think someone would come into our cellar and steal our food now that we are back home?" Mollie asks as she carries the last bit of apples in through the back door.

Mary quickly locks the door, saying, "I'm not sure anymore. This war seems to have taken all decency out of everyday people."

After visiting with the couple next door, Mary tells Mollie, "I'm so grateful no one has stolen our neighbor's cow. We're fortunate they like to barter for apples, so we just may have milk, butter and cheese. They say to stay inside as much as possible and try not to let it look like anyone lives here. Apparently, my sister had quite a few visiting soldiers, and we don't need them coming around here anymore." Mary takes a hammer and begins to pull nails out of two boards under the rug and continues, "We'll keep some of the food on the shelves by the stove, so if someone does rob us they'll think they got everything."

"Can we hide down there too?" Mollie asks.

Her mother shakes her head, no. "I don't think there's enough space for you and me to hide, and anyway, too many loose boards would move and squeak, giving our hiding place away. Even if I could get it to not squeak, how would we get the rug back over us? No, we will run out the back door to the cellar and lock ourselves inside it to hide."

"Last nail is out." Mollie watches as her mother hammers the nails back in and bends them flat on the back side of the board. "Why are you doing that, Momma?" Mollie asks.

Her mother looks up and says, "Well, Mollie, if someone pulls back the rug, the floor will look like all of these loose boards are nailed down. Now, start handing me the jars first—then the other things to go under the floor here."

"OK, Momma. Then can we bake when we're done with all this? I think I would like your biscuits and honey—or maybe gravy."

"Sounds to me like someone is hungry," her mother replies. "How about we save that for in the morning, and tonight I'll make cornbread with that last little bit of collards from the cellar? With sugar the way you like? Mollie, after dinner we will talk about the war, your daddy, and this." She lifted her dress to show the pistol on her leg.

After dinner, the two sit close together with only the light of one small candle instead of the oil lantern, which throws off too much light. They want to stay unseen.

Mollie begins first. "Momma, our house smells so good when you cook. Do you remember when Daddy used to tell you that?"

"Thank you, Mollie. Yes, I remember." Mary looks away and sighs, feeling her heart break even more. She knows there is no time for grief, just survival, and says, "You and I are in a very dangerous situation. Yes, we have our house and some food, but for how long, we don't know. We don't have a man around to protect us from the war and from all the bad people who now visit our streets at night. We'll have to protect each other. The guns your daddy taught us to use all went up in flames in the wagon except this one on my leg, and you've never shot it before. Here—hold it, learn how it feels, and remember all the safety precautions he taught us. Mollie, if you or I are in danger, one of us might have to use this gun."

CHAPTER 4

CORNBREAD MAN

"Mollie, there is one more thing I need to tell you," Mary says. "I have always told you that you are two years younger than you really are. Your daddy and I both thought you were an exceptionally beautiful child. Some men have inappropriate admiration for a young girl like you, but I don't expect you to understand that now, and I want you to enjoy your childhood. Your tenth birthday coming up is really your twelfth, and that is the reason you are developing so fast. I need you to promise that you will continue saying that you are two years younger than you are. You have some added protection with some that don't believe that the age of consent should be ten years old. There may come a day when being two years younger will be an advantage to you. I'll explain it more later..."

Mary knows that Nashville is occupied with many Northern soldiers. She thinks that some of these occupiers, from several northern states with an age of consent of twelve, may have misgivings, either legal, moral, or religious, and leave Mollie alone if they think that she is only ten. Even in Tennessee, where the age of consent is ten, many locals have convictions about such things. If it only stops one person from hurting Mollie, it's worth telling a little lie.

Mollie remembers her mother insisting that she was eight years old when they suddenly moved here from Virginia and never understood why, since she was certain she'd celebrated her ninth and tenth birthdays already. Or why she all of a sudden had an aunt that she had never heard of before. But her mother's tone when discussing such matters made Mollie realize there was no room for discussion on either issue.

Suddenly they both jump when someone starts banging on the door and rattling the handle, trying to come inside. Mary blows out the candle and puts her finger to her lips to quiet Mollie. The banging on the door gets louder, and she hears a man's voice. "Celia, let me inside! Why is the door locked? You can't be closed. It's Smokey Row. Nothing closes here. Open up, honey—I just got paid."

Mary and Mollie slip out the back door and head toward the cellar just in time as the front door is met with a ram of the man's shoulder and he's now inside. As she looks back, Mollie sees streams of light from his lantern through the windows. She looks over at her momma with her big blue eyes, frightened to death as they hear the man say, "Celia, where are you hiding? You finally cleaned the place up. Looks great. Where are you? Lookee here. You've got food, Oh my, this cornbread is delicious." As he reaches over and feels the warm wick of the candle, he wonders why Celia had to leave in such a hurry. The man takes the rest of the cornbread and leaves, pulling the door closed behind him as he shouts, "I'll be back!"

Another visitor comes in a short while later—much heavier because he makes the floor crack loudly as he walks across where Mary pulled the nails from the boards. He doesn't notice the squeak in the floor because at that moment his lantern lights up food on the shelves in the kitchen. He shoves the food jars and everything else on the shelf in a sack, and without saying a word, he quickly departs.

The two stay in the cellar until daybreak. When they come out and go back inside, the front door is wide open. The second intruder took everything, including the box of matches. The only saving grace is that the hiding place under the rug appears to have been untouched. The food they have under there now is all there is. Mary says, "Mollie, first thing on today's to-do list is, get some boards out of the shed and secure the front door so we can be safe at night...the back door too!"

That night, Cornbread Man comes back banging on the door. "I'm back! Wanting me some more of that cornbread—best I ever eaten." He tries and tries to push the door open. This time he doesn't get in, but just to be safe, Mary and Mollie are ready to dash out the back door. "I'll be back tomorrow night!" he shouts as loud as he can.

The next night, Mary leaves a pone of freshly baked cornbread on the front porch, hoping he will take it and leave. No such luck. He sits on the porch, eats it, and talks. They can hear as he rocks back and forth in the chair. Suddenly they hear the man as he loudly argues with someone. "You need to go on and get! I protect this house—no visitors."

That man makes it a habit to show up every night, always expecting cornbread, and he sleeps on the porch, chasing off Celia's old customers. One night he comes and finds an empty box of matches in the empty cast-iron cornbread skillet. The man gets the message, and the next night he brings matches, meal, flour, eggs, and bacon.

Days go by without their leaving the house except to get fire-wood and trade apples for milk next door. Although they are eating less and less, trying to stretch out the food as long as possible, it is getting dangerously low. Long days hiding inside turn into weeks and then months, until there is no more money and no food.

CHAPTER 5

UNCLE BILL

After not showing up for a few months, Mary and Mollie hear the man say, "Celia, I'm here, honey. Sorry I've been away for a while." To his surprise, the door opens, and Mary steps out on the porch to meet the self-appointed front-porch guard. He's a Union soldier, rough cut, but with a smile that says, "Trust me. You're not Celia," he proclaims. Then the smile on his face shows he is pleased as he stares at her chest. "You're much prettier than Celia."

"Celia is my sister," Mary says. "She is not here anymore. If you will get me some cornmeal, I'll bake you a pone of cornbread."

"Yes, ma'am," he replies. "That would be nice, but would you be willing to do what your sister did? I'll pay good money."

"How can you talk to me like that? I'm not my sister," Mary snaps back. "Get out of here, and don't you come back," she says as she slams the door.

The man can hear Mary crying behind the door. He smiles and slowly turns away, only to return the next night with some cornmeal. When Mary opens the door, she bursts into tears. Between the sobs, she finally gets out, "I guess in your own way that you mean well, but I can't feed my daughter and me on just cornmeal."

Mary looks the man straight in the eye and with as much strength as she can muster says, "We have somehow survived ten months since my husband was killed. I never thought I could say this, but you say you are willing to pay me…pay me if I do what Celia did for you? I'm almost out of food, have a child to feed…and we are down to eating the last of the pecans off the ground out of the back yard."

"Yes, ma'am. Let's go in and get down to business right now," he exclaims as he quickly walks toward the door.

"No, not here. Not under my dead husband's roof. I will meet you at your tent. How much money?" she asks. Ashamed, she can't believe these words coming out of her mouth.

"Well you're real pretty, and you're a first timer. I'll give you a dollar, but that won't buy you much in the way of food. Bacon, coffee, butter, flour—all of it is five times higher than before the war. The five guys in my tent are all disease free. Come back with me, and we will use only you and keep it that way. That'll be six dollars a week, enough for you and your kid to eat. What do you say? Come back with me? I'm anxious to do a newbie, and it'll be fun…you'll see." As he is looking her body up and down, he continues, "What's your name, anyway? My name is Bill, and my buddies will love to meet you too."

"Six," Mary exclaims. "What? I can hardly stomach the idea to allow one man to touch me, much less six." She stands at the rail and thinks she might get sick. Her pulse quickens, and the back of her neck is on fire; sweat drips down her spine. Then she sees Mollie's face peeking out of the curtains and remembers that she said to her that she would ask the man for food. "Let me go in and make sure my daughter is safe and remind her how to lock the house up while I'm gone. Bill, I'm afraid. What if I can't do it? I think I'm going to be sick, and my name is Mary Smith," she rambles on as he guides her to the door.

"You'll do just fine, Mary Smith. It's OK with me if you want to close your eyes and make believe I'm your husband. You can touch me tenderly like you did with him. If you have sex, Mary Smith, you might as well enjoy it."

Mary is in a daze as she walks inside. "Mollie, the man will give us food, but I have to go to his tent to get it, and it's too dangerous for you to go with me. You know how I put the boards across the door? That's how you are to do it when I leave." Mary pulls up her skirt and hands Mollie the pistol, saying, "You're my brave little girl. If by some chance someone does try to break in, you run and hide. I know that you know how to use this gun. If they find you… just shoot them. I'm not sure how far away the tent is or how long this will take. You get some sleep, and just know we'll have something good to eat when I get back."

"Momma, you take your gun. I have a knife," Mollie says as she holds up the blade and waves it back and forth and tries to look mean.

Mary kisses her daughter on the forehead. "You keep the gun. When I get back, I will knock on this side of the house wall three times, count to three, knock three more times, count to three… three more knocks. You then look out the window to make sure it's me before you open the door. There are men who are capable of doing bad things to women and little girls and I don't want anyone to see you."

"OK, Momma. Three different knocks of three. I can't wait to see what you bring back. Will you get some sugar? We can bake cookies. Please?"

Mary smiles as she shuts that door of her life and opens an unknown other.

Mary and Bill walk to his tent, silently most of the way, until she confides, "I went to my family and some neighbors earlier to beg them to feed us or take Mollie in because I can't take care of her anymore. They all said no. Well, except for Celia. She says that she'll take her, but she is going have to put her to work in the business. I'm horrified. Then she says I'll soon have to start spreading my legs and 'screw' people for food like all the rest of them. Is that another word for sex? I've never heard that before."

Bill's smile grows even bigger when he realizes what innocence he is about to enjoy in the tent. He wakes up the tent mates to share the good news and to collect the money. Mary nervously waits outside and starts to reconsider. "What in the world am I doing?" Then she feels the hunger pangs and thinks of Mollie's pretty little face.

Bill comes out with a lantern in one hand and gives her money with the other. "Mary, please come in and meet everyone." She takes a deep breath and goes through the flap of the tent.

It is daylight before the last one finishes. Mary feels filthy and can't wait to leave. She wakes Bill to take her home to Mollie and somewhere to buy supplies. "Bill, wake up and take me home. My daughter's alone, and I need to buy food for her."

Groggy, Bill wakes up with a hard-on and thinks he's dreaming and not in the middle of a war when he sees her pretty face. He wants more and is going to take it. Mary struggles, but he is much stronger than her small body. As he mounts her again, Mary thinks that she has never hated someone so much in her life as she does Bill now. She is glad to get out of the tent without being forced to do another round with all the others.

Bill agrees to take her home safely, but first he takes her by the mess tent and gets enough bacon and coffee for the both of them. She is more furious with him than hungry now and has to ask, "Why did you do that? Forcing yourself on me?" she shouts. "I performed for all of you like we agreed. And another thing: y'all smell like pigs. Next week, get a bath, or I'll leave."

He laughs at her and says, "You're officially a whore now. You have no rights. No one cares. It's a dangerous game, so get over it. It's the life you live now. Someone else will probably do a lot worse to you than what me and the men did anyway. If we can get a bath, we'll do it, but you bring cornbread. Now, let's get your supplies at the store. I have work to do."

"Will you continue to stay on our porch and protect us?" she asks with great concern.

"Do you really think I stayed on your porch to be some kind of hero? Once it was obvious Celia didn't live there any longer, it became just as obvious that a female who cooks and cleans did. Because of the locked doors, I thought you hadn't got in the whore business yet and you were probably clean and free of disease, so I just waited you out until you got hungry like all of the other southern widows, and you did. You came to me. Didn't figure you to have a kid though."

Mary's face shows her disappointment as she sees the price of the basic staples and knows she's going home with a lot less than she had anticipated.

Desperate, Mary succumbs to the life of a prostitute for food. Weekly she comes to Bill's tent, and one week asks for more money or more food as payment. Six dollars is not enough to feed two people. She asks Bill to bring more men into the group and to let her come to the tent more frequently. He says no to new customers.

One morning when she comes home, Mollie is missing. The house is wide open and in disarray. Luckily she finds Mollie with her friend Sissy, who lives down the street with her grandmother. Mollie tells her that a team of bandits roamed through the streets of the red-light district earlier in the morning and raided several of the homes. Mollie quickly thought to escape under the floor by reaching out with her long arms and carefully pulling the rug back into place before allowing the floorboards to drop into position. She had just barely slid under the floor into the crawl space when the house was raided. When she reached the outside wall of the crawl space, she kicked several boards out and escaped with her knife and Mary's gun without notice.

The next week Mary reluctantly decides to bring Mollie with her, thinking that Mollie will be safer. At first she has Mollie wait outside, but then Mary realizes it is just too dangerous and asks her to come inside after explaining, "Mollie, I do things with these men like what we saw Aunt Celia do the first night we came home from Alabama. I don't like it, but it's what I do for food for us. I don't know how to get a job or food any other way. I hate that you're here and that you have to see, but it's extremely dangerous to leave you at home alone anymore. I pray you are safer in here with me. I'm sorry to put you through this, Mollie. Please someday forgive me."

As she takes Mollie's hand, they go inside the tent. Mary looks at all the men as they see this pretty little girl given instructions by her mother to sit in the corner on a blanket and be quiet. "Don't look at her. Don't touch her. She has nowhere safe to go, and that's why she's with me," Mary defiantly says. Mollie has absolutely no experience or standard to judge whether what her momma is doing is right or wrong.

For over a year, Bill comes over many nights, usually with some type of food from the mess tent, and is relentless, pressing Mary constantly for sex at the house instead of in the tent, but she is adamant about honoring her husband's memory and makes him stay outside.

Mollie trusts her Uncle Bill. He protects their house and gives her momma money for working, which she uses to buy food. Sometimes it's hard to find food to buy, and Uncle Bill brings his food from where he lives in the tent. While Mary cooks inside, Bill allows Mollie to sit on his legs with her back against his big, warm chest. He gently rubs her arms and legs with great kindness as he tells her that she is pretty. She leans back against his firm body and looks up at him and says in a whisper, "I love you, Uncle Bill. You're like my daddy now." He wraps his strong manly arms around Mollie's tiny waist and gives her a good, loving squeeze and then keeps his arms rested on her lap while she continues to read.

As he gives her a piece of taffy wrapped in paper, he whispers, "Mollie, don't tell your momma I say you are pretty. I don't want her to become sad and think I like you better than her. Do you understand?"

"Yummy—my favorite," Mollie says as she jumps off his lap.

"I'm going to give Momma half."

"No, Mollie," he replies, as his arm catches her from getting away. "That piece is for just you, because I do like you better than her." He smiles at her and kisses her on the cheek. "You're more fun, but that's our secret, all right?"

Mollie nods her head in agreement as she unwraps the tasty candy. "Do you want me to read to you from my learning book?" she says proudly, "It's my friend Sissy's book. All my books got burned in the fire in Alabama, but I remember them. Do you want me to tell you about them?"

Mary comes out the front door and is pleased to see Mollie reading to Bill, a man whom she can trust through very strange circumstances. "OK, you two—we're having biscuits and gravy for dinner again. Sorry, but flour is about the only thing we can afford. The gravy is made with salt and water, not milk, since the neighbor's cow was stolen. But the good news is, I found sugar, so we're having apple pie." All three wear great big smiles.

The routine is the same night after night. Bill shows up after work, Mollie reads to him on the porch or tells him about her day with her friend Sissy as Mary prepares a meal. After months of Mary's visiting the soldiers' tent with her daughter, Bill asks, as he gently rubs the full length of Mollie's hair while she reads, "Mollie, how old are you? Does it bother you to come to the tent with your momma?"

"It did at first. Momma would always be sad when we came home, but now she's neither sad nor happy. I'm glad you put the lantern close to me so I can read while Momma works. It's boring to watch Momma work the same way each time. It's always the same, but I'm still glad we go because you always have food to eat. I hate being hungry, Uncle Bill. Oh, I have a birthday coming up at the end of the week, Uncle Bill," she blurts out, as she catches what she is about to say, "and I'll be twelve years old."

His eyes get big, and he removes his hand off of her lower back. "You're how old? I thought you were at least fourteen or so. *Going* to be twelve, you say?" He stresses the word *going*.

Bill is leaving soon for yet another battle and can't stop thinking of Mollie. How will he convince Mary to go along with his future intentions?

Sitting on the porch after dinner, Bill opens a bottle of whiskey and pours Mary a glass half full. "Try this, Mary. It'll relax you. You're always so tense. Go ahead—it'll help, I promise."

"I don't know how to drink that. Never had it before. Besides, I haven't been eating much. I don't think I should."

"You're no fun, Mary. Why do I come here anyway, to sleep in this stupid rocker every night to protect you and Mollie from this horrible neighborhood? And then I work all day. You and your stupid grief. You don't realize how good I am to your Mollie, and you never invite me in for one meal. Some people's guard dogs get better treatment and are even welcome inside. I'll just leave you to your misery. Say goodbye to Mollie for me. Nice knowing y'all."

He began walking across the yard when Mollie screams, "No!" at the top of her lungs. Mary is so devastated at all of this uproar that she takes the whiskey and drinks it in one gulp and swallows hard. If this is all it would take for her man guard to stay, then down it would go. Mollie runs to Bill and jumps up, throws her arms around his neck, and holds on with a death grip. She has to stop Bill from leaving. He is her only security as well as a means to get fed, and she can't let him go.

Bill is amazed at how easily his plan is falling into place as he leads Mollie to the porch. "Let's talk, Mary. I see you drank the whole thing at once. Silly you. It's going to hit you fast, I'm afraid. I have honored your wish and not come into your house up until now, but I want to sit on the comfortable sofa inside and hold your hand and Mollie's hand and not think about all the horrible battles I will most certainly face in the near future...I may not live to return. Can you give me that much, please?" he says with great sincerity.

Mollie looks down at her mother, "Momma, please! We can't let him go."

"Mary, it'll get cold soon. Am I expected to sleep outside here until I go away to battle? There're a lot of women in grief in this war who might appreciate having a man around to protect them more than you do, Mary. I think I'll be better off on my cot in a warm tent than on your porch."

Mollie lets go of Bill and desperately jumps in front of her mother, screaming, "Momma, it's my house too! I want him to stay! Remember the bandits? They'll stay away if they know a man is here. Daddy is dead. All I have is his saxophone, and it doesn't keep away the bad guys."

Mary slowly stands and feels the effects of the whiskey and says, "Let's all go inside. Please come inside, Bill." Bill is highly pleased with how the night is unfolding. He may just have a chance to win a bet with his tentmates after all.

All three are on the sofa holding hands when Bill states, "If I could stay in your comfortable house instead of the rocker outside, I would still leave very early to get back before all the men in my tent wake up. Ever since this war started, I'm good on about three hours of sleep."

Mary falls asleep much more quickly than Bill expects due to the large amount of alcohol she guzzled to keep Bill from leaving. Bill secretly smiles as he carries Mary to her bedroom. Back on the sofa, he has a perfect situation for the grooming of Mollie to begin. He begins tickling Mollie and says, "I'm ready for some fun and laughter. How about you, Miss Mollie? Do you feel like laughing?" Mollie squeals for more. As he pulls Mollie's favorite taffy out of his pocket, he says, "Let's play 'hold hands.'"

"OK, Uncle Bill. Thank you for staying. I promise my momma will start being nicer to you, and so will I."

"Since you look and act so much older than your age, do you want to play an adult game with me? But you can't tell Momma. She likes to play this game with me, and she'll get jealous if you tell her. But we will do it only if you want to play, Mollie."

"OK, Uncle Bill, I love games and you!"

"I love you, too, Mollie," he says, as he reaches over and kisses her cheek. "That's what you do when you love people. You kiss them on the cheek." She nods in agreement with a big smile on her face. "Sit over here on my knees, Mollie, and let me tell you about a game I know," he says with a sly grin. She obediently complies and straddles his legs to sit on his knees. She loves to please Uncle Bill.

"OK, are you ready to play the tickle game?" Uncle Bill asks.

"It's past my bedtime, Uncle Bill. Momma will be mad," Mollie replies.

"We don't have to play, Mollie. I can leave, or maybe Momma will play when she wakes up."

He completely confuses her about what's going on. "No," Mollie cries. "Don't leave. Please don't leave. I want to play your game."

Mollie says yes to playing the game with Uncle Bill. He puts her on the couch and begins to tickle her sides, and she immediately balls up in a fit of laughter as he sneaks in a kiss on her neck at the same time.

Mollie enjoys the game, and now it's her turn to tickle Uncle Bill when Mary, still drunk, opens the door and says, "Bill, it's...

ah...past Mollie's bedtime...mine, too. Are you coming to bed?" Mary falls back into bed and again passes out from the drink.

"No more reading or games for tonight. I'll take your momma and tuck her into bed. Do you think she will like to work for some food money tonight while she sleeps? Maybe they'll have eggs at the market tomorrow, and you can bake your first cake for me. How does that sound?"

Mollie's face is full of disappointment; she wants to play the game, and he'd rather go work with Momma instead. "OK, I'll play better the next time, I promise," she says, as she holds back tears. I'll help change Momma to her sleep clothes for you." As Mollie pulls back the sheets and covers, she says, "Lay her here, and I'll take off her shoes first. Will you make sure the house is protected while I change her? She is still out like a light."

"No need to change her," Bill says. "Just take all her clothes off so she can work better." When Bill arrives back in the bedroom, he is delighted at the sight. Mary is completely nude, and he has only seen a picture from one of the guys back at the tent of a totally naked woman since the war started. This was a sight for his sore eyes to see, and he says, "Mollie you go on to bed. I'll put the nightgown on her after we work for egg money. Now go on to bed as your Momma asked you to do." He touches her cute bottom and slowly guides her out the door. "Good night, Mollie."

Early in the morning, Mollie wakes up to Uncle Bill sitting beside her on the bed. He leans over and whispers, "I like you better than your momma, but let's not tell her about the games we're going to play. OK? She won't let us play anymore and probably won't let me stay and protect you. Do you want to play another game tonight after your momma goes to sleep?"

Mollie sits up and brushes her long blond hair out of her eyes. "I won't tell, Uncle Bill. I like to play games with you," she says, nodding her head up and down.

He places a piece of taffy on the bedside table and winks at her. "See you later, beautiful Mollie."

Bill is back at the tent when all the other men begin to wake up. He has half of a day's chores finished already and is eager to set the rules for the bet takers. All of the soldiers have extra money from a battlefield bonus payday, and they can't wait to spend it on Smokey Row. But to prevent disease, they have agreed not to stray away from Mary. They are to depart soon to Mississippi for the great battle of all battles, according to rumors of the day.

Bill wants to have Mary come as much as possible until then but also wants to challenge the others to use the money for a bigger prize. "Let's pay off Mary to give her consent for us to have that beautiful daughter of hers at least once before we depart. If I can pull this off, I get a fifty-dollar jackpot, and we can double Mary's fee from the agreed fifteen dollars for our last three days to thirty dollars. Anyone up for the bet?"

One of the men asks about Mollie's age. "She is twelve," Bill replies, "and the age of consent is ten in Tennessee, so we really don't need her mother's consent, but her mother will be useful getting Mollie's consent. Listen, men. We represent the US Army here, and I for one would be the last to do anything illegal or immoral."

The man who asked about Mollie's age says, "Well, the age of consent is twelve where I come from, so twelve is old enough. I guess I'm in."

Bill looks around to five grinning faces, all willing to participate. "You really don't have anything to lose. Go to your death for your country and know you just serviced the last virgin in Tennessee, or die with money in your pockets and let some Johnny Reb take it? You guys ought to feel lucky that I share my plans with you because I'm doing it anyway. Just thought I'd include you guys in on the fun. I know it's the whole paycheck and bonus. So what do you say? Are you all in? That's five dollars each to pay off Mary; then you each put in ten dollars for the jackpot for me... not mine unless I can pull this off. That's fifteen dollars total to play in my game, and you get all your money back if I can't do it...

minus the fifteen original for Mary. Mollie's birthday comes up right before we leave. That'll be the date. Good—by the looks of your nods, we're all in the game. Help me find some eggs to take there tonight."

Bill arrives at the house with the promised eggs. Mollie's bright, shining face makes it worth the extra effort. "Mary, you seemed to like the alcohol last night. Let's try it again, just not so much that you fall asleep." Mary doesn't like the taste but agrees with Mollie that she will be more compliant and therefore accepts the glass. Bill gives Mollie a piece of taffy, and Mary doesn't notice him wink at her.

Bill suggests, "Let's sit on the sofa, hold hands, and talk about the future. We're about to leave for another battle in Mississippi. Our commanding officer is a rich guy and gave us a battlefield bonus from the last fight. I want you two to have mine. Mary, the soldiers at the tent want you to come stay for the last three days, and they will offer fifteen dollars for constant availability. We don't know if after the battle we can come back here…that's if we live. I worry how you will survive after I leave, so I want to stay here with you two as much as possible and protect you before I go. We'll get any extra food we can to give you before we leave.

"Mary, to be honest with you, I slept in your bed with you last night. I'm not sure if you remember that or not. We broke your golden rule under your dead husband's roof. It was great grinding into you on a real bed instead of a cot. In my opinion, I think, since my buddies want to pay you so much before we go, it will be nice for you to offer to bring them here, and they'll clean up real good, the way you always like. It'll be safer for Mollie too. She knows the guys, and it's not good for her being around so many horny soldiers at the camp about to go off to battle. It'll remind them of home before they go. Mollie, we can get extra supplies, and you can practice your baking skills for us."

Mary is speechless. She had sex with him in her bed and didn't remember it. He is leaving. No more weekly money, food, or protection. What will happen to them? As she drinks the whiskey and holds out her glass for more, she realizes that he and the other soldiers are offering to help her as much as possible before they have to leave. She thinks that she would be crazy to turn down such a generous offer. She wonders how the circumstances in her life have left her so out of control and turns to Mollie to see how she feels about the matter.

"Momma, we don't have a choice. People want to help us. Let them. We don't have anyone else. It has been almost two years since Daddy died, and without Uncle Bill and his soldiers, we would not have survived this long. At least you'll be here for my birthday, the day before you leave, Uncle Bill," Mollie smiles.

Mary feels the buzz from the whiskey and asks Mollie to go to bed early while she and Bill have a grown-up conversation.

Bill turns up the charm on Mary by telling her she is the most beautiful woman he has ever met, and he begins to describe the different parts of her body that he had the pleasure to explore and enjoy immensely the night before. As he begins to kiss her with his tongue, gently at first and then more forcefully, he pulls her body close to his. Her husband never kissed her this passionately before. She leads him to her bed and slowly takes off all of her clothes while he watches. He too undresses completely, lays on his back, and has her straddle his face; she puts her hands on the wall above the headboard as he buries his face into the soft folds of skin between her legs and brings her to a level of ecstasy she hasn't experienced before in her life...total delight.

The rest of the night she is his to do with whatever he pleases. Around three o'clock, he quickly dresses and once again goes to Mollie's bed before he leaves. He touches her hair to awaken her and then begins to softly smooth it to keep Mollie relaxed and off guard. She loves him. He's her Uncle Bill, who protects her and her momma like her daddy did and brings them food and money. He pulls the blankets back over her and says, "See you tonight. Remember I love you more than Momma." Then he adds,

"Tomorrow all the soldiers will be arriving to stay here. I'm so glad you're going to be safe at your house and not at the soldiers' tents."

"Momma says I can bake you a caramel cake if you buy us sugar and butter and cookies too."

She smiles, and he leaves the room muttering under his breath, "I win…I win…"

CHAPTER 6

THE GAMES BEGIN

B ill tells Mary he is deeply worried about her survival while he is away. They only have so much time to prepare her home for safety before he leaves. He makes Mary feel like the most important person in his world and wants to be with her after the war and take her back to his family in Pennsylvania. Mary gleams like she hasn't since before the War started.

Bill loves giving Mary whiskey. She'd do anything for him now, and he knows she thinks she is in love and is almost expecting an engagement proposal for when the war is over…the absolute last thing he would really want…a whore from the South and her kid.

Over the next three days, Mary stays busy as promised as the six men rotate in and out of her soft, warm bed. Mollie happily bakes with all of the supplies the men bring into their home. Tomorrow is her birthday.

Bill makes a proposal to Mary that night in bed after he passionately makes love to her. She agrees to anything her lover asks. "Mary, the soldiers all love being here in your house. Before we have to leave in two days, they have bonus money also. You said Mollie was going to be twelve, right? They all want to double the amount of money you make—that's thirty dollars, more than you'll ever see working these tents—for your consent to have Mollie. I'll go first and be slow and gentle. She's already been letting me tease her a little bit and responds well."

Mary's in shock...the man she loves wants to steal her daughter's innocence and, even worse, force her to do it with multiple men.

"Come on, Mary. The age of consent in Tennessee is ten years old. Mollie is well older than that. You have to talk her into this, and then you'll have enough money to survive until we get back. You or she can't be with anyone else but us. If you don't take this offer, you will be reduced to taking her on the streets, and you know she'll get a disease.

"Look all around you. You know us. We only have been with you because you were new...you were fresh, and we didn't want syphilis or gonorrhea. You'll starve, and she'll be on the streets with just anyone. Do you want to starve, or would you rather talk her into letting us lovingly and with your help take her virginity?"

Mary knows Mollie is really going to be fourteen, and her breasts and hips have become those of a very mature teenager, but Mary is eaten up with jealousy that the man she is in love with wants to be with her daughter, who in his mind will be only twelve the next day.

CHAPTER 7
MOLLIE'S BIRTHDAY

"Momma, just like you told me, I'm twelve years old today. Is that why you made me take a bath? Is that why we went visiting all of our relatives and neighbors again? Aunt Celia doesn't want me. She doesn't even like me, and it's kind of like you don't want me either? Why don't you want me, Momma?"

"Food" is all Mary Smith can say to her beautiful young daughter. "They don't have any. I don't have any. You are going to starve. Simple as that. Not one family member, friend, or neighbor wants to help. Not one, and I'll never forgive them. Now, I have to take you home to a life I never wanted for you. If I take you back home to what awaits us, I feel sure you will hate me forever."

As Mary puts her face in her hands and begins to sob and cry, Mollie tries to comfort her. "No, Momma, I heard Uncle Bill say he wants to protect and provide for us while he is away. I heard him."

After spending all day trying to prevent Mollie from the life of prostitution by sending her to live with others, Mary brings Mollie back home to be taken by the soldiers, at such an early age. Knowing that there really are no other options, she makes the decision to give her permission. She repeats to them that Mollie is twelve years old, the age of consent in most Northern states and

43

well above Tennessee's age of consent of ten. She hates herself for being forced into this situation, but she also knows that it is the only way for her and Mollie to survive.

Mary helps Mollie undress out of her only nice clothes and lays her daughter back on the big stack of pillows. "Momma, where are my old clothes?" Mollie asks.

Jealous of the fact her lover has desires for her daughter, she invites Bill into her bedroom, along with the other five. "Mollie, tonight you're twelve and well old enough for any of these men to have sex with you. We have been paid thirty dollars today to consent to that, and that's enough money to help us survive while our soldiers are away. Besides, Bill tells me he's been teasing with you at night, and you like it and are ready."

Mollie feels betrayed by her mother but even more so by Bill, who must have revealed their secrets. She is not ready for or understanding of Momma's work for food. Bill walks up to the bed, clean-shaven, and drops his clothes to the floor. Mollie screams, "No!" and covers herself up with a pillow.

Mary ignores her daughter's protests as Mollie says, "I'm only twelve years old today. Momma, you said I was to say that I was only twelve years old. How is it helping me to say that now?"

"Honey, you are…really much older than you think. I'm sorry. Sometimes we have to do things we don't like, but it will be all right," Mary says as she lowers her head. "Bill, you have my consent."

Uncle Bill is not listening and apparently has no sympathy for the situation that the mother and daughter are in. He approaches Mollie and tells her it will be all right, and he won't hurt her.

"No!" Mollie yells at Uncle Bill again. "Momma…make him stop…Momma!" Mary is distraught and closes the door behind her. She takes a big swig of whiskey out of the brand-new bottle Bill brought just for the occasion of Mollie's birthday.

"Let the party begin, boys," Bill says. Mollie escapes…in her mind…to another place where they can't hurt her. Staring at the ceiling, she hears Uncle Bill say, "I win. I win the bet. I got the virgin for us before the battle. Pay up and put your ten dollars on the bedside table for me. My wife and five kids back home are really going to appreciate the money. Thank you, Mollie."

One by one, all six men have their birthday virgin, but she is not there.

CHAPTER 8

RUN, MOLLIE, RUN

Hours later, it's finally over. While they sleep, Mollie thinks about what has happened. Her mother sold her and the only interest her Uncle Bill had was the bet to take money for her virginity and give it to another family and not come back for them after the war after all. Why had he been so nice? Mollie is confused about it all as she dresses quietly and notices every part of her body hurts, especially her abdomen and the space between her tender thighs. She knows that she must leave for her own safety.

Mollie sees the world differently now. She's filled with hurt and betrayal and is angry as hell when she sees her mother passed out on the front porch, smells the whiskey from three feet away, and sees a half-empty bottle. *How could Momma do this to me?* she thinks as she reaches in her mother's clenched hand and takes the thirty dollars without regret.

"I put a curse on you, Mary Smith—no-good mother of mine. You sell me like livestock to the highest bidder. I wish for you to die." Then Mollie takes the remaining whiskey and pours it out on the front porch. She carefully lifts Mary's dress, unties the pistol and straps it to her own leg along with her knife.

Then the vision of fifty dollars on the bedside table comes to mind. She thinks to herself, *I was the bet. It's more my money than it is for a comfortable family away from the war back in Pennsylvania.* She creeps back inside the dark room, careful not to step on the boards that creak. She then picks up the biggest pile of cash she has ever seen and shoves it into her dress with the other thirty dollars.

As she turns, Uncle Bill grabs her wrist. With one quick motion of the knife, she jabs his arm deep enough that he has to let go. Mollie takes off as fast as her legs will go through the house, across the porch, into the yard, and down the middle of the street, faster than she has ever run before.

She hears Bill's loud voice shout from the front porch, "Mollie, you little thief! you whore! Get back here!" He starts to run after her for the fifty dollars that he thinks he rightfully earned. Mollie knows she can't outrun him for long, and she needs a place to hide, fast. First she thinks of Sissy's house, but her grandmother has soldiers there too. Next thinks of Aunt Celia, but she's mean and would make her do the same things as Mary. She decides to double back, cut through familiar backyards to her own house, and hide right under their noses.

When she gets back home, she removes the boards on the outside wall that she kicked loose to escape on the day of the bandits, slides inside, and quickly puts them back in place as she tries desperately to quiet her loud breathing from the soldiers above. Next, she takes one of the empty food jars and puts all of the money but ten dollars inside, with the lid on tight. She digs a hole with her hands in the corner and buries it in the opposite direction of her entrance and away from the loose boards in the house. That way, if she gets caught or robbed, she won't lose all of the money.

Mollie takes one of her shoes off and carefully makes a slit on the inside of the leather to hide the money she will keep to survive. So that she won't be noticed, she takes the dark blanket previously used for hiding to the far wall and rolls up in it to blend into the darkness. Then, if someone should come through the boards in the floor to look for her, hopefully, she wouldn't be seen.

Within a few short minutes, all the soldiers are up, and Mollie hears everything. Bill walks outside on the porch and yells, "Wake up, Mary! We need to know where the kid will go to hide. She stole my money, and I want it back…now."

Mollie listens and contemplates to herself, *Now I'm a kid again, and hours ago that didn't matter.*

The other soldiers began to laugh and tease Bill. "You thought you were so smart, Bill," they laugh. "You were outwitted by a twelve-year-old—a girl no less. You take advantage of everyone's weakness and fear, then she takes advantage of your greediness."

"Funny how all that works out," laughs another soldier.

Another wakes Mary, still sleeping on the porch, and brings her inside as he twists her arm behind her back. They all turn and smell her when she comes in. "Tell Bill where you think Mollie will hide with all his bet money," one says.

Mary says, "Bet money? What bet? She took my thirty dollars. I want her found as much as you do, Bill."

"Bill bet us all ten dollars each that we could get a piece of that young virgin tail, and we paid up. Then Mollie took the money, stabbed Bill, and ran out with his fifty and your thirty."

"Let's go find that kid," Bill says. "We only have until dark before we have to be back at camp. Let's hurry."

As Bill fires everyone up, Mary rats Mollie out, "I bet she went to that little girl Sissy's house down the street. The butcher shop is her grandmother's. We can check there first. Leave one of your soldiers there in case she should come later. She knows where my sister Celia lives. We went there yesterday on River Row. One other thing, Bill—she has my gun, and she knows how to use it, but don't hurt her. I just want my money back. She doesn't know what she's doing."

"I say winner takes all, and Mary, you're going to take me to her," Bill yells as he pulls her out the door by her hair.

As frightened Mollie listens, she can't believe that her mother has sold out even her probable location…again for money. It wouldn't be a surprise if her mother led them straight to her. Mollie thinks to herself that if she goes to sleep and doesn't wake up, then God must want her in heaven with her daddy. If not, then he wants her to stay in hell and wake up in a few hours after the bad guys are all gone to camp and off to battle. *Why did Momma stop taking me to church after she started working for food?* Mollie ponders as she drifts off to sleep.

Mollie is startled awake by footsteps but can't make out any noises, when suddenly light comes pouring in from the hole under the rug and boards being removed. It's Mary first and then Bill, both with big, bright lanterns. "Looks like a rathole down here," Bill spit in disgust. Mollie does not look in the direction of the lanterns, knowing that her eyes would glow like an animal's.

Maybe because it's a new day and a guardian angel is looking over her, but the chase for Mollie ends at that moment, when one of the soldiers yells down the hole to Bill, "It's almost dark. We've got to head back to camp. Give it up, Bill. She got your money. Maybe you'll run into her again one day, and she will pay you back," he chuckles.

Bill hands up both of the lanterns, and as he climbs out, he pushes Mary back inside, causing her to fall to the ground. "You're the whore that caused all this. I think you should stay in this hole and live like a rat," he laughs. He places the boards and rug back and then tells the men to add a heavy piece of furniture on top.

Mollie listens as Mary wails and sobs in the dirt, locked under a house in the red-door district of Nashville in the middle of the Civil War of the United States of America. "Why me?" is all Mollie can understand her to say. Around daybreak, Mary locates the loose boards and fortunately is able to move one enough to get her hand out and slowly slide the piece of furniture out of the way. The men may have not had the same animosity toward Mary as Bill did…it was not a heavy piece of furniture. She puts the boards and rug back when she leaves.

Unknown to Mary, Mollie got quite used to staying under the floor for long periods of time when Mary went away to work. It is OK with Mollie to stay as long as it takes for people to stop looking for her. She hopes all the soldiers that know about her having large amounts of money will all be gone by the time that she plans to come back out. Uncle Bill stuffed her pockets with taffy for two days before her birthday, and that's all she needs for now. She finds a jug of spring water by the empty food jars. Her body needs rest and recovery. She goes to sleep again until dark.

CHAPTER 9

MADAM MOLLIE

Real hunger wakes Mollie. It's time to go see Sissy. She hears no one in the house, but her mother may still be asleep. Cautiously exiting the crawl space, she goes straight to Sissy's bedroom window and starts to open it up but realizes someone is in the room with her. She waits in the bushes until that person leaves, and then she gives the secret bird whistle to let Sissy know that she is there.

Sissy walks to the window as if it's just another day and says, "Hi, Mollie," as she lights a hand-rolled cigarette. "I knew you'd come by. You have everyone in town looking for you. They say you're a thief. Do you want to come in and talk? Cigarette?" Sissy offers Mollie the dish of tobacco.

"No, no, no. What's going on with you? Who's that in your room? Why are you smoking? You're only eleven. What's happened?" Mollie implores.

Sissy leans out the window and puts her arms around her best friend, and Mollie flinches in pain. "OK," Sissy says, "I'll answer first. The soldiers that took over my grandma's butcher shop will only feed me if I do for them what grandma does. I got hungry. I do as they say. It's really not so bad. Not all of them are mean, and some of them are nice, but mostly I feel like I'm in a jail…grandma too. Here, have this chicken leg the last soldier gave me." As she pulls it out of her skirt pocket and gives it to Mollie, she adds, "Now tell me what happened to you, Mollie. You look terrible."

She waits for Mollie to quickly eat and even suck on the bone. Mollie puts the bone in her pocket to suck on later. Before Mollie can catch her breath, Sissy adds, "I know this, Mollie. You had a bounty on your head until the entire camp had to pack up and move on yesterday. That's why it's so quiet around town tonight. A new group will come in a couple weeks. Italians, I heard this time."

Mollie describes what happened to her on her birthday with Uncle Bill and her traitor mother, Mary. She wishes them all dead. "I'll help you, Sissy. I don't know how yet, but I'll come back around this time tomorrow."

Mollie sets off for Aunt Celia's, glad the streets are quiet for a change. Once she arrives at her aunt's house, it's pretty much the same…southern women at the mercy of men from faraway places, dressed in blue. On the walk back home, Mollie devises a plan for all three households to unite as one to protect one another and the children. Arriving home to a drunk and passed-out Mary on the porch, Mollie decides to sleep in the house and appoint herself in charge. After all, she has the gun and the money.

The next morning Mollie leaves early to buy supplies. The prices have gone down slightly since there's a surplus with so many soldiers departing, and she buys extra. Mollie then stops by Sissy's house to convince her and her grandmother to live with them, to team together to survive. As much as she hates it, Aunt Celia and her working partner are also invited to come to Mollie's house.

Mary finally wakes up on the porch and has no idea what is going on in her own home. Mollie quickly informs Mary of the what fors: "I'm in charge of this home, and everyone in this house backs me. Mary Smith, you are dead to me, and I have no use for you. You are a complete failure as a human being and as my mother. You did have the only gun in the house, and still you let six grown men attack and rape your twelve-year-old child while you got drunk and counted your money. The only reason I let you stay is that Celia begged me. I'm in charge of this business and will make sure that we have food and, with our numbers, safety."

Mollie reads the newspapers and now realizes the dangers they are all in with the rampant spread of disease. "First thing we all need is to see a doctor," Mollie says. "Before we open for business, let's go over basic rules. We will set certain hours and days of the week. We'll ask the doctor what to look for in symptoms and basic understanding of how to stay safe and healthy. Every man that walks in the door gets a health look-over. Some of them smell bad. May even want to wash their bottoms…what do y'all think?" By asking their opinions, Mollie established that all would have input and some say-so.

Two days later, the group of six is at the hospital for prostitutes in downtown Nashville. A nurse steps out and says, "Mollie Jones."

As Mollie quickly stands and takes Sissy with her, she turns and looks at Mary and says, "You heard that right, Mary Smith. I have a new name. It's because of you that I'm here, and I don't want any connection to you…ever."

The doctor walks in with his nurse, and their faces indicate they are surprised at the youth of Mollie and Sissy and look around for a parent as Mollie speaks up, "My name is Mollie Jones. I'm twelve years old. This is my eleven-year-old sister, Sissy Greenleaf. We were forced to do things with grown men we didn't want to do because of our parents and this war. Unfortunately, we don't have a way out of it without starving, and we don't want to die of a disease or have a pregnancy. A few days ago, I was the prize of a bet and was brutally attacked by six men. I am now in charge of a team of six women, and I want you to examine all of us and give us guidance on how to stay safe and healthy. Don't worry. I have money, and I will pay you for this advice and visit."

The doctor, who normally speaks with a cold, unfeeling manner, says, "Our lawmakers think it's acceptable for an adult man to have intercourse with a ten-year-old child. I find it unacceptable. Mollie, you are very wise to be of such a young age. This war has a way of aging all of us, including you. I wish all women would approach this necessary occupation with as much wisdom as you have."

After completing all six examinations, the doctor invites them into a room with a table and chairs and gives them their results. "Ladies, I have good news. Preliminary results indicate you are all disease free, which is a miracle in this town. None of you appear to be pregnant. I suspect it's the little amount of time you have been in the sex industry. I would like for you to come back once a week to keep an eye on your health. My nurse is going to give you about an hour class on the sex industry that I hope will help keep you all safe and alive."

Nurse Valerie puts on her teacher hat and is no-nonsense, blunt, and straightforward from her opening words. "Ladies, some of the things I tell you might just save your life, and we're going to start off with a diagram for you to understand your lady parts and Johnny's parts. Here's the female. This is the labia—in other words, your lips. The urethra is where you urinate. The clitoris is what makes you feel good. The vaginal opening is the hole, and the anus is what you call your butt. Common names for the vagina are *honey hole, crotch, cooch, snapper, snatch, cookie, muff, kitty, tulip...* or you can call yours whatever you like...my husband calls mine... the 'Lady V,'" she says as she giggles.

"Now here's a picture of a man's genitals. This is a man's scrotum, the bag or sack that holds the testicles. You may have heard them called balls or nuts. This is the penis, shaft and head, and where a man's brains are...just kidding. There's no proof that this is true, but I personally think it a possibility." She turns, smiles at the women, and continues, "Common names for the penis are *doodle, tool, shaft, member, rod, arm, ding-dong, goober, jim dog, prick, joystick, woody, johnson,* or *tallywhacker...*I call my husband's 'johnny.'" She turns again to the women. "Honey, y'all can call it anything you want...men don't really give a crap when they are fixed on you. And let me tell you something, and you listen to me...don't for one minute think you are powerless. If you use it to your advantage, you have more power between your legs than any man in this country...use it."

Nurse Valerie looks around the room and sees Mollie absorbing every word. Pointing at the pictures, the nurse adds, "Of course, this is his anus, the butthole...and another piece of advice, judging from what you have and will experience, you may think that a butt hole is all a man is. But, ladies, there are good men out there. Not all are buttholes, but when you do meet one, it's up to you to decide how big a butthole you want to work with."

She carefully rolls up the diagrams and continues on, "The reason I show you all this is that most prostitutes never even get a look at the man's parts. Her dress is being pushed up, and he's in before you know it. So, step one on staying healthy is to make it a habit to always look and examine his parts first. If it looks like something's wrong with it, you can bet there's something wrong with it. Sometimes you don't see anything, but it's better to weed out up front as many bad ones as you can.

"As you know, the point of the sex act for a man is to ejaculate, have an orgasm, or come off, and it doesn't have to get you pregnant..." Nurse Valerie tells them all the most up-to-date options to keep from getting pregnant and then concludes, "Of course, the best way to keep from getting pregnant is to talk him into wanting to stick his little tallywhacker somewhere else."

She turns to Mollie and says, "Mollie, you have nice breasts to be so young. Remember, you can't get pregnant or get sick letting them screw your boobies. You may be surprised to find that some think it's taboo and like it even better. And of course, there is the hand job, the mouth, between the legs, and yes, I probably know a lot more than a good Christian woman should, but the main thing, ladies, is that you cannot get pregnant or sick those ways. Explore your own ways to do the trick…heck, you may discover that in some cases you will be able to wiggle your butt and collect a coin.

"Another thing, ladies, that I would highly stress…get out of Nashville. The diseases are at a record high. There are madams in some cities that like to bring in traveling girls that are clean. I'll give you the name of a place in Memphis when you leave. I think it's a wonderful idea that you are joining together as a team. We have a morgue full of young women who walk the streets alone. If you do stay in Nashville, please do as the doctor asks and come back once a week. The Union Army pays for the checkup. They want everyone involved in the business to stay clean as much as you do."

Nurse Valerie looks around at the ladies and asks if there are any questions. Sissy speaks up and asks, "This one soldier was just too big."

"Oh, honey, don't you worry about that. Just tell him how big he is to stroke his ego, and earn your money another way.

"Let me show you what you need to worry about." She reaches in a cabinet and pulls out two big fruit jars and stacks them one on another. "Was he bigger than this?"

"Well, no," Sissy replies.

Nurse Valerie holds up the two fruit jars and says, "This is what will be coming out of you if you don't follow my advice. Any more questions? No questions? Then I'll see you next week…y'all be safe out there."

She turns to Sissy and, with a most sympathetic voice, says, "Honey, I didn't mean to scare you. You'll be fine. I have a hunch that Miss—or should I say Madam—Mollie is going to take very good care of you."

A few minutes later, the women are saying their goodbyes to Nurse Valerie as she gives them the address of the madam in Memphis and hurries away to her next appointment.

On the way home, the six women discuss the information nurse Nancy shared and giggle at all of her nicknames for body parts. Mollie says, "Sissy, you and I will screen all the johnnies before they get to anyone, and we will collect the money at that point."

"That's right, Mollie. Get the money up front. I learnt that the hard way," Aunt Celia chimed in.

Mollie turns to Sissy and tells her, "Sissy, you and I will do hand jobs only and always be together, never alone. We're too young for all that other…aren't we, ladies?" Mollie says, looking more at her mother than anyone else. Her face softens a little and she continues, "Truth is, we must all look after each other like our families did at one time. I hate that we have to do this to survive. You four will be the main workers. I'll keep us all as safe as I can, I promise. I'm going to start right now by sending a telegram to Fannie Walker of Memphis on our way home. Until we hear back from her, we'll operate from here for now."

None of the adults admits it, but they are all grateful that someone is taking charge. Now they don't feel so alone, ashamed, and isolated.

Mollie receives a telegram from Memphis and has another health check for everyone per request. Because the rail system is strictly for war purposes, she buys stagecoach tickets for six, and they pack up what they can for the trip. What they can't carry, they hide under the floor. The front and back doors are boarded from the inside, and Mollie exits through the floor, being careful to replace the sideboards on the outside wall of the house. "It'll be a surprise to me if no one breaks in while we are away," Sissy says as the six begin their journey to Memphis.

Their arrival at Madam Fannie Walker's on Memphis's famous Cotton Row on the riverfront is nothing like anyone expects. It is almost noon, and no one is stirring in the big, fancy house except the help, and they ask the group to wait in the parlor. All six notice the elegance in the house and suspect they don't fit in. Mary looks at their shabby clothing and says, "We don't belong here, and they're not going to want us. We better leave before they come in and turn us away."

Mollie shoots a how-dare-you look and replies, "You're not in charge here. I am. And we're as good as anybody else in the town. We're staying! We spent all that money getting here, and we are not wasting it." Just at that moment, Fannie walks into the room and says, "I like that take-charge attitude, kid. You're the boss of this crew, the one that sent me the wire? How old are you and you?" she asks as she points to Sissy. "I don't allow children to work here."

Mollie begins her new career with what will become a habit of changing her age to suit the situation she is in at the time and says, "I'm fourteen. Right, Momma?" Mary nods her head up and down in agreement. "Sissy is thirteen, but we don't go all the way with the men anyway. That's what these four ladies do—and only hand jobs for us."

"Interesting" is all Fannie can say as she looks at the health report papers Mollie has brought for her. "I have a boardinghouse down the street for you to stay while you're in town, and I will insist that you use my clothing while you're here. My wealthy clients like their ladies on the fancy side. You will meet some of the most influential men of the cotton industry, riverboat owners, and the officers of the Union, but no soldiers.

"Two weeks is all I can use you ladies for. Then you rotate to Madam Lou Wooster of Birmingham. She is a real hoot. You'll enjoy her spunk, and her house is right across the street from city hall, so you'll get lots of rich politicians, lawyers, judges, and businessmen. You will spend two weeks there also. Then you will move on to Jesse Case of Shakespeare's Row at the port of Mobile for two weeks. There you will find many wealthy international visitors, and sea captains frequent her place. Then you go home for two weeks and make the loop all over again. Men like variety, and that's why we keep changing it up."

Mollie and Sissy both succumb to going beyond hand jobs and into the world of being prostitutes with their family. Two years of being on the travel circuit begins to take a toll on all six, and a break is taken back home in Nashville. One day Mollie discovers old letters left behind in furniture in what was her daddy's office.

She immediately confronts her mother, saying, "Mary, I have tried hard to bring it in my heart to forgive you for forcing me to sell my body to survive, but now...are these letters true? When you forced those men on me, did you know that my daddy had a cousin in Savannah, Georgia, where there is no war right now?" Mollie screams. Mary begins to sob in her hands. "According to these letters, she wanted us to come there instead of Alabama. So, if I understand things correctly, you have chosen not to take me there, but rather you kept me in a dangerous war—and, even worse, prostitution? What kind of mother are you? Are you really my mother?" Mary sits silent and looks away, knowing that for Mollie to have a new life in Savannah, she wouldn't need emotional ties to her. God willing, she would one day have the chance to explain.

The next day Mollie begs Sissy to go with her to a better life, only to be rejected. "I can't. My grandmother won't leave Nashville for very long. She keeps thinking Grandpa will come back one day, even though she hasn't heard one word since he was taken away by the Confederate soldiers. I've learned a lot from you, Mollie. They need me to manage the business," Sissy says, crying. "Go, Mollie, make a better life for yourself, and leave all of this behind."

"I will come back for you, Sissy. I promise. I will come back and make sure that you are OK."

CHAPTER 10

SAVANNAH

Years after introducing her daughter to the prostitution industry, Mary sees Mollie off on a stagecoach to Chattanooga. From there she'll take a train into Confederate-held Georgia to Atlanta and another to Savannah, to stay with her daddy's cousin Lucy, who married English cotton merchant Charles Green.

After traveling on a train for the first time, and alone, Mollie arrives at the Savannah Station with her suitcase, saxophone case, and a little money she saved from working the circuit. The city seems almost normal compared to Nashville's military presence. The air smells sweet like the jasmine perfume some of the women she works with wear.

Mollie arrives at 14 West Macon Street on the northwest corner of Madison Square, to a Gothic Revival–styled home. The house has a beautiful cast-iron portico at the entrance, and on three sides of the house is a covered porch surrounded by ornate iron work. She walks past the concrete pond with goldfish, going right up to the carved, wooden, nine-foot front door. She uses the door knocker to announce her arrival and begins talking when the door opens. "I am Mollie, daughter of Professor Harrison Smith from Nashville, Tennessee."

As her breathing quickens, Mollie is a little nervous in front of the strange woman, who is the head servant to the massive estate. She begins to fear that she is not good enough to be here and will bring shame to this house. Exhausted from the long trip and perhaps dehydrated, she feels weak and lightheaded. Mollie finds it hard to concentrate and hands the woman the letter she found in her daddy's desk, mumbling, "This letter is why I'm here."

As she tries to compose herself to keep from fainting, a beautiful woman who looks like her daddy walks up from behind the servant to see who has arrived. Overwhelmed by the woman's striking similarities to her father, Mollie's head is spinning, and she feels her world go dark.

The owner of the estate, Lucy Green, and the servant woman catch her. Carefully they take her to the guest bedroom upstairs. The servant gently gives Mollie a bed bath and places her in a nightgown while Lucy curiously opens the envelope, pulls out what appears to be her own letter, and begins to unravel the arrival of her mystery guest.

When she awakes, Mollie is confused and not sure where she is. Does she hear someone singing as she slowly becomes aware of the feather bed with silky smooth linens? She knows she is in Savannah, but how did she get in this bed, and who is singing? The singing gets closer as Mollie sits up and stretches her arms above her head and asks, "Hello, who is that singing so beautifully?" An elegant, beautiful woman with white blond hair, just like Mollie's own, stands in the doorway, smiling.

In her hand, she has the letter Mollie brought from Nashville, the proof. "Let me look at you, sweet angel. I'm Lucy Green, your father's cousin. We were as close as brother and sister back in Virginia." Lucy pauses for a moment and, with obvious resentment toward Mary in her tone, adds, "Before he married your mother." As she moves closer to Mollie's bed, and with trepidation, she asks, "You look just like my Harrison. Please tell me he's alive."

Mollie shakes her head. Lucy already knew by the look of her physical condition that he was not. All she can do is provide comfort, love, and safety as she wraps her arms around Mollie's frail shoulders. Mollie long ago stopped her own tears of grief, but she knows that news of her daddy's death is new to her daddy's cousin, and she hugs Lucy back as hard as she can.

"This disastrous war," Lucy says as she shakes her head and looks away for a moment. Then she smiles back at Mollie. "You look so much like your father, with the sky-blue eyes and your hair and flawless skin. Did you know our family was from Sweden? I can't wait for you to meet my eight children. They're studying with the governess at the moment. Some of them look just like you, and I will do all that I can to provide for and protect you. Once you've had enough bed rest, I'll show you around our beautiful family mansion and tell you more about this part of your family.

"Mollie, I can and would like to provide the best of everything as though you are one of my daughters, and that, young lady, includes education, etiquette training, music classes, dance lessons, and ballet. Of course, we will have the seamstress create a wardrobe. Until then, I'll have the department store send some things off the rack.

"Mollie, you are going to love it here. Besides my family, my other love is God. Next door is St. John's, our family church, and we are very active, usually having a small group Bible study Friday nights here at the house. My worldly passion is our equestrian estate.

"Our entire family is crazy foolish about horses." For the first time in four years, Mollie's face lights up with joy and a big wide smile. "Oh my goodness, dear. I have been rattling on and given you no chance to talk. Tell me about yourself, precious."

"You love horses too? I love horses," Mollie squeals with delight and kicks her feet under the covers.

CHAPTER 11

ETIQUETTE FOR MOLLIE

Lucy and Mollie share their common love for horses with both swapping stories until they are startled by a redheaded, conservatively dressed young lady standing in the doorway without making a sound. Irked, Lucy snaps, "I hate when you approach me without making a sound." Embarrassed by her own poor manners, her tone changes to that of kindness. "Please, come in. Mollie, this is your private governess, Mary Roxon, of England, my husband's home country. Ms. Roxon is twenty-two years old and will be your full-time companion and escort, making your schedule and arranging all your classes. As I might imagine, you have fallen behind in your studies."

Mollie hates the name Mary but reaches out and shakes Mary's hand like a man, saying, "Very nice to meet you. I'll be a very eager student and appreciate all that you'll be doing for me."

As the teacher pulls Mollie's fingers out of a tight grip, she places them in a proper position with four fingers out for the greeter to clasp. Mary looks at Mrs. Green for approval while saying in her heavy British accent, "Today we will begin with etiquette, Miss Mollie."

Lucy's head nods in agreement, and she says, "I'll leave you two alone for now. I'm expecting tea guests downstairs in a few minutes, but first I'll send word to Rich's department store to send some things over."

As Lucy pulls the door closed, she blows a kiss to Mollie. Mary's body language changes, and her proper language falls by the wayside as she says, "What the bloody hell? I have been with this family for years, and they still treat me as an outsider. But you, a bloody Civil War survivor with a good story, drop in from out of nowhere, and they take you in with open arms, and all the little ones are clamoring to meet you."

Mollie interrupts, "We are family."

Mary either ignores or doesn't hear her and blabbers on mostly to herself, "Now it'll be on me to teach you basic manners before I can introduce you to the family." Shaking her head, she continues, "I can just tell you don't have any, and I'm betting that your table manners are a nightmare. If I could only find a husband, I could get away from this treatment." Mary Roxon freezes in place and says, "Family…did you say family?"

Mollie shakes her head up and down to confirm that yes, she is family.

Mary's body stands more erect and professional. "Please accept my apologies, Miss Mollie. I am so very sorry. I don't know what came over me. Please don't tell the Greens."

Mollie replies, "I won't look at you as an outsider, Mary. Not at all. I will look up to you with respect as I learn all that you have to offer me. Yes, I am far behind in all areas but never in my wildest dreams did I think I would be blessed with professional training by a governess. I am grateful for you. The past four years of my life have been a living hell since my daddy died. I'm ready to move forward and put it behind me if I can. Can we start?"

Mollie pulls the covers back, climbs out of bed, and shakes Mary's hand the proper way she was shown earlier in a gesture to prove she is sincere. Mollie met bitches like this on the traveling circuit and knows that she must keep her guard up at all times.

Mary stands erect and begins her professional training. "The foundation of proper etiquette is behavior that is accepted as gracious and polite in social, professional, and family situations. Good manners can mean the difference between success and failure in all aspects of your life. Knowing and exhibiting proper etiquette is essential to the entire civilized world. Being rude only serves to make you appear boorish and selfish. Rules for the family are respect for one another's privacy and belongings, don't interrupt, be on time for meals, use polite language such as *please* and *thank you*, don't yell, pick up after one's self, and mostly obey parents. Also, I would prefer you not be in your nightgown while I teach, so let's go to the sewing room. Maybe they'll have something that fits."

Mollie follows behind the governess as she looks about the extravagant home for the first time. She has never seen such fine interiors. Mollie hears the ladies chatting away in the tea parlor from the floor below as she remembers the cruel world of Nashville from a few days before. Mary talks with the seamstress as she begins measuring from the stride, back, shoulders, hips, and waist.

The seamstress raises her eyebrows across Mollie's large bust and says, "I have a large dress already made that might fit over these. Give me a few minutes to take in the waist and hips. People notice wealth through one's clothing, and a properly fitting garment is the key. I'll bring it to your room when I finish, along with undergarments and shoes."

Stiff-faced Mary escorts Mollie back to her room, where the staff has set up for her a quick bath and two formal table settings per the governess request for today's first lesson in basic table manners. "Mollie, please, have a seat." Mollie does as instructed as Mary shows her how to let one push a chair underneath you as you sit. As she seats herself, Mary very mechanically begins, "Wait until the host or hostess is seated to unfold your napkin. It is then that you can place it in your lap. When the meal is over, fold your napkin and place it to the left of your plate. Each piece of silverware has a specific purpose, and we will begin at the right and work our way around the plate. Remember, you'll always work your way from the outside toward the plate as the meal progresses. If uncertain, just follow the lead of the hostess. This is a fish fork, meat fork, salad fork, plate, napkin, place card; on the other side of plate, working our way out, salad knife, meat knife, fish knife, soup spoon, and oyster fork. The glassware is next. The champagne glass is at the top. White wine glass, sherry glass, red wine glass, and water goblet. To the left, back across the top of the plate menu card, ending with the bread plate and bread knife to the left of the plate. You'll need to study this every day before I deem you ready to dine with the family."

Without hesitation Mollie looks at the setting and begins to recite, word for word, "Wait until the host or hostess is seated, then unfold your napkin and place it in your lap...ending with the bread plate and bread knife to the left of the plate."

Mollie looks up for praise and gets the most disdainful look on Mary's face instead. "Apparently I am being mocked, and my services are no longer necessary," Mary says, quite irritated, and abruptly stands.

Mollie touches her hand, "I'm not mocking you. I have a good memory. My daddy said it was a gift from God. Seems like I never forget anything...the good or the bad. Because of this, I will be a very easy student and anything you want to teach me, I'll remember it. I would like for you to give me all of the books you think appropriate for me to read in my spare time, and I do mean *every-thing*. I am so far behind, and I have so much to catch up on for my age. I never dreamed of being given an opportunity like this, Mary. I don't want one minute to go to waste. Thank you for spending time with me," Mollie says with strong conviction.

Before Mary can react, there is a knock at the door, and one of the staff announces a shipment of clothing has arrived. Mary shakes her head in disbelief at all of this outpouring being given to a basic stranger, while she is only allowed to wear dark, unbecoming clothing. This requirement is common with younger governesses so as to not compete for attention from the man of the house. The house seamstress arrives with the tailored dress for Mollie, and then she chooses from the rack of items those that she can alter until she sews Mollie's complete wardrobe.

Later, Mary leaves an odd book on the bedside table from Mr. Green's most recent library addition, *Journey to the Center of the Earth*, by Jules Verne. She laughs, thinking Mollie will hate it or not understand it at all.

Mollie is served meals alone in her room all day, always being encouraged to rest and relax per busy Lucy's request. Late that evening, well after Mollie has finished the fascinating book, Lucy comes to her bed and kisses her on the head and then gets on her knees and begins to pray over Mollie. She thanks God for the wonderful blessing Mollie has brought to the Green family today, regardless of the rumors of the Civil War atrocities coming to Georgia.

"Mrs. Green, thank you for taking me into your home, praying for me, and teaching me. I've never felt so loved...not since my daddy died."

"Oh, Mollie, your father and I were like brother and sister. Call me Aunt Lucy."

As Mollie shows Lucy the book that Mary gave her, she replies, "Aunt Lucy, Mary gave me this book to read. Do you have other books that you think I need to read? I read a lot, whenever I can."

Lucy begins to laugh. "I wonder why she chose this book for you, with so many others in the library that would be more suited for a young lady as yourself. Tomorrow after your lesson, I'll tour you through the house, including the library, and I'll introduce you to my children. They are very excited about meeting you, Mollie."

Mary knocks at Mollie's door before sunrise and is surprised to see Mollie dressed, the bed made, and Mollie eager to start her lessons. "My, my, Miss Mollie is up early," Mary says as she looks straight ahead and as if reciting again. "Today we will continue with fine table dining and table manners. Remember to take your cues from the host or hostess. Never talk with food in your mouth. Don't cut all of your food before you begin eating. Cut one or two bites at a time. Never blow on your food. Wait until it cools. Scoop your soup away from you..." Mary goes on for ten minutes and then hands Mollie a book entitled *Fine Table Dining Manners* and concludes, "This is the gist of everything in this book."

"Mary, will it please you if I recite the rules back to you, to let you know I pay close attention? Thank you for this new book, and here is the book you gave me yesterday. I love to read. Mr. Verne is sure a great writer. Do you have other books by him?" she asks as she returns the novel.

"No" is all Mary can say.

CHAPTER 12

MOLLIE MEETS HER NEW FAMILY

Later in the morning, Lucy comes to Mollie's room, happy as always. "Good morning, sunshine. I hope the staff has kept you fed, and you're getting plenty of rest. If you're up for it, I'd like to show you around our home—and more importantly, Mollie, your home too.

"Let me start from the beginning. Charles is my precious husband, who came to America from Liverpool, England, at fourteen years old. He has worked hard his entire life, and he is now a successful cotton merchant and ship owner. We have three sons from his first wife, who died. When we married, I was twenty-two, and he was forty. We have five children together and another on the way. I hope this one is easier because the last delivery nearly killed me.

"Charles has been arrested and is now detained in Fort Warren, Boston Harbor, for acting as an agent for the Confederacy…his sister, Mrs. Lowe, too. They have no proof, and we have friends and family working on his release. They let her go, but did you know that she did have papers from England twisted up in her hair that she later delivered to Jefferson Davis? Charles's papers are in his red boots, but they'll never find them. You see, Mollie, every family has dark little secrets. It's called life during the war. Do you want to share with me your story? I have plenty of time today. You can tell me anything, Mollie, and it will not go any farther than me. If you can't talk about it yet, I understand."

Mollie listens to Lucy intently and can't decide what to reveal. How much is too much? She walks to the door and looks both ways down the hallway and then locks the door behind her. She looks at Lucy. "Are you sure?" is all she can muster to say, not sure how it will all sound once it is all said out loud. Lucy's loving smile and nod is all it takes. Unfortunately, Mary has a glass to the wall in the adjoining room and listens to everything.

Hours pass, and rivers of tears by both women create a solid bond of trust that will last forever. Lucy knows she'll have to be overprotective of Mollie with Charles's older sons, as all three are lady charmers. Mollie has to ask, "Why didn't my mother tell me about you? Why didn't she come to you for help? Why didn't she bring me here instead? No, she chose to deliver me to a life of hell."

"I never understood your mother's insecurities over your father and me as they are ridiculous and so unfounded. Harrison and I are the same age, and our mothers were best friends. We did everything together. Your mother considered our friendship incestuous, and she began plotting a move to Nashville, as far from the state of Virginia as she could get.

"I suppose that to keep the peace, Harrison went along with it and took a job at the university there, leaving me and the state of Virginia forever. They didn't even come to Virginia when I married Charles or when we moved here to Georgia. Both of our mothers and most of our family died of the bubonic plague, and we never saw Harrison at any of the funerals. Your mother banned any contact with me. He even asked me at one point to stop our correspondence. I'm sure it was her jealousy. It must have bothered her that you and I look so much alike. Do you suppose she was thinking of me when she put you through all of this pain? I hope not. That is just pure evil.

"I wrote Harrison that last letter, when I heard that Nashville had fallen to the Union, urging him to come to Savannah. It must have been Mary who hid the letter from him, because why else in the world would he choose Athens, Alabama, over Savannah?"

Afterward, they both sit silently for a long time, taking the time to absorb all the new information. Mollie asks, "Lucy, one more thing about my daddy...he said our last name was Smith, so I use the name Jones just to be different from my mother. Mother said that we were both wrong. What did she mean by that?"

"Mollie, my poor child, your family name is Teal, not Smith or Jones. My maiden name is Hunton, but your grandfather, who came from Sweden, was a Teal. That's your real name, Mollie. You're Mollie Teal. It's most disturbing that Mary would go to that extreme effort to keep him, and you, hidden from his family. We can talk about this further at another time. Let me give you the tour while the house is quiet."

Mollie says, "Thank you for the new clothes. They make me feel like royalty. It seems like such a long time ago, but my daddy loved to dress me up and take me to the university where he worked—as he would say, to show me off. He made sure I had beautiful riding attire also. My mother must be a lunatic. Sorry to keep talking about all of this, but it's all so new and confusing. Aunt Lucy, I would be honored for you to show me around your lovely home... my home too."

Lucy had obviously given the house tour many times before as she did it with such ease and grace. "Mollie, Charles spent more money on this house than any other home in the nation—$93,000 to be exact, competing with his brother-in-law, Mr. Lowe, to build the biggest in Savannah.

"Let's start at the front entrance, which has three sets of doors. The heavy outer double doors fold in and form a small closet on either side of the entrance. Of the other two sets, one has glass panels to give light, and the third set is louvered for ventilation. The woodwork on the main floor is American black walnut.

"There are marble mantles in each room in the house, the two in the double drawing rooms being of Carrara marble. Other original adornments in these rooms are the matching chandeliers and the large mirrors in gold leaf frames, which we brought from Austria. The graceful curved stairway with skylight above is a feature that I love.

"The library has thousands of books for you, and I want you to make yourself at home in here. Actually, it's one of Charles's favorite rooms in the house." The library is also the favorite spot of Mollie. She and Lucy spend some time there, selecting some books for Mollie to read. Next is the indoor kitchen; it's so nice to smell the food being prepared inside the house. Upstairs, Lucy continues, "This is the girls' shared room and the young boys' over here. The older boys have rooms down the hall. We have a staff of eight slaves to run our home that we all love as our family. Mollie is shocked and thinks, *I've never been around slaves, and I don't think I want to start now.*

As Lucy ends the tour, she brings Mollie into the spacious music room and has her sit in a very comfortable sofa while she signals the staff to bring in the children. As beautiful as a picture book, five adorable cottontop, blue-eyed children walk in a single line, with their music teacher following close behind. They are all grinning from ear to ear as they first lay eyes on Mollie. They see the resemblance to themselves and their mother immediately. One swoop of the hand by their teacher, whose husband is an officer in the Confederacy, and they all begin to sing "The Bonnie Blue Flag," a favorite marching song of the Confederate Army and a symbol of secession, self-governance and state sovereignty:

"We are a band of brothers,
And native to the soil,
Fighting for the property
We gained by honest toil;

And when our rights were threatened,
The cry rose near and far—
Hurrah for the Bonnie Blue Flag
That bears a single star!

"Hurrah! Hurrah!
For Southern rights, hurrah!
Hurrah for the Bonnie Blue Flag
that bears a single star.

"As long as the Union
Was faithful to her trust,
Like friends and like brothers
Both kind were we and just;
But now, when Northern treachery
Attempts our rights to mar,
We hoist on high the Bonnie Blue Flag
That bears a single star.

"Hurrah! Hurrah!"

They continue until they have sung the entire song.

When they finish, the room is eerily silent as Mollie follows Lucy's cue and claps joyfully to smiling faces. Lucy then asks them to come and meet their cousin Mollie. The smallest, Lucy, is the first one to climb in Mollie's lap and touch her hair. "You're beautiful and look just like mother. I'm four," little Lucy says as she shows her four tiny fingers. "My name is Lucy." Then she wraps her little arms around Mollie's neck. Anna, seven, and Douglas, eight, are right behind Lucy, wanting to see and touch a relative whom they didn't know about and who oddly looks as beautiful as they do.

"We are excited to finally meet you, Mollie," Anna giggles and curtsies, while Douglas hands her a single daisy from the garden.

Gilbert, twelve, and Edward, ten, step forward and properly shake her hand but are both suddenly too shy to speak.

"Children, Mollie's dad and I were first cousins, which makes you second cousins. She's family and going to be living here with us from now on. She's one of us," Lucy says, with so much happiness that the children jump up and down and clap their hands, cheering. Overwhelmed and unable to control how she feels and with tears pouring down her face, she embraces all six and lets their love fill her empty soul.

"When our father gets home, he'll love you as much as we do, Mollie," says a smiling Edward.

Across the room, sour-faced Mary whispers into the music teacher's ear, "She's an outsider, and it is up to us to protect the children until we get to know more about this stranger. Mrs. Green is too gullible to make wise decisions while Mr. Green is away." The teacher nods, knowing that the governess is in complete control of the children's daily schedule of activities and lessons, but more importantly she has the ability to make life difficult for all the household staff.

"We can use this as an opportunity to teach the children not to trust strangers so readily as their mother does. Plant seeds of doubt about Mollie in your music classes. She'll soon be joining you," Mary orders. Mary spends the day giving the same directions to other instructors and the house staff. Most of them are in disbelief, because—since Mollie's arrival, the house has been full of excitement, joy, and happiness during this sad time of war.

In the afternoon, Mollie is introduced to the three older sons: Benjamin, twenty-six; Charles, twenty-one; and Andrew, eighteen. Later, the close family goes to worship at the church next door. Mollie finds such comfort to sit in a pew for the first time in years, this time with nine family members and God. Lucy looks across the full pew filled with her family, so pleased and feeling blessed; she smiles upwardly.

That evening, for the first time, Mollie is included at the family dinner against Mary's advice, and she fits perfectly in with all her newly acquired table skills, pleasing Lucy.

CHAPTER 13

STAR

The next few weeks go by so quickly, with Mollie establishing a bond on many levels with all eight children. Some days, Mollie takes classes with the others, but many days her lessons are private. At least four days a week, the family goes to the horse stables. Each child has his or her own horse and trainer. On Mollie's first day, she is given a short history about three different horses and is given a choice to pick her favorite. The decision is easy... Star, a shiny black thoroughbred with a white star on his forehead. Star displays a well-chiseled head on a long neck, high withers, deep chest, short back, good depth of hindquarters, and lean body with long legs and stands almost eighteen hands tall. He has been brought from England and is a trained show horse.

The trainer smiles as Mollie introduces herself to Star with a cube of sugar, loving the feeling of his soft muzzle and whiskers on her palm. She rubs his star and down the length of his nose and offers him another sugar cube before making circles with her fingers beside his eyes and on around his ears. Another sugar cube, and her hands move down his long neck and back up to the mane. She so wants to throw her arms around his neck and take in his smell, but she knows to continue trust building first. With his brush, she takes the time to go over every inch of him, making use of periodic cubes of sugar.

The trainer watches as Star doesn't stammer or switch his legs. He stands still and snorts a few exhales with his eyes closed as she moves her hands from his legs down to his hoofs. While using both her hands, she finally explores his big broad chest, making large circles as she moves in closer, bringing her chest to his, wrapping her arms up around his neck, deeply taking in his scent, and bringing their hearts together. Star lowers his head onto Mollie's back. Mollie realizes how blessed she is as she smiles, looking up to give God praise.

She turns to the trainer and asks permission to mount him. He recognizes she has obviously been around horses and says, "Miss Mollie, I see this is not your first time around a horse. I can see that you do have a natural way with horses, but you have been taught by someone."

"Yes, my daddy," Mollie replies. "He always told me that you have to become one with the animal."

"Well, he is right, and you do appear to have that ability. Of course I give you permission to ride, but first let me tell you more about Star." He brings her up to date on Star's many abilities of racing, jumping, and other obstacle-maneuvering talents.

Throughout the day, pregnant Lucy stops in to see Mollie's remarkable progress. Lucy is so happy to see Harrison's love of horses in Mollie's eyes as she watches, thinking how pretty Harrison must have thought his daughter looked in her English riding clothes and the boots he gave her. Mollie thoroughly bonds with Star and displays her riding ability, while Star...Star becomes a show horse again.

CHAPTER 14

BEN AND MOLLIE

Weeks turn to months as Mollie is groomed to be the finest of southern elegance and sophistication. Even though in the middle of war and pregnant, Lucy continues with her social and civic obligations, quite often proudly having Mollie accompany her to balls and elegant dinner parties along with the aloof oldest son, Benjamin. Lucy represents the family while her husband is away.

It has been months since Mollie's arrival and her appearance has changed for the better as her confidence has soared. She is well beyond her years in knowledge due to all the time spent in the library and on the circuit. Because of the light, the window seat is her favorite place to read. Oftentimes one of the other children would be in another window seat in a different room and wave at her through the glass.

Mollie enjoys getting up extra early and going to the stables to feed Star and muck out his stall. After a few mornings, she notices Benjamin is there early too. He usually doesn't give Mollie much time, but today is different, as he approaches her with a warm, friendly smile. "Good morning, Miss Mollie."

Mollie, also with a beautiful smile, continues to shovel manure out of the stall and replies, "Hello, Benjamin. It seems you like it here as much as I do to get up so early before your busy day as a cotton merchant."

"Mollie, it seems you're a victim of staff manipulation. I once had it happen to me, and I want you to know I see right through them. The problem is that Mary has dirt on me. She wants the staff to doubt your authenticity. She tries to put a wedge between you and the children. The younger ones don't fall for it. They love you wholeheartedly, and why not? For crying out loud. You do look just like one of them.

"Charles and Andrew are all about their future inheritance and don't want to slice the pie one more way...greed, plain and simple. Mary is exploiting their weakness. You should hear how they go nuts every time Lucy announces another child is on the way, practically wishing her dead. They forget she is the one who raised and loved us after our own mother died. Lucy tries to only see the good in people and overlooks their evil ways."

For the first time, Benjamin shares his caring nature, revealing to Mollie his true inner self rather than his usual cold persona. Mollie is surprised by his unusual openness and honesty and asks, "What kind of information do they have on you? Or me?"

"Well, Mollie," he sighs and hesitates, almost rethinking his decision, "They accuse me of not liking the ladies and preferring same-sex trysts." Mollie's past exposed her to such situations, but who is she to judge? She knows that she is the biggest sinner in the family.

"I am so sorry, Benjamin, that someone would put you through this anguish. What do they gain by saying such? What do they claim to have against me?" A question she will forever regret asking.

"Control and power," Benjamin replies. "Mary controls Charles and Andrew against me, saying my father, Charles Green, could never be my real father. You, they say, are a professional lady of the night who heard about the generosity of Lucy Green and the similar appearance. They say you're an imposter who takes advantage of Lucy while she is in a weak state of mind with a child. Mary thinks she can tell my father when he returns, and he'll run you out of town. Look at you…you're a fine, sophisticated young lady. Where do they come up with such nonsense? I have read the letter that you gave to Lucy, and I know that you are family."

Mollie's heart stops in her chest, and her throat begins to tighten and cut off air. Before either can react, they hear Lucy screaming for help from the other end of the stables. "Lucy's in labor," Mollie cries.

With no time to wait for a doctor or midwife, Mollie jumps into action and has Benjamin fetch her clean rags and something sharp to cut the cord. She makes a bed with horse blankets in the hay for Lucy to lie on comfortably. There's a problem when the head starts to crown, and it seems stuck upside down. Benjamin brings water and cloth, but he is clueless about how to help.

"Don't push, Lucy," Mollie says, "The baby is stuck. I saw this happen in Memphis, and the midwife had the woman flip over on to her hands and knees with her bottom in the air. Somehow it makes the baby flip over and come out normally. Lucy, we must try it now before the baby suffocates in the birth canal." Mollie helps her sit up and flip over, careful to protect her privacy with blankets, as the horse trainers start to arrive and become spectators. "Someone please go get the doctor," Mollie shouts. "The baby is coming out straight now. Lucy, push—push hard. I'll catch it. Push!" Mollie commands.

Mollie looks down at her hands and notices them tremble and wonders how she got into this, but she can't let anything happen to Lucy's baby. "Benjamin, please help. It looks like your little brother or sister is about to make an entrance, big brother." Benjamin, like most men, is lost as to what to do. He hands Mollie the only knife he can find. "Is that all you could find to cut the cord, a dull knife from the workshop?"

Mollie lifts her dress up to her thigh and pulls out a long, sharp blade. The baby's head and shoulders are out, and in one more second, the rest of the baby girl slides out. Mollie takes the baby and slaps her bottom, causing her to gasp, take in air, and begin to cry. Mollie takes the cord and cuts it close to the baby's belly. Lucy is unconscious when the doctor arrives.

Benjamin gingerly holds the baby while Mollie wraps her in cloth rags to keep her warm. "You saved the baby's life, Mollie. You're a hero. I hope the doctor can save Lucy too. I'm really afraid, Mollie," he says as he sways the baby back and forth. "She almost bled to death when baby Lucy was born. If I judge by that knife you have stashed on your leg, what I asked about earlier is true? How did you know what to do about Lucy's delivery? Memphis? Who are you really?"

"Later, Benjamin. Let's make sure Lucy is all right first," Mollie interrupts.

After the doctor examines Lucy, he gets her ready to move home to her own bed.

About that time, Mary shows up and snatches the baby out of Benjamin's arms, saying, "A man's arms are not a proper place for a newborn...right, baby Mary?" She sneers at Benjamin with disgust.

"Baby Mary?" he and Mollie say at the same time.

"Yes, you heard correctly, Mr. Green gave me the news on my birthday several months ago. It surprised me too, but I'm flattered. I'll be off now and take her home to the au pair."

Mary turns quickly to leave. Mollie touches her arm and says, "Leave if you will, Mary, but Lucy wants to name her Catherine, after her grandmother, not hired help."

Mary stops suddenly and turns back around and snaps, "You two just bloody wait to when Mr. Green returns. He'll put a stop to all of your shenanigans."

Mollie steps close into Mary's face and without raising her voice, so as to not wake the baby, says, "That's if you last that long, Mary, to get your comeuppance. For now, I am the eldest female family member, and Ben is the eldest male. We are taking charge of the home while Lucy is incapacitated and Mr. Green is away. You need to stay in your quarters until we come and talk to you. No gossip to other staff members, either. Do I make myself clear?"

Mary's mouth drops wide open in disbelief and nods her head as if to say yes. Then she quickly turns around again to leave. Mollie notices Benjamin has the same shocked look on his face and says, "Ben, is it OK that I call you Ben? It suits you better. I won't stand for her disrespect of you or me anymore. You're right about her gossip behind my back; the seamstress barely speaks to me. Some of the slaves won't look me in the eye. We're going to get things straightened out right away when we get home. Thankfully, Charles and Andrew will not be home. Ben, why do we have slaves anyway? We can afford to pay for hired help."

She looks at Ben for answers, and he is smiling. "Mollie, I don't know if *slave* is the right word, but one thing I do know is that I thank you for standing up for me. No one has ever done that for me, and, yes, Ben does sound nice. Lucy pays all eight of the servants. They have houses of their own. Charles brought them from England. They have been a part of our family my entire life, and their children are free."

Mollie shakes her head. "Perhaps, but they're still slaves. Have you ever been made to do something against your will? I have, and I hate it. I was made to do things, unspeakable things as a child, just to survive, to eat. That's why this family, house, money, and lifestyle seem like a dream compared to where I've been."

"Let's go by church before we go home," Ben says. "There we can pray for forgiveness of our sins and guidance, but mostly, let's pray for Lucy." Mollie reaches out and takes his hand, confident she has made a family bond. For the first time in his life, Ben feels acceptance for who he is and that he is not being judged negatively.

After church, Ben and Mollie rush home to tackle the divide Mary has caused in their home, where they find Mary not in her room as ordered but holding prayer vigilance at Lucy's bedside.

She's burning candles in front of a statue of Mother Mary and repeats rote prayer after prayer.

Rather than cause a scene, Mollie has a meeting with the servants and finds out Mary came home and filled their heads with all sorts of made-up nonsense that she has to straighten out immediately. Ben loves being around this strong, take-charge woman.

During the meeting, Ben and Mollie learn that the servants haven't had a day off in…in as long as they can remember. Mollie suggests to Ben that since it may be slow around there for a few days until Lucy recovers, they be given the next day off, starting now. Six of the servants are delighted to have a day off, but two refuse, saying that there is no way they would ever leave the baby and Mrs. Green. By the end of the meeting, Mollie and Ben have their loyalty…not that it was that hard. The staff knew that the eldest son would have priority over Mary, and besides that…Mary just hadn't made a lot of friends in her years with the Greens. "Please don't forget to pray for Lucy," Mollie tells them as she closes the door behind her.

She turns to Ben, saying, "It was nice of you to say that you were going to get with your father on his return and see about a raise for the servants. As for tomorrow, we can pull up the slack while some take the day off. Myself, for example…I can cook. Look, they have already plucked the chickens. If you get the firepit outside ready, I'll make my special white sauce that I make with mayonnaise, vinegar, salt and pepper. It's better when it sits for a while. I'll save one chicken to boil to make soup for Lucy and maybe add rice to put a little weight on her. She seemed frail this past week before giving birth." She stops talking and then asks, "Why do you stare at me Ben?"

Ben smiles and replies, "You have a certain way and sureness in yourself that encourages me to do the same and in all the right ways. I'm so glad you are part of this family, Mollie. I hope you're here when Sherman arrives. They say he is burning a path of destruction across Georgia to the sea, and that's us. You've seen the war in every way, while my family has been sheltered. I don't know how we will handle it, but with you here, I'm sure we'll figure it out."

Mollie walks toward the door to go get the seamstress to help prepare food, and she stops when she hears Ben tell of this news of war in Georgia that is soon coming to them. "Ben, I haven't heard or talked anything about the war since I've arrived. I don't know what will happen. I need to read the stacks of *Savannah Morning News* that I have deliberately ignored, trying to forget the war. For now, let's focus on the problem we have right under our nose: Mary. I suppose she plans on becoming indispensable in Lucy's recovery, which is good until Lucy wakes up."

Unexpectedly, the seamstress walks in to speak with the cook and is surprised to see Mollie preparing to rub down raw chickens with seasoning. Mollie says, "Perfect timing…grab an apron, and start peeling and cutting these potatoes for frying, and I'll cut the vegetables for Lucy's soup. All the servants are on a much-needed day off, so we'll all pull together. You're on board, right? It's for the children; they need to eat."

Miss Brown's back bows up, and she says, "No, I am not a servant hired as a cook. That's what the slaves are for, and what on earth gave you the authority to give them time off? They don't get time off!" she almost shouts.

Mollie immediately replies, "So, you're telling me that you have another employer lined up to pay the ridiculous amount you are paid here in the middle of a war? Well then, don't let that big door out front bump you on your way out, and don't expect a glowing reference, since you'll be leaving us in a time of need, with Mrs. Green unconscious after the childbirth today. I hope she survives. At least say a prayer for her. She has always been so kind to you. And no, you can't take anything with you. I'll have only what is yours delivered to your new address. Good luck," Mollie says with obvious sarcasm.

"Please stop. I don't have another job. Mary says you are trouble, and I seem to be caught in the cross fire," Miss Brown pleads as she ties the apron behind her back. "Mary says you're a fraud and to keep an eye on you. I've never prepared food myself, but if you can touch those dead birds, I can cut a few vegetables."

"Then please forgive me, Miss Brown. You have been nothing but kind to me since I arrived, and I may have been a little overdramatic." Ben comes back inside and is amazed that Mollie actually has cooperation.

Mollie shares a story from her past. "You see, Miss Brown, when you starve—I mean when you are so hungry that you dream to suck on a chicken bone—to be able to hold fresh food like this is a privilege and a dream actually. The war is coming our way, and there are no guarantees we will survive. Enjoy what we have for today, for so many have lost everything. The war caused me to lose my dignity and even worse my daddy. It's best to be prepared and be grateful for now."

Miss Brown says, "I've never known anyone who actually witnessed and lived through this war...only stories of others. What parts of the war did you see? Where was it?"

"Well, let's see. It all started in Nashville for me. I watched my daddy murdered in Athens, Alabama, by a Union soldier. My starving mother thought the only way to survive was to sell me to men when I was only twelve back in Nashville. To survive, we traveled to different cities like Memphis, Birmingham, and Mobile. Many of the places we went through, things were burnt or otherwise destroyed. I've seen and done more horrible things as a fourteen-year-old than most people will see in an entire lifetime."

"You are only fourteen? I can't believe it. I'm so sorry. Mary tells such terrible tales about you, but you seem to speak the truth, without an agenda."

Mollie spears all the chickens with two long poles and asks Ben to carry them to the firepit. "Do you know how to cook on an open fire, Ben?" she asks.

He shakes his head sideways and says, "I'm sorry, no, Mollie."

"That's OK. I'll teach you. Come outside with us, Miss Brown, because you need to learn also. When the war gets here and civilized people are reduced to savages, this may be the only way to cook."

Before they get to the door, the smaller children come into the kitchen from their dance lessons, hungry, looking for a snack, and surprised to see the kitchen help gone and replaced by Mollie, Ben, and Miss Brown. Excited and wanting to join in on what looks like fun, they practically shout in unison, "Can we play too?"

Mollie speaks up over them, "Yes, kids," Mollie says with fun and excitement in her voice. "We are having cooking classes. Your mother had baby Catherine this morning, and now she's sleeping. We are going to make her some soup, and you can help. But first we are going to learn how to cook chickens outside on the open fire. Let's go."

She shows Ben how to secure the poles over the flame and explains that they must be rotated often so as not to burn. The three younger boys want to assist with this chore, or any chore that involves fire, but Mollie makes sure Miss Brown and the young girls play a part as well. "They all need to know how to survive if the war comes, and for certain, it'll steal their innocence."

After the chickens are ready, Mollie continues the lesson back inside, showing everyone the proper and safe ways to handle a knife and letting everyone cut carrots, onions, and cabbage into bite-size pieces for the soup. The potatoes are the most challenging for the younger ones. Miss Brown tends to the stove while Mollie gets out all the ingredients for cornbread. The kids love to break the eggs and stir the dry with the wet. It's the first time anyone in the family has been involved in preparing food for themselves, and it turns into a joyous party when it's time to eat.

Later they meet their baby sister for the first time and watch the nurse feed their mother with food they themselves made for her.

Mary vanishes to her quarters without a word.

Mollie announces a field trip to the Savannah Bee store on River Street, planned for the next day, to see Lucy's beekeeper, Ted, who promises to show them how honey is made.

Excitement erupts and the children all hug and love on Mollie. She looks at Ben and Miss Brown and insists they go along. Miss Brown has never eaten with the family before and enjoys the company. She readily agrees to go along, as does Ben.

CHAPTER 15

MR. GREEN RETURNS

Days turn to weeks, and Lucy's recovery is very slow. Mary continues to teach the children until the day Mollie learns that she has been insisting to the children that the baby's name is Mary Catherine and telling them to refer to the baby as Mary. Mollie makes the grave mistake of dismissing Mary, thereby creating a situation where Mary is not close by for Mollie to control or have knowledge of her actions as much. A few days later, Confederate soldiers begin to show up at the house asking for Mollie. Yes, Mary is handing out advertisements with Mollie's name and address.

Word arrives that Mr. Green has been released and is on his way back home. Lucy, still very weak and thin, wakes for a few minutes at a time several times a day, excited for Charles's arrival and for him to meet the new baby.

Mary is living at a boardinghouse and continues to fill her days giving out pieces of paper with Mollie's name and address to the soldiers.

The day of Mr. Green's expected arrival, Mary waits at Tybee Island until she sees his ship. He is met at the port by his trusted governess, Mary, where she has ample opportunity to fill her boss's head with her version of how this awful opportunist has invaded and taken over his home while his wife is in recovery and not able to make sound decisions. "Mr. Green, I warn you, Mollie, or whatever her real name, is a very conniving young woman. She even has all the younger ones believing anything she says. Why, even Ben escorts her around town to galas and such, with her on his arm with pride."

"Ben?" Mr. Green asks.

"Yes, Ben. She changes the way he dresses and cuts his hair differently too."

"Is that not a good thing, Mary?" he asks.

"I'm warning you, Mr. Green—she is in everyone's lives on every level, except Charles and Andrew. Those poor men have been working around the clock in your absence...they don't like her either. She is a fraud, and I want you to be aware of what you're walking into at your home."

Charles arrives home with Mary, to all his family and staff awaiting his return in the large parlor. Lucy insists on being out of bed and dressed beautifully for her husband. Frail and weak, she is propped up with pillows in a large chair.

Charles greets the children with gifts and hugs and, to everyone's surprise, meets his new baby and calls her Mary. He gets on one knee and presents Lucy with a rolled piece of paper as he kisses her hand and cheek while he admires her beauty. "Another deed, my dear. More land has been added to your beloved estate in Virginia." He smiles.

Lucy quickly introduces him to Mollie with such enthusiasm. "Why, thank you, Charles. This is my beloved cousin Harrison's daughter, Mollie. Isn't she beautiful?"

"Why, yes, she is indeed—and most certainly bears a striking resemblance to you and our children. Mollie, may I speak with you further at a later time? Right now, I would like to be alone with my wife." He then scoops up his fragile wife, whom he has missed so much, and carries her up to their bedroom.

Mollie thinks to herself, *I sure hope they're just going to talk. It could kill her to get pregnant again.*

Later in the afternoon, Charles is furious as soldiers continue to arrive. In the library, Mary says, "Mr. Green, I am absolutely horrified to walk down the streets with Mollie. Men in both directions stare at her, waiting for her to look back. Why, they look right through me as though I'm invisible. They know something." Charles chuckles to himself. He knows why...she's stunningly beautiful, with big boobies.

Mollie is reading yet another book when Mary arrives at her door with a smug look on her face, "Mr. Green summons you to his library," she says as she scurries away.

Mr. Green greets Mollie wearing a stern business face as he invites her to sit in a chair next to his desk. Mollie can't help but notice that Mary is already sitting on the other side of the desk. Mollie asks, with a great deal of concern, "How is Lucy feeling—is she all right?"

Charles is surprised by her sincerity. "Lucy is sleeping. Let's get right to the point, Mollie. Mary has a long list of accusations against you, including a reputation which causes me great concern for the security of my family. She claims you gave the slaves a day off, went in our private bankbooks, and doubled their pay without permission. She further says that you had my children doing manual labor in the absence of the servants and says you spend most of your time reading my books. Mary told me that you've altered my son Benjamin's appearance and attitude—and worst of all that you invite all the soldiers to our home. Yet strangely enough, I couldn't help notice the pride Lucy had when she introduced you today and the praise she gave to you in private later. Anyway, what do you have to say for yourself, young lady?"

Steaming on the inside that she let Mary get one over on her with her very own family, smiling and confidently she begins, "First, let me begin by thanking God for keeping me alive long enough to meet you and Aunt Lucy and all the children—plus the house staff and even the slaves. I feel absolutely blessed and very privileged to be in this beautiful home. I learn new things every single day. My daddy was killed before my very eyes when I was only ten by a Union soldier on a white horse. My mother for some reason didn't reach out to Lucy at that time but rather chose to put me in constant danger with men for food in return. After two years of living in hell on earth, in the middle of a war that I don't completely understand, I found a letter from Lucy to my daddy begging him to come to Savannah before the war broke out.

"I did so many unspeakable things for money to get here. I privately confessed all of this to Lucy the first day after I arrived. Mary must have eavesdropped on our conversation and spread it about town to the soldiers. I have also confirmed that she has spread this through the house staff, slaves, and your older boys."

Mary interrupts, "Mr. Green, are you going to let that little tramp lie about me like that?"

"That's OK for now, Mary. Let her talk," Mr. Green replies.

Mollie continues, "I was made to do things that I desperately did not want to do in my lifetime, so I felt sorry for the slaves. I know it's not my business, but I don't like it, so Ben and I thought that a day off would increase morale, and, sir, we...I did not give them a raise, but I guess that I did talk Ben into speaking to you about a raise when you returned. I know, sir, that I'm not a financial expert, but I really think a raise might make them feel better and be grateful to be with this nice family instead of a mean family, and I thought everyone likes a day off. Sir, they dance and sing while they work now.

"I used the opportunity to teach everyone to cook in order to survive if the war should come here too. Young Anna took to baking after that and just last week baked an angel food cake all by herself. Ben's confidence was stolen by vicious gossip here in his own home. I helped him dress and act like the wealthy young bachelor that he is. It was my pleasure to be on his arm when we represented the family at charity events that Lucy couldn't attend. Now, he walks with pride, as he should. I'll admit, I helped change him."

She stops and takes a breath and looks around at all the books and continues, "Lucy granted me permission to read any of your books. I do spend all my spare time in here, and I have read all of the books on the wall behind you but not those on the other walls. My favorites are those on architecture. The most curious of them is *Journey to the Center of the Earth,* a science fiction novel by French author Jules Verne. I had dreams about that book for weeks. How could someone think to write about such things? That led me to the adventure novel *Five Weeks in a Balloon.* Could you just imagine traveling around the world in eighty days by air? How wild!" Charles smiles as he enjoys listening to this bright young woman.

Mary interrupts, "That proves it. No one can read that many books in less than six months; she is a liar. Mr. Green, your family is in jeopardy with her here. Just look out the windows at the soldiers who constantly come by. Your children don't need to learn manual chores. It's beneath them. Admit it, Mollie, you are a soiled woman and bring shame to this family. Where's the proof of this letter you speak of?"

"Sir," Mollie interrupts, "she only asks because she has already stolen it from Aunt Lucy's room. Ben read it, and of course Aunt Lucy."

Charles interrupts in a loud, commanding voice, "I've heard enough. Mary. Go to your quarters until I call for you."

Mary pleas, "I have no quarters, Mollie humiliated me in front of the children when I showed them the baby's birth certificate that Lucy had me acquire, and then Mollie dismissed me out into the streets. I'm devastated without your family in my life." She begins to cry. "I've given up everything in England to work with your children and for you and Lucy. Please don't let an outsider do this to me—you must believe me."

Mollie speaks up again, "Please don't tell me that you put Mary on the birth certificate. Lucy told me that she wants the baby's name to be after her grandmother Catherine, not you, Mary. It appears that you arbitrarily put your name on it anyway without her permission. That's sick."

Charles takes sobbing Mary to the door. "Go to your old quarters until I send for you." He almost reaches out to touch her face and comfort her but catches himself and stops. Mollie notices the spark. He closes the door behind her for privacy and then opens it back to find her standing there with her ear to the door, listening. "Go now, Mary, I say!" Charles orders as she cries and runs off.

Leaning back in his chair, Charles says, "Mollie, you seem to be a delightful, smart young lady. Why would you claim to have read so many books? Where is the letter? Why would Mary change the birth certificate? I have so many questions."

Mollie responds quickly, saying, "I have the ability to read extremely fast and somehow remember it all. My daddy said it was a gift from God. Except for those not on the wall behind you, pick any book on the shelves, open it, and ask me a question. It's not a parlor trick, Mr. Green."

He randomly picks a book off the shelf, *Governors of the Northeastern United States,* and flips it open. "Who was the governor of Vermont in 1823?"

Mollie responds, "Governor Cornelius Vann Ness took office October 10, 1823, followed by Ezra Butler 1826, Samuel Crafts 1828, and William A.—"

"That's enough; no one knows anything about Vermont on purpose." He closes the book and returns it to the shelf. "So you can remember everything?" Mollie nods her head up and down to confirm. Somewhat in awe, Charles says, "You could do wonders in a business world with a gift like that—know everything about everybody before a meeting and be able to recall it on the spot. I would love to have that gift. Does that bother you, having so much information? I mean, does it ever confuse your thought process?"

"No, sir," Mollie replies. "It's just there for me to grab when I need it. I've read all your books and daily newspapers on this war, and although I may have the information, I don't always understand. This war has forever scarred my life, and I'm not sure I understand why all the civilian population of the South has to pay the highest price. Less than five percent of the population owns slaves, but the rest of us are hunted down, starved, stolen from, and towns burned like we are all guilty of something. Men are taken from their families and forced to fight, and in many cases, they have no idea what they are fighting and dying for.

"I've also read in your books and old newspapers about the high tariffs on people like you, who export. The North wants the South's money, but they don't like how it's made. It's so hypocritical. Can't the leaders in Washington work it out and leave the rest of us out of it? I want to live without fear. Other than Mary's little games with my life, I love it here in Savannah with no war."

"Mollie, you are wiser than anyone would probably size you up to be. Use that to your advantage throughout your life. I, as an Englishman, am not supposed to interfere with American matters, but yes, as a businessman, the tariffs put me at a disadvantage. Many businessmen would prefer the tariffs be lower. It was eighty cents on the dollar at the start of the war. Does that seem fair to you?

"The insulting part is that the Northern politicians take our so-called tainted money and build up their cities by building manufacturing plants, bridges, train depots, ports, higher education schools, and hospitals. The only upgrades in the Port of Savannah in the past twenty years I have paid for myself. Why doesn't the southern tariff money stay here and build us more efficient railroads? The politicians on both sides and President Lincoln should have handled all this without a war, but their enormous egos and regional biases wouldn't let them.

"Did you know that our president started colonies for a resettlement of the slaves in the Caribbean? Five hundred went to Île-à-Vache in Haiti, a complete failure because of money. He told many black leaders the move would get rid of the violence. The black ministers did not believe him.

"Things aren't as they seem, Mollie," Charles continues. "I was in New York City after the Emancipation Proclamation was signed and the local white Irishmen didn't want to be drafted to the war. When riots broke out, there was total bloody mayhem for five days. They didn't want to lose their jobs to all the free slaves arriving from the South, so they lynched and burn all the blacks out of New York City.

"Like all wars, it's about the money—always about the money. The slavery issue was added to get more people to support the war and join the army, but that didn't work, so they import immigrants with a promise for a better future after they fight in our war.

"I know I own eight slaves, and I should have freed them a long time ago. However, ours are more like family. Lucy has always insisted that I pay them, and we treat them well." Charles's voice begins to fade as he hears his own words out loud.

Mollie shoots back, "It doesn't matter how well you treat them or pay them. They are humans owned by other humans, and it's not right, and you know it. Yes, I've learned from your books. I learned that slavery of all colors of skin happens all over the world...in many cases to build great countries, from the pyramids in Egypt to the Great Wall of China. That doesn't make it right just because it's always been around."

Mr. Green stands and walks over to the window. Staring out, he finally turns and says, "Perhaps I have no dog in this hunt, Mollie. It took a child to open my eyes. I already pay my slaves and give them homes. I trust they won't leave me if freed. Cotton, even with labor for growing and picking added, will still find market, whatever the price is. If the northern representatives will quit meddling with regulations and tariffs on the South, things will be fine. They got fifty-one percent of the vote, and now they stick it to us. Why can't we all just follow the Constitution? I'll begin the paperwork immediately. My slaves will be free.

"I hope they decide to stay, because our family loves them all. Since you seem to be wise beyond your years and Lucy is not ready yet for deep discussions, I will use you to devise a plan. Sherman has left Atlanta in flames as he scorches the earth on his way here. I plan to meet with the local politicians and convince them to surrender because we don't have a chance. Maybe if we offer him our beautiful city on a silver platter, he won't burn Savannah.

"As importantly, I have twenty-five thousand bales of cotton in my warehouses that I don't want him to burn—or the port I paid for. This war is almost over, and we may as well save what we can so that we don't have to rebuild it all again later. Heck, I think I'll offer him this fine home, rather than let them take it. There's plenty of room for all of us."

The thought of being in the same house with soldiers terrifies Mollie to the point of causing her to stutter. "You...ah, you, you would have them stay here? Here inside, with your children and your wife? They're monsters. They'll hurt us. Please don't," Mollie begs.

A knocking at the door startles both of them. It is the butler with a well-worn letter for Mollie. "What on earth? Surely it's not from one of the soldiers out on the street. I can't believe Mary is causing all of this; she's a horrible person," Mollie moans.

"Open it, see who sent it, and leave it alone about Mary changing the baby's name. Catherine was my first wife's name, and it will only serve as a reminder of our loss. I don't know what Lucy was thinking when she mentioned it to you," Charles says in a cold voice.

Mollie opens the paper to find it is from Sissy in Nashville. She feels a huge sense of guilt for leaving her behind.

My dearest Mollie,

This may be the last time that you hear from me. My grandmother has passed away, and your mother is near death at the prostitute hospital. They don't give me a whole lot of hope either. I am so glad you got out of Nashville before all the new foreign soldiers arrived carrying a syphilis disease from Europe that is a death sentence to all the women in this business. Your mother, me, and more than a hundred other women were rounded up by General Rosecrans and charged as having cyprian behavior. We were all banished onto a steamship called the *Idaho* to Louisville, Kentucky. We were not allowed to dock when they found out we were on board. For over thirty days, we were on the ship with little provisions, as no other town allowed us to dock either or even gave us medical supplies. Finally we were brought back to Nashville, where your mother and I were brought to the hospital for mercury treatment. Thank you for taking care of all us. I love you.

Sissy Greenleaf

P.S. I wish I had gone with you.

As Mollie finishes, she folds the paper in half. This is the last thing she expected after the ordeal with Mary. Without much compassion, Charles asks Mollie to return to her quarters. "We both have a lot to think about," he says.

Mollie figures that Mary has been available to Mr. Green in more ways than just a governess and is why she felt empowerment to challenge Mollie from the start. She takes care of the boss and uses it to her favor. Mollie knows she has been outplayed by Mary, and she understands the odds that she is up against now. She sees the bigger picture.

As the library door locks behind Mollie, Mary steps out of the sliding bookcase from a secret hallway and begins to unbutton her blouse, smiling at Charles. "We need to make up for lost time."

CHAPTER 16
MR. GREEN AND MOLLIE

Charles knocks at Mollie's door and then enters immediately, quickly closing it behind him with a toothy grin and his upper shirt unbuttoned and open. He has something naughty on his mind as he stares at her breast, and Mollie wants no part of his advances. Smelling the alcohol, she knows she has to act quickly. She pulls out a chair and practically forces him to sit while he grabs at her top. Clearly, he is a wealthy man who usually gets whatever he wants.

"I assume you've seen a doctor since you've been here and that you are clean?"

"No, sir, but that's not the issue," Mollie says, lying through her teeth. She saw a doctor before she left Nashville, and she is only saying this to make a horny man think.

"Mollie, Lucy took a year to recover from her last child, and it doesn't look like this time will be any different."

Mollie interrupts, "Why get her pregnant if it endangers her health?"

Charles snaps back, "Because that is what a woman does for her husband, to bear his children. I provide well for her and love her, as you can see. That's why I'm here. I can't stop thinking how much I want you. I'll put Lucy in the nursery while she recovers and move you into my bed. I'll give you money. You'll like that, right? So many things that I will teach you." He begins to touch himself at this thought.

"Stop, Mr. Green, I'm only fourteen," Mollie pleads, knowing that she is actually sixteen. "I have business in Nashville, and I intend to leave in the morning. If you wish, I will leave right now."

Charles turns and sits on the bed. Looking up into Mollies blue eyes, he says, "Oh, Mollie, I don't want you to leave. Surely with what you have seen you don't blame a grown man for trying. I know it's wrong...Mary, too—but, Mollie, you just may be the prettiest woman I have ever seen. Look at you, Mollie. Perhaps you still think of yourself as a little girl, but, sweet Mollie, you're a woman, a beautiful woman."

Yes, Mollie has seen this situation before and actually feels sorry for the man. "Sir, if I ask you to leave...would you?"

"Yes, Mollie, I'll leave. Sorry," he replies, and starts to get up. "Is it possible that you may change your mind and take me up on my offer?"

"No, I need to leave. Besides, Mary would always be trying to get me. I want you to know that Mary is not the only au pair or governess in town. Mr. Green, watch your step...that woman is trouble."

Charles starts to leave but turns to Mollie. "Please consider staying here, but if it's not in the cards, be safe. You are always welcome if you choose to return...no strings attached." He pulls a wad of Confederate dollars out of his pocket and places it on the dresser. "Spend it quickly, Mollie. It will be worthless very soon."

CHAPTER 17

PLANS FOR MOLLIE'S ESCAPE

After he leaves, Mollie uses the secret hallway that she found when she tried to figure out how Mary knew so much about her confession to Lucy. She taps on Ben's secret door and quickly steps inside his room, which the two have done many times since the baby was born.

Mollie climbs under the covers, and Ben smiles. "Will you tell me more stories about the men like me in Mobile again?" He then notices the worried look on her face. "What is it, Mollie? You look like something is on your mind." He wraps his arms around Mollie as she trembles.

"My mouth is too big, and my past life has caught up with me. Ben, I should have kept my soiled life to myself. The first man that my mother sold me to said, 'Once a whore, always a whore.' I thought my life would be different here in this home, but it's not. I have to leave, Ben," she sobs onto his shoulder.

After a few minutes of deep breaths per Ben's instructions, Mollie retells the day's events: the library scene with Mary, the idea of letting Sherman stay here, Mary being the baby's name, and the letter from Sissy—but she leaves out the proposition of being a full-time live-in mistress in Lucy's bed.

"I love Lucy, but you know that I can't stay here," she says, exhausted as she falls back into the pillow.

"That little bitch Mary!" Ben says. "There's no telling what she might do if you did stay and squeeze her out. She will go nuts if she loses her power over you. I bet she will try to poison you or some other untimely death. You're doing the honorable thing, Mollie, for Lucy, but why Nashville? You need to head south to Florida, away from the war...not right through the middle of it. Sleep on it. We'll come up with an idea together. Maybe I should go with you. What do you think? I have lots of cash, but I've heard the currency will fail. People here in Savannah still use it, but in a lot of places, it's useless paper."

After a few hours of sleep, Ben wakes Mollie with an idea. "Mollie, wake up—we need to act fast if you're still determined to go to Nashville. I have a friend that owns the stagecoach station in Athens, and he's here in town right now. I'll pay him what it takes to get you there...I hope in front of Sherman's troops before they burn the tracks for the train to Chattanooga. That's as close as I can think to get you. I'll ride as far as the coach will take you, and then I'll return here. I promise to tell Lucy about Sissy and how much you love her."

Groggy, Mollie rubs her eyes. "When do we leave?" Ben walks closer, sits on the bed, and takes her hand. "Mollie, I realize you're determined to save Sissy, but I wish you wouldn't put yourself in such danger. I want you to get her, and you both come back to Savannah." What happens next almost causes Mollie to faint. Ben puts a large diamond ring on Mollie's finger. "This was my mother's ring. Mollie, I would like for you to marry me when you return. Since your arrival, I have been happy. You make me laugh, I can be myself around you, and you know my secrets. I love you, Mollie Teal."

"Ben, we can't get married, I'm too young, and besides you're, well...different. I'm not what you want or need—not to mention all the family drama. Your father will disinherit you, and you know it to be true."

"Mollie, I will love and protect you like no other, that I can promise as a gentleman. I just won't have those sexual desires for you, and I'll keep that private between us, as I do now. Together we can stand up against my family. I'll purchase us a home while you are away.

"Mollie, my father had me marry Isabelle Stoddard when I was twenty. As you know, it didn't work out, because she didn't truly know me like you do."

"No, Ben. Although I appreciate very much what you're trying to do, the whole idea is foolhardy at best. I can't marry you for many reasons," Mollie says as she tries to put the ring back in his hand.

"Mollie, keep the ring. Just don't wear it—someone will rob you for it. However, if you need to sell it to survive, then that's OK too. Please make it back, Mollie. Go to your room and pack quickly. We have to go soon, before the children wake up—because you know they'll be shattered and cause a big scene and won't let you go. They fell in love with you too. Only you could make learning to cook meatballs the highlight of their week. Who else will show them how to do gymnastics on the back of a horse?"

Mollie is scared out of her mind and doesn't know what may lie ahead but takes the ring and pulls up her dress while tying it in her gun holster. She travels light, with very few things and her daddy's saxophone. Mollie looks back over her shoulder at the expansive black walnut foyer with magnificent artwork and indoor live tropical plants. She shudders to think of this beautiful oasis soon becoming part of the hell that she ran away from but now heads directly into. Tears flow from her anger and disappointment that this will all be but a wonderful memory. *Why?* she asks herself. *Why is this war so determined to take away my will to live?* "I'm not going to let you win," she shouts into the night sky as she closes the front door for the last time.

A short time later, Mollie waits in the carriage as Ben is at the door of the stagecoach depot, discussing the future journey toward Atlanta and not away from it like most other people. The man throws his hands in the air and slams the door. Undeterred, Ben knocks again. When the man opens the door this time, Ben has a case full of cash opened for him. The man pulls him inside immediately. This is probably the most exciting and scary thing Ben has ever done and not quite the boring bookkeeping that he usually does.

Mollie watches the two men come back out a few minutes later and quickly proceed to harness up six large horses. Naturally she thinks of Star, wishing she could go to the stables one last time, take in his smell, and say goodbye—for how long she doesn't know…maybe she will never see him again.

CHAPTER 18

SAVANNAH TO MACON

The journey to Nashville begins out of Savannah at two o'clock in the morning on a high-speed stagecoach, after the driver introduces himself with, "I'm your driver, and I'm crazy for doing this. Make the money while you can, they say. This is a special Abbott Downing Company stagecoach. It weighs over two thousand pounds, and they employed leather strap braces under the coach to give it a swing motion instead of the jolt up and down of a spring suspension. I tell you this because we usually go five miles an hour with nine passengers, luggage, and mail. With just the two of you, we are going to push it to eight miles an hour. This is a dangerous trip, and I want to make it as fast as I can. For this reason, I'm going to use the Macon trail. The Atlanta trail is very crowded with refugees fleeing south. It's one hundred and sixty miles to Macon, but we should be able to make it in twenty hours by changing teams of horses twice. Are you up for this dangerous ride? And please God, tell me you brought pistols! The trading posts where we change horses are known for holdups." Mollie nods yes and insists on saying a prayer before boarding.

The driver passes and swerves around heavy wagons drawn by long teams heading in both directions at high speeds. The road is often narrow and steep, with sharp turns. Once, the driver, while quickly swinging his horses around a bluff, suddenly comes up on a wagon struggling up the hill. Only the driver's great skill prevents a collision. Going downhill, he has the horses at a full gallop—surely twelve miles an hour on the long stretches. Even climbing uphill, the horses are at a fast trot. At one point, the stage comes very near the edge of a steep drop. The earth gives way to the outer wheels, and for a moment the coach leans over a little, but due to the speed of the horses, it quickly straightens itself out.

At midnight they arrive at the Stagecoach Inn in Macon. The town is wide awake and busy with more refugees than they have seen in days. People are fleeing out of the door at the inn as the three walk inside to inquire about rooms and fresh horses for the morning to go to Athens. The innkeeper laughs at the exhausted three travelers, saying, "Everyone else here is fleeing for their lives, and you want to check in? I guess you haven't heard. The Union has about twenty thousand troops from Nashville camped one mile outside of town. We've been told that they'll burn Macon come sunrise. So, do y'all still want a room? Help yourselves. I'm looking for a way out of town," says the innkeeper.

The driver looks at Ben. "I'm leaving now too. We can get way ahead of the bluecoats and stop at the river about twenty miles back the way we came. There we can rest and water the horses. I don't think I'll sleep any though."

The innkeeper asks for a ride, promising that he'll bring plenty of cooked food. Ben is terrified for Mollie, but she insists she can make it to Athens after resting at the inn. She reminds them the soldiers aren't coming until morning. The innkeeper offers her his horse and tells her where it's hidden as he gets inside the stage-coach. Mollie hugs Ben and kisses him on the cheek. They already said their many goodbyes during the trip. "I'll see you back in Savannah," Mollie says as she locks the big door at the inn from the inside, adding the large board crosswise and turning off the oil lamps to make the place look vacant.

The innkeeper also tells her to use his bed, with a feather mattress, at the end of the hall on the second floor. She finds the still-warm stew that was left behind but isn't able to eat much. Delighted to find the room has several big locks, she temporarily feels safe and climbs into the comfortable bed.

After a few hours of sleep, Mollie thinks she hears thunder and decides to get up and go. It isn't thunder, but it is the all-too-familiar sound of thousands of feet pounding the ground that she actually feels. She quickly gathers her things, and before she opens the door, she hears voices of soldiers in the hallway and freezes in place, kicking herself for sleeping too long. She will have to make her way out onto the roof and look for a different escape.

It's still dark, and she thinks she can make it to the alleyway, find the hidden horse in the warehouse, and be on her way before they arrive in numbers. She notices more soldiers arriving on horses in front of the inn, which is where she planned to climb down the side of the front porch. She needs another way before it gets too light out.

That's when the whole world changes for Mollie. Directly below her is the face of a man seared into Mollie's memory for life, the blue giant from Athens, Alabama, who stampeded her daddy. He stands alone, with the reins in his hands next to his big white horse. Mollie becomes so emotional and angry that she goes a little wild and crazy. She would shoot him dead on the spot, but the noise would attract attention and prevent her escape.

Next, Mollie does something dangerous and stupid when she jumps onto his horse's back. All the soldier sees is the side of a saxophone case as it hits him, knocking him to the ground. Mollie takes off in the opposite direction of the troops. The now general quickly jumps back up and kicks the music case. Why is it familiar to him? He bellows orders to nearby soldiers to chase the horse thief immediately. He also orders other soldiers to search all over

Macon in case the thief doubles back and to hold off on any fires in the town until his horse is found.

This is his hottest temper flare-up of the war. That horse has survived with him throughout this war, and he isn't about to lose him now. The soldiers' tired horses don't have a chance up against the well-rested white stallion. Mollie runs the horse as fast as he can go through the vacant streets until she reaches the dead end of Georgia Avenue and sees something she's read about in the Savannah newspapers…the four-story, red-brick, eighteen-thousand-square-foot Italian Renaissance Revival–style mansion built by the Johnson family, known as the Palace of the South.

Mollie heads straight up to the grand entrance and intends to speak to the family as though she knows them personally.

At the Huntsville courthouse, Judge Stewart comes down hard with his wooden gavel, with a loud, thunderous whack, as the crowd in the courtroom comes back to reality. The sound of the striking gavel almost makes her come out of her seat. "Lord have mercy, Your Honor, have I been objected to again?" Sissy asks, with some sassiness in her voice. "Or are you just trying to scare me and see how far I can jump up off my chair?"

"Well, Miss Sissy, I'm sorry about that again, and there haven't been any objections…but for the life of me, I can't understand why. I'm starting to believe that all sides are forgetting there is a trial going on here. Not only is it past my supper this time; it's almost dark. You can continue in the morning."

"But, Your Honor, I was just getting to the good part, where Mollie meets Herman Deeley. You know Herman, Judge—he lives down on the river now at Taylorsville."

"Yes, Miss Sissy, I believe that I have met Herman, and I assure you that we will all be here in the morning to hear what you have to say about the man. What he would have to do with this case is beyond me, but if it's anything like today, I doubt anyone will object." With some laughter in the courtroom, the judge calls for the court to reconvene the next morning. As Sissy stands up and straightens up her dress and elaborate hat, the judge thinks to himself, *She is cute when she jumps.*

CHAPTER 19

HERMAN DEELEY

Back in time to Macon as Sissy continues her story in the Huntsville courtroom the next day...

A small young black man, wearing a horse-jockey suit, comes out of the stables. He waves Mollie over to him and says, "The Johnsons took all of their slaves to Ohio except me. I'm a free man—always have been. They left back a couple of months ago, when the Georgia invasion began."

Mollie quickly interrupts him. "I don't mean to be rude and interrupt, but I'm being chased, it seems, by the entire Union Army. Is there a place we can hide this horse? I mean really fast, because the Union soldiers are right on my tail."

"I can understand that...been hunted down myself before. Let's tie him up behind the hog house, where there's a stream. I've got to warn you—it stinks to high heaven," the young black man says as he helps Mollie down and takes the reins to lead the way.

The black man notices the rank on the horse saddle and other gear and interrogates, "So what's a young lady as yourself doing on a Union horse...that of a general's to boot? You must have some bounty on your head. How did you get away? How many are chasing you?"

"I don't know. I think I went a little bit crazy. That's what this war does to people—makes them do stupid things that they normally wouldn't do." Together they remove the saddle, rifle, and other supplies, including a saddlebag full of papers. She leads the horse to the stream and attaches a long rope to his harness. Then the unexpected happens: the horse begins to play in the water. He kicks his feet about and scoops up water with his head and sprays it toward the two humans. Then the giant beast bows down on his front two legs, like a puppy that just wants to play when he submits to a big dog.

Next he completely immerses himself, flips over, and jumps out, continuing to prance up and down the bank. Mollie speculates that he must never get the saddle taken off and groomed, but joyful horse play is exactly what Mollie needs to calm her nerves and clear her head. "Do you mind if we groom him here? I want to get to know him," Mollie asks as she teases the giant beast's muzzle.

The man looks at the animal and says, "Miss, that is the whitest horse I have ever seen. Bet you can see it for miles. You want to make it shine more? Putting some mud on it might be better with those soldiers chasing you. I'll bring back blankets, brushes, and maybe an apple or two, but you need to get that horse in a pigsty or a closed and hidden horse stall quick. Miss, my name is Herman Deeley, and yours is?"

"Mollie Teal...Mollie Teal is my name, and thank you for hiding us." She almost ignores Herman to connect with the horse.

Mollie takes two hours to groom and talk to the new horse as she closely inspects all of his scars and wounds from the war. Herman goes to the racetrack to find out the latest information about the troops.

When he finally returns, he says, "Miss Mollie, you did a fine, fine job grooming that horse...he's stark white now, but he is beautiful," Herman says.

Mollie comments, "Well, you may be right about standing out, but I just can't put mud on him. I think he's some kind of show horse, but every command I use, he looks confused or ignores me. I've gone through some of the general's papers, and if I'm correct, I think he's Russian. If I could look at a language translation book, I could use the right commands on the horse. Did you find out any news at the racetrack?"

Herman replies, "Yes. It was hard though because everyone is spooked with all the bluecoats on our streets, so I didn't ask too many questions and draw any extra attention. Here's the strange part: Macon was sent a telegram yesterday to evacuate our citizens before they torch us. Now, the general, General Turchin, has ordered every home to be searched for his horse. There must be something more to it than a horse. I think the answer is in those papers you're reading."

"Well, good," Mollie says. "Tell that bastard if you see him that I got something that he wants."

"If I see him, I just might do that," Herman shoots back. "There's a large library in the house. The Johnsons did travel in Europe for five years. We can look for one of those translation books you mentioned."

Herman is well acquainted with the home and seems proud of it. On the way to the library, he tells Mollie all about it. "Miss Mollie, the Johnsons asked me to stay here while they fled. Oh, it's a big house, over eighteen thousand square feet, and the things in it are as modern as any home in this century. We have hot and cold running water to all the bathrooms, central heat, gas lighting, a speaker-tube communication system, in-house kitchen, French lift, and an elaborate ventilation system. Unlike many of the Greek Revival–style homes being built in the South, this Italian Renaissance Revival–style home is chiefly characterized by arches and curves."

Mollie interrupts, "Herman, are you quoting that from memory?"

"Why, yes, ma'am. Sometimes the Johnsons would ask me to show some of the guests around. I learned it word for word. If

I may continue…Miss Mollie. The central block of the house is flanked by two wings, which are identical from the exterior. The three-story octagonal cupola serves as part of the ventilation system and acts as a chimney which draws hot air up and out of the house."

They walk up the large circular staircase that leads onto the elaborate porch. As she glances back out over Macon, it's as if the outside front steps disappear, and you appear to be looking out over a balcony to the river in the valley below. As they walk through the entrance, Herman continues, "These nine-foot pine doors are often mistaken for bronze because of these carved lions on the front." Herman goes off-script, saying, "What surprised me the most is they left without the *Ruth Gleaning*, the marble statue by Rudolph Rogers. It's their prize piece. Look in here. They made a room just for her, with special natural light," Herman says as he walks into the room off the large ballroom to show her.

He catches himself doing yet another tour and turns to Mollie. "I reckon those Union soldiers are not going to wait for me to give you a tour. Let's take the straight route through the marble hallway over to the owner's office and library to get started on these papers before the troops show up. Actually, I think you should wait until dark to travel."

Herman watches in amazement as Mollie quickly reads each page of the *International Language Translator Guide*. After she reads seven pages of the general's papers, Mollie looks up and says, "You're right, I'll wait until it gets dark to leave. These are the war strategy plans and maps written in Russian—how brilliant. Not many Southerners could ever read these. I want to make my way through these cities where the least amount of soldiers will be." She points to the map and a straight line from Macon to Athens.

"I'm trying to get to Nashville to help my sister and my mother. Both are seriously sick. Judging by this map, the rumors about the Union not destroying the rails from Athens to Chattanooga are true. They bring in reinforcements and supplies up the Tennessee River, across Alabama to Chattanooga, and then rail them into Georgia." She points again to Athens, Georgia, over fifty miles northeast of what is left of Atlanta.

Herman opens a book of maps to Georgia and says, "You have to go to the capital, Milledgeville, to be able to cross Lake Sinclair. There's no other way around it. It's a preplanned, centrally located city, with the Oconee River on one side and the lake to the north. All roads lead there. If you can sneak out of Milledgeville, it'll be an additional seventy miles for you. Keep going north to Eaton, Madison, and Watkinsville and finally to Athens. Mollie, you may look older, but I suspect that you're no more than sixteen. I'm afraid that you will have a hard time managing the dangers you will face. You'll need help. Heck, I can't be a jockey for the Johnsons anymore...started growing too fast. But they did educate me well, and I know this area. What can I do?"

"I will survive off of the will to live and pure determination. I won't let this war take that or any more people I love from me. I can't!" Mollie almost shouts. "Besides, I'm stronger than you think, and I have what the great General Turchin wants as much as his papers—his magnificent horse. Papers that I have read say the horse's name is Belyy, which translates to 'white' and sounds like *belly*. I found some Russian commands that I will certainly try with him.

"Herman, I could use your help to get out of Macon. I need some supplies to camp, hunt, and fish, plus enough food for Belyy and me to live in the woods for a while so I can stay out of sight of both armies. Also I'd like to get rid of the general's saddle for a smaller one."

"Yes, ma'am," Herman says, looking at Mollie, "I think I know what you mean. I've rode a few horses myself."

Mollie innocently continues, "Well, I can take it if I have to, but a smaller one would feel better. I have wads of Confederate money to give to you. Is it still useable here?"

Herman laughs and shakes his head and replies, "No." He is taken by this young woman's bravery and strength. For some reason, he admires her and trusts her with very private information. "Mollie, I'll share something folks around here don't need to know anything about—and better yet, I'll show you after we eat. It's the way for you to escape, or you could just give him back the horse— have you thought of that?" Mollie doesn't answer but watches as Herman slides the false panel to the hidden pantry for her to pack food supplies for the journey. Herman reminds her, "Make sure and slide the wall back until it clicks; otherwise, thieves or soldiers will steal everything."

Butter pops, sizzles, and smells incredible as Herman cooks two-man-cut ribeye steaks in a cast-iron skillet with onions. Mollie didn't realize how hungry she was and enjoys every bite.

After eating, Herman and Mollie climb the beautiful staircase, and just past the large stained-glass window at the landing, he shows her a secret hidden room behind a rotating wall. "This is where I want you to hide if they show up before you leave," he says. They continue up to the top floor and then up into the attic, to a spiral staircase, which leads to the outside at the top of the cupola.

Mollie almost bumps her head on the short door as she steps out into the refreshing wind and says, "The view is incredible from up here, but I almost feel like I'm going to fall this high up."

"See the bridge on the river? That's where they'll have soldiers and roadblocks," Herman says as he points southward. He turns and points to another part of the river, saying, "That's where I'll take you to cross; the water is low. Once across, you need to head straight north toward that mountain." He points in the distance. They are both pleased to see only one fire in Macon and no troops in sight. Herman says, "In a strange way, you and the stolen horse have saved Macon from total destruction. Let's go to the stables and get you ready for your trip."

Mollie chooses a different saddle and saddlebags for Belyy. Herman closes the large stable doors and places a latch across the middle with a large board as well. He quickly goes into the tack room and comes out with a long white riding cape, which belongs to Mrs. Johnson, "It feels like colder weather is coming. Please take this to stay warm." Mollie thinks it is beautiful and gladly accepts as she places her arms in it while Herman holds it for her.

Herman decides to offer Mollie a revolver, "You'll need this for protection." About that time, the cold metal slips out of his hand. He juggles and almost catches it with the other hand, but it hits the ground.

Mollie laughs, trying to make light of it to not embarrass Herman, and asks, "Is that some kind of circus trick or just 'happy fingers'?" Herman smiles as he quickly picks up the gun.

He then leads her down to an empty stall and lifts up the flooring, which is more like a huge door that leads down a steep bricked path into a tunnel. Herman lights a torch and leads the way down, with the horse and Mollie following close behind. As Herman releases a rope to lower the door overhead, he explains to Mollie that the tunnel leads to a large cave system that continues for three miles and comes out at the Ocmulgee River.

"You'll cross where the river is low and be able to stay out of sight. Old Clinton is twelve miles north, about halfway to Milledgeville. Stay off the roads as much as you can. I don't think they'll go north looking for you," he says. Mollie notices this is a well-worn route through the cave and chooses not to ask any questions, and Herman offers no information.

He shows her how to make a hoot owl call by grasping his hands tightly together and blowing air between his thumbs. She does the same, and it surprises her at how much like owls they sound. She begins to giggle, but quickly realizes she can't be silly for now and stops.

They come out into the daylight, and it's almost sunset. Herman makes sure all the bags are secure, and he wishes her well and insists that she cross the river before dark. Mollie remembers what he said in the kitchen—"folks around here don't need to know about." Mollie thanks him for his help and kindness, and then she realizes his detachment is because he has been on this journey before. She suspects that he has helped slaves to escape on this route. She decides to answer his question about giving the horse back. "The Russian killed my daddy," says Mollie as she directs Belyy into the water.

Herman arrives back at the stables and quickly covers the hidden door with hay. He knows the soldiers will come, so he opens all the horse stalls and the large doors at other end of the barn into a corral. Then he opens the corral gates, setting the prized horses free so that they won't become war service animals. He does the same for the hogs and chickens.

When he gets back to the house, Yankees are coming up the drive. A soldier comes up to him and points a rifle with a bayonet on the end in his face, while another grabs his arms from behind, aggressively pushing him to his commander, now on the front porch.

"Do you know about a young woman on a stolen white army horse, which belongs to—?"

Herman answers before he finishes and says, "Young white girl on a beautiful white stallion?" Herman holds back a grin as he sees the man flinch and grind his jaw. "She was here early this morning. Caught her red-handed as she opened all the gates to the horses and other livestock. She said, 'Tell the Russian to be careful of what he burns as his horse may very well be hidden inside, not to mention other things.' I think that is what she said before she laughed and took off down the drive from which you came, yelling, 'Tell him, I got something that he wants...I got something that he wants.'" Don't understand it; that woman crazy or something?" Herman tries not to notice the general's still-clinching jaw and continues, "I've tried all day to find the horses, but no luck." Just as Herman finishes, a soldier confirms that all the livestock is gone.

CHAPTER 20

THE WHITE DOVE

Mollie crosses the river with ease and comes out on the other side to a well-traveled footpath, which follows alongside the main road going north. Occasionally she ventures out onto the road to let Belyy run at a full gallop. It's an easy ride due to the moonlight. *Herman's right—it is colder,* Mollie thinks to herself, and pulls the cape tight to her chest like a blanket.

After riding all night, Mollie is looking at the Russian's map and hears the unmistakable sound of a battle—the report of sharpshooters' rifles, the crackle of muskets, the rapid firing thunder of cannons, the pounding of hoofbeats and soldiers' boots coming from the direction of Griswoldville. Fortunately, that's a few miles east of her. Mollie ponders will the smell of gunpowder always represent death? Will I ever get these sounds out of my head?

Pushing forward through the graying dawn, she avoids the Union soldiers at a checkpoint that guards the railroad tracks. In Old Clinton, she meets Mr. McCarthy, whose family is kind enough to feed and water the horse as well as offer her breakfast. Mollie tells them about the evil foreign Russian killing their fellow citizens, including her daddy. "If they do come asking questions, tell the Russian he may be burning his own horse in the next fire he starts, and don't forget to tell him that I said, 'I got something that he wants.' Where are the rebels? I haven't seen any graycoats in days." He can't answer her question about where the Confederate forces are and moves his head side to side, shrugging his shoulders in defeat.

Mollie rests for about two hours and continues on toward the capital, off the road by way of trails. She finds a spring off the trail where she can make camp. It is also a good watering hole for Belyy. After eating jerky with an apple, she feels the diamond ring from Ben tied on her gun holster and hopes Sherman doesn't harm the Green family. Surely Charles sent them away to safety. For now, she makes a safe place in a makeshift hammock high in a tree to hide and sleep.

It's still daylight when she wakes up and decides to stay put until dark. She reads the rest of the translation book and tries a few commands on the horse. Her Russian words fall on deaf ears, so she tries hand signals. "Hooray," she shouts as Belyy kneels like he did back at the pigsty. Now it makes sense to Mollie. If this horse is a show horse, naturally he can't hear in a noisy and crowded show arena, and you would rely on hand signals. After an hour, she has discovered many of the horse's tricks and dances.

Mollie saddles Belyy, puts on the long white cape, and prepares to break camp. Realizing that she has to climb back up the tree to get her food bag, still tied to a limb, she uses Belyy as a ladder. Untying the bag, she hears the branch start to crack beneath her feet. Mollie is about four or five feet up in the thick tree canopy and surveys that the saddled horse is right under her, so she pulls the cape back to avoid snagging it and drops like a bird, letting the cape fly after clearing the tree. Being a show horse, Belyy seems to think nothing of it when Mollie lands up straight in the saddle.

It's still daylight and not safe to travel, so she kills more time and tries to do some tricks on his back as Belyy, thinking he is back in the circus, walks in circles. Due to natural ability and dance lessons at the Greens, eventually she is able to stand on one foot with the other leg straight out to the sky and her arms spread out from her sides like a swan.

Startled by the crackles in the near woods, she drops with one swoop into the saddle and listens. Hearing the voices of the men, women, and children on the other side of the tree line, she realizes field slaves have been watching her and decides it's time to skedaddle.

She could have never known that her time teaching Belyy show tricks and consequently falling out of the tree onto his saddle was what would make her an icon among slaves and whites alike. She was merely playing with her talented horse. But the slaves peeking through the trees saw a being dressed in white flying out of a tree and landing on a white horse. In an instant, Mollie became the White Dove—a symbol of freedom and of peace to all Southerners who longed for a world without war.

Mollie plans on riding all night to make it through the capital and across the lake before sunrise. She travels at a slow pace except for on long stretches of the main road where she can see ahead in the moonlight. Then she lets Belyy run wide open, with white blond hair and the white cape blowing in the wind behind her, knowing that she might appear ghostly to an onlooker. She smells the army encampments well ahead of time and goes off in the woods to avoid them.

In the meanwhile, back at the Johnsons' mansion, the soldiers search the stables and report back to their commander, "Sir, there is a tunnel under a fake floor in the barn, and it leads to a huge cave system."

As all eyes turn to Herman, he explains, "The family that lives here bought slaves in Savannah that never became slaves at all, but they were taken up North somewhere and made free. Mr. Johnston bought me off that awful ship and freed me immediately. He treated me like a son and said I was too small to make it in the world without his help and an education. He trained me to be a jockey for his racehorses, but that's all gone now because, well, I started growing, and due to the war." Herman shook his head. He didn't know what else to say.

Another soldier comes out of the house with two dirty plates. "Sir, don't believe a word his says. He has aided the Confederacy and should be detained until we get the truth." That's all it takes for Herman to scoot under and between the group of horses and run until he reached the woods where the sprint of his life begins with gunshots hitting the trees in front and behind him. That day, for the first time, he is glad his physical size and endurance have increased in the last two to three years.

He whistles for his fastest horse, which he saddled earlier, figuring something like this might occur. It was perfect timing for the horse to show up as he reached the stream and jumped on to ride her down the shallow water in a shortcut to the bridge. Across the river, Herman runs the racehorse as fast as she can go. He knows it's only a matter of time before the soldiers will go through the cave and perhaps follow the path to Mollie. He has to warn her.

A couple of miles outside of Milledgeville, Herman comes upon a group of slaves, their hands tied to ropes as they walk on the side of the road behind a wagon driven by a well-dressed black man. They all joyfully sing their hearts out. Out of respect, he slows to pass them. He keeps the same pace as the wagon. Herman asks the cheerful driver, "What do y'all have to be so happy about? Look at them. They have a spring in their footsteps."

The driver smiles, "They saw a white dove dancing on a big white horse. The white dove transcends all cultures and traditions. It's symbolic of new beginnings, peace, love, fidelity, luck, hope, and prosperity. Some believe the white dove is the Holy Spirit. Like the rest of Georgia, up until now, they have had a fear of being burnt to death. My name is Mr. Joy, and I haven't a choice but to be happy and joyful...do I?" he laughs.

"What did they see exactly...the slaves?" Herman presses on. "Where?"

The driver says, "Listen to them—they're still chattering about it. They're absolutely happy. I'm happy their owner is so spooked and he has me move them to his city place in the capital. I'm a free man and work for him for wages. They don't have anywhere else to go, so they don't try to escape. I saw the White Dove run her horse at full speed under the moonlight last night, and it did feel lucky to witness, but those lucky souls saw the White Dove fly out of a tree and land on the white horse."

Herman can put two and two together. His mind starts to think how he can spread the word of good luck to the slaves across Georgia so that each slave community will welcome and protect this idol of luck, thus meaning the Union may not burn the town as an added benefit.

South of Milledgeville, Mollie arrives at a large hospital campus. She feels sick when she hears the desperate screams coming from the patients' windows. She rides close enough to talk with one woman, whose arms are dangling between the bars. Cautious, she asks, "Lady, why is everyone screaming? What kind of place is this?" The woman gradually lifts her skeletal face out of the shadow and locks her dead eyes with Mollie's. After a long silence, she speaks, "This is the Georgia Lunatic Asylum, the largest insane asylum in the world. Wealthy men put their wives here to teach them a lesson. Some of us have been left here to die. Mix anyone in with the real crazies long enough, and it begins to wear off on you. You see, I've plotted my husband's murder for almost twenty years in here. I hope this war doesn't kill him first. Most of the inmates are upset, for they've heard Sherman will come here to burn them alive in these locked hall-ways." Mollie is horrified to hear this and, if true, wants to help the woman and others escape rather than let them be burned to death.

A small group of black women, whose work shift just ended, notice Mollie and begin to rejoice at her sight. "You're the White

Dove? My grandmother told me about you. We'll all be saved. Hallelujah!" one nurse exclaims.

Mollie is clueless as to what they refer to but senses she can get their help. "Do you think all the people in here deserve to go to their death in flames when Sherman arrives? Will you help me let them out? Do you know how to unlock the hallways so that they may escape?"

They know that they may get in trouble, but they show Mollie how to get inside and where the locked hallways are located but don't want to stay and help. Mollie knows this delay can get her caught, but she feels like it's the right thing to do. She goes to the find the woman in the window first and uses her to open all the locks she can but quickly leaves when she hears the familiar sound of large troops marching nearby.

She has barely escaped into the pecan groves when she looks back down the hill and sees the campus flooded with escaped patients as hundreds of troops arrive. "That should slow them down some," Mollie laughs, and wonders if the woman in the window has begun her journey to murder the husband.

Mollie races through the woods and ends up at a vacant plantation. "Rose Hill" is on the beautiful gate. Seeing a light in one of the upstairs rooms, she walks up the front steps in between six cypress columns to an open front door. "Hello? Anyone home? May I use your stables for a few hours to rest and feed my horse?" She steps on a board that creaks so loud in the silence that it scares her. She sees a grand piano in the ballroom and next to it a mirror that reaches from the floor to the ceiling. It calms her to think of all the joyful songs and good times that happened in the house before the war.

With the people's faces at the asylum still in her head, she hears a woman's voice from the top of the staircase say, "I'm up here in the front room—please help me. I'm hurt." Perhaps Mollie is still spooked from the insane asylum, but the voice sounds eerie, and it frightens her. She is not sure what to do, but she really doesn't want to go up there.

Mollie calls out, "If it's OK, I'll just use your stables for a bit—then be on my way."

"Help me!" the woman cries.

Reluctantly, Mollie begins to climb the big wide stairs. She hates to leave Belyy unattended. Once on the second floor, she goes straight to the room glowing with the light that she saw from the front of the house.

A beautifully dressed woman with brown hair greets Mollie at the doorway, "Please come in. I usually only entertain handsome men, but when I saw how beautiful you look atop your horse as you crossed my lawn, I had to meet you. My name is Emma."

All Mollie can think to say is, "I thought you said that you were hurt. You seem fine, so I must be on my way." She turns to walk out of the room, and there's Emma in front of her, blocking her way to the door. Mollie quickly glances back where Emma was and just as fast back to the door...Emma is gone. The room is dark, and suddenly Mollie feels very cold.

Mollie doesn't hesitate one bit as she runs down the stairs, looking back as she reaches the landing...nothing is there. She practically glides down the wooden rail, not even sure if she touches any of the seventeen steps she counted going up, and out through the open door to waiting Belyy. Scared out of her mind, she takes off through the woods and heads north.

Mollie arrives in Milledgeville before sunrise, and the streets are still quiet, so she stays on the main road and hopes it'll be the swiftest way through town and over the lake before the sun comes up.

While enjoying looking at the beautiful homes near the governor's mansion, she notices a few people are up and about. A black woman begins to sing and dance about as she sees Mollie approach. Others hear the joyful sounds and come outside to witness and join in the merriment. Quickly a crowd of black and a few white people surrounds Mollie and apparently are honored to be in her presence. All she can hear is, "Glory to God, the White Dove cometh...Glory to God, the White Dove cometh." She doesn't understand but can't afford to be delayed any further. She tries to get Belyy to move forward. The horse doesn't budge but rather enjoys the rubs and admiration—almost similar to the circus.

Away from the crowd stands Herman and his horse, all smiles. He makes the hoot owl sounds with his hands, catching Mollie's attention. She cups her hand and makes the same sound back. "Praise the Lord" is heard throughout the crowd. Mollie gets down from her horse, smiles, and greets the crowd while making her way over to Herman.

"What in the world are these people doing? Why are they so happy and who do they mistake me for?" puzzled Mollie asks.

"Some of the slaves saw you at the spring where you made camp the other day fly out of a tree and stand on a white horse looking like a bird. They call you White Dove, a sign of good luck. They believe their homes won't be burned now because they've seen you.

"I raced straight here to spread the word before you arrived and to warn you that the Yankees found the cave and are on your trail. I believe that we can get the people's support to help you on your journey. As Sherman heads this way to take the capital, we need to get across the lake quick, and these folks will help. They want to protect you. They'll hide you in the middle of the crowd or whatever it takes until you get across that lake. Others will help you farther along.

"With your permission, I'm also here to help you escape to Nashville. Anyway, they're after me now, too. They know I helped you. I'm not as superstitious as some, but who knows? You just may be the White Dove."

Mollie took Herman's hand, saying, "Thank you, Herman, and of course I accept your help. In fact, I need all the help that I can get. I'll go along with this White Dove thing, but between you and me, I'm no white dove."

"Good," Herman says. "We'll make camp for the day about halfway to Eaton. Let's get a move on, Miss Mollie White Dove."

The word spreads quickly about the White Dove, and the crowd grows larger but is unnoticed by the soldiers as they are accustomed to seeing large numbers of refugees flee towns before Sherman's arrival. Once on the other side of the lake, Mollie and Herman mount their horses.

Mollie turns and with the white cape flying in the breeze, says to the following crowd, "Tell the Russian that his horse, Belyy, will be hidden, so be careful what he burns. Also, taunt him, saying, 'She said that she had what you want.'"

As Mollie is about to leave, she looks over at Herman and stands up in her saddle on one leg, the other stretched out behind her covered in the white cape and arms out like wings. She makes a click sound with her mouth, and Belyy moves forward, bows down on one knee, stands tall, backs up away ten steps, turns, and trots off. The crowd goes wild and begins to sing and chant, "White Dove."

Out of sight, Mollie looks over at Herman, saying, "I admit... it's kind of fun."

CHAPTER 21

THE AMBUSH

Only four or five miles down the road, instinct tells Mollie to set up camp well off the road. Mollie's hearing heightens as she wakes up to the sound of horse hoofs in the distance. Climbing to the edge of the cliff, she watches two Union soldier scouts on horses meander their way up the path and come toward her. She scoots back down to camp. Herman is awake, and she tells him, "Herman, big problem. Two Union scout soldiers are coming up the trail and will be here in five minutes. We don't have time to run, and a gun battle is the last thing we need…someone could be killed."

Herman picks up the general's Spencer repeating rifle, the first to be issued, and chambers a round. "Miss Mollie, I don't see where we have a choice. God willing, it won't be us."

"Wait, wait. I have an idea. When I distract them away from their horses and guns, you get the jump on them with that fancy general's gun. Then we can tie them up and escape."

"OK, Mollie. We'll do it your way, but I may have to shoot them. When will I know that they are distracted?" Herman asks.

"Oh, you will know—trust me, you will know," Mollie replies.

She rushes back to the cliff and climbs out on a boulder that is directly above the path, takes her cape and coat off and waits for the two unsuspecting soldiers to pass below. As they get close, Mollie says in the sweetest Southern accent, "Hey, down there." The soldiers reach for their rifles but stop when they see a woman. "My daddy left me here two days ago while he went to find some food. I think he'll come back for me, but I'm worried that something happened. What do you think? Surely he will. He has to know I'm starving by now."

Mollie jumps up, which cause her breasts to bounce up and down, catching the soldiers' eyes.

"What do you want us to do?" asks the younger man.

"Well..." She pauses and stands tall with her shoulders back, presenting her breasts front and center. "I sure am hungry—could you spare me any jerky?" she asks as she smiles.

"Sure" immediately comes out of the younger man's mouth.

But almost instantly, the older man says, "Wait just a minute. I get a say-so here. What do we get for a piece of jerky? Maybe a peek at one of your boobies?" says the older guy.

Mollie pretends embarrassment. "Gentlemen, I declare. I never entertained the idea of such an act. I'm not one of those whores y'all see every night." She pretends to be defeated. "I am hungry though—how about two pieces of jerky?"

"Yes," the younger man says with excitement.

"Two pieces from each of you," Mollie negotiates, "and I have two boobies. Two pieces for each booby from each of you—that makes eight pieces. Do you have that much for me?" she teases as she pulls her long hair across her chest, accentuating their size.

"We have that much. Now show us your beautiful boobies," says the older man.

"Well, show me the jerky first," Mollie requests. "How do I know if you'll give it to me once I show you?"

The older man says, "You come down here off that boulder, and we'll give you the jerky when you show us the goods. Then we'll give you two extra pieces if you let us watch your boobies while you eat the jerky. What do you say? Deal?"

Mollie pretends to think for a minute and then nods her head, agreeing to let them watch. "I'm not coming all the way down. You'll have to reach up the rock ledge and hand it to me. OK?" As she slowly makes her way down to a lower ledge, pulling her dress up at times, both men are looking at her but still glancing over their shoulders…after all, they are trained seasoned soldiers, scouts as it be, and it could be a setup. Still, the power of a woman makes a man not reason with his brain, even if he is well trained and seasoned.

The younger man gets off his horse first and attempts to give Mollie the jerky but can't quite reach her. He throws it to her, and as she puts a piece between her lips, she starts unbuttoning her blouse. When unbuttoned, she puts another piece of jerky between her lips and slowly pulls her blouse apart, suddenly releasing her boobies. The young man gazes on her bare nipples as she chews the jerky.

Mollie is concerned that the older man has not dismounted yet. She leans over the ledge and with her breasts still protruding, asks the younger guy where the rest of her jerky is. He turns to his partner and says, "Get over here with your part. The view is better from here anyway."

"I reckon," the older man says. "Guess I'm just being too cautious."

As he starts to dismount, Mollie gets a good look at his horse and the way it ruts, snorts, and stammers…It's Jack, she believes— Jack, her daddy's horse that she had to sell years earlier. As the man is walking toward Mollie, he is spooked by something and turns to grab his rifle. As Mollie pulls up her dress and draws her pistol, she whistles for Jack as she did so many times before on the farm. The horse bolts toward her, knocking the soldier down. He jumps up and starts to go for a pistol but stops when he see Mollie's pistol pointing straight at him. "I wouldn't do that if I were you, sir," she says. "I assure you that I know how to use this."

"You going to take us both on, pretty lady?" he tells her as she pulls back the hammer.

"Gentlemen, thank you so much for the jerky. Now, please put your hands on the top of your heads before I have to use this."

"Think you can get us both?" he replies.

"Don't have to...I just need to get you. Thanks to your commander, my friend 'happy fingers' over there has a Spencer repeating rifle on your friend." Herman steps out with the Spencer pointed at one and Mollie's pistol is pointed at the other. "Drop your pistols," Mollie commands.

"You boys better listen," Herman says. "She's crazy."

Mollie walks around the back of the boulder and comes down.

"Mollie...Mollie," Herman whispers. "Mollie!"

"What?" Mollie snaps back.

"Button your top," he says. Mollie looks down and seems actually embarrassed.

"Sorry, I forgot. Please forgive me," she replies.

The men can't believe this is happening to them. Finally one figures it out and says to the other, "Dammit, it's that White Bird woman. She probably has the general's horse around here somewhere too."

With tears flowing down her face, Mollie runs over to Jack and wraps her arms around his neck. She knows he remembers her too. "Jack, oh, Jack. I never thought I'd see you again. Have they been good to you?" Judging from his appearance, she knows the answer. She takes in his smell as he does hers. Never did she think she would see anything of her daddy's again, much less Jack. Herman doesn't know what he is witness to but understands its importance completely when it comes to the connection with a horse.

Mollie turns to the two soldiers and tells them that she is sorry for the ambush, but it was the only way she knew to disarm them without a gun battle, where someone could have been killed. She lets them know that her only goal is to get to Nashville to help her family. As they talk, it seems that they are not bad men after all.

Mollie hands the young man a rope. "Sorry, but please tie your buddy up to this tree over here," she tells him as she waves the gun in the direction of the tree. "Now tie your feet up for me by this tree," she says real nice to the young man. As he ties himself up, he is grinning from ear to ear.

He has just seen the bare breast of a woman for the first time in his young life and says, "Ma'am, this is a screwed-up war, but the whole damn war was worth it to get to see those." He continues to stare at her as she securely finishes tying him to the tree.

Mollie asks the soldiers, "Where's Sherman? I don't want to run into his troops."

The older guy is a seasoned soldier. He replies, "White Bird lady, he's a day away. The plans are to skip Madison, per Sherman's orders. Hear he's honoring the promise and handshake of a West Point colleague to spare each other's home towns in the event of war. Instead, in a few days, they'll head directly north to Athens. I normally would not tell you squat shit, but the war is about over. Like you, I just want to go home. We're scouts with General Turchin's troops. Our encampment is on the other side of the main road about a mile north of here, but he has us all mobilized chasing his damn horse.

"All of the people in these small towns dance for joy about a white bird, a sign the war is coming to an end and their homes will be safe. Where do they come up with these myths? The war is coming to an end now, so maybe you are a white bird or dove…or whatever they call you. I don't know.

"Either way, General Turchin has ordered the burning to cease. That's good. The war's almost over. I don't want to burn anything."

While he looks at Mollie's face, he smiles and says, "If we were going to get took, at least we got took by a pretty Southern lady."

"Turchin, huh?" she pauses and thinks better to say anything. "I don't want y'all to freeze to death," she says as she puts blankets over their shoulders and tucks the corners in the rope to help it stay put from the cold wind. As she leans over them, the men inhale her close scent. Unexpectedly, she asks the men to open their mouths so she can give them some food, the beef jerky they gave her earlier, saying, "You got to have dinner."

She smiles and walks away, stops, and then walks back. "I estimate that you will be able to work out of those ropes sometime today. If you promise you won't say you saw me, I'll leave your guns here and a horse a couple miles away. Otherwise, it could be tomorrow before you get back to camp, and who knows who might find you first? What do you say, men? Keep your mouths quiet?"

They both chew for another minute or two, and the older soldier speaks up, "Little lady, now you know that I can't do that. It's my duty to tell what I know to be true but nothing else, and that I will promise you to do."

The young man chimes in, "I will never deny seeing you. It's been the best thing of my sixteen-year life. I'll say you headed toward Savannah, in front of Sherman. How does that sound?"

The old soldier turned to the kid and says, "No, you won't. You will tell the general the truth or nothing at all. Just give the general back his damn horse, lady, and let's let this war be over."

"Who says I have him? He may be in someone's barn or home for safe keeping," Mollie says. "Anyway, I wouldn't if I did have him...that Russian bastard killed my daddy."

CHAPTER 22

ON TO ATHENS

Herman tells Mollie, "There is an Indian spiritual ceremonial ground on the north side of Eaton that most white people avoid, so that will be a good place to camp." He begins describing how they will travel on the lake and cut over on the north side of town. He tells Mollie of the Rock Eagle, a two-thousand-year-old effigy of a bird that he imagines is a white bird if you could see it from the air. It is made of white rocks and is ten feet high and over one hundred feet across from wing tip to tip.

"Seems appropriate, given you're a white bird also. It was built by the early Indians as a place of religion, just like the white bird in Christianity and African myth. Most even still know the Indian myth that it's sacrilegious for white men to trespass. I'm black, and you're a woman, so we'll be fine. No one will bother us there. We can rest the horses for a day and come up with a plan, but we have to leave here soon. These woods will be filled with Yankees with those two telling tall tales about meeting the legend herself."

After setting up a small camp at the Rock Eagle, Mollie falls into a deep sleep while Herman skins, cleans, and cooks a rabbit he hit with a slingshot. Something profound happens to Herman as he stands guard. He sees this woman has more grit, will, and determination in her than anyone he has ever met. She just may be the White Dove, and it's his destiny to travel with her in the mist of the dangers of war.

The next morning, Herman says with a strong conviction, "I had a dream last night that an angel came to me and instructed me to help you with your journey as far as it takes. God be willing, I'm happy to oblige." Mollie smiles at the thought of God protecting her. Herman is right. Nobody ever comes to the Indian ceremonial grounds.

The next day, they make their move north up to Madison. After they arrive, word spreads quickly that the White Dove is there, and there is a welcoming town reception at Heritage Hall. It is another Greek Rival home, with six huge columns in the front. It is also the home of Dr. Elijah Evans Jones, a Confederate doctor. Everyone in town shows up to see the White Dove and to be grateful that this religious prophecy will spare everybody's homes and businesses from being torched.

Herman seems to know the black leadership in almost all the communities. An elder at the Johnson estate who was a black Freemason often took young Herman to meetings in the area under the jurisdiction of Prince Hall of the Savannah Court.

Before Mollie goes inside for refreshments, she notices that Herman turns over the care of the horses to a man with whom he has a special handshake.

Mollie tells the crowd of people surrounding her, "I'm no hero. I'm a fourteen-year-old girl who is running for her life from an evil giant Russian general named Turchin. Please help me hide from him so that I can make it to Nashville before my sister and mother die." She hears a marching band approaching, and it's filled with men too old to fight leading a parade in her honor. Mollie thinks to herself, *this is a little too much.*

Inside the house, she finds Herman next to a marble fireplace. He stops speaking to a group of men when he catches the concerned look on Mollie's face and moves her way. "They love you and are treating this like a celebration day." Herman smiles.

Mollie shakes her head. "I feel like a fraud. I told you they'll spare Madison because of a college handshake, not me."

"Mollie, three long years of war is all any of us have known. You give me—all of us—hope. It's real. Look at their faces. Not just here—everywhere we've been since you've been on the run. I've learned from the group of men over by the fire that you have created a seventy-mile swath of a no-burn trail thus far. See, Mollie, like it or not, you're their hero. You can't argue with facts. It just so happens you represent a symbol of something strongly positive at last to civilians, slaves, and poor people alike. They otherwise have no hope, and it's contagious across all colors." Mollie begins to soften and understand that it's not her exactly but what she represents...hope.

Mollie feels ice water pour down her back, and a woman urgently tells her, "Leave, hide. They'll kill you too." Mollie swirls around to no one there.

With big eyes, she looks at Herman. "Did you hear her?" Her arm reaches around to touch her back. Amazingly, she touches a dry back.

Herman says, "I didn't hear anything. What did you hear? You look like you've seen a ghost. Are you ready to go?"

"Yes," Mollie says. "We have to get out of here now!"

"OK, but you will be the legend of this town for years to come," Herman says as they walk back through the fourteen-foot-high front hall, past the staircase to the front door.

They say their farewells to all and remind them to tell the Russian that he could be burning his own horse in the next fire he sets—and not to forget to also say, "She said that she has something that you want."

Someone rides up in a rush. "We can hear the Union on the march, south of town. We've already spotted their leading scouts. Ride, White Dove, ride!" shouts the young-boy lookout rider.

The crowd begins to repeat, "Ride, White Dove, ride," as the two quickly escape with the white cape flowing behind Mollie as they head thirty miles north to Athens.

While they rest the horses at the Eagle Tavern Stagecoach Inn at Watkinsville, Mollie tells Herman about the woman's voice and the ice water. His eyes get as big as hers. "Ghost," he says. "All these old houses are known to be filled with ghosts. I've never seen one myself. You really hear someone?"

"Yes, I thought you also would have heard her say, 'Run, or hide! They'll kill you too,' and you didn't hear it? It scared me to death when I felt cold water on my back, but it was dry when I touched it. A different woman spoke to me at a vacant house outside of Milledgeville, and then she just vanished."

"Are you some kind of special person, Mollie? I watched you read like I've seen no other and your way with horses, men, and now ghosts?"

Mollie gives him the short version of her life with no apologies. Just as they begin to get back on the stagecoach trail, a crowd starts to gather and rejoice at the sight of the White Dove once again. Herman sees and smells fields of unpicked cotton on fire. He shakes his head in disbelief every time he sees another fire and then says, "Sherman promised to 'make Georgia howl,' and he's doing a good job of taking us off the map. I hear he hates Georgia boys. Says they're the meanest and toughest fighters in the war. This is his payback, to put the fear of God in the civilians, burn everything, loot the farms, and confiscate the livestock in the hope to break the will of the people for support of the war. Look around—everyone has lost the will to fight. Then along comes you. You have given folks hope that the nightmare will be over soon."

They ride mostly on the main trail as they get closer to Athens. A decision is made to call on the hospitality of Colonel Hill's horse farm for the night.

Turchin's army bypasses Watkinsville and goes straight to Athens. His assistant rides up alongside the general. "I've located the perfect house for you, sir...another one of the big, beautiful Southern white houses. This one has thirteen columns on it, one for each the original thirteen colonies. It's the mansion of Confederate General Robert Taylor. I get a kick when we occupy a rebel general's house. How's that for a good sign? The widow fled in a hurry. All the servants are still there. It'll be nice to eat some good cooking," he says as he rubs his empty belly, and asks, "Do you really think she'll come straight to you in Athens?"

CHAPTER 23

CC TAYLOR

Herman stays at the colonel's horse farm just outside Athens, with Belyy and his horse. He plans to meet Mollie and Jack in Nashville if she doesn't return in one week. He will try to visit area farms for information from Athens citizens and let them know the White Dove has been in town.

Mollie decides not to follow behind the troops to Athens and instead opts to go to the Winterville depot, six miles east of town, so that she'll already be on board with Jack when the train arrives at the Athens train station. All goes well as she boards the freight car with Jack. Thanks to Colonel Hill, she's wearing an oversized Union soldier uniform with a very tight undergarment across her chest.

Mollie's heart begins to pound as the train slowly rolls into Athens station. The loud freight door opens to Mollie's backside. Jack has a loose shoe. With a horse hoof over her knee, she taps the shoe back into place and hears, "Hey, we weren't told of any freight in this car from Winterville. Where are you going?" asks the Union soldier.

Mollie waves her hand hello but doesn't stand to look at the man with questions and says with as deep of a voice as she can muster, "Major General George H. Thomas's new horse." The soldier knows of the new commander of the Army of the Cumberland up in Tennessee and sees nothing unusual. Mollie pulls out the forged papers she wrote the night before at the farm, using Turchin's papers for information, and holds them up in the air, obviously busy with her hands full.

"Yeah, I heard about the president replacing Rosecrans," he says as he looks at the orders that he can't read and folds them, giving them back. "Good luck with that shoe." Mollie exhales as he leaves the car. Something strikes the soldier as odd, but he can't put his finger on it.

The same soldier checks on the wounded Confederate soldier in the next car up. The man has been sent home in a war exchange effort from the Rock Island prison in Illinois. His family has connections, and he has come home to die. Unfortunately, when he arrived in Marietta last night, the town square, the depot, and all the plantations had been burned to the ground. No one was left.

Christopher Columbus "CC" Taylor, a private in the Confederate Army who fought so hard to get home, is ready to die, so he stays on the train to Athens. The Union soldier has orders to remove him, so he hoists the weak body over his shoulder and carries him to the side of the depot and places him against the wall. Then he goes to a nearby well and gets water for the wounded man. Before he leaves, he takes off his winter coat. He knows he can get another, so he places it on CC, who tries to reject it, saying, "I want to die. Please let me go."

Additional cars are added to the train in the idle time, and Mollie's stomach is in knots with an all-time high level of anxiety. Thankfully, the whistle blows, and the car slowly starts to roll forward for about two hundred feet. Then it suddenly stops. Nervous sweat rolls down Mollie's neck and chest. The door opens. It's the soldier from earlier. Mollie's mouth is dry. He enters the car and says, "Something about you struck me as odd. You have a bare neck. It's cold, we all have long hair, and no one gets a haircut in the middle of war. Who are you really?" He pulls her cap off, and her long white braid falls out. "You're her, the White Bird lady that we've chased for the past one hundred miles. Where's the horse? There's a bounty on you, and I'm the lucky one to get it. Hot damn. You are awful pretty too." He smiles and tries to grab her arm.

Mollie pushes a pistol into his side, "You're going to be quiet, and shut the door," she says.

"No, ma'am," he replies as several armed Union soldiers point their guns at Mollie. He takes her pistol.

She never really thought that she'd get caught. *What in the world have I gotten myself into, and just one month before Christmas?* Mollie thinks to herself as she is led out of the car. Just for the attention, the soldiers tie her hands, untie her long braid, and then let her hair flow in the cool breeze. Next they put her on Jack to parade her through town and show off their catch in hopes of demoralizing the population of her followers.

Instead the civilians are so excited to see the White Dove with their own eyes that they chant her praise, "White Dove! White Dove!" and to the astonishment of Union soldiers, the people begin to celebrate in the streets—the young, old, black, and white. Some of the soldiers secretly take pride to be seen so close to her, especially if it means they can go home before long.

Word has been sent to the Taylor house, 634 Prince Avenue: "General Turchin, we have captured the 'White Dove.' The crowds are larger than expected while we are in process to deliver."

Turchin is anxious about her arrival as he thinks to himself, *why is this Southern woman derailing my mission? Who is she? What does she look like? Where is she from? Where is she going? Who would be so foolish to ambush me and steal my horse, rifle, and very important papers, the plans to go to South Carolina after Savannah? She's been too busy on the run to give them to the Confederates. Why? Why is she the White Dove, and why am I obsessed and waiting so long to see this woman?* He paces up and down the main hallway through the house, waiting for her arrival.

Herman has followed Mollie and watches at the depot as Mollie is hauled off to her predator as he fears for her future, his own life, and his beautiful state of Georgia. He stands with the cold wind to his face and notices that the wounded man on the ground has managed to stand up and hold his hands to heaven. "Thank you, God. Thank you for giving me the will to live again. Thank you for sending me an angel...Amen."

Herman himself has felt such a divine occurrence recently, and he knows it's God's will to protect Mollie. He doesn't question why, but he just witnessed it happen to another man.

Herman holds out his hand. "My name is Herman Deeley. I see you have been touched by the Almighty himself," he says, with an engaging smile. "Could you hear where the soldiers are taking her?"

"Yes, my name is CC Taylor. An hour ago, my life was over— farm, family, friends, and the whole town gone. Then in the middle of all the war, death, and destruction, God wakes me up and shows me an angel. Damn Yankees took her as prisoner. They called her the White Dove and took her to the general for the reward. I will recover and help her escape. That's God's message to me, and now here you are. Are you the one that God has assigned to help me heal and rescue her?"

"I'm not much on caretaking of people," Herman says, "but I do know a good bit about horses. Is it your shoulder or arm?" Herman asks with genuine concern.

"Both," says CC. "I got some kind of terrible fever when I was in the hospital, and they let my wounds turn bad. I knew all they intended on doing was to cut it off, like they did all of us rebels. I laid there in bed and watched it all day long—piles of arms and legs built up so fast they used wheelbarrows to haul them off somewhere.

"My Grandma, bless her heart…" CC almost tears up. "She was good at writing letters, and boy did she ever write them. Grandma wrote President Lincoln a letter every single day I was in the prison hospital. She pleaded for my release, explained to him I am the only member left in the family to carry on the Taylor name and to please have mercy. It must have worked because they exchanged me for a Yankee and then put me on a train to Atlanta, just in time to see it burn…my hometown too."

Herman puts CC on the back of his horse and then gets in the saddle and takes him back to the colonel's horse farm. They are met at the gate like heroes once CC takes off the Union blue coat. CC sits down and rests on the front porch. It's a beautiful day, peaceful and quiet except for the woodpeckers. They create the sound of drums as they peck on the hollow cypress wood columns above. The colonel's grandpa laughs and says, "Dang birds hear themselves make all that racket and think they're the size of elephants."

The ladies begin to tend to CC's wounds first, using whiskey made from the corn on the farm for cleaning, and it burns to high heaven. Granny explains, "That burn is where we are chasing the devil out of you. If we can stop the burn, we may save your arm." Then trays of food are brought in. Granny feeds CC as she tells him of the family members who fight or have died for the Confederacy. The family is so happy to help this soldier as they believe to it's his destiny to save and protect the White Dove.

CHAPTER 24

WHITE DOVE MEETS GENERAL TURCHIN

The Union soldiers make barricades on each side of the corner lot to keep spectators and the curious away. Mollie is taken to a very elegant mansion, not camp tent headquarters as she expected. The house reminds her of the Greek Parthenon, which she saw pictures of in the Green library.

Strangely, the house is decorated for the holidays already, with green wreaths, garland, and red ribbons. Then she notices a baby Jesus in a manger scene in the front lawn, and Mollie begins to weep and thank God for showing her such beautiful reminders of Christ and all that he endured before she is about to be thrown into a Yankee jail.

That's not typical of Georgia, she thinks as she notices big ant mounds at the tree trunks, in the middle of the well-groomed lawn. She's escorted up the stairs in her Union disguise, past the large columns to the dark mahogany front door, which is surrounded by glass panels. She is still on the arm of the soldier from the depot; he knocks and says to her, "I really do hope you bring an end to this war. If Johnny Rebs would just quit and not fight back so hard...I mean they fight with everything they have, even after they are wounded and defeated. I guess I would too if strangers invaded Connecticut."

The formally dressed butler opens the door and receives, as ordered, just the two of them into the large foyer, leaving the remaining men outside. Mollie stands on the enormous rug under a crystal chandelier and awaits her punishment.

Turchin stands at the top of the ornate wooden staircase, so tall that he makes the eight-foot grandfather clock next to him look average. "Behold the White Dove's presence!" he says, not expecting that he would respond this way to seeing her but never imagining her in a Union uniform or with dirty black smudges on her face. He slowly walks down to her, but now all the questions he thought of earlier cease to exist.

"I am Brigadier General John Turchin," he says with little Russian dialect. He notes she is staring him directly in the eye, as if trying to get in and burn his soul. "You must be uncomfortable in that uniform. Please follow the servant to your quarters. They have drawn you a bath...you smell like horse manure. Surely they have clothes to fit you somewhere in this enormous house. We'll talk over dinner."

He walks in the direction of the grand library, where officers are in a planning meeting, but stops when he hears, "*Svin'ya*," which Mollie has said in Russian as she pretends to spit on the ground, intending complete disrespect. He feels her anger and rage from across the large hall, and although he finds it stimulating, he is astounded as to why she would insult him in his native tongue.

"American woman?" He shakes his head and then continues on to the officer's meeting.

Turchin orders his officers to continue the march to Savannah with Sherman while he holds enough soldiers to guard him and occupy Athens. He explains that he has had recent health problems after having a heatstroke and will remain here until he recovers. After he leaves the room, there are snickers among the officers, but all admire him and his leadership. They don't blame him for taking a break. He has fought hard in every battle and endured many injuries, but they're suspicious of his obvious obsession for his prisoner, the White Dove, and just a little curious along with being envious.

Two female black servants take Mollie off to a nearby bedroom and help the White Dove take off the many layers of the army uniform. They are surprised to see her own dress, shoes, knives, and holster under it all. One of them takes the dirty clothes outside to the washroom. She is excited to put the word out on the street that the White Dove is here safe and the town of Athens can celebrate.

Mollie gently slides her tired, aching muscles into the warm bath. One of the servants grabs a washcloth while the other servant pours scented bath oils into the tub and then uses the remaining oil to massage her shoulders and back. Mollie thoroughly enjoys the two servants' attention as there's something very comforting about another woman's touch, let alone two women. She has been on the run for so long that she is almost relieved it's over, but still curious as to why she hasn't been thrown in jail yet...maybe to not upset the civilians who believe in her.

The two servants proudly and carefully brush Mollie's long hair. They pull it into a high ponytail and then braid the loose hair. They give Mollie a beautiful hoop dress to wear for dinner, but Mollie is not happy and blames the Russian for selecting it. The girls say no, that they just know it would be beautiful on her. The tight corset seems over the top, and she has them loosen enough so that she can breathe. The servants feel special to witness the beauty of the White Dove and be in the same room with them. They will talk about it for years to come.

Mollie recognizes that they probably look at her as an idol, and she puts her arms around both the girls in a three-way hug, saying, "Thank you. Thank you for the comfort of your touch. This terrible war has made everyone so cold. Maybe if we can all embrace one another's touch, we can find peace." Both girls hug Mollie with happy tears, chanting, "Praise the Lord...praise the Lord... the White Dove cometh."

Mollie's arrival is announced to the Russian as "Miss White Dove" when she enters the enormous dining room. He smiles, stands, and removes his hat as she enters the room. He opens his arms and gestures for her to join him at the fireplace to talk before dinner. She accepts and comes across the room. He greets her, saying, "You must forgive my staring, but in my lifetime I have been in many military battles, including this bloody war, and you seem to be an oasis in a desert. Please have a seat." He stands behind a chair for her near the warm fire.

"I'd like to start over. Please call me John. Your real name is? Why would you call me a swine? It seems as though you hate me by your body language, yet you're the one who steals my horse and other belongings in the middle of a war. You can be tried as aiding the Confederacy, yet you're here in this beautiful home with me and not a jail."

Mollie says, with built-up anger, "Mollie Teal, and you really should have searched me because I can have my fingers on a knife and twist it into your evil heart until it stops anytime I choose."

John asks, "Shall I have the guards outside the front door join us for dinner? Where does this violence come from in such a lovely woman?"

Mollie's crazy anger takes over, and she jumps up with both hands and goes for John's neck. When she does, the shoulder shawl drops to the floor, exposing her bare shoulders and the top half of her chest and cleavage. John is able to quickly take Mollie's wrist, all the while enjoying her exposed flesh. In her furious state, Mollie tries to kick and punch the man who killed her father. All efforts of thinking rationally are out the door, and pure hatred and rage flow from her petite frame. She struggles, but her twists and kicks are no match against this large man. Mollie wears herself out, and her struggles eventually stop. Her arms flail as she tries to fight, and her body goes limp in defeat. He catches her and holds her up against his broad chest as she begins to sob tears on his jacket and then suddenly begins to viciously pound on his chest. He doesn't make her stop but allows her to get all the years of pent-up pain, anger, and sorrow out until she finally tires in complete exhaustion and then goes silently limp like a rag doll.

He concludes, when she keeps her head still, that he can gently put her back in the chair. Then he places the shawl back over her shoulders. Bending down on his knees, his face close to hers, he lifts her chin and begins to wipe her face with his handkerchief, truly appreciating the beauty of a woman's face compared to all the men's faces he has seen on the battlefield, both dead and alive. Mollie feels his warm breath blow across her face and opens her teary eyes to see his dark-brown eyes staring in to hers. His shoulder-length dirty hair is tied at the back of his neck, with only a few lose strands around his face.

John stands slowly and never dreamed he would be so close to this lovely a creature. "Please forgive me, Miss Mollie. I realize my smell is that of war, and that has you upset. I'll go find a change of clothes and will return shortly. I'd like to talk before dinner." As he gets up and quietly walks toward the door and pulls the door closed behind him, Mollie realizes that he did reek of gunpowder and smoky campfires. How did she end up this close to the monster that had ruined her life? Now she's confused as to why he is trying to be so nice to her.

Mollie thinks long and hard how she will keep her emotions to herself and decides to tell him boldly what he did on the very day she arrived in Athens. She wishes to tour the home while she waits and asks a staff member to escort her through the common areas and then to the library. Mollie reflects on all the homes she has visited since Savannah. This one is impressive as well, inside and out, and makes her think of the unfortunate family that had to flee from this home. She is delighted with library's enormousness; according to the plaque on the wall to the donors, it duplicates many books from the nearby University of Georgia. Mollie begins scanning the ornate mahogany wooden shelves and pulls out several books that she will read after dinner.

"Here you are," John announces in his overbearing presence. "So you're a reader—how interesting."

A startled Mollie turns around, trying to contain her emotions, and says, "I choose the library for our conversation before dinner because it is a room full of collected knowledge and wisdom—that is how I wish to keep our conversation...intelligently stimulating without any emotions that merely distract." She stops when she observes his very well-groomed appearance. "Why, I don't recognize you."

He apparently had the staff prepare him a bath as he has flowing, clean brown hair. He also trimmed the overgrown mustache, beard, and nails. John laughs heartily. "Do you think I look like the fancy carriage driver in this suit? Am I overdressed? The only clean clothes that fit were that of a large slave. He said it's his driving uniform when he took the Taylors to fancy galas before the war. I wished I'd visited the South before all the destruction; it must have been really extraordinary, except perhaps the slaves."

Mollie can't believe she is distracted by this man's pleasant appearance, mostly noticing his broad chest and large shoulders, with a shirt slightly too small for his upper frame. He walks closer. Although she is tall for her age, he towers over her at six feet, two inches. He smells of the same bath oils she bathed in and has a fresh, clean scent. Not sure why her hatred for him is softening, she walks around to the other side of a long table, keeping it as an obvious buffer between them.

Mollie stands tall with a defiant poise of confidence and sternness and blurts out, "Athens, Alabama—you murdered my daddy. I witnessed it with my own eyes. I made vows to always hate you.

I've tried for years to get your face out of my mind, out of my nightmares. Just when I thought enough time had passed, you show up underneath the roof that I was forced to jump off of in Macon.

"I was on my way out of town before all of your soldiers showed up to burn everything. I wanted to get here to Athens, Georgia, to board the army supply train to Tennessee. My sister and mother are sick and dying in a hospital in Nashville." She takes a slight pause to clear her throat and continues, "John, if you know what's good for you, don't ever trust me. I'll always want you dead."

John's happy demeanor turns ominous. "Now I remember you! You're the girl that bit my leg and pinched my horse that almost threw me off." John goes before Mollie on one knee and takes her hand, eyes tearing up and trying to hold back his emotions, "Please forgive me. Please. I'm so sorry. I will never forget the look on your face that day. It haunts me to this day. Forgive me for being a part of your terrible war nightmare."

Mollie asks most defiantly, "I thought I read that you were court-martialed in Huntsville, Alabama, for your war crimes in Athens. Why aren't you in jail? Why are you still in the army?"

He replies without hesitation, "I did have a federal trial in Huntsville. Mollie, sometimes I truly wish I'd stayed in jail there. It's a beautiful town, with mountains and rivers, with nice people. I considered staying there after my jail term.

"I'm thirty-five years old and have spent most of my adult life fighting wars for the Imperial Russian Army. I proudly became an American citizen. I love this country so much, even more than the motherland. That's why, when the United States government asked me to serve in the Union Army, I said yes. I want to protect America from ever becoming like Russia.

"That day in Athens was a huge mistake. I had become weary and frustrated with the war here and used tactics that were used in the Crimean War, using pain and fear. If a farmhouse shoots at my soldiers, I order my men to rampage the place and then burn it down. I admitted this in court. I wanted to pay the price for my mistake and go to jail. The army wanted me back, so President Lincoln stepped in and promoted me to brigadier general, a position that can't be court-martialed. Then, they sent me right here to Sherman to do the exact same kind of war crimes in Georgia. He wanted to adopt my country's vicious war tactics, and I became an adviser on Russian tactics and strategies. Again, I am so sorry, Mollie."

Trying to stay unemotional and certainly detached, she says, "John, I will always want you dead."

Completely ignoring that statement, he says, "May I ask you other questions? How did you read my maps and know which towns were safer for you? They're written in Russian. Did you see all the plans? Look at the books you're holding—*Economies of Asia* and *Religions of the Middle East.* Who are you, really? Are you special in some way? Who is White Dove?"

Mollie takes a few deep breaths and carefully ponders how to answer that barrage of questions and finally says, "I am special because I have a voracious appetite to read. I thoroughly enjoy reading a lot—so much that I read really fast as well, and I remember every word. Your observation serves you well that in fact I did read a translation book at the house in Macon that had a limited amount of Russian, mainly to understand Belyy and his commands. The map is easy. After Savannah, you are going to South Carolina.

"While being hunted by your soldiers, so as to not get caught, I traveled at night. One day while I was killing time waiting for nightfall, Belyy let me practice ballet standing in his saddle while I wore a white cape. As you can imagine, since Belyy was at one time a show horse in a circus, he was doing show tricks when a group of slaves saw us.

"From that one farm, it spread all over Georgia, the word of peace and good luck. They had seen a symbol from their religious beliefs back in Africa, a white dove. People are sick of the war; they clamor for something that gives them hope of a better tomorrow. Even if I am their White Dove, I still want you dead." He's speechless after she answers all his questions and needs a moment to collect his thoughts.

"Mollie, I must insist that we have dinner even if you want me dead." He quickly nods to the staff member at the door. "You sure know a lot to only be eighteen years old," he says as he stands up. She isn't sure where he got that age, but she would go with it for now. As they enter the elegant dining room, with its stunning chandeliers and ornate ceiling, John asks the server to move the two place settings from the ends of the twenty-foot table so they can be across from each other in the middle. They immediately accommodate John's request and also move the flowers and candles to not obstruct their view of each other.

Like a gentleman, he pulls her chair out and scoots it in for her as she sits, picks up the napkin off the center of the plate and places it in her lap for her. He gets situated across from her, and soup is served. After waiting for Mollie's cue to begin, he picks up the correct spoon, scoops it away from his mouth, and begins to eat. Mollie notices all the details of his impeccable table etiquette as the meal proceeds—and to think…a few hours ago he was the dirty, vile Russian monster, the villain in all her bad dreams.

He suppresses his emotions for Mollie and changes his demeanor to a pure, professional manner and asks, "Did you show, tell, or repeat to anyone about the map and the plans? And if so, who? Anyone in the Confederacy?"

Mollie spouts off, "Of course, I told General Lee himself. Are you kidding me? I have been on the run for one hundred miles, with little sleep or rest. Forgive me if I didn't give the war priority over my safety."

"I take that as a no. You showed the papers to no one?" he asks.

Mollie dodges the question and says, "I destroyed your papers, but I remember everything that I read." Pausing for a reaction, she continues, "After ruining my life when you killed my daddy, leaving us penniless and without the protection of a man in the middle of this terrible war, I eventually found relatives in Savannah. Then the word comes that Sherman has his sights set to burn Savannah, and about the same time, I get a letter from my sister of her illness." Mollie leans forward. "Can you get me to Nashville?" Mollie asks.

"Sorry—I'm not letting you go anywhere with the information you know until Sherman takes Savannah. You're under house arrest here with me. Did you read about the White Dove in a book and plan this?

"Where is my horse, and why did you say he is a show horse? He is not. He's a war horse," John declares as he finishes pelting her with questions.

Mollie finishes her meal, places her fork upside down on the plate and her napkin to the left. Although he isn't near finished, the Russian follows her lead and ends his meal as well. Mollie asks, "Where is my horse, Jack? He's my daddy's horse that somehow ended up in your brigade. You can't keep me here. I have no part in this war," she yells.

"Let me go to what I have left of a family. Your horse, Belyy—he's my insurance so that I get to my family while they're alive."

John replies, "You know that I can't let you go after what you just told me. Let's just have faith that Sherman does win quickly, hopefully before Christmas. Besides, there are over sixty thousand troops here in Georgia, and it's too dangerous for you to travel. Relax, rest, be safe, and read the entire library if you want.

"I have taken a leave from the war to recuperate from a heatstroke. You'll be very well protected here. There are two guards at every door, all over the lawn, and there are barricades on the street. No one can get to you here," he says as he tries to comfort her and likewise to let her know that what protects her also imprisons her.

He fights to remain platonic, but secretly he can't help but want to seduce her. He justifies it by knowing that any man would take advantage of this once-in-a-lifetime opportunity, even if he were married.

"Prisoner, that's what you mean, isn't it? Your prisoner!" she shouts angrily, pushing away from the table. The Russian stands, giving her the signal to wait until he comes around to pull her chair out. She waits, stands when he assists, thanks him for dinner, and tells him she going to retire for the night.

Picking up her books on the buffet, she asks the servant to show her the way back to her quarters, and then she turns back to him. "Savannah will be given to Sherman on a silver platter with no resistance. Mark my words, and remember the name Charles Green. He will help make it possible. Now that I have given you war secrets, will you let me go?"

"Thanks, Mollie, but, no," he says.

It takes two ladies to help Mollie out of the dress. She requests something practical for the next day. Reading another book, she sees footsteps pass her door, up and down the hall, very late at night.

The general paces up and down the hall and tries to understand a very complicated woman. He can't stop thinking about her, her beauty, her unique gift of knowledge, and the White Dove symbol people claim to love. Has she put him under a love spell too?

The next day, the Russian is up early to select some books he has already read, in hopes to get Mollie to read them quickly and later discuss the books as a means to get close so she'll let her guard down. He senses she needs "fatherly love," and he will make her feel like a loved princess..."Apple of my eye," he laughs. Yes, she's smart but young. He has to be careful playing this woman's heart. She is capable of stabbing him in his heart, and not with a knife.

Mollie decides that, if she'll be in the "house jail," she will read in the library to avoid John.

"Good morning, my beautiful princess. I have something for you." He boldly kisses her cheek and picks up her hand. "Look, isn't it beautiful on your wrist? I knew when I saw it. It is perfect on you." As he closes the clasp on a diamond bracelet he has taken out of the now unlocked safe upstairs, he finishes, "You deserve diamonds all over, Mollie—more than any woman in the world."

Mollie steps away. "Where is the diamond ring that I had in my gun holster when you captured me? And my gun?" Mollie kindly asks.

"I will inquire to all involved. For you, Mollie, I will find them."

Mollie is concerned about his amplified kindness as he continues, hardly taking a breath, "Your dress is very becoming, although last night's dress will be hard to beat. I like when you dress beautifully. I like the idea of both of us dressing up in the clothing that's of this region while we wait for news from the war front. Why not? It's nearing Christmas; it'll be fun.

"I've thought of other things you might enjoy. Today's weather feels like it'll be warm—let's take advantage and have a picnic out in the English garden in the back lawn. Look, I have picked out some of the books that I have read. Perhaps you can start to read one so that we can discuss it at our picnic?" He gives her random books, from sword fighting to poetry and vodka making. "Come on, Mollie—it'll be a fun distraction away from the outside world. Just you and me and a way to get to know one another. I'll tell you all that you want to know about me, and I want to know every single detail about you—everything. You're amazing. Look at you. Who wouldn't want to know everything about you?" he says as he smiles and looks into her eyes.

Confused but acting flattered, she agrees to play along and gives him several books to choose to read from that she has already read, including a cookbook. The two go their separate ways to prepare for their lunch date.

John greets Mollie with a splendid blanket picnic, including flowers from the hothouse, spread all about. Smoked meat, cheese, and bread are on plates within reach. Mollie wears a white spring dress without the hoops and carries a parasol that matches. Her hair is pulled around to the front in one thick pony tail. He wears a maroon shirt that is unbuttoned at the chest, with a sports jacket that does not go unnoticed by Mollie. She knows it's strange and doesn't understand why she is attracted to her captor.

They discuss the books of medieval warfare and sailboats. He's surprised she actually reads so quickly and remembers every detail. For fun, he opens books to random pages and tests her.

Their outing is disrupted when Mollie notices many big black ants. "John, let's go before these bullet ants sting one of us. I spoke with the gardener, and he said they came in on a load of tropical plants from Brazil that the owner purchased in Savannah. Before everyone fled, all the neighbors were working together to stop them from spreading—with some success, since the only mounds left are in the front yard. Their sting is very painful, like burning fire, and can last for twenty-four hours."

"Yes," John replied. "I have had an encounter with those devils...stepped on one the mounds in the front yard...thought I had been shot in the leg."

As they walk back to the house, he is convinced that the picnic went very well as a way to get closer to Mollie as he planned.

Dinner that evening is a formal dress-up occasion. John presents Mollie with a diamond-studded necklace and insists that she wear it every day, along with the bracelet. He gently kisses her shoulder before he lets her hair down after he clasps the necklace from behind. Mollie has reservations and is very skeptical but admits to herself that his attention feels good. Is he trying so hard to make up for killing her daddy? She realizes this is the first time she has found a man attractive. Why now? Why this man?

While the weather is mild, the two meet for breakfast each morning on the veranda. She always picks up more of his books to read, and then they meet for lunch on another exquisite site on the property to discuss them.

Dinners have progressed to an after-dinner dance in front of the fireplace. She loves the way her body tingles when he touches her shoulders and back or arms. Shivers actually go down her spine at his touch. John's aroused again, and he wants her to make the decision to move a step further. So far, she has resisted his charm and excused herself frequently.

Back in her room, she tries to focus and read but finds it impossible. She becomes easily distracted and thinks about her handsome John now and not the evil Russian. So many thoughts spin through her head at once. What are his intentions? He's older and makes her feel older, special, and good about herself. He says he has never met anyone as remarkable as her, and he's so handsome.

Then she begins to hate herself as she thinks of her daddy, a face she can barely remember. John has already said he's going back to war and will meet his troops outside Charleston. Why get attached, and then he's killed too? She's never met someone so attentive. He makes her heart race. Of all the men in her past, none of them has wanted to know her or ask her questions about herself or her thoughts on anything. Why John? She thinks that she needs fresh air to think clearly, and suddenly it hits her...the answer is no. She must honor her daddy.

John's tension is building to an all-time high as he lies in his bed thinking about a naked Mollie on top of him. Tomorrow he will take her in his arms, declare his love, and make plans for their future after the war. Whatever it takes—he only had so much time to play before he heads to Charleston, and he wants to make the most of each day...primarily in his bed.

Mollie gets up early and again goes straight outside to the private balcony off her bedroom in her nightgown and listens to the birds sing. Didn't they know to expect cold weather at the week's end, according to the newspaper? She closes her eyes and feels the morning sun warm on her face. She is happy, in an unfamiliar way. Her future is uncertain, as it has always been, but for now she is content on sharing her days with her villain turned charmer. She smiles as she pictures his eyes looking into hers.

She opens her eyes to the bright light of a camera flash from the nearby stairs. A man comes out from under the cloth behind the large camera. "Perfect," he says. "The people are going to love to see a picture of the White Dove." He packs and runs off with his camera as Mollie runs inside and screams for someone to catch him.

Finally she sees John and shouts, "You said that I was safe here, protected with guards, and this man gets within feet of me right outside my bedroom. For crying out loud, I'm not even dressed, and he takes a private photograph. Please catch him, John. There can't be that many cameramen around this small town."

He smiles and can't help notice her thin nightgown. "I'll find him. I'll find him for you. Anything for you, my Mollie. I'm here to protect you, and don't you worry, I'll be back in time for our breakfast. I want to talk about our future—yours and mine, Mollie." He places diamond earrings in her hand, "There's never too much for my princess. Wear these for me today my precious, Mollie." He kisses her forehead and rushes out the front door.

Of course a photographer got that close. John paid him. He knows Mollie goes out on her private porch early in the morning. He wanted a picture that would reveal Mollie, knowing she would never pose for it. He hopes the photograph looks as good as she did just now in the thin nightgown.

Mollie's hosting their breakfast on the huge front porch when John arrives and says, "I see where you have added extra soldiers outside, so I thought we would enjoy one more day of very warm weather for December. Strange, Christmas will be here soon. What will be of our lives by then?"

"Yes, my beauty." He adds, "I did post more soldiers for your protection and got rid of the loafers that were on duty earlier, and all parts of the city and countryside are being searched for the photographer's wagon." He smiles with the photograph in his pocket.

John sits across from Mollie, and he pours on the romance, saying, "Mollie, I'm not sure why or how our lives have crossed. I do know I started to fall for you the early morning you jumped me. You sent a bolt of lightning through me, stole my horse and my heart. I had to chase you, and I am so glad I did. In the short amount of time that we've spent together, I've gotten to know you. You are a very intelligent, witty, loving, and caring woman...a fireball at times but in a good way. Combined, that's the real you, and now I gladly give you my heart to love or to stab.

"I know I broke your little heart when I carelessly took away your father. I want to spend the rest of my life and somehow make that up to you. I want to make plans to spend our lives together. I love you. I'll provide for you; I'll protect and treasure you like no other man in this world. Will you spend your life as my wife, Mollie? Will you marry me and go to Chicago? We can have a wonderful life far away from this war." He smiles as he slides a diamond engagement ring on her finger. "You don't know how hard it was to find an engagement ring in Athens, Georgia, with a war going on. This is the ring that was on your holster. Does it have significance? Can we use this until I can buy you another? We'll be happy together, Mollie. You'll see."

You could knock Mollie over with a small puff of wind, and it shows on her face. This is the last thing on this earth that Mollie was expecting, and she says, "That's an old family ring, John. Are you asking me to use it as an engagement ring?"

"Yes, I want you to have something to wear. We'll have a big wedding when we get back to Chicago if you would like, or better yet we can get the army chaplain to marry us now, before I go back to fight." He smiles ear to ear. "We'll spend the holidays here in this big, beautiful mansion on our honeymoon. I'll gladly go back and fight to end this war and get home to you."

He stands, takes her hands, and puts one on each side of his neck, allowing his big chest to press into hers. He holds her face with one hand and the back of her neck with the other as he stares into her eyes. Then, as his eyes slowly shift toward her mouth, his fingers glide across her lips as he takes in a deep breath, brushing his lips across hers. Slowly he presses harder against her lips and presses his body into hers. His tongue glides over her lips and savors the taste. His mouth opens hers, and their tongues meet; they dance and twirl as they embrace with faces locked together.

Mollie feels every inch of her body light up and tingle. She is in a daze because she was taught early on to never kiss a man because it involves your heart. Mollie is able to pull away for a moment, barely able to breathe, and asks, "Is this what happiness is?"

"Yes, my beauty," he replies as he kisses her neck and face and then back to her mouth. He briefly stops, saying, "You are so loved, Mollie. Please be my wife soon. It's hard for me to see you and not want you." His arms wrap around her waist; he pulls her in close and lifts her off her feet and twirls around the porch, kissing her.

He lets her down and asks, "You haven't said anything. Am I pushing too hard? If you want to save your family first and then have a big wedding, I understand. Yours truly can wait," he says reluctantly. "It's just a shame. We could remember Christmas in this house and our honeymoon forever. It's only once in a lifetime that you get to stay in a home like this, and we have it all to ourselves." John thinks to himself that he has to make this work—she is so sensuous. Mollie stands up with all the diamonds sparkling in the sun that John gave her from the home, knowing that they are not his.

"John, I feel faint. I need to rest. We can have lunch together," she says, and quickly goes inside.

Mollie gets to her room and flops across the big stuffed bed with her head spinning and starts to ask questions out loud to herself, "Is this too good to be true, and does he really feel that bad about Daddy? He's in such a hurry. I've never felt so excited to be in the presence of another person. It's intoxicating, so why not? It's a chance in a lifetime, and he loves me. I love him, I think. But this is all so fast—yet he makes me feel like I am the most special person in the world. I hope he doesn't think that I'm famous because of the White Dove thing. He's a general in the army and has vowed to take care of me," she rambles on.

Then it hits her so hard her throat becomes tight and dry... her past. The past that seems to follow her always chases her from safety. How could she forget even for one moment? How could she ever forget? Now, she dreads to see him. The past few weeks were so pleasurable that she somehow blocked all the bad memories.

John begins to feel a tad bit guilty that maybe he poured it on a little too thick earlier, but who cares? He is ready to be a newlywed. He begins to shove breakfast in his mouth with the manners of a soldier. He will press on until she can't resist, no matter what excuse she gives. He will have her.

For lunch John has the staff bring a big tub of warm water into the parlor and place it in front of a comfortable chair. Finger sandwiches and tea are on the side table. He sends a note to Mollie's room to attend lunch barefoot.

Mollie goes to lunch with intentions of flat-out refusing John as her life is too complicated as it is. She walks in the semidark parlor, with only a few Christmas scented candles for light. John stands and comes forward to meet her and touches her hand. "Thank you for continuing to wear all the diamonds. They make you look like royalty, and so will this." He pulls out a diamond headband from a tight-fitting jacket and places it in her hair, "Now that completes the look." He greets her with a small kiss to the cheek and takes a good long stare in to her beautiful blue eyes, pulling away slowly as he smiles. Moving his long hair away from his mouth, he licks his lips and deeply inhales to take in all her smell. *Soon*, he thinks to himself. *Soon*.

"John, I'll wear these jewels while we're here, but they're not mine to keep."

"Yes, they're yours, 'To the winner goes the spoils,' and I'm winning this war. Come over here—I have a surprise. In one of the books in the huge pile that you have read, I found one on Chinese acupressure. Today I will give you the beginner's version and help you relax. I didn't mean to get so excited and put so much pressure on you earlier. I've never felt this way before. I want to capture it and keep it forever. I've seen so much death. You are a light in my life, so forgive me for being so excited.

"No more talking. Let's put your feet in the Epsom salt bath to soak." He places a blanket over her lap for privacy, slides a smaller chair up to her side, and says, "I'm going to start with your hands like the book suggests." He holds her hand in his and then takes his index finger and ever so slightly draws tiny circles all over her palm and then brings his lips to her hand and begins kissing it. He uses oils that smell like flowers to massage her hand and applies pressure at the pad and heel, pulling fingers one at a time, especially the thumb. Both of his big hands rub her wrist and forearm with long, firm stokes.

Each time Mollie starts to speak, he shakes his head and says, "No." She leans back and enjoys the present and relaxes her shoulders. John moves his chair to her other side. Mollie thinks about how she went from a nightmare to a daydream. Next, he moves his chair, dries her foot, and places it on his leg. He applies more oil and begins to massage and apply pressure as he refers back to the diagram in the book. He notices that she lets out a slight moan when he touches her beautiful milky-white calves. John tries to disguise it, but all he can think about is where these two long legs meet at the top.

Very relaxed after lunch, Mollie tries again to tell John, "There's more to me than you know, John. I have a past…a very horrible past. You deserve someone so much better."

He interrupts her again, "It doesn't matter what has happened in your past; it's the past and before we met. You would run for the hills if you knew of all the gruesome things I have done, so let's leave the past alone."

He walks behind her chair and picks up something, saying, "I have a wedding gift for you, assuming that I'm not being too presumptuous." He smiles as he knows this one item will seal the deal for this "daddy's girl." "Close your eyes." He opens her daddy's saxophone case and places it in her lap. "OK; open wide."

Mollie is so surprised. She has been so busy on the run and in a daze since she has been here with John that she completely forgot losing it when she attacked him in Macon. She's truly touched that he chose to keep it. "How did you know?" Mollie asks with a smile as happy tears flow over her cheeks.

John tells her, "I remember you pitching the case in the shrubs before you bit me that day in Alabama. You had it again when you jumped me in Macon. Even if I had figured out how the two were connected, I would never have guessed it would've turned out like this. Do you play?"

She shakes her head. "No, it was my daddy's," Mollie replies as she wipes away tears with the handkerchief John gives her. As she smiles big, Mollie asks, "Do you think this is a good sign or maybe a blessing from him, a blessing for me to forgive you and accept your offer? Yes, my darling. The answer is yes." She holds out her hand with the ring on it.

"Yes!" John shouts, as he pulls Mollie out of the chair and into his arms, twirling her around the room.

"One last time, John. I have a very bad past. Are you sure you don't want to know about it?"

He thinks, *Bad past—ha. So what? She probably killed someone that attacked her.* He wants his young virgin bride tonight.

"Let's get married tonight in the big ballroom over there. I'll get the chaplain. You do want to do this right away, don't you? Why wait? We only have so much time before I have to go. I want to spoil you in every way I can before I leave," John says with a huge grin.

Mollie asks, "Once we marry and you go back to the front, will you help me get to my sister and mother in Nashville? We'll be there in Chicago, at the parade they'll throw in your honor when the war ends."

John replies, "Yes, ma'am, and anyone else in your family that we can help. We can live anywhere—Chicago or Nashville—but keep in mind the South will never be the same. Believe me, it's destroyed."

"I'm going to see the chaplain and get him here right away. Oh, Mollie, thank you so much. I know you'll make me happy, and I know you'll be a good wife. I'll do all that I can to make you happy.

"Guess what else? There is a long wedding gown that the staff has been ironing on all day that I asked them to prepare, hoping that you would say yes. They say it came from Europe. Wear your hair down. I like it that way." He gives the butler a list of orders regarding the meal, flowers, his clothing, and of course the bedroom before he sets out to find the chaplain.

CHAPTER 25

THE GAMES MEN PLAY

General Turchin goes to the local tavern and meets with his two favorite officers who are allowed to drink alcohol. He's got a huge smile on his face and asks for a double vodka, saying, "Which one of you wants to be the chaplain this time? You owe me, you know. I did it last, for you both, in Mississippi. Who has the cross necklace?"

The slightly inebriated first officer speaks up, "Well, well, Russian, I'll be damned. Neither one of us thought you could do it to this one too. I bet she's fine. There are all kinds of stories that float around out there about her. She actually held up a couple of our boys in the woods. Both are under her spell and even now appear to cover for her, we believe but can't prove. Wish I was in your shoes, General. I'll do it, if only to see her up close."

"Then I'll play the witness," says the second officer, "so then I get to touch her as I escort her across the room. Mm, mmm, mmm, I can't wait to smell that woman up close. I hope she puts me under a spell too. It sure beats reality. You good-looking, lucky devil you. We all thought you were nuts for chasing down your horse through all of these towns without burning them, but now we get it...The little head rules."

"Here's to the little head," the fake chaplain toasts as they all clink their glasses in triumph and order another round.

"Think you can find a way for us to watch?" pleads the witness.

"Oh, hell no. You almost blew it before with your moans from the next room. You'll have to wait for me to tell you how she feels as I push deep into her for the first time. The inviting look on her face that's mine, all mine—a real southern belle. I've seen her boobies through her nightgown. Great glory to our God above, he blessed this woman," he laughs as he brings his drink under his nose and raises it high in the air, saying, "Salute!" He orders another round while thinking about his devious seduction.

He'll prolong the process, make her long for the inner-most sensuality she doesn't know she possesses: desire. She'll be another desperate and easy Southern woman. "There are numerous young female slaves that I've enjoyed each night in my bed. You're welcome to any of them after the ceremony," he coldly suggests to his comrades in deceit.

Yes, as do many other officers and some enlisted men, the general intends to go home after the war to his devoted loving wife. It's all a game they play. Their wives hardly ever find out, and if they do…the wife will just have to deal with it. *Besides, it's war,* he selfishly thinks to himself.

Brigadier General John Turchin arrives back at the mansion with two fully dressed Union officers and sends them to the bar as he heads to his bedroom to bathe. His room attendant shaves his beard, mustache, and chest and then dresses him in a clean uniform. He's pleased with the flower petals on the sheets, fresh flowers from the green house fragrantly spread about the room, champagne bottle on ice, and English toffee on fancy foil paper close by on the table. The scene is perfectly set.

He heads down to the bar to join the "chaplain," who is wearing the fake cross, while the "witness" talks with two female black slaves in the back of the room in the butler's pantry. "Thank you,

Chaplain," John says, slapping him on the back as he walks around the bar to pour more vodka. "I don't think we have camped out in a house this nice before. The owners were loaded. I found a safe full of jewelry and cash…too bad it's Confederate. There are so many servants running around to keep everything just so. There's even someone to undress you as you take a bath, and they practically bathe you too. Very odd, having so many black people waiting on your every need. I could get used to having my own servants. Those two with our buddy over there are the best at answering any man's needs."

Mollie wants her hands to stop shaking before she starts downstairs. She can't believe she's getting married to the same person who caused her so much pain. Doubts start to roll in her thoughts: I'm sixteen, and he doesn't know that. He's much older and needs to know about my past. What am I doing? I can't do this.

A knock at the door startles her. "We're ready to take you down to your groom," announces a woman. Mollie opens the door and looks at the group waiting to hold the extra-long train for her.

"Today, I follow my brain, not my heart," she says to herself as she pulls the veil over her face, hearing the piano start to play.

Mollie slowly descends the stairwell. The train is so long that the ladies at the top are still holding it as she reaches the bottom. They slowly come down behind her. A man dressed in a formal army officer uniform takes Mollie's arm and escorts her down the hall. He stops at the entrance to the ballroom and intensely looks at the newest bride and thinks the Russian uses his good looks to get the best ones. He deliberately leads Mollie slowly to the flower-adorned altar so he can unapologetically stare at her up close as her groom and chaplain gawk at her beauty. John thinks she looks like a sophisticated royal queen and loves the off-the-shoulder, tight-fitting white silk dress. Mollie is wearing all of the diamond jewelry he's given her, and her beautiful light-blond hair hangs long under the diamond headband, truly looking like an elegant white dove.

When Mollie reaches John, her eyes meet his, and they gaze at one another. She sees his ruggedly strong, handsome face for the first time without hair. He has a long square jaw with high cheekbones, a chin and nose that look like they were perfectly sculpted out of marble, full luscious lips, and passionate brown eyes that adore her.

Boldly and slowly, Mollie gets the strength to say, "No, no, John, I can't marry you," and exhales deeply. "How could I ever have true feelings for you? I will hate you forever for killing my daddy," Mollie coldly says, with her face covered. "This is some kind of twisted, manipulated control for you to want to marry me. Something is definitely not right here. I can feel it in the depths of my soul."

From somewhere in the house can faintly be heard, "Hallelujah... Thank the Lord."

John lifts the veil off and softly strokes her face and lips with the back of his finger. "Such beauty," he says as he ignores her admission. She studies his face as he leans in while pressing her waist forward against his and passionately kisses her. He escorts her across the ballroom to a table full of refreshments. John introduces the "chaplain" and "witness," and opens a bottle of Champagne Charlie bubbly to loosen her up. Struggling, Mollie accepts one of the female servants' assistance to unhook Mollie's cumbersome train for her.

"Everyone gets the wedding jitters, Mollie. Here, have a drink to relax you," John says as he hands her the crystal flute.

CHAPTER 26

SAVANNAH HONEY

A loud commotion comes from the front door. The butler is arguing with a drunken soldier who insists on speaking to the general. The drunk places his foot in the door and begins to holler down the large foyer; his voice echoes, "I bought this picture of the White Dove from a photographer. She ain't no White Dove! She's a 'soiled' dove. I was the first to have her in Nashville. Her momma sold her to me and all my buddies two years ago. She's nothing but a no-good little whore. Do you hear me, General, sir? With all due respect, please forgive my intrusion, but I thought you needed to know, sir. She also stole my money."

John watches as Mollie's face turns from complete shock to unfiltered anger. "Oh, my God!" Mollie screams, "Uncle Bill, you monster! I'll kill you." She angrily turns and runs for the front door in a fit of rage, holding up her wedding dress, trying not to trip in the long gown. John orders the butler to stop her immediately as he gives chase.

Mollie looks around for anything to use as a weapon and finds a glass quart jar of her favorite Savannah honey that the butler apparently laid down to answer the door. She grabs it with both hands up high and with a forceful blow lands it square on Uncle

Bill's forehead and nose before the butler has a chance to stop her. "I should have cut your throat when I had the chance that night, you son of a bitch."

Uncle Bill's nose cracks as blood spills down his ugly distorted face. "She broke my nose!" screams Uncle Bill. "Yep, that's her: blond-hair whore with big boobies, and full of spitfire."

John grabs her hands from behind and holds them over her head before she has a chance to use the glass to cut his throat. Drunk Uncle Bill's hands and face are covered in sticky, sweet honey. "Let me go, John! I want just one hour, one hour with that devil, and I will show him what a living hell looks like! That's all that I ask," she pleads. As he shakes the broken honey glass out of her sticky hands, it shatters on the hardwood floor. He takes the photograph of Mollie out of the butler's hand and puts it in his jacket while he pulls the resisting Mollie down the hallway toward the staircase.

The "chaplain" and the "witness" detain Uncle Bill at the door while John comforts Mollie. He isn't about to give up on getting her into his bed. "Is what he's saying true? Your mother made you into a prostitute? You poor thing," he says as he wraps his arms around her.

Mollie screams, "He raped me for hours on my fourteenth birthday with all five of his filthy disgusting buddies. They had a bet as to whether my mother would sell me or not, and she did. I demand you court-martial him for raping a civilian child and lock him away where he'll never see the light of day ever again. And if you won't, then let me at him!"

John's powerful voice interrupts her frenzy, "Mollie, I can't allow you to just kill or harm one of my soldiers while I stand by and watch."

John lets her arms down and puts his hands on her shoulder and questions her. "So, you're only sixteen?" he asks in disbelief.

She answers his question with another question, "What if I don't hurt him? Just tie him to that tree out front, and let me scream at him until I get out all this pent-up anger I've been hanging onto all this time. I can't keep it in me for the rest of my life. I just can't. I hate him too much."

"OK; I'll honor your request and have him tied to a tree for one hour, and you can scream at him, if that'll make you feel better."

They go out the door, and Mollie points at a particular tree. "That tree." The general orders one of the soldiers on the horse closest to the porch to use his rope and tie the drunken soldier to the tree for one hour. The soldier securely ties him to the tree at his waist, pinning his arms but leaving his forearms and legs free. After all, the drunk is a soldier like them.

That will be his punishment for public drunkenness and any other crimes against civilians that he may have committed. The soldiers, now gathering around, think the general is doing the right thing by only giving out a light punishment.

Mollie slowly walks toward him. Uncle Bill waves his arms and hollers and slurs to her. Her voice quickly changes from angry to seductive, "Hey, Uncle Bill, you big man. I love honey, don't you?" she asks as she licks the honey on her hand and with a finger spreads some on her lips, with the finger slowly going on down across her breast. John looks at her with great confusion but is yet quite amused at this side of Mollie that he has not seen in the past week.

"Come on over here, and have your way with me, pretty Mollie. You know how much you love it. Don't pretend you don't. I bet you're even better now than before, you little whore," Uncle Bill slurs in a drunken gruff voice. Mollie seductively moves in closer. The general could easily put a stop to this unfolding seduction scene at any time, but knowing that this is a diversion from just being stood up at the altar and still amused, he stays back.

Mollie starts to sway her hips and presses her chest out as she draws near him, smiling and looking in his eyes. "Uncle Bill, not just honey, but Savannah bees' honey—it's the best around. Did you taste it?" She slowly licks it off her middle finger and then seductively pushes her entire finger in her mouth in and out and in and out again, sucking in and out while still looking him in the eye. "Here, hold out your hands. I'll let you try it," she says, as she takes the honey still on her breast and puts it on the tips of his fingers. He eagerly licks his fingers, trying to imitate her and suck. "Hold your hands out again, Uncle Bill," Mollie says with such a sweet, seductive tone of voice. She rubs the remainder of the honey on her hands onto his big rough hands.

"This time I want you to rub it where you want me to taste it on you." With long tongue exaggerations, she licks off the honey remaining on the inside of her wrist. Uncle Bill complies, reaches down in his pants, and rubs the honey all over his now-obvious full erection. "Here you go. Put a lot down there—everywhere you want my lips to touch you, anywhere you want my tongue to lick and taste. I'm going to treat you so good, Uncle Bill." As she slides her tongue back and forth across her lips, besides pulling on his hard-on, he rubs honey on his stomach and chest.

"Hear that, boys? She wants me. I'm getting lucky," he shouts to the envious witnesses, including John.

She says, "Oh no, I'm almost out. Rub some of the honey that's in your hair on your face and neck and even your ears, if you want me to kiss you there too. Would you like that, Uncle Bill? Do you want me to kiss your face? Did you get the back of your neck too?" He moves his head up and down, broken nose and all, smiling, still rubbing himself.

"Eat your heart out, jackasses. I'm about to get me a piece of the White Dove again," he boasts. "I taught her everything she knows, boys. And all you can do is watch. She wants me. Look at her," he yells again. "All mine. Come here, sweet baby—show

Uncle Bill what you have learned since I saw you last. Bring out those big, luscious titties too."

More soldiers arrive, and they laugh at the drunk but are still envious as Mollie rubs her fingers through the soldier's hair. With honey from his hair dripping from her hand, Mollie saunters over to a huge ant mound just five feet from the tree she picked. She drizzles it back to Uncle Bill, creating a honey fuse, and wipes it all on his boots and legs, pretending to be sensually rubbing him, while he stares at her rather large cleavage as she bends down to expose more of her breasts.

"Enjoy, Uncle Bill!" she smiles as she comes up and then turns and walks to the horse where John stands waiting. John is of course sexually turned on and speechless at what he and all the other soldiers just witnessed.

Uncle Bill calls to Mollie, "Wait, honey! You're not going to leave me now, are you? Mollie, you come back here right now!" he yells as he struggles against the rope.

The "chaplain" and the "witness" begin to laugh at the entire scene as they finish their drinks. Mollie says to the horse-mounted soldier, "One hour. The general promised me one hour. Not one minute sooner. If I were y'all, I'd make friendly bets on him surviving the ant pile before the hour is up…ants love honey." Mollie turns to John and says, "John, as agreed, I did not harm him. I'll let the ants do that. One hour. You allowed me one hour."

Uncle Bill starts to yell from the tree, "The White Dove is nothing but a no-good little whore. Once a little whore, Mollie, always a little whore. Get over here and untie me, damn it." If the soldier would stay still and not hit at the South American bullet ants as they climb all over him and into his pants, the ants might be content just to eat the honey for the next hour. As he swats at the ants, he starts screaming and says, "I'm coming to find you in Nashville after the war. I'll make you pay, you'll see. I'll come get you, and your mother too."

Still angry, Mollie climbs the steps to the front door, stops, turns, and loudly yells, "I hate all of you Union soldiers—more exactly, I hate men in general...at least most of you," before slamming the door so hard it rattles the house windows.

A soldier arrives with a telegraph for the General; it reads: "Dearest John, although I'm pregnant, I miss you terribly and will arrive in Athens on Dec. 25 for Christmas. Loving wife, Nadine."

John waits a few minutes to give Mollie time to calm down, but he knows that he now doesn't have much time left to seduce Mollie. Now his fantasy with her has to transition from a virgin to a professional prostitute. Either way, he will have her.

John stands at Mollie's door and knocks. He hears her cry and say, "Go away! I will be a war prisoner in my room until you let me go. Please leave."

He opens the door and sees her sitting on the side of the bed. "Not a chance, Mollie. I'm not going anywhere." He walks to the bed and scoops her up in his arms and carries her out the door to their honeymoon-ready bedroom.

A big fire and candles light the room with a glow, and he gently lays her across his bed. Then he stares at her with unbridled lust. Playing with her mind is half of his fun, and she knows this now.

She sits up, glares at him, and decides to go out to the balcony to enjoy this last day of warm temperatures and to check on Uncle Bill. John follows with two champagne glasses. "No, thank you. My mother got drunk the night she sold me. I don't want to even try alcohol. I saw what it did to her."

As she pushes the glass away, John says with care, "You are not your mother. You don't have a child under your care. Here, drink this to relax. You need it. Look at all that has happened in just the past two hours. I won't let you get drunk, I promise." She takes the flute by the stem and drinks it and has quite a pleasant reaction to the bubbles.

"John, I tried to tell you that I'm not who you painted me out to be—this White Dove symbol and all of that business—and that I have a horrible past. The truth is that she started taking me to the soldiers' tents when I was only twelve, the year you killed my daddy. Is this what you want to hear? Does it shock you to know how I got started?

"We were hungry and absolutely starving, John. Do you know what that must have been like for a mother who had always been taken care of by a good man to not be able to feed her child? Even our hidden supplies got robbed because the house got broken into often. Uncle Bill seemed to be a good guy, our protector, at first. I sat on his lap and read books to him. I don't know if he could read or not. I loved to bake cakes, pies, and cookies with the supplies he provided. I totally and completely trusted him. I trusted my mother too.

"My first time sexually was horrifying. I was held down and raped by six soldiers until early the next morning. Uncle Bill went first. I could barely walk, but after I stole his big pile of cash, I had to run. Every inch of my body hurt, but I ran fast. I just couldn't let him catch me. I hate him as much as I do you, maybe more. What a sick jerk!"

The faint cries suddenly begin from the tree. The soldiers are now back at the barricade across the street and don't hear him, but Mollie and John hear and see it firsthand. It looks like Uncle Bill has passed out, but then all of a sudden, his legs start to jump like he is walking on hot coals, one knee up in the air higher than the other; then he holds them up in the air, being held up by the rope. His relief only lasts a few seconds before his legs come down and his arms start to dance in the air, and then he swats all over, the screams of agony growing louder as he begins to beat on his head. "Make it stop! Make it stop!" are the only words they can make out of the screams.

Mollie looks at John and smiles. "I know you must think I'm some kind of sick person, but I'm finding a certain amount of pleasure from all this. I screamed similar words years ago when I asked my mother to make them stop…make them stop. You can stop it if you think you should," Mollie says as she hands him her glass for a refill.

John returns with two filled-to-the-top glasses and says, "Are you joking? You can't stop delivering the pain until it's over. That's how it works. Once you start, there is no stopping." John looks at his pocket watch. "He has nine more minutes—no stopping."

Mollie clicks her glass with his, saying, "To sweet revenge—how good it tastes." As she closes her eyes, with each scream, she is able to release a scream from her own past.

When the hour is up, the soldier on horseback rides up to untie him and is horrified at what he finds. He immediately calls for a medic. "I wish I had a medic that night. It is so strange, but this really has helped. Thank you, John, for helping me heal. Let's go inside and finish our conversation, shall we? The temperature has started to drop, so no more spring dresses while I'm your prisoner."

CHAPTER 27

LESSONS FOR MOLLIE

"Let's talk about that now, why don't we? First off, are you really only sixteen?" She nods yes, knowing that sixteen is her real age. She tells him the truth and doesn't follow her mother's advice to always tell everyone that she is two years younger than she really is. "I would have bet a paycheck you were at least eighteen. You have the body of a full-grown woman, and you carry yourself much more worldly and mature than a sixteen-year-old."

"I suppose war ages us all," Mollie says, shrugging her shoulders, suggesting there is nothing she can do about the realities of her past.

"So you were a prostitute against your will at first, and then reluctantly went along with it after a while, right?" he asks her.

"I know that you are speculating, but yes. I wanted to tell you, but you didn't give me the chance. After being raped, I traveled the circuit for about two years," she replies.

"The sad news, Mollie, is, once a prostitute, always a prostitute. Even if you stop, it'll follow you throughout your life.

"But the good news...it just happens to be a fantasy of mine to train the perfect prostitute...from a man's perspective, that is. What do you say, Mollie? Let me teach you to enjoy what you do and to love every man you're with as though he's the only one in the world. Let me teach you to be the best you can be, and you can charge any price. I'll teach you to only associate with men of power and wealth, the people that run things—business, politics, military, and law enforcement.

"Please let me be your teacher. It'll help you be the most successful at this business as you can. Let's have fun, shall we? I know you don't want to be with me as a husband, but could you be with me as a man? A man who desires you in this profession? You have no idea how aroused you made me and every other man outside with the honey. That's the Mollie I want. That's the woman every man wants.

"Mollie, you've got that 'thing' men dream about. Let me teach you how to get any worldly possession that you want with that special gift. Life has thrown you a bad hand that will stick for the rest of your life, so let's make the most of what gifts you do have. Enjoy life when you can with what you have—and you, my beautiful Mollie, have it. It's up to you to decide what you will do with it.

"I am sorry to be the one to tell you this part...men will likely never love you in the end. I know it's hard to accept, but they won't—they just can't get past it. The wealthy will pay any exorbitant quantity of money to be with someone as beautiful as you if you let me teach you. Do you want to be average like everyone else, or will you learn to be the one that every man dreams about?"

He gazes into her eyes. "I could force you, and given your past, no one will care, but I don't want that. I want the 'willing and turned-on you.' We've kissed, and I felt your desire. Give in to it. We are in a war. It's almost Christmas, and I'm not letting you go anywhere until I know either that Savannah is on fire or Sherman accepts its surrender."

"Why do you ask this of me, John? It cheapens our feelings."

He interrupts, saying, "Because you hate me, and that's your true feelings. I'm sure you've been with men you hated before. So,

I suggest you hate the fact you desire me. Let's have fun, Mollie. I'll eventually let you go, and you can keep on loathing me forever. Meanwhile, enjoy, and you'll learn some things. You like learning, Mollie. I know you do." He moves his head up and down, trying to get her to agree.

By now, Mollie realizes John likes to make the decision on most things, and she goes along with it. However, she also likes that he's firm and in control. John has one of the two female servants remove his uniform and asks Mollie to watch. He sits on the foot bench while they remove his boots and unbutton his cuff links. Slowly, he unbuttons his untucked shirt, slightly exposing the bare skin of his chest and stomach. He stands with his hands behind his back as he pulls sleeves down to remove his shirt and confidently watches her face for a reaction once it's completely off.

By the smile on her face, he can tell she is pleased. She hates herself for desiring him. Next, he knows she wants to touch, so he picks up her hands and places them on his muscular chest, looking into her blue eyes. He kisses her lips softly and, with his eyes closed, inhales her breath and smiles. He laughs a little and says, "Go ahead. Touch me—explore. I see it in your eyes. I know I will love it, and I will love touching you too."

Mollie doesn't remember that the servants are still in the suite as she makes small circles with both her hands on his chest and notices that every muscle of his stomach ripples as it disappears into his trousers. Her hands spread across his broad chest, up his neck, and across his shoulders as she takes in his manly smell. She focuses on one arm and feels his hard muscles there.

"Now it's your turn. Stand on the tailoring box so you'll be up high. That way I can watch them take your dress off." She's not sure why, but she does as he asks. Meanwhile, he opens more champagne and brings her a glass. While two black female servants unbutton the pearl buttons at her wrist, Mollie takes notice of how beautifully John has the room decorated with fresh flower arrangements and petals on the bed. What a romantic! He's so thoughtful in every detail.

"Take everything off her except the diamonds," he tells the female servants as he puts the glass on his lips and enjoys his drink. "Turn her around, and let me watch you as you reveal her back. It's my first time to see it, and I want to remember every detail of tonight forever." He loves it as they pull the sleeves forward. The gown comes down, and Mollie steps out. "Take her shoes too. Turn around, Mollie, while they untie the corset." He wants them to hurry, but yet he wants to savor her innocence in the sensual process as well. The slip comes over her arms, baring her big but perky breasts. John stands and comes closer to get a better look.

The two servants gather up the dress and leave the room. John's big hands are overflowed as they go underneath each breast, lifting and caressing as he moans, saying, "Feeling your breasts for the first time is amazing. I'm a bit captivated. Seeing how firm your nipples are is wonderful. Men have little ones." He places Mollies hand on his nipple. "See? We are quite similar, but female nipples are so big comparatively."

Mollie smiles as she watches this handsome man with such pleasure on his face. "Visuals are amazing. Seeing the curve of your tulip through your pantalets is incredible. Any man would love to touch you—feeling the sponginess of your mound through fabric is incredible," he whispers as he touches Mollie in the valley, giving her pleasure.

"I call it my 'special place,'" Mollie says. He looks at her with some slight amusement and tells her.

"Now I want you to give me a gift. First, finish removing your undergarments, slowly." He watches intently. "Now, put on a show, a dance. It was supposed to be our wedding night—do a wedding dance for me."

Mollie only knows ballroom dances from her classes at the Greens' mansion in Savannah. She remembers once she saw Gypsies dance in an erotic way by the fireside, but they were dressed. She decides she'll make it up as she goes, but she really doesn't understand why she is doing this. Is it the attention, the affection, or the alcohol?

Mollie turns her back to John and pulls all of her hair forward, which brings complete focus on her plump round bottom. Then she begins to sway back and forth, moving her hands to the silhouette of her body. Slowly she turns to face John, again showing him where to look with her hands, first around her face and neck, as she pulls her fingers through her hair across her face and then kisses her fingers while her hips are moving slowly side to side.

John's seductive smile lets her know that he approves so far. Her hands move to her breasts as she makes circles with her fingertips around the nipples; her hands then slide under the globes, and she lifts as if to offer them to him. Her hands continue down her sides and slide across her hips. Then bending forward, with chest out, she touches the sides of her thighs to her knees and slowly comes back up the inner thigh to the top. She stops and turns back around.

John loves the show and tells her so. Then he adds, "Stand on your toes, alternating your weight back and forth from foot to foot. Oh, yes...perfect. Go faster! Your butt looks beautiful as it shimmies, wiggles, and pops up and down." Her bare hips move in and out in ways that would drive any man wild.

Surprising herself, Mollie likes to dance for John. It's fun. She is aroused as she watches him watching her. But all the while she is still confused as to why she is going along with this and why she is so attracted to someone she hates. She figures it must be lack of experience in the matters of the heart. The dance continues as Mollie begins to spin round and round, with beautiful hair chasing behind her in the glow of the fire.

John is so turned on that he goes across the room and picks her up in his arms and says, "Wow! Now that's a wedding dance,

Mollie. I bet you'll get lots of proposals when you perform like that for men. I wish you weren't a prostitute, Mollie, or I really would marry you. I would wear you down until you said yes, but I know I could never forget all the other men, so it would end in disaster. I am proud to know you as a professional," he says. Then he smiles and sits her on the edge of the bed, admiring her gorgeous young body.

Disappointed, Mollie asks, "Why do you do that, John? Take us from the heat of the moment and throw me back in the reality of prostitution?"

"It's simple, Mollie. I'm trying to teach you a very important lesson as a woman. If you want to understand men and not get hurt emotionally, then you'll listen to me. Men keep everything in separate compartments. Imagine boxes, if you will. Each box is for a different category. One box is for your work, like war. Another box is for family, one is for your friends, one is for health, one is for love, and one is for emotions. Maybe even one is for hobbies—and, yes, a big box is for sex. But the rule for men is that we never, ever, mix the boxes...never!

"Now, women, on the other hand, mix it all together in one box...all of it. It's crazy and confusing to men. Women are like a book with many separate chapters, but they don't list them in order. Women mix them all together and shuffle the pages like a deck of cards. Then they'll even add another book in the mix, sometimes more, which only further complicates their view of the world. One big, messy box is how women see things, and all at the same time.

"So in order for you to survive and thrive in the sex industry with men as customers, you don't need to get complicated and mix emotions with raw sex. That's what I want to prevent you from doing right now. You can't show how you feel and have emotional attachments at work. You can't mix up the boxes. That will kill you in the long run."

Mollie contemplates what she is hearing. This is the first time in her life that she has had such a conversation with a man, and he wants to know her and to teach her how men think for her to be successful and survive. But why does he try to psychologically redo her thought process? Is it kindness or destructiveness?

John snaps her out of her daydream as he pushes her shoulders back on the bed while her legs dangle over the edge. He spreads her legs apart and says, "Let's get back to the lessons." Mollie is scared and shocked as she sees a long sharp blade in his hand.

"Why, John? Why? Why would you want to threaten me or cause me harm? I've gone along with you and have done everything you've asked me to do so far. You don't need to hurt me, John. Think about it. Please. I don't want to get hurt," she cries.

He takes her trembling hand. "No, precious, I will never hurt you. I promise," he tells her as he shows her shaving cream and a lathering brush. Mollie has gone from frightened to confused. He touches the hair between her legs. "I'm going to get rid of this, the hair," he says with a naughty smile as he spreads the cream with the brush. Mollie props up on her elbow, curiously watching through her breasts as the activity progresses between her legs.

"Most men don't take the time to truly look at a woman down here, and they don't know what they're missing. It's truly beautiful!" he says as he gently shaves her. "I want you to do this for me this one time so you can appreciate the raw sensual touch and erotic feel of your tulip. The trick is to always use a sharp blade and always douse yourself with alcohol afterward to prevent a razor rash. Why are you laughing?"

"Because you are so focused, John. Do Russian women shave like this?" Mollies replies.

"Yes, some women I know back in Russia shave, but it's rare. And of course I'm focused. I have one box open now, and I'm concentrating on it. I'm not cluttering it up with other boxes. I bet most men don't even know there are lips into the entrance," he answers as he uses a soft cloth to wipe her and clean up the excess shaving cream. "Beautiful! Take a look and see. Feel how smooth you are, Mollie. You will make an impact with every client with this. I will never forget this sight."

She sits up and takes a look, and she feels like a little girl again at first, touching her smooth silky skin. It's odd to look at yourself bare, she contemplates to herself. Why is he doing these strange things? Why train me? What does he get out of it? What do I get out of it?

John snaps Mollie out of her thoughts as he begins to pour champagne across her smoothness, reminding her, "Don't forget to pour alcohol to prevent razor bumps." He uses his tongue to taste her wetness. "Mmmmm, Mollie" is all he says as he gives her pleasure like she has never experienced before. When she is on the cusp of feeling ecstasy, he stops. "I want to teach you how to please me now." Again, he leaves her disappointed and confused.

John teaches Mollie things from a man's point of view. She welcomes this because she has really never understood the opposite sex. He admires her ample, voluptuous chest and begins, "Many younger guys have never touched a woman's tulip or breasts, nor have they had a female touch their johnson or whatever a man calls his thing. By the way, what do you call it?" he asks.

"Jim dog," she replies.

Cute, he thinks, and says, "Just seeing your breasts is going to make any man's jim dog stand at attention.

"For now, let's start with you pleasuring me." He demonstrates and says, "This is how to handle a johnson. Always be careful with the sensitive head, and pretend it's a lollipop. That's right, Mollie, get it nice and wet and stroke it." He lets her watch him for the proper technique. "Now, try these different ways to hold it, with your full hand grip—oh, yes, Mollie, that's good. Try just the thumb and forefinger, OK, and gently swipe the head and tip," he instructs as he reaches over and plays with her breasts and rubs her nipples on his johnson. "Lick it, and then stroke it—make it wet and slippery, yes," he moans. "Lick the tip while stroking.

"Mollie, you are really good, baby," he tells her as he takes in a deep breath and has her stop. "Now, let's start over from the beginning. Mollie, this is really important. You do this right, and men will travel miles to come see you." He pulls up his drawers and trousers, buttoning them, and then hands her a pair of short silk panties to wear.

Mollie looks at him, saying, "John, you are strange. Twice now you have prolonged it for both of us, but I'll keep going along with you for now."

John says, "Delaying pleasure will make things more intense when you finally do let go. Pay attention, Mollie. Open the flap. Keep your eyes on me—yes, that naughty smile of yours is perfect. And keep your eyes on mine. Now, undo the button, and pull down my trousers. Yes, you can smile, baby—look how big you've made it." He watches her pull down his pants and compliments her saying, "You're so beautiful. Please kiss the ridge of my johnson through my underdrawers...oh, baby, you're so damn attractive to me. It's extra amazing if you're topless and men can see your lovely breasts."

As his fingers touch the soft skin of her smile, John continues on with the lesson, "Pull down my drawers, Mollie, so just the tip of my johnson peeks out." She slowly pulls down his drawers, exposing the head, and rubs her hand up and down, eventually pulling his drawers all the way down, exposing the full length of his erect member and his full large testicles. She can tell that he intensely wants her to touch him, and he's squirming with excitement.

She has him so horny his breath quickens as she turns around so she can spread her legs over his face in the "favor-for-favor" position. John pulls Mollie down, holding her to him. Not wanting to stop, he finally says, "Oh, Mollie, I'm loving this." Mollie is gasping as she rapidly breathes in and out, making a soft moaning noise. "My, my, the way you move, Mollie—you are on fire."

The pressure is at its height for Mollie also, and just then, John begins a cruel move and takes it away. With his muscular arms, he lifts her and lays her on the bed beside him. Next, he says, "Last lesson for the night, Mollie…it's not about how you feel—only the customer counts in your business." He then lifts her up off the bed in his arms and looks deeply into her eyes. "You are truly every man's dream, Mollie," he says as he carries her across the room to the door and out into the hallway.

Mollie is breathing so deeply, not knowing what else to expect from her villain, captor, lover…teaser…John. They enter Mollie's room, and he drops her onto her bed. She anxiously waits for his next touch, his next stroke of attention, to continue the fantasy. "Mollie, we will pick up with the lessons tomorrow," he says indifferently as he walks across the room and closes the door behind him.

As John walks down the hallway to his room, he motions for the two young black servant girls at the end of the hall to come to his room.

That night is crazy for Mollie. She tosses and turns, stares wide-eyed up at the ceiling and tries to understand exactly what just happened. Why is John's mind so full of twists? Perhaps because he's foreign; she speculates that probably most of these things he learned in Russian brothels. On the other hand, maybe it was an older, lonely Russian countess who taught John these things when he was young. That could even explain why he has been so persistent in his pursuit of young Mollie, now that he is the older teacher.

Christmas is almost here, and for the past week or so, every day and every night, John has taught Mollie a new lesson, which always involves sexual encounters, fantasy, positions, and role-playing.

Mollie has lost track of days while enjoying all the special attention. She continues to wonder where all of these strange lessons are coming from in just one man—perhaps, because she has never really known a man other than just on the surface. Maybe all men confuse her with their many boxes.

It's Friday night, December 23, 1864, two days before Christmas. Beautiful, fresh-smelling trees and garland are decked throughout the house. Herman sneaks into the house as a music man, with help from the house servants. He sings and plays festive music at the grand piano and is able to talk to Mollie in between songs. He explains, "Mollie, the entire house is surrounded by soldiers around the clock. God sent you another helper besides me. I met him at the train station when you were captured. His name is CC Taylor. Believe it or not, this is his uncle's home, and he was able to draw the layout of the house on paper. I'm sorry, but we are not able to find a safe way for you to escape yet."

⇒⊱ ⊰⇐

It's Christmas Eve. John reads the latest telegram from his wife. Although he has tried to slow her travel, she is due to arrive early the next day, just in time for Christmas.

Mollie stays warm at the fireplace while she waits on John for dinner. She is determined to tell him what she expects tonight… sexual relief. Each night he has built up the tension to a maximum and has always stopped before either has reached a sexual release. Tonight is going to be different.

John admires Mollie's beautiful dress tonight. He appreciates her efforts in her appearance, and she continually wears the many diamonds he adorns her with daily. "How's my beauty tonight?" he asks as he kisses her deeply. "Do you need my coat? Are you cold and trembling?" He holds her hands between his large palms.

Mollie replies, "A little cold, but that's not why I'm nervous. I realize you like to be in control all of the time. Sometimes you have me be submissive and sometimes not. You frequently keep me in check by reminding me who and what I am.

"John, it's always your rules, your way, and your outcome. As the prostitute you have so eagerly trained, I should be in charge, not you. John, tonight we will not stop," Mollie says with more confidence than she realizes she has.

"You're so right, Mollie. Tonight will be the grandest of them all. I thought we had longer, but tomorrow we must part our ways. I just received word, and General Sherman has taken Savannah as his Christmas gift to Lincoln. The information you gave me was right. Not a shot was fired, and Sherman is staying at the home of Charles Green as we speak.

"Tonight will be our last, and it'll be the grandest of all of our nights," he says with a grin as he pulls her body into his. I've made arrangements for your safe passage to Nashville tomorrow—right after you give me my horse. I dueled my brother to his death over that horse…a stupid brother fight. I didn't know he was a show horse as you say. You will bring him back to me. Your horse has been well taken care of while you've been here.

"I need to tell you about your father before you go. He was a double agent spy. He was one of the reasons to raid Athens. His real name was Teal before he took on the new identity of Smith. You might consider him a hero for the Confederacy. That's all you need to know. I shouldn't have even told you that much. Don't ask me any questions." Before any of this information can sink in, he changes the subject, not allowing her a chance to ask anything.

"Now, let's skip dinner and take advantage of what time we have left and get started here, in this room. Strip for me one last time. Do the dance you have perfected for me as you listen to the music man singing in the parlor."

Mollie's head is spinning, but for whatever reason, she complies and slowly dances out of her clothes. She notices John's officer friends are peeping at her through the cracks between the doors of the butler's pantry. Did John invite them to watch? she wonders. Mollie stares into his eyes as she touches his erection through his clothes. Then she slowly unbuttons his pants and begins teasing John with her tongue, lips, and hands—just how he has taught her. She knows she is also playing to an audience.

"Hey, music man," Mollie calls out. "Play something fun and fast beat!"

She hears Herman reply, "I only know one fast song, ma'am, and the Union soldiers aren't going to want to hear 'I Wish I Were in Dixie.'"

"Oh, yes, they will. It's perfect. Start in two minutes, please."

Mollie realizes that she has many sets of eyes on her, from the closet and from behind furniture and the large floor-to-ceiling drapes. Would they complain about the music? No. This song will be burned into their memories forever after tonight, Mollie giggles to herself.

For a reason unknown to Mollie, she accepts her fate as always being a prostitute, and like John says, she will be better at it than anyone else. She looks at John. "You want your friends to see the White Dove dance? Get them all out in the open," she commands. John leaves himself exposed as he watches Mollie from the sofa.

He says, "Come out and watch the show boys. It's your Christmas present from Uncle John." On one hand, Mollie hates that John is deceitful and exposes her without consent, but on the other hand, she is aroused by so many men admiring her naked body, while knowing that they can only look and not touch.

The piano begins playing and Herman starts to sing, "Wish I was in the land of cotton, / Old times there are not forgotten; / Look away! Look away! Look away! Dixie Land. / In Dixie Land where I was born, / Early on one frosty morn, / Look away! Look away! Look away! Dixie Land..." Mollie dances and swerves to the tune, her hands moving to the shape of her body. She teases them more by slightly touching her hard nipples with her fingertips. Her ballet training comes back to her as she does minuets standing on her toes. Across the room, she goes through the men, looking like a ballerina until she stops, stands up straight on her tippy-toes, and throws her hair around as she looks back over her shoulder. Each man knows that she is looking just at him when she wiggles her ass.

Mollie knows that she is getting turned on herself, which breaks one of the rules from her lessons…she is letting emotions into her "one" box. I can handle it, she tells herself, and decides to put on a show for these officers they'll never forget.

Some of the men are now moving in rhythm with the music. Mollie seems to almost float in the air like a lovely bird as she leaps from the floor to a chair, to the long dining table. It is during the war in 1864, and most of the men staring at Mollie's perfect nude body high up on the table have never witnessed such a show. They are mesmerized…and have no idea "Dixie" is playing.

Mollie sashays up and down the table with an alluring walk that seems to accent her flawless hourglass figure. As her nude figure thrusts from side to side, she makes eye contact with each man, making each think that the dance is just for him. She continues to use her hands up and down her body to make every man in the room dream of having her. The crescendo rises until Mollie feels the timing is right. She stops and straightens her back, letting her quick breathing accent her breasts and stomach. Her whole body is shaking as she throws her head back, allowing her long hair to flow down.

John is mesmerized. He can't believe what he has just seen. Mollie reaches out her hand for one of the officers to help her off the table and lets them watch her erotically and slowly step back into her dress and hoopskirt. Mollie finally understands the power over men that she has, and now she knows how to use it.

She slowly walks across the room and sits in the large leather chair next to the roaring fire in a confident position, indicating it is OK to line up and let them pay homage to her. The men abide and come to her side, each removing his hat to his chest. The first officer places a gold coin on the table beside her as gratuity, saying, "Ma'am, on the darkest nights, when trying to sleep on a blood-soaked battlefield, I will close my eyes and think of this very evening, and a smile shall come to my face as I think of you. And I'll try not to hum myself to sleep to the tune of 'Dixie.'"

So the other officers follow suit. Mollie realizes the money is most likely stolen, as are the many diamonds that John has given her, from all the homes they have pillaged previously. As the men leave the room, they feel thoroughly entertained in a way they won't soon forget before they head back to the war.

John watches Mollie intently and admires how she carries herself with such elegance and charm. He carries her to his bed, pulls out his knife, and hurriedly cuts her dress off. She is scared and excited simultaneously. Sadly, she still treats him as a lover and not as a client. She's involved emotionally.

Mollie looks at John, his big arms bracing the headboard above her. His chest looks wide, strong, and beautiful as she explores his muscles and face with her fingers and on through his long hair as it hangs loose, his eyes locked with hers. At last they reach the very prolonged moment of ecstasy as their bodies shudder together.

An hour later, John sleeps as Mollie stares at the ceiling, wondering if she will ever feel this good again. Why does he have me wonder about all of it? The uncertainty is stressful. Eventually she falls asleep.

CHAPTER 28
THE ROAD TO NASHVILLE

In the middle of the night, Mollie wakes up hungry but in her own bed again. *Maybe he just likes to sleep alone,* she thinks. She puts on a thick cotton robe and heads to the kitchen for a snack. The staff isn't around, so she searches and finds a whole roasted chicken and ears of corn in an icebox. Cold as it is, it tastes great. One of the kitchen staff hears Mollie from the adjoining room and comes in to assist.

Mollie is pleased—it's her trusted courier that she has used to send Herman messages since her arrival. She asks her to contact Herman once more to announce their escorted departure for Nashville in the morning. Union troops will join them about three miles outside of town. Herman is to hide the Russian's horse, Belyy, about a street or two away for negotiations, insuring that everything goes well. Under the guise that he is a cousin from Nashville and very sick, she has gotten John's permission to allow CC ("Percy Taylor") in the carriage with them.

She finishes her meal and decides to sleep the rest of the night in John's arms. She quietly opens his door. The fire has died down, and the room is dark. Although it is hours later, the room still smells of sex as she slowly walks barefoot across the cold wooden floors. As she gets closer to the bed, her eyes adjust; she sees movement under the covers and smiles, glad he's awake. Possibly another fulfilling sexual encounter before her early departure comes to her mind. Giggles come from the covers as a young servant pushes the cover off her head as if gasping for air, exposing John's naked body glistening in dripping sweat. Mollie hears the squeaky noises of the bed while the young girl rides him hard. There's another young slave woman with long, dark, slender legs straddled apart across his face.

Mollie is stunned, in disbelief. She feels betrayed and humiliated. What kind of games has he played with her every night? Her disbelief turns to raging anger. "What in the hell is going on, John?" she loudly screams at him, totally frightening the two young black girls.

He sits up, calm and smiling. "Oh, hi, Mollie. Perfect timing! Please come join us, and make all my fantasies come true," he says as he extends his hands out to hers.

"What? What's your sick, twisted game? You're a foreign, mentally ill, sick bastard," she screams. "You play with me all day, all night, and tuck me away wanting more. Then you make these young girls finish you off. You're a sick pervert, John. They're younger than I am. Did you give them a choice? I bet not. You are no better than the masters that owned them. Yankees here to free the slaves, my ass! Nothing more than hypocrites, all of you!"

"Now wait just one minute here, Miss White Dove. We went into this agreement to have fun...that's it! No strings or unnecessary complications, remember? I taught you better than to get all emotional, Mollie. Otherwise this business is going to eat you up and spit you out. You can't afford to get personal, Mollie. You know that. Now get over here," John says with a big, inviting smile.

Mollie is shaking and enraged with clenched fists at his coldheartedness—but mostly at herself for letting this villain who murdered her daddy get the best of her like this. She stomps off in a huff, looking around the room for something to beat him with. Seeing just what she needs, she picks up a bag of silver and gold coins, squeezes it as if to throw, and then suddenly changes her mind because she doesn't want to hit one of the girls. She decides to keep the coins instead and storms out of the room, slamming the door hard behind her and probably waking everyone in the house. She lets out an immense scream of frustration, anger and sadness.

The two naked servant girls are still frightened out of their minds and huddle up together in the corner. John orders, "Come back over here, girls. There's nothing to be frightened about. Besides, we're just getting started."

The girls stand up, holding each other's hands as they tremble. "We've made the White Dove unhappy and brought bad luck to all slaves," one says as they both begin to cry, picking up their clothes and quickly leaving the room, contrary to John's demands.

⊷ ⊶

Early Christmas morning, Mollie prepares for a long, cold trip to Nashville. She wears men's pants under her dress for warmth, uses the pockets for coins and ammo, and ties to her leg the holster, gun, and knife that John returned. In a small bag, she packs the white cape the servants cleaned and all the stolen diamonds. In the kitchen, she has the staff pack her three knapsacks with dried beef, pickled eggs, pecans, peanuts, hard cheese, and a dozen apples. Mollie smiles. "Do you have any of your peanut butter fudge made? Is it in the candy case?"

She walks into the butler's pantry, retrieves her sweet delight for her travels, and overhears two drunk officers' voices from the dining room. "Damn the Russian. He has the little White Dove, all those slave girls every night, and now his pregnant wife will arrive sometime today from Chicago to share Christmas in this big house with him. Now that ought to be interesting. That lucky bastard. We don't have diddly-squat except this fully stocked bar of fancy liquor. How much do you think we can carry with us?"

The other officer replies, "Yep, he uses those good looks of his to always charm the pants off these Southern belles. I bet he's had half a dozen virgins in this past year alone."

"How many times do you think we have faked a marriage for him?"

"Sure was a bunch of them in Mississippi. He's probably left a trail of Russian babies throughout the South."

"Stupid, desperate women is all that I can say. We can't say too much. He did help us both with our fake marriages. We need to take all the liquor. Don't need to leave a drop for the rebels to find once we leave."

"Do you think he'll let us pillage the rest of this house before we leave? He's already got the safe opened somehow."

"Everyone thinks that there was more in that safe than just worthless Confederate cash and the diamonds he drapes on that little whore."

You could knock Mollie over with one finger. She leans back against the cabinet and shakes her head in further disbelief, squeezing the wrapped fudge. The Russian has gotten into her mind more than she realizes or acknowledges. All manipulating lies. Fake marriages based on more lies. Including theirs that almost happened. Babies too. How low can one man go? Pregnant wife for Christmas. Now he intends to rush her out by escort to Nashville so his wife will never know about his devious schemes.

Mollie goes back into the kitchen, more furious than she was earlier in John's room. She asks the staff to arrange for delivery of Jack and another horse to Herman, with the finest carriage on the estate, when Herman arrives and to have the carriage loaded.

It's still dark outside. Mollie decides to walk through the large house one last time as she waits for Herman. She reminisces about all of the time shared with John in each room. Remembering how it all started over books. She recognizes she has been duped by a real scoundrel. She thinks about leaving all the diamond jewelry for the home's owners when and if they return but changes her mind when she remembers that the two drunk officers in the dining room plan to clean the house out before they depart.

The sunlight barely peers through the drapes when she sees Herman riding high in the carriage seat in the front yard, with Jack tied beside him. She goes out to greet him and unties Jack. "Herman, go ahead and leave in the carriage. I'll take Jack, and we'll catch up with you long before we meet up with the troop escort. We'll get Belyy on our way," she tells him. Her brain tells her to leave now, but the strong emotions of an angry woman push out all sensible logic. She makes the excuse to Herman that she needs to ask John to finish his story about her daddy. Everything is pent-up in one box as she climbs the stairs to give John one last piece of her mind.

She stands outside the bedroom door, takes a deep breath, and then chickens out. She's about to leave when the door opens. John stands in only his trousers. "Mollie, come in. Let's talk. That outburst last night was uncalled for and very immature. I was not only put out by your child like actions, but you woke up everyone in the house. I tried to warn you—check all your emotions at the door in this business—but you just wouldn't listen, wouldn't learn. Now look at you, all hurt and full of venom toward me. It didn't have to be this way. We should part as friends, Mollie."

He takes her small hand and walks her across the room to his bed one last time. Mollie is furious with him and does everything in her power to not show him her true feelings. She's in utter disbelief that he is still pursuing her. Then Mollie does something very unexpected. She turns around with a most seductive look... and then a wicked smile. She yanks a curtain tie off the wall, locks the door, walks toward John, and surprisingly says, "You've been a naughty boy, John, and you're going to get spanked. You do like that, don't you?"

He smiles from ear to ear as he anticipates one last time together before his wife arrives later that morning. John freely holds out his arms as she puts his hands on each side of the tall heavy wooden bedpost and ties his wrists together as tightly as possible. "You have been such a bad, bad boy, John," she devilishly whispers in his ear, kissing the side of his face as she touches his awakening erection through his trousers. She takes the gold silk scarf off his uniform jacket and rubs it across his muscled-up stomach and chest. Then she softly kisses his nipples, making them stand at attention, taking in a pleasant deep breath.

She ties the scarf around his eyes as a blindfold. He stands still as she kisses her way back down his front side and excites him even more as she unzips him. "My bad, bad John likes it when I spank him. Don't you, dear?" she coyly whispers as she pulls his trousers down to his ankles and slaps him on the ass with her bare hand several times. He is again intensely stimulated as she caresses his thighs and now rubs his fully hard erection. He moans deeply. "Oh, yes, Mollie, you know how much I like your touch. So you do remember all that I taught you—naughty girl."

Her hands glide over his strong body for the last time as she reaches over to the nightstand for the general's pistol. She puts the cold metal of the barrel against his face and says in a stone-cold voice, "It appears that I do still hate you," as she intently pulls back the hammer.

A jolt of lightening shoots through John's entire body. "Mollie, you don't want to do this! Honey, it won't bring back your daddy or free you of the hurt and anger. Take one of the rolls of US dollars out of the nightstand and go. Let the past go," he pleads.

Mollie is overwhelmed by her high emotional state of confusion, anger, love, hate, revenge, and a thousand other emotions that now flood her mind. She lowers the gun and pulls open the nightstand. Not seeing clearly in the early morning light that what is thought to be $1 notes are actually $100 bills, she takes two of the many rolled bundles of money and the sticky photograph of her on the porch. *The son of a bitch owes it to me*, she thinks.

Turning to leave, she's becomes self-aware of her undeniable rage, and she points the gun directly at John's heart and screams, "This bullet should go in your cold heart, you murderer! You lied to me and led me on, you slept with the slave girls, and now you have a pregnant wife on her way!" She pulls the trigger, only to move the gun at the last second, discharging the gun into the wall next to his head.

The loud sound of the gun firing is deafening, especially with a blindfold on, and John thinks for a moment that he's been shot. He falls back and hits his head on the footboard. "Maybe now you won't hear me scream so loud, you bastard!" Mollie shouts in a fit of rage. "That's for my daddy and the life you forced me to live!"

Throwing the gun on the floor next to the bed, Mollie has only seconds to escape. She doesn't need to hear his lame story about her daddy anyway. She leaves him just as he is, tied up with his trousers around his ankles, for his wife to find.

Mollie rushes out of the room with a satisfied smile on her face as she heads out the balcony door and whistles for Jack. She quickly climbs over the rail, jumps to the landing below, and runs down the long flight of steps in the backyard to her waiting horse. She cuts through backyards just in time before Union troops are swarming everywhere like disturbed wasps.

Mollie catches up with Herman and calmly pulls Jack up close to the carriage. He sees her and slows down as she climbs in and ties Jack to the side. "Where is Belyy hidden? We need to go there and get moving fast, before the Russian changes his mind and comes after me," Mollie says, out of breath. Herman looks at Mollie, turns, and pops the reins to signal to the horse pulling the carriage to speed up. All the while he's thinking, *I really don't want to know.*

⇒⊹ ⊹⇐

Two officers from the parlor greet the pregnant Mrs. Turchin in the foyer, when suddenly they're startled to hear a gunshot from upstairs. All three immediately climb the stairs to search for the general, cautiously watching in case a gunman is still somewhere in the house. They reach his room at the top of the staircase and tell his wife to wait outside in the hall. She will have nothing of it. After the officers break the lock, she charges in with them to find her husband pulling his pants up, his pistol on the floor by his side. He's somewhat dazed from the gunshot still ringing in his ears as Mrs. Turchin runs to his side while the officers stand confused in the doorway. There's no gunshot wound—no injuries to be found. More soldiers come in and head out to the open balcony door. No one is in the backyard except for troops now scurrying about.

Turchin regains his composure and sits down on the edge of the bed. "What is going on, John?" his wife frantically asks as she hovers over him. She looks around and demands, "Go find who did this to him. Find who nearly orphaned his child."

The general holds up his hand over his ear, saying, "No, darling, let it go. My gun just hit the floor when I tripped and fell putting on my pants. I'm so embarrassed." He looks at his men and, for show, says, "There will be no other word about this except that a gun accidentally discharged...understood?"

Yes, the handsome general has defied the odds again and escaped being discovered for who he really is. As his good luck would have it, the curtain ties were old and rotten. He quickly broke the ties in just enough time to push them and his scarf under the bed, getting his composure to stand up. In a way, he has Mollie to thank. If she had not acted like an angry jilted woman, they would have been in bed together when his wife arrived. The only mistake he made, in his mind, besides the roaring in his ear, was that his lieutenant did not get his wife's arrival time correct. Arrival times by railroad travel are so unreliable in this war. *Mollie's good*, he thinks as he chuckles to himself. *How did she know that would excite me? I never taught her that side of myself.*

⊷⊶

After they pick up Belyy, Mollie and Herman meet the Union escort about three miles outside of town. The sergeant approaches the carriage and says, "Good morning, Miss Mollie. An honor, ma'am, to meet the legend. I see you have the general's horse as agreed." He turns to another soldier and tells him to carry the white horse back to the general.

Mollie, crying, says her goodbyes to Belyy. "I'm going to miss you," she says, sobbing as she finally turns to climb back aboard the carriage.

"Are you still going to escort us to Nashville?" Mollie asks.

"Yes, ma'am. I can now that you have returned the horse. I guess for some reason the general didn't entirely trust you. War tends to do that to some people...well, all of us, actually.

"Now, ma'am, who's the man in the carriage with you?" the sergeant asks.

"He's my personal confidant and my special angel, sent by God for me to protect. His name is Percy Taylor, my cousin. He is partially deaf...hears sounds but doesn't always understand words. He is stupid, too. Drinking rum at the Pirates House in Savannah got him abducted, taken through underground tunnels to their ship, and nearly beaten to death. Realizing he couldn't hear, they threw him overboard, and he swam ashore. He's lucky to be alive. He tried joining the war, both sides actually, and neither wanted him because he's stupid. But what can I say? He's my family. I'm

198

all he's got, and I will not allow anyone to make fun of him. He's going to Nashville with us to rescue my sister and my mother in the hospital."

"Stupid, huh?" the sergeant inquires as he looks inside and tries to talk with the cousin.

CC has heard the entire conversation, and as they discussed earlier, he plays the role perfectly, his mouth wide open as though his jaw is loose, his shoulders rounded forward. He acts restless, and he shifts weight from one side to the other, all the while bobbing his head as though he is hearing music that the rest of them can't hear.

"I talked with General Turchin about Percy. He said it was OK," Mollie finally says.

The sergeant turns the orders over and apologizes, saying, "I'm so sorry, ma'am. It is here on the back. Sorry, Mr. Percy. I trust you will enjoy your trip. Let's be off…if it is OK with you, Miss Mollie."

"Thank you, Sergeant," she says, thinking that at least the son of a bitch kept his word. Mollie winks to her passenger, acknowledging he still has to play the role awhile longer.

Twelve Union troops join the carriage as it readies to continue on to Nashville. The soldiers are completely mesmerized by Mollie, the White Dove. They are actually proud to protect the legend. They want the war to end too.

The group quickly moves forward. At rest stops, Herman and Mollie talk when the opportunity arises. Mollie asks Herman if he is sure about CC. Herman replies, "He is sent by God to protect you. I saw the man change from welcoming death to answering God's call after he saw you for the first time at the train depot the day you were caught. I believe he will protect you, Mollie. We both feel you will save many more people's lives. I've helped him recover from his war injuries over the last month while you've been captured. He's a sharpshooter. The army made him an assassin until the Union soldiers got him first. I've watched him. He's the best I've ever seen with a rifle." With his white riding glove, he pats her on the hand and nods his head for positive reassurance.

Mollie's face turns sad as she wonders if she would have been spared all the heartache had Herman and CC rescued her from CC's uncle's home. She thought she knew how to handle the Russian. Perhaps she was guilty, as are many other women, of thinking that she could understand the complicated man. *Yes, I may still have "one box," but I need to toss that idea or at least put it in another box*, she thinks to herself.

Mollie and Herman share their mutual concern for everyone's safety as they travel with only twelve men, in blue coats no less, in the thick of a Georgia that has recently been savaged by Sherman's total destruction. They feel more like targets as they pass desperately hungry civilians who have lost everything. Some of these once-good citizens have become bandits, along with others that have been robbing and stealing and just up to no good all of their lives.

An unescorted carriage would not make it to Nashville, but everyone, especially the soldiers in blue, knows that there are still a number of dangers for even an escorted one. Also, the soldiers have an extra problem...with all that this war, and recently Sherman, has inflicted on the South, they are a blue-coated target for not only bandits but likewise for a lone gunman's revenge, even at Christmas, until this war is officially declared over. Day by day, mile after mile, it is the same...burned towns and plantations with refugees who search for help.

As luck would have it, the soldier in the rear moves up to the sergeant and tells him that they are being followed. Looking straight ahead, the sergeant asks, "How many?"

"Not sure, sir, but more than ten," the soldier replies. The sergeant knows that trouble is coming, and a lot of it. He pulls up close to the carriage and, ignoring CC, tells Herman and Mollie that if they have guns, get prepared.

Fourteen bandits appear at the edge of the woods about a hundred yards away. They yell at the caravan, saying that the troops are surrounded and all they want are the valuables and any food they have. The sergeant looks around, knowing at that distance accuracy is not guaranteed, but he needs to keep them a distance away from the carriage. He nods to his men, and with no warning, he commands, "Fire."

Six bandits fall dead in and around the woods. The others scatter to a safe distance of more than three hundred yards and turn to assess the situation. Two more rifle reports come from the carriage, and in the distance two more men fall to the ground.

Although the raid is over and the sergeant has not lost a man, he is concerned and pulls up next to the carriage. Percy's gun is still smoking. "Mr. Percy, where did you learn to shoot like that? Who are you?"

Mollie quickly replies, "Sergeant, he can't understand what you're saying. Marksmanship is a gift that he has. He can't hear, but his eyesight is sharp as an eagle's."

The sergeant looks down at the rifle Percy has. "Mr. Percy, that is a Spencer repeating rifle that you have. I don't have one. None of my troops have one. Sir, where did you get it?"

Mollie, again, answers for CC. "Sergeant, it's my gun. The general thought that I might need it for my trip and gave it to me as a Christmas present."

The sergeant looks somewhat befuddled but replies, "Well, Mr. Percy, a couple of those bandits may come back, if for nothing but revenge, and we may meet more. See if Miss Mollie will let you keep 'her' gun close." He turns, shaking his head. Under his breath, one can barely hear, "I always wanted one of those."

The sergeant never knows just how good CC really is. Four bandits were sneaking up behind as the troops faced the others in the woods. The first four bullets in the Spencer's magazine went to them.

CHAPTER 29
BLACK-EYED PEAS

The weather takes a turn for the worse as Georgia is hit with a rare winter storm that forces them to stop at a vacant farm. The barn has been burned to the ground, and the two-story farmhouse looks as though it has been ransacked by both sides, but it provides excellent shelter from the outside elements. All of the towns and farms, left soaked in blood and ashes, are now under a blanket of pure white snow that temporarily disguises the reality below. The storm has delayed them another day.

The next morning, New Year's Day, 1865, Mollie opens her eyes and realizes that it's Sunday, the first day of a new week and a new year. Before she pulls the blankets from the carriage back, she recites her long list of things for which she is grateful: "God, Jesus, good health, Sissy, the beautiful morning sunshine, Herman, CC, the twelve Yankees, the Green family, all of the strangers who helped our escape, and this shelter..." Nowhere does the Russian's name come up.

The soldiers don't like for Mollie to let strangers who arrive at the doorstep to come in from the cold. However, as Mollie walks down the creaking wooden stairs, she smiles as she sees the living room floor covered with warm bodies and notices the smell of

202

horses scattered through the rest of the house. Apparently more refugees arrived after she went to bed. Thankfully the Yankees took turns standing guard and took them in.

The beautiful sunshine blinds her as she opens the door. She and a few of the soldiers look for firewood after they take the horses outside. She remembers how she had to argue with the Yankees to bring all of the early arrivals in from the subzero cold last night and to use the large dining room and parlor as a stable. Anyway, keeping the horses inside has another benefit...they help to heat up the house.

As much as Mollie wants to share her food, she knows her provisions will have to last awhile. This weighs heavily on Mollie's heart as she looks for firewood in the snow. When she notices a large, snow-covered broken branch that's still attached to the tree as it creaks above her head, she backs up for safety and continues to look for smaller fallen branches. When she does that, she notices that the shadow of the branch on an empty silo make a perfect cross rising above the white snow.

Mollie is moved to tears and truly believes that Christ is still in her life and that through him, God will answer her prayers. She immediately drops to her knees and says a small prayer before the shadow of the cross, not for herself but for all of the starving people who have started to come out of their hiding places in the untouched woods, caves. and structures. "Jesus, in your sweet name, I pray for food for all these hungry people in the house. Amen."

As she walks back to the house, she trips over something in the snow. Pulling herself up out of the soft snow, she feels around and realizes that she tripped on cut trees to be used as fence posts. "We can't eat wood, God, but thank you. It'll keep us warm."

Something draws her attention back to the silo-and-limb cross. She knows that the Yanks would have taken all the livestock, and what they couldn't use they would usually slaughter, or they would have burned the silos with the grain that kept the livestock alive. She thinks it must be empty, but maybe they left just enough to feed all these people a small meal?

Mollie goes to the opening at the bottom, takes a deep breath, and partially slides the door open. She jumps back in amazement as the trough begins to fill with black-eyed peas. "Thank you, Jesus, for delivering my prayers to God. Thank you, Father God."

She sees Herman and CC near the horses and frantically waves her arms for them to join her as she jumps up and down in her excitement. "Look, can you believe our good luck? Now we can make sure all of those hungry people will have a hot meal on this glorious first day of this new year. Thanks be to God. Let's go to the smokehouse," Mollie tells CC directly into his ear as she catches herself almost saying "CC" out loud. "Percy, see if we can find large pots to cook all of these black-eyed peas. Herman, follow my tracks that way. You'll find a pile of fence posts that we can use for a fire to cook the peas."

Mollie is so exhilarated that she skips through the snow to the smokehouse. As she expects, it is stripped of all the smoked meat, but the fatty hog jowls were left. She finds three large pots and takes them to the silo to fill. Herman starts the fire for the stove and suggests, "C...ah, Percy, while I get this second stove started, go out there by the horses and get the salt lick; they don't like it in cold weather anyway. We can use it to season these peas."

Mollie tells everyone, "I put a half of a pound of hog jowls in each pot. It'll taste like bacon, and we all need the extra fat. No time to soak them. These big pots are going to take a while to come to a boil, and that will have to serve as the soaking time. Once at a slow boil, we are two hours to dinner.

"Let's search the cellar for anything the Yankees might have missed. Also, we need to look for loose boards in the floors or other hiding places in the house for a stash of supplies the owners may have left hidden or even forgotten."

The hungry refugees are more than happy to help with the New Year's Day meal. The cellar was empty, but to everyone's surprise, one of the refugees searching did find a small stash of flour and cornmeal under the floor along with a few jars of canned collard greens. Additional refugees begin to arrive; no doubt the smell of cooking food has traveled out in the cold countryside.

One of the Yankees says, "Mollie, that sure smells good, but the reason that they left the black-eyed peas is because back home it's cow fodder. Are you sure it's fit for humans to eat? We don't eat that back home in New York."

Mollie looks at him, laughing, and says, "It's the only hot, home-made meal you're going to get at all on this New Year's Day. Moo if you must, silly man, and enjoy. We've been eating these down South all of my life. God gets the glory for this glorious meal today; in Jesus's precious name, we pray. Amen," Mollie finishes the dinner prayer.

"Amen! Praise the Lord," says the crowd of hungry people.

Mollie adds, "May we always give praise and remembrance to God's endless mercy every New Year's Day and eat this fine food as a tradition. Pork is for luck, peas are for pennies, collard greens are for folding dollar bills, and the cornbread is for gold. Happy New Year! Let's eat."

Everyone eats with gratitude for the food. One young black woman remarks, "Praise you, Jesus. The White Dove is with us," not knowing that it's true.

As they are finishing the cleanup after the feast, one of the soldiers comes running back into the house and eagerly tells Mollie, "Come look—you're not going to believe this!" Mollie grabs her coat and runs out the door to see that standing in the snow beside Jack is Belyy.

He stands on all fours and is so excited when he sees Mollie that he rears up on his back legs and paddles his front two legs in the air. Then he begins to run to her as fast as he can. He gets to her, nostrils flaring, and bows on his front two legs, snorting as though to say, "Get on." She gladly climbs on his back and throws her arms around his big neck and hugs him with such love. Mollie prances him around, doing a few tricks and showing him off to all. Then she slides off the other side to get close to his face. "How did you find me? How did you get here? We left over a week ago. Where's your harness?" she whispers to him.

The sergeant is touched by the reunion of White Dove and her horse and thinks of it as a New Year's Day miracle, but he still tells Mollie that he's sorry, but he must later take the horse to Decatur to be returned by train. One of the soldiers, seeing the emotional reunion and the tears in Mollie's eyes, walks over to the sergeant and whispers, "That's not the general's horse, sir. You saw the tricks it was doing. That is a trained show animal…probably ran away or got separated from the circus. Won't hurt to let the woman believe it's the same horse, will it?"

The sergeant looks at the young man and whispers back, "Son, you don't really believe that?" He walks over to Mollie and says, "Knowing that I personally turned the general's horse over to be returned to him, it appears that this horse cannot be the general's. Probably lost from a circus. I've been with the general longer than anyone, and he has never mentioned that he rode a show horse… lots of white horses in the world. We are almost to Decatur, Georgia where we'll get on a train and as far as I'm concerned, you're stuck with a lost horse."

CHAPTER 30

DETOUR TO HUNTSVILLE, ALABAMA

Their slow journey in the snow continues by land until they reach Decatur, Georgia, where all of the horses and even the carriage are loaded onto a military train bound for Chattanooga, Tennessee. While they bump down the tracks heading north, Mollie asks the fourteen men to swear that they will stop telling all they meet that they are escorting the White Dove. She explains that the White Dove thing is in her past and she must move forward. As they reluctantly swear to keep the legend to themselves, one man leans over to another and whispers, "Legends never die."

The soldiers have to give Mollie the bad news as they arrive at the Tennessee River. "We can't cross over to Chattanooga. The damn rebels won't quit fighting around these parts of Tennessee. It's not safe for you to travel. We are going to take a military supply boat to Huntsville, Alabama, and go straight north to Nashville from there. It'll be safer." They buy what few supplies are available at the trading post before they board the ship.

Everyone is packed together pretty tightly on the water portion of the journey. As the soldier said, "Legends never die." Herman and CC have committed their lives to protecting Mollie. The Union soldiers…well, they just want to go home, so why take a chance on the legend getting hurt or killed? If keeping the White Dove alive will bring peace and an end to the war, then so be it.

Despite the war all around them, they experience the most beautiful scenery in the south on the river. Sporadic gunshots fire from the shore. CC's ("Percy's") rifle occasionally fires, and they all know he may have just saved one of their lives again. All are ordered to stay on board while military supplies are unloaded at certain stops.

On the river somewhere near Guntersville, the ship stops, and they are allowed off. Mollie meets a local woman waiting for her family to arrive at the Stage Coach Inn and Tavern. She tells of the latest news that she got from her last group of refugees from Huntsville: "The Yankees occupy all the homes in downtown. They tell everyone that they are here to protect the slaves, but I have heard the truth from the distraught owners. They are devastated that their slaves, some of them their own children, are being whipped and beaten for being a nuisance to the soldiers as they beg for food.

"As more and more starving slaves came to the headquarters, some of the soldiers' patience ran out, and they even began lynching some of them to send out a message to all the slaves to stay away. The military feels that they have a war going on, and they have no time to take care of slaves, freed or not.

"You know that most of the Yankees that occupy Huntsville are Dutch foreigners? They are especially mean, and they mock the Huntsville citizens as being 'lint heads' because of the cotton-based economy. But compared to how they treated Guntersville, Huntsville is pretty lucky for being spared. You can get any supplies you need there, unlike here, where there is no food, no post office or railroad." Mollie begins to think that war-spared city of Huntsville might be a good place to start over after the fighting ends.

Farther down the river, there is serious trouble as cannonballs rain down from the top of Wallace Mountain. The attack on their riverboat scares Mollie to death. The ship speeds faster than normal due to the captain's claim that he had made "special modifications" to the engine. The captain is giving all the boat has to throw off the cannon's fire "lead" time. None of the troops nor CC returns fire back on the Confederate troops.

CC whispers to Mollie, "Without a lucky shot, they are way too far away on that mountain to hit us. I'm more worried about the captain's jury-rigged engine blowing up this tin-clad boat. Don't worry, Mollie, I'm here to protect you."

The ship arrives at Ditto Landing, just south of Huntsville. On the ride into town, Mollie remarks on the beautiful countryside and lush green mountains—no signs of war anywhere. The Union headquarters in downtown Huntsville is another story. It appears to be a civilized occupation, but Mollie remembers the woman's stories about the refugees that once lived in these beautiful homes and their slaves who were mistreated by the occupying forces.

The Union escorts check in at the Huntsville headquarters and show the signed orders from General Turchin. The receiving officer mutters that it's unusual for a female civilian and her companions to be given a security team of armed escorts in the middle of this bloody war. Still, he signs the papers and gives directions to the depot. Then he explains their itinerary: "The train to Decatur, Alabama, leaves in one hour. There you catch another straight to Nashville. You'll be there tonight."

Mollie is happy to hear the good news that they will arrive earlier than she expected. She prays she makes it in time for Sissy.

⇥⇤

The train slowly pulls into the Nashville station. The occupied Tennessee State Capitol is on the hill to the left, with Union camps covering the lawn. The entire group is anxious for Mollie to find her mother and sister in time. As the train door opens, the familiar disgusting stench of the large army encampment burns their nostrils. As they wait for the horses and carriage to be unloaded, Mollie looks around at all the men who have bravely brought her here, closes her eyes, and prays, giving thanks.

The recent Battle of Nashville has claimed St. Mary's Catholic Church as another military hospital. Mollie marvels at yet another Greek Revival structure, with large columns at the entrance. All of the men wait outside the church. The bishop's large home is used as the prostitutes' hospital. To Mollie's surprise, it seems clean and orderly, with army doctors and the nuns from St. Celia Convent as nurses.

Mollie speaks to a friendly nun's aide, Laura Ann, about her mother. "Sadly the news is not good for Mary," Laura Ann says. "We're currently treating her with mercury for syphilis. She's been here for two months. I pray with her every morning, but she has simply lost her will to live and welcomes death.

"Now your sister, Sissy, she's a different story altogether. The mercury cured her, and she has chosen to stay here. She even volunteers to help the other patients. Let's find her first—she'll be so happy to see you. She talks about you all the time. Why, I feel like I know you already."

As they walk down the hallway, Mollie asks, "Is my mother well enough to travel by train? I want to get her out of Nashville."

Before the nurse can answer, the squeal that can be heard across town comes out of Sissy's mouth as she sees Mollie, "I knew you would come back for me!" she says as she runs and jumps on Mollie, wrapping her arms around Mollie like a child. Sissy pulls her head out of the hug just long enough to say, "I told everyone that you promised God that you will always take care of me, and now here you are, just like you promised." Her arms and face clamp down on Mollie again with great joy. "Come, let's go see your mother. I'm so glad you made it before she passes. She's not going to last much longer. Your mother is very weak."

Laura Ann opens the door to the room, which smells of death and medicine. Mary's frail body is lying on her side with her back to the door. Mollie is relieved when she sees her mother's chest rise and lower. Sissy cheerfully goes to the bed and gently says, "I've got a surprise for you, Mary."

"No thanks, Sissy. I just want to sleep," Mary replies as she closes her eyes.

Mollie touches her hands. "It's me, mother...Mollie."

For the first time in two weeks, Mary's eyes open wide, and she slowly sits up on her own. As she reaches out to embrace her daughter, Mary says, "Oh, my dear Mollie, it's really you. You're back. I must get something off my chest before it's too late. I'm so sorry for all that I put you through. I know you can't forgive me. No one should forgive me, but I'm so truly sorry. While I have the strength, please let me tell you the story about your father." Tears of pain and joy flow down Mary's cheeks.

"Your father was a hero for the Confederacy. When we lived in Virginia, he worked as a spy. They gave us a new name and identity and moved us to Nashville. That is why we had no contact with anyone in his family. It would have put their lives at great risk. Celia Hall's husband was your father's friend in Nashville. We are not related. In addition to Turchin's bloody war tactics in Athens, Alabama, he probably had orders to assassinate your father.

"I read the records of the court-martial of Colonel Turchin, and there is no mention of your father's death. No record of him anywhere. It's the politicians in Washington who are completely responsible for this war and your father's death...all of it because it's about the money...always about the money. The government knew he had too much information on them. They could have stopped this war before it ever started. Lincoln promoted your father's murderer to brigadier general to protect him from court-martial.

Our last name is Teal, not Smith, and we are not related to any Smiths in this town. It's all make-believe. You need to know the truth. That's all I have wanted to tell you...the truth before I die."

Laura Ann and Sissy's faces show their surprise, for they haven't heard Mary speak this much since she's been here...much less such a confession. "Momma, I forgive you. Thank you for telling me the truth. We will have lots of time to talk about it. Momma, you are coming to Huntsville with me...now," Mollie tells her mother as she sits on the side of the bed and wraps her arms around her. Uncontrollable sobs and tears help to release years of hate and pain for both mother and daughter. The long, hard journey from Savannah was worth it to be in her arms and feel the love that only a mother can give.

Mollie regains her composure and tells Sissy, "Gather both yours and mother's belongings. We're leaving Nashville right away." She bends over and puts her arm under Mary's knees and one under her arm and across her back and picks the tiny body up. She walks carefully, carrying her mother outside to the waiting carriage. A few of the soldiers actually clap, relieved to know they got Mollie here in time to see her mother alive and rescue her.

Mollie asks, "Sissy, is our house still standing?"

Sissy nods yes but is curious as to why Mollie would ever go back there.

"I was sorry to hear about your grandmother."

"Yes," Sissy replies, "and I had to witness her being robbed and murdered."

Mollie hugs Sissy, thinking, *No wonder she stays at the hospital. It is much safer than the streets.*

Mollie asks the Union escort soldiers if their obligation to her has expired. Giving relief to Mollie, with a smile, the sergeant says, "No, ma'am. The orders clearly state...to your final destination beyond Nashville." She briefly thinks of the Russian. He didn't have to provide her with such extravagant security, but Mollie knows the truth. Turchin is a low-life, foreign jerk, trying only to get her out of town before his real wife arrived for Christmas. Mollie knows she must get better control of her anger.

She wraps Mary in blankets for the trip. Laura Ann says her goodbyes, and Mollie replies, "Look us up if you're ever in Huntsville. That's where we're going to go to start a new life."

Laura Ann's face lights up, saying, "I'm a member of the Hobbs family of Huntsville, down on the Tennessee River. I was here attending school when the Union took over the church. Maybe we'll run into one another there someday."

Mollie responds, "Thank you for caring for my mother and Sissy, and for the extra mercury and morphine too. Yes, I have a feeling that we will meet again."

Traveling through Nashville's Smokey Row with a Union escort has a different feel for Mollie compared to just one year ago. She has traveled, learned, and met so many types of people since leaving Nashville. Most of it was good.

Soon after, they arrive at her old house. Herman, CC, and two soldiers walk with her to the door. Things are the same. Aunt Celia and others work as prostitutes, trying to survive another day. They greet her warmly, and she returns the kindness. Mollie tells them that she has left something under the floor and will be right back.

They watch as she pulls off her dress with pants on underneath, pulls back the rug, lifts out the boards, and lowers herself to the dirt below. With her lantern, she goes straight to the corner where she buried the cash. She looks for a good long while, but it's just not there. *I shouldn't have gotten my hopes up*, Mollie thinks to herself.

About to climb back up into the living room, Mollie decides to close her eyes and picture herself hiding under the floor in the dark. Realizing she has been looking in the wrong corner, she goes to the opposite wall. Sure enough, all the cash from the bet and her mother's selling of her is still there in the glass jar. Feeling she is about to have a panic attack, she hides the jar of betrayal money in the pockets of her pants and scurries fast to get out of this hole once and for all.

Mollie dusts her pants off, and then she pulls on her dress again, saying her goodbyes. Quickly she is out of the door with the group, on their way back to the train station. She and Sissy catch up on the train ride while Mary sleeps deeply because of the morphine. She shows Sissy the jar, vowing to never open it. Herman and CC, as promised, stand over Mollie like guardian angels.

Mollie speaks with the train conductor on the trip from Decatur, and he tells her that the Lowry home off Meridian Pike belongs to his relatives, who are temporarily seeking refuge out of town until the war ends. He tells her the home is available as a boardinghouse.

They arrive back in Huntsville the next morning, tired and hungry. The sergeant and his men have done their job and are ready to mount up for departure. It actually becomes a tearful departure for the Union soldiers and the band of Southerners they have protected. Mollie gives each soldier a hug he won't soon forget.

The sergeant shakes Herman's hand and wishes him the best in what will be the new South, and he tells Mollie that he is thankful to be a part of getting her to her mother. He then turns to "Percy" and looks him straight in the eyes. "Percy, thanks for your help. You saved a few of us, and we will always be grateful." Then the sergeant leans over and whispers into the supposedly deaf man's ear, "CC, the war will soon be over. Let's both let it go and return home. Promise me, CC, that you're going home." CC looks at the sergeant, with a tear in his eye, and just nods in agreement.

As the troops mount up and leave, CC reflects upon the sergeant and his words. He thinks again about the war. It is truly brother fighting brother. He is delighted to not have to play the part of an idiot any longer.

⟛ ⟛

The judge's gavel comes down hard again, calling for a recess for lunch…with the same startled reaction from Sissy, except this time she says nothing. Sissy looks around at the engrossed courtroom, glares at Celia Hall, and says, "I was in Mary Smith's hospital room when she told both Mollie and I that she had no relatives. That it was all made up for their new identity." She turns to the judge and says, "Your honor, I've had enough for today. Can we pick up again tomorrow?" The crowd starts to get disorderly as one man says, "No, you can't let her stop now. The day is not over. We want to hear more. What happened next? Did her mother live? What about the money? What did she do with it?"

A newspaper reporter says, "Y'all are going to read about black-eyed peas tomorrow. We have them every New Year's Day, and nobody could ever answer where the tradition started or why. Now we know it was the White Dove. Wow, what a story."

As he darts out of the courtroom, a friend of Mollie's and Sissy's says, "I'm so glad Mollie was able to save you and Mary from a hard life. She really did love you, Sissy."

David Overton stands silently in the back corner with a sour look on his face, always present as a constant reminder to Sissy that he will never stop hounding her until he finds the whereabouts of his brother. Meanwhile, secretly hidden at his home is the one thing that would break Mollie's heart.

CHAPTER 31

THE LOWRY HOUSE

The Lowry house has a beautifully landscaped lawn with a cast-iron fence around it. The home and friendly staff turn out to be the perfect medicine that they all need to rest, far enough outside of town for peace and quiet.

Herman takes comfort as he notices the quilt that covers a window. It's full of symbols for the Underground Railroad, code for escaped slaves seeking freedom in Canada.

The vastly overweight cook at the Lowry house is happy to be feeding large groups of folks once again. She makes freshly ground sage sausages, fluffy scrambled eggs, buttermilk biscuits with gravy, fried potatoes, and creamy grits loaded with sugar and butter or honey. After breakfast, Mollie makes sure her mother is comfortable, takes a warm bath, and thinks of the Russian again as she climbs in a thick and fluffy feather bed, with soft sheets and blankets that have a wonderful fresh-air smell and feel. She falls sound asleep.

After two weeks, with plenty of bed rest and no war sounds outside, Mary starts to show signs of improvement and is strong enough to come down the stairs for meals. Sissy comments at the table, "Mary, it's as if you've got your will to live again." All Mary could do is smile and look at her daughter, Mollie.

Mollie agrees with Sissy. "Momma does look much better, and so does everyone, actually. Could it be the peace and quiet? Sissy, look at you—so much healthier with extra weight. CC, it looks like you're moving your shoulder better. Herman, I haven't seen you stop eating since we've been here. You'll be a foot taller than me in no time." Everyone at the table smiles as Mollie compliments all.

Herman says, "I'm a growing man now. I haven't had so much food since those two steaks we cooked back in Macon. The day you showed up with Belyy seems so long ago. Well, I take that back. I'll never forget New Year's Day food as long as I live. How about you, CC? Remember how good everything tasted and all those hungry people Mollie took in?"

CC laughs, saying, "I'll never forget how we all found enough food to feed everyone. Even the Yankees ate it up, thinking the black-eyed peas were cow food."

Mollie looks at Sissy and Mary and explains, "We will keep that New Year tradition alive forever. You two will be a part of it next year. Sissy, Herman has the carriage clean and is going to escort us to a ladies' dress shop for some nice things to wear for our tour through Huntsville. CC, I think Huntsville has too many Union officers here for you to be seen around. One of them may recognize you. I think we should keep you out of sight here at the house, just in case. At least until the war is over."

CC isn't happy about staying behind but agrees and says, "Well, guess staying here is not so bad. Better than playing an idiot and shopping with women for dresses. I always meant to ask you, how did you come up with the plan that I should pretend to be deaf and an idiot so quick?"

"I had the sergeant with the pirate part," Mollie replies. "The rest was just made-up fun to keep you protected and make no one suspicious. I figured none of them would ask you any questions if you were stupid and deaf. They all avoided you like the fever." Everyone laughs, as CC puts on a "silly" face as if playing Percy again.

Hours later, Mollie and Sissy enter a dress shop on the Square as Herman sits high in the carriage out front. Mollie unknowingly chooses the most expensive dress in the shop and picks another, just as elaborate, for Sissy.

The clerk notices their shabby clothes and begins to follow them around the store, assuming they won't be able to pay for their high-priced items and might try to steal the clothes instead.

Mollie finally realizes why the clerk is so cool to them, so she puts a stack of gold coins in front of the woman and says, "This should help your business. I understand retail has been slow these past few years. I think we'll take one of everything you have. My mother is ill and needs a very small size. We need new hats and parasols as well, and perhaps new shoes. Let's not forget all-new undergarments. Anything else, Sissy?"

Sissy shakes her head no, astonished at how Mollie took control of the situation in her favor, while she has never seen someone buy up so much so quickly.

"Please be a dear," Mollie says, handing the clerk her old clothing. "Dispose of these, and have all the other things delivered to the Lowry boardinghouse for me."

Impressed with the confidence of this new woman in town, the clerk says, "You're staying at the Lowry home? OK, my sons and I will package everything and deliver it today. Welcome to Huntsville. This morning I was considering closing the store permanently. Nobody has any extra money, and if they do, they're not spending it. Deliver to the Lowry house, right? What is your name?"

"Yes, the Lowry house for now—that is, until I buy my own house. My name is Mollie, Mollie Teal," she smiles.

"Nice to meet you too. My name is Mrs. Cabaniss."

CHAPTER 32

BUYING REAL ESTATE
MOLLIE'S WAY

Herman drives through town with the two ladies, and they enjoy the beautiful homes, none of which has been burned. Only a few church bells are missing. They were melted to become cannons for the Confederacy. Huntsville is such a contrast compared to other parts of Alabama, Georgia, and Tennessee. Except for all the bluecoats everywhere downtown, you'd hardly know that there is a bloody, horrible war going on.

Herman drives through the poor and black neighborhoods as well. Mollie takes notes in her mind about certain areas she likes. They stop at the Oak Avenue general store to pick up a few items. All three are thrilled with the abundance of supplies; it is unlike anywhere else in the South.

As Herman helps Sissy into the carriage, Mollie is approached by a smiling young man in a police uniform. "Sheriff Oscar Fulghum, ma'am. May I make your acquaintance? You must be new to the area. If there's anything I can help with, I'm your man."

"Well, Officer, it is more than my pleasure to make your acquaintance. Please meet my driver, Herman Deeley, and my sister, Sissy. My name is Mollie," she says, and then even slower, "Mollie Teal." She notices him biting his lips due to nervousness.

"Yes, there is something you can help me with, sir." Mollie continues, rubbing her soft lips together as she locks eyes with his. "I'm new to town and responsible for the care of my ill mother, my sister, and a cousin. I want to purchase homes rather than renting rooms at a boardinghouse and throwing away all that money. Do you know who might have property for sale? I understand homes are cheap and widely available because of the war."

He replies, "Yes, ma'am, but you're a woman and can't own property. You're at least over eighteen, right? Maybe put property in your cousin's name?"

"Sheriff, that just won't work for me," Mollie replies softly as she gives him a naughty smile. "It's in my name, or maybe I'll just leave and find another town. Did I mention that I want five houses? I have the cash and will pay a finder's fee."

By this time, the young sheriff can't disguise his attraction to Mollie, and she uses it to her favor. Mollie moves a little closer and leans in, partially covering his ear with her hand and whispering as she uses her other hand to shield her words from being heard by anyone but him. The sheriff's eyes get as big as saucers, and he gets a huge grin on his face. "Do you think we could have a dinner meeting at the Bell Tavern this evening? You know, to sign papers and witness things. I will sure like having the sheriff as my very special friend, if you know what I mean. You work out that ownership thing, and I'll have Herman bring me around—say, six o'clock?" She smiles and waves to a speechless sheriff.

He spends the rest of the day collecting real estate information and the right owners for his dinner meeting with Mollie.

Mollie arrives looking more radiant than she did that morning, and everyone notices her as she walks into the Bell Tavern. Herman delivers her to the table and returns to the carriage to wait. The sheriff introduces his lawyer. "Mollie, this is my lawyer, who is now Judge Greenleaf. He's making me your legal guardian, which allows me to purchase all the property in your name. He will make all of the necessary paperwork legal. Just to keep things above board and make you comfortable, I also got you your own lawyer, Septimus D. Cabaniss."

As they eat, Mollie makes pleasantries with the men but studies Judge Greenleaf for a resemblance. Is it a coincidence that he has the same last name as Sissy? Yes, she convinces herself—a fluke. The sheriff describes the different real estate options he's seen today and gives Mollie his recommendations on the five best. He has asked Mr. Cabaniss to prepare contracts and deeds for the different properties. Mr. Cabaniss tells Mollie that he has also reviewed the method of ownership for her and agrees that this is the best way.

Trying to build a bond of trust and hopefully a long-lasting relationship among them all, Mollie tells the men that she is depending on them and they have her trust. Mollie agrees to buy the houses sight unseen. They don't need to know that she has already looked at most of these houses today from the street, while driving through the neighborhoods. She suspects that the sheriff may be using inside knowledge to get the best deals.

Mollie signs under the sheriff's and the sellers' signatures. The tavern owner signs as a witness on each document or deed transfer. All the men stare as she counts out the exact purchase price for each property in $100 greenbacks. She asks each man to send her a bill for their services, and then she lays down enough money to cover the group's dinner, with a generous tip.

"Congratulations, Mollie," says the sheriff. "You are the proud new owner of five homes on or near Dixie Place." Police Chief Wilks walks by and asks about the celebration, but it is only a ruse to get closer and meet Mollie. However, Mollie's eyes are only on the sheriff for now, making him feel like the only man in the world. The judge, the police chief, and the tavern owner are envious of the attention she pours on Sheriff Fulghum.

Mollie secretly slides her shoe off under the table and stretches her long bare leg out, touching him in between his legs with her toes. The sheriff's face brightens with excitement as he touches her silky smooth calf as far as he can reach without being noticed. "Sheriff Fulghum, would you do me the honor of having a drink with me to celebrate our business relationship?" Mollie says with the most mischievous smile, ordering a bottle of their best wine.

The other men excuse themselves and leave, with only the bartender remaining. Mollie excuses herself long enough to go outside and tell Herman of her success in acquiring all five houses and to wait just a little longer for her to celebrate the deal with the sheriff.

Mollie smiles on returning to the table, knowing that she has the sheriff under her finger. She tries to not think about the Russian but only to remember his lessons. After one drink, Mollie nonchalantly unbuttons the top two buttons on her dress, feigning that it is hot in the pub. Of course, her breasts push out until half of them are almost fully exposed. She is completely bare underneath. Mollie is a good conversationalist and continues talking, although the sheriff appears to not hear a word, with his mind focused somewhere else. The sheriff attempts to make some small talk, and Mollie reminds him to breathe as she smiles at the eager sheriff, never taking her adoring eyes off of his.

"I'm sorry, Miss Teal. I just have never met a woman quite like you."

"You can call me by my name, Mollie."

"My name is Oscar. Please call me Oscar," the sheriff replies nervously, remembering he already told her this information.

"OK, Oscar, but can I sometimes call you 'Sheriff'? I think it's powerful, and I love your uniform too." The sheriff looks around to see if anyone is looking. The bar is empty except for the bartender washing glasses. He leans over as if to talk and reaches under the table. Mollie pretends that nothing is happening and partially spreads her legs as he rubs high up on her soft, milky thighs.

The bartender startles them both as he tells them that he's about to close down the bar. The sheriff turns and says, "Thanks— we were just about to leave anyhow."

Walking out the door, he says, "I feel drunk and haven't had but two drinks. You make me feel incredible, Mollie. How did I get so lucky to run into you today?" He didn't need to know that she had looked for him first. Mollie walks over to a private, secluded alley way next to the bar and turns, facing the adjacent brick wall. With no one in sight, she leans back against the building, saying, "Let's finish our celebration here, Sheriff." She pulls up her dress, exposing her beautiful legs and her mound through her panties. "I love to see a man release himself as he rubs my special place through my panties. Would you do that for me? Please?"

Well, Mollie doesn't have to ask Sheriff Oscar Fulghum twice.

He later walks her to the carriage, where Herman is asleep in the seat. The sheriff says his goodbyes and adds, "Always, Mollie. I'll always protect you. I swear. You only have to send for me, and I'll be there," he says with genuine sincerity.

As Mollie was preparing to leave, out of nowhere, she sees the police chief. "Good—I thought I might see you again, Chief," she tells him with a beautiful smile. "How about you show me some raw land that I might like to purchase tomorrow morning, and I'll let you take me for a picnic on the Tennessee River for lunch?" She winks before he can answer. "Pick me up at the Lowry home in the morning. Let's say nine o'clock."

And with a nod, Herman is at the door and assists her into the carriage.

CHAPTER 33
NEWSPAPER HEADLINES

Early on a beautiful spring morning, Mollie announces her intentions to the group: "I've read in the national papers that the war is about to end. Thank you, God! We don't know what is left for the South. We are now, and will be for years to come, under reconstruction. The Confederate States will remain under the control of the United States government, and this will be enforced by the Union troops like those that occupy Huntsville today. I feel sure that local folks who supported the Confederacy will not be represented in local elections, leading to them having no power, influence, or money...only resentment.

"On the other hand, Union officers receive a steady paycheck. A colonel makes two hundred and twelve dollars a month, and even captains make one hundred and fifteen dollars per payday. Northerners will move south with money, trying to buy things up cheap.

"Entertainment is the common thread. Gambling, booze, and women are common vices of men with money, especially when they are away from their homes and families. I have been given an undesirable position in life as that of a prostitute. There's no getting around that. I have come to accept this and will try to make the most of what life has given me. I also accept that no man will ever truly love me because of this fact. I now embrace this life and will help the four of you in any and every way I possibly can.

"Rather than risk my health and that of you two women, I will embark on the rest of my life as a madam. I intend to run everyone else in this business out of town with the best-trained and cleanest women. With no competition, our prices can go up.

"The wheels are in motion. I have bought property on Dixie Place, and I have very important connections with the sheriff and the police chief to keep us protected. A judge or two are in my close circles too. I likewise hope to make the acquaintance of General Mitchell. I heard he's a real grump, but I'll just have to change that." Mollie grins.

"Sissy, I need you as a manager. You know the business. I don't want you to ever have to touch a man if you don't want to as long as you shall live. You'll receive a large cut of the profits.

"Mother, I want to build us a beautiful home someday for you to live out the rest of your days. Herman, it would be my honor if you would be my very-well-paid male bodyguard, assistant, and driver. CC, you can't stay in town. It's just too dangerous with Federal troops around. You'll be recognized by a Union soldier one day, and they'll feel justified to kill you on the spot.

"I'm head over heels about a piece of property on the river. It snugs up against Wallace Mountain...you know, where we took cannon fire coming into Ditto Landing. I want it to be a farm but also more. We will build a horse track with benches for the fans to sit, and we will have concession stands for alcohol and betting plus really nice stables to attract the big-name owners from all around. Herman knows many jockeys from the racing world in Georgia—if they survived.

"After the war is over, people will come to the South, and we'll be ready to entertain them. I have an advertisement in the local papers looking for clean, inexperienced women to train. It'll cost them five dollars to join our team, and they have to pay fifty cents a week to see a doctor. All the money will go into a fund to take care of any girl that gets sick or pregnant. I want each woman trained my way, the right way, to have the best bordello in Huntsville."

Amazingly, no one says a word except Mary. "No, Mollie, I don't want you to do this. I'm so sorry for taking you down this terrible path in life. Surely there is a better way to start over."

"Perhaps, Momma, but from my experience, there is no other way. It follows you. I know. I found out the hard way more than once when I went to Georgia. I've accepted this life, but it will be on my terms and no one else's."

⊷⊶

A deliveryman arrives later that month with a large envelope and a letter. Inside the envelope are the two opened letters she sent earlier to the Greens in Savannah—one to Lucy and the other to Ben—along with the newspaper articles reporting the deaths of both. Benjamin at only twenty-six died of consumption, and Lucy died during another childbirth. The handwriting on the envelope is definitely that of the governess, Mary Roxon. Mollie's hands tremble as she considers that Mary may have had a hand in both premature deaths. She slowly looks down at Ben's ring on her finger and decides to keep it rather than return it to his brothers.

The second letter is from the Grady family, the new owners of the house in Athens, Georgia. Mollie had mailed them asking for instructions for returning some items she had borrowed when she had been held captive. The letter informs Mollie that the previous owner, General Taylor, "has passed, and the widow sold the home with all contents. Any baubles you may have borrowed during your stay, you may keep. Thank you for your honesty." Mollie smiles—she truly did want to return the carriage, but more importantly the jewelry.

⊷⊶

Weeks pass. Mollie has three of the five bordello houses up and running full time and is about to open a fourth house with freed former slaves and mulatto women only. Mollie, Mary, and Sissy live in the nicest house, and Herman lives above the carriage house, where every evening soulful or upbeat music is heard over the gardens as he either plays the piano or Mollie's daddy's sax.

Mollie prefers any business she conducts to be held in a sterile hotel room. Many of the Union officers stationed in Huntsville are from Illinois, and they often leave copies of the *Chicago Tribune* in the hotel lobby. Mollie reads in disbelief: "Chicago Welcomes Home War Hero 'General John Turchin' to a Grand Parade."

April 10, 1865, newspapers across the country read: "The War Ends: General Lee Surrenders."

The April 15, 1865, *New York Herald* reads: "Assassination of President Lincoln: The President Shot at the Theater Last Evening."

CHAPTER 34

THE PAINTING WINDOW

In 1870, years after Mollie moved to Huntsville, a knock at the door reveals a census reporter. "Yes, sir, my name is Madam Mollie Teal, and my mother says that I was born on August 20, 1852—or was it 1850?—in the state of Tennessee. Don't you want to wish me happy birthday? I'm eighteen years old today," she says as she smiles and flirts with the man. Well, her mother did say that, even though Mollie knows for a fact that she is twenty and has childhood memories that are not in Nashville.

The reporter has heard of Mollie for years, and he jumps for joy that her address is on his list today. However, he can't believe she's only eighteen and is the most desirable woman in all of Huntsville, madam or not. He gladly congratulates her. "Why, happy birthday, Miss Teal," he says as he happily finishes the survey and takes a little longer than actually required.

⟩⊹ ⊹⟨

Two years later, it's a Saturday, and Mollie has put on a church dress as she tries to shop at the nearby general store on Dixie Place for basics that all her women need. Usually the owner only lets her shop while he is closed on Sunday morning, when all of the reputable folks are in church, but never during regular business hours. His excuse: it's to protect her from all the jealous women, when in fact it is an unwritten rule that unescorted ladies of the evening not even be allowed at the ice cream counter. Of course, he mainly wants to protect men who recognize her in front of their wives. "Please, there is no one else in here. I'll just grab a few things and be on my way," Mollie says with a smile.

The store owner raises his eyebrows toward the stairs. "There's a church lady up there now, Mollie, and I bet she has never seen the likes of someone like you. She could easily spread it around that I let you shop here and then wham, I could be out of business. Here she comes now. Please go," he says as he walks her to the front door.

The young church woman asks, "Sir, why are you making this woman leave?" Turning to Mollie, she inquires, "Is he harming you?" Mollie shakes her head no without looking up.

The store owner threatens. "Miss Hobbs, I'll ask your daddy to not drop you off alone here anymore if all you're going to do is start trouble. Besides, you're supposed to be painting a picture of the bank on top of the Big Spring from my upstairs windows with all of your new oil paints from New York City."

"Sir, it is not my intent to stir trouble, but I might remind you my father hasn't paid for these expensive paints. I could tell him that you ordered the wrong kind, and you'll be stuck with them. You'll lose my father's business after my mother hears how mean you are to women."

All of a sudden, Miss Hobbs recognizes Mollie. "Your mother is Mary from Nashville, right? I'm Laura Ann Hobbs. We met at a hospital in Nashville near the end of the war. Remember? I told you I was from here. So how are you?" The women excitedly embrace as the confused store owner watches.

Laura Ann pauses and turns to the owner, "Sir, my subject is here to be painted. We'll be upstairs enjoying all my new paints.

Oh, and would you please be a dear and have cold refreshments sent up? It's rather warm up there, so sweet tea for the both of us, please."

Laura Ann holds hands with Mollie as if they are best friends as they climb the stairs to the painting window. "Help me open these windows, Mollie. We'll burn up if we don't. How's your mother? Did she survive? Sissy? Please tell me you all started over to a fresh new life here in Huntsville. Do you mind if I paint you while we talk? Your face has perfect symmetry and bone structure."

Mollie smiles and holds up her hand for Laura Ann to slow down, and she says that she really doesn't want to sit for a painting for any longer than twenty minutes. Laughing a little, she says. "You talk a lot and ask a lot of questions, Laura Ann. And you have a lot of spunk to stand up for me, especially to a man like that in public. But let's start with the fact that the store owner doesn't allow me or any of my girls into his store during regular business hours. Yes, I'm a madam now. That's why I get treated this way. So, do you still want to paint me?"

"Let me think, Mollie. You actually perform sexual activities with men for money?"

Mollie speaks low so she can't be overheard, "Yes, ma'am. For money and power in certain areas—and knowledge about things most women would never know. I invest in things where women are not normally allowed to venture, such as real estate.

"Laura Ann, the reason I'm so popular is that I give a man the time of his life, and I enjoy my job with all my heart. I suspect many of the women who are prostitutes don't like what they do. I treat my man in the moment like he's the only one on earth. They know this and come back for more, and I can charge them any amount I want. If one of them does complain about the high cost, there's always another right behind him who is willing to pay any amount for their time with me.

"Matter of fact, any of the girls that work for me that get negative and start to complain, I run them down the street to Mattie's whorehouse. All those poor, deranged women like that need to stick together. I'll have none of that bad behavior at Madam Mollie's houses. Laura Ann, God put people like me on this earth for a reason. It's not up to us to always question why. Now, do you want to paint me or not?"

Laura Ann is speechless, but finally gets out, "Yes, yes, I think I would."

Every Saturday for months, Mollie meets Laura Ann at the painting window. They always discuss a variety of subjects. Laura Ann loves to secretly meet with Mollie. It feels sort of naughty for her to know a madam. But most importantly, she loves how much she learns from Mollie's vast knowledge of so many different topics. She even mentions, "Mollie, I really think you're smarter than any man I've ever met.

"I don't really understand men. Do you? I ask this in a nice way. I don't hold it against you…what you do for a living, that is. We both lived as civilians through Grant's sending endless numbers men as soldiers into the saw of Lee's army for slaughter. I've worked at many different hospitals during that time, where many of the soldiers were here alone from Germany, Holland, Italy, and so many other countries. They fought and died in our war, but it seems to me like they were only bodies to the generals." Sadly, Mollie nods in agreement.

"Everyone's emotions are still so raw here in the South. The war changed the whole nation. My point is, I met and prayed over many men, but I didn't get to know them, and I still don't understand them." Mollie walks to the top of the stairs, where she checks to see if the store owner is still listening to their conversation as he loads up Mollie's list of this week's supplies. He still keeps the other girls out altogether.

"You know that he eavesdrops on us. He's a bigger gossiper than any woman," Mollie whispers. "The reason you didn't understand any of the men you've met is because they were operating mentally out of a certain box, a box called war. You didn't fit in their box.

Women don't have boxes like men. We jumble everything together all at once—emotions, feelings, love, family, health, friends, even food. It all factors in with us in our decision-making. Men can't do that. They process one category at a time.

"Remember this, Laura Ann, and it'll help when you get married. If your husband worries about the crops and is not showing you affection, it's because he can't mix the two."

"Did you learn this from studying all the men you meet at work?" she asks, looking down the stairs again for the owner.

"First of all, being a madam affords me the luxury of not having to sleep with men I don't like. Actually, I only have a handful of influential men that I work with, and it's all about who you know—a little bit like politicians. No, not all the men taught me this…only one," Mollie says as she presses her lips hard together. Holding back any emotion, she focuses on writing the bordello address over and over on small pieces of paper that she has cut into perfect squares.

"What impresses me most about you, Laura Ann, is your complete, unwavering devotion to God and to service to others. You never expect any gratitude or recognition. Where or who does that inspiration come from?"

Laura Ann grins. "God, Jesus, and my mother, silly. Would you like to study the Bible with me, Mollie?"

"I know the Bible well enough to know that I'm considered a sinner," Mollie says, smiling, and accepts Laura Ann's invitation.

Laura Ann, happy that Mollie is open to studying the Bible, says, "Each year I work at the Convent of Visitation School in Mobile, Alabama. After spring planting, I usually go back to volunteer with the Order of the Visitation of Holy Mary to tend to the poor and sick at the hospital. I'm very humbled to do God's work. Would you like to join me this year? I leave at the end of the month and stay for four weeks."

Mollie laughs. "Do you really think the nuns will welcome me, of all people? You're being silly. Oh, and how would your family feel for you to travel with a madam? I bet that will never go over well. Have you finished your painting yet?" Mollie asks as she picks up the large bundle of daisies that Laura Ann brought as a prop.

"Yes, I finished a month ago. I use the painting as an excuse for us to continue to meet. You're the one person on this earth that I can talk with and not feel judged," Laura Ann replies as she turns the easel around with great expectations for Mollie to like her portrait.

Mollie's mouth falls open. "That is so beautiful, but I don't look like that—the white dress makes me look angelic," she says, smiling and admiring Laura Ann's talent.

"Let's keep meeting, and say it's not finished yet," Laura Ann suggests. "I'll keep adding little props in the background, like I added the flowers today."

"OK," Mollie says, "Next Saturday we'll meet as usual." As she stares at her eyes in the painting, the eyes seem to follow her. The two ladies depart separately.

Mollie heads toward the bank on the square. She smiles at the men while they conduct their business on Cotton Row. Remembering how Mary spread the word in Savannah so effectively, she gives them a daisy in one hand, a piece of paper in the other. A businesswoman never stops. After all, it's Saturday, and she has houses full of beautiful women.

CHAPTER 35

THE RUSSIAN COMES A-CALLING

Four weeks later, it's a warm, breezy Saturday morning, and Mollie is sitting contently on the back-porch swing. She is looking forward to her visit with Laura Ann that afternoon, before her trip to the coast. Mollie considers how odd their relationship is compared to each other's lifestyle. Sissy is her best friend for life. They have common experiences and can talk about anything. Her friendship with Laura Ann is on a much different level, but it is equally important—probably because of Laura Ann's higher education and unwavering faith.

Mollie hears the front door chime, and Sissy announces, "I'll see who it is, Mollie." Then a long silence as Sissy steps out on the front porch, intending to explain that this is a private residence, not a place of business. This is a frequent problem, as everyone wants to meet Mollie. Sissy stares at the most attractive, well-dressed man she has ever laid her eyes upon in her life, and she doesn't say a word.

The tall, well-built man speaks with a slight accent. "You must be Sissy, as beautiful as your sister describes you. Is Mollie available?"

"You're him" is all Sissy can think to say.

"So, she mentioned me to you?" he smiles. "May I see her?"

"How did you find us? Why are you here? What do you want with her? No, I won't let you see her. You need to go!" Sissy says as she reaches for the doorknob. But then the man slightly touches her arm. Sissy's embarrassment shows on her face as his touch sends thrills all over her body.

"Please," his head hangs abjectly. "Please, I need to talk her. I've looked years for her. A military friend of mine from Illinois is here because of Reconstruction duty. He wrote to me of the town's most beautiful woman, who owns a big white horse that sounds like one that ran away from me or went missing in Georgia. I read his description of the lady, and I knew it was her. I got on a train immediately, and now I'm here. Please let me see her. I have so much to say."

Sissy lets him inside, acknowledging, "You did provide her with armed escorts to rescue us out of Nashville. Come inside. I'll tell her that you're here. That doesn't mean she'll talk with you, though."

He stands at the dining room window and observes his gorgeous Mollie outside on the veranda as Sissy breaks the news to her. It's not the welcome he was hoping for. As Sissy says, "It's the Russian, and he's here," John sees Mollie's lovely face change from happy to a horrible look of concern.

Mollie sits for ten minutes by herself to think before she comes inside. Before Sissy becomes scarce, Mollie tells her, "Don't let Momma know he's here. He killed her husband, my daddy, and she'll climb out of her bed to kill him. Then she would only die in jail." The syphilis hadn't killed Mary, but the morphine addiction was causing her to waste away.

With only one glance at him, Mollie's stomach churns. The fronts of her thighs seem to weaken as she says to John in a very controlled voice, "What brings you here, John? I thought I would never lay eyes on you again."

She sits in a chair to his right. He cups his right ear. The roaring has lessened but has never stopped since she nearly killed him in Athens. "Thank you for seeing me, Mollie. I wasn't sure if you would or not. First, please let me apologize for the way that I treated you in Georgia. You were the White Dove, giving people hope—even my soldiers believed in you. Instead of building you up, I tore you down. I didn't know you were so young when we first met. You acted so grown up and sophisticated. I'm sorry for all the bad things, Mollie. I truly am. It was war, and I used that as an excuse to mistreat anyone in the South, and that included you. I have so many regrets with you. If I could do it all over again, I would do it so differently and treat like you should have been treated. For years, there hasn't been a day that's gone by that I have not thought about you—the way your skin feels, the fullness of your lips when we kiss, the way your long hair smells, your hands exploring my body, and especially the way our bodies melt as one.

"Please tell me you have some good memories of our time together too. My hopes are that you'll have me, and that we can have a life together. Everything I said to you about a man never being able to love you, I was wrong. I do love you. You are lovable, and I know now that I can forget your past. I thank God that I finally found you. Please tell me that we have a chance."

Coldly is the only way that Mollie can handle such an unexpected, devious visitor from her past. She couldn't become his victim again...ever. She couldn't let him know she thought about him daily, dreamed about him nightly, and never can stop how she feels emotionally. She still longs for his touch. No, she couldn't let him know that. She closes her eyes when other men touch her. She always pretends it is him. No, she says to herself, he shall never know.

Mollie says, "No, John. You have a family already. I have done exactly as you taught me. I have become the best prostitute in town, and I stay emotionally detached. Remember, no room in the box for feelings. Perhaps you are a victim of your own lessons and taught the student too well. But I do have one question, though. Why did you teach me all that about how to be the best sex partner? Where did you learn so many things? What would make a man want to teach someone to be a prostitute?"

"That is more than one question, my sweet Mollie, but for you I'll try to answer. First, I'm thrilled you're speaking with me. I wasn't sure if you would or not, so thank you." John charms her with his handsome smile, but Mollie refuses to break her iciness.

John begins, saying, "I grew up at military boarding schools, and in the summers my busy father would ship me off to stay with my aunt, who happened to run a bordello. She is to this day a big, red-headed success in Russia. I probably had more sex with more women before I was fourteen than most men have in a lifetime.

"When she brought in new clean girls, I was playfully used as a model on training day. Not that I'm complaining, but I'll admit my view on things might be a little skewed. But honestly, I think two people can do a variety of things to please one another's bodies, and it's not strange to give pleasure, is it? I want our bodies, arms, and legs all twisted together again. Mollie, I go to sleep thinking of you and only you. Before I open my I eyes in the morning, I fool myself and think it's you that I'll wake up next to—you, with your beautiful body, and I'll take you in my arms. Will you please have me once again, Mollie?"

"John, I have put all those days and memories behind me…you taught me well. I own four operating houses in Huntsville, all in my name. I have more money in the bank than most men in town. Yes, you heard me right. I'm the only woman in town to have a bank account and own property. It's all in who you know—and you taught me that too, John, to only associate with affluent people who can help me or my business."

"We can read books together, Mollie. I know that you love to read. Look at all the books you have here. We can share that once again," John pleads.

With all the indifference in the world, Mollie says, "John, your timing this time is very poor. I travel to Mobile tomorrow, and I will live at a convent for an undetermined amount of time."

"Wait a minute!" he says, almost laughing. "A what? A convent? You're serious. You can't do that, Mollie." He studies her face to see if she's lying but is surprised when he realizes she's telling the truth.

Mollie's hands tremble as she opens the door for John to leave. She prays for the strength to close it behind him. He turns and says, "Mollie, please reconsider. You have too much vitality to live your life like that. Mollie, darling, you're a lover—my lover. I'm at the Huntsville Hotel. Please see me before you go."

He reaches out with his big arms and tries to embrace Mollie, only to hear, "Yes, I know where it is." As she closes the door behind her, she then bites her lip and holds her breath so as to not come apart in front of him. She watches him as he walks down the sidewalk and down the street out of sight. She crumbles up on the floor in front of the window and wails in pain for her lost love, the villain, the most-hated Union officer in northern Alabama.

Upon hearing Mollie cry, Sissy hurries into the room to find her best friend devastated, uncontrollably crying and shaking, barely able to utter a word. Not sure what to say, Sissy lies on the floor behind Mollie and spoons her. As she strokes Mollie's long hair, Sissy says, "I love you, Mollie Teal. Let it out. It's been in there for a long time, so just let it all out."

A few hours later, Mollie composes herself, dresses very modestly, and packs a trunk with plain and bland clothes to take to Mobile. Mollie will miss Sissy the month she is away, but she has to depend on Sissy to keep the business going while she is absent.

"Sissy, you're my favorite person in the world. I love you with all my heart and trust you more than anyone I know. Just think of me when you have to make decisions, and you'll do just fine. I need to do this, Sissy."

"I'm going to miss you so much, Mollie, but I understand. I wish you weren't going. I have a bad feeling about it," Sissy says with deep worry lines between her eyes.

Sissy follows Mollie out of the house where they meet Herman. "Herman, please pull the carriage around. I need to meet with Laura Ann at the general store," Mollie says.

"Mollie, Sissy told me what happened. I'm so very sorry. I don't want you to go. I have seen you every day of my life since Macon, and I will miss you." He looks at Mollie with fear in his eyes for he suspects that it's her power in town that keeps him safe.

"Herman, please don't make me cry. Besides, you're going with me. We're taking our carriage down to Mobile by train and trading it in for a new one. I will have the finest carriage in all of Huntsville." She laughs, knowing that her carriage rides make her more money through gambling than she could imagine.

"Sissy, once I'm gone, please deliver this letter. It's to the Russian. I'm giving him Belyy back. That horse is a constant reminder of him."

Before she can say anything else, Mollie is interrupted with, "No, Mollie, that horse loves you. If he sees the Russian after all this time, it will bring back all the memories of war. You ride him and Jack almost every day. Remember how he acted when you tried to give him back the first time? He found you somehow—a miracle—and he is happy to be with you. I say you must keep him," Herman pleads.

"Herman, I have always known that the horse didn't accidently find me. The sergeant knew it too. Thank you for what you did back in Georgia. To this day, I don't know how you pulled it off, but I was aware that two of the black refugees that New Year's Day at dinner somehow brought Belyy to the edge of the woods at the farmhouse...I suspect to keep the White Dove legend alive. Let's talk about the horse track. We are going to the river after I see Laura Ann."

CHAPTER 36

TRIP TO THE RIVER

Laura Ann is waiting at the usual spot by the window when Mollie arrives. "I've never seen you dress so...boring. What's gotten into you, Mollie? Is everything OK? You look upset. What is it? You can tell me. I keep all of our secrets."

Mollie announces, "I have unexpected good news for you. I'm going to Mobile with you tomorrow. That's why I'm dressed this way, so as to not bring any attention or to embarrass you. I need this trip. I'll have a whole month to tell you the details. I have business to attend to on the river today before we leave tomorrow. Would you like for me to meet your parents before we go?"

Laura Ann's apprehension shows. "Oh, no. They know your name and reputation. They think I come here and meet a pupil from the Huntsville Female College to paint, not you. I gave you a name, Merry Perry—that's easy to remember...Merry, as in Christmas, since you always strike me as joyful, and I like the holidays. They'll love to meet you. I told them how smart you are, and now I see why the conservative dress."

"You lied to them about me. That's so unlike you, Laura Ann," Mollie says as she pretends to try to shame her.

"Well, let's just say there is another side to you besides being a madam, and that other you needs an identity of her own. I hope you don't mind, but I talk about you all the time, and I have to call you something. Otherwise our visits will be over. I can't believe you are going with me. It's very rewarding to serve God and others. Come meet my family. We live on the river, on Hobbs Island Road, at the foot of Wallace Mountain."

Mollie mentions, "That's right in the same area as my business of horse stables and a racetrack."

Laura Ann gasps. "You're the owner of the horse track, where there's gambling and alcohol?"

"Yes, ma'am. If it's a sin, I can make money off of it. If not me, then someone else will do it. But hush up—no one needs to know that I'm involved as I have partners. You know, women aren't supposed to own anything. We can head there now, just leave a note, and let your father know you are with Merry Perry and going to the river ahead of him. How funny—Merry Perry." She laughs as the sound of it rolls off her tongue.

Laura Ann is concerned. "You want me to go to the horse track with you? You can't be serious. I can't go there. You know someone will see me and tell my father. No thanks," she says as she wipes her sweaty hands just thinking about it.

Mollie reassures her. "We won't get out of the carriage. My other partners can come out to us." Reluctantly, Laura Ann agrees.

Laura Ann quietly listens as Herman and Mollie discuss the horses, jockeys, betting odds, and types of liquor, and what gets her attention the most is that Herman drives Mollie's high-end clients, each with a lady of his choice, to the track. This is the reason for the very plush carriage she seeks to buy in Mobile. This is a very large moneymaker for Mollie as many very wealthy men use this discreet service to carouse with the women, gamble, drink alcohol, and most importantly lose their money.

Once they arrive at the track office, Herman goes inside to fetch CC. "Laura Ann, these two friends, and I mean true friends, stuck with me all the way through the terrifying trip from Georgia, to Nashville and Huntsville. You don't know just how dangerous everything was near the end of the war. Battles all around—starving people everywhere you looked. That's when you and I met too. These two were with me that day, and I'm grateful for their courage and bravery. We make a great team.

"Before you ask, no, I have not, nor will I ever, have sexual relations with either of them. Our bond is on a much higher level... let's just say that there are stories that we've all agreed to leave in Georgia. They both claim God sent them in my life."

Herman knocks, and Mollie unlocks the door. Laura Ann feels uncomfortable as the two men get in and lock the door, especially as CC cuts his green eyes towards her and says, "Hello, ma'am. Christopher Columbus Taylor, but you can call me CC. Very proud to meet you."

After the meeting, CC goes back inside the racetrack. Laura Ann can't shut up with the questions. "Who is this man? Did you see his gorgeous green eyes? His curly blond hair? Why did he look at me that way? You saw him look at me, right? Am I a box to him? I feel all sorts of new feelings right now, and I don't know why I am having them. Take me seriously, Mollie. My heart rate is higher. I felt kind of naughty too, you know, to hide in a locked carriage with a handsome man without a male escort. Oh, Lord, I can hear the women at the church talking now. Good thing we leave tomorrow. I don't need to feel lust. Is that what I'm having, Mollie? Feelings of lust? I'm pretty sure it's a sin, no matter what you call it. I'm very confused, Mollie."

Only after Laura Ann takes a deep breath and stops talking does Mollie answer her, with the sweetest smile on her face. "If it makes you feel better, I'll bet CC has the exact same confused state of mind as you. I have never, ever seen him so quiet. If you're asking about love, I don't have good advice for you as I quit on love, I think. Get your advice from your mother. Let's go meet her now. My business is finished here."

Laura Ann's parents are delighted to finally meet Merry Perry and excited about her traveling to Mobile with their daughter.

"How did you come by the name Merry Perry?" Laura Ann's father asks.

"Oh, don't be so nosy, you old coot," her mother tells him.

After leaving Laura Ann's house, there's about an hour's worth of sun in the sky as Mollie and Herman come back to town from the river. Herman sees bellowing smoke north of town and asks Mollie if it's OK to drive a little out of the way to investigate. Mollie agrees, and as they're driving up Meridian Pike, Mollie notices a young black woman, alone, with her hands held high. The woman is screaming uncontrollably to God. Mollie sees a small girl who hides behind her, in the fabric of her skirt. A few minutes pass, but the vision has disturbed Mollie so much that she has Herman turn around and go as fast as he can to find them.

Sure enough, the woman is still in the same spot, with hands still high, and seems to be going through a highly emotional break-down when Mollie gets out of the carriage and greets her.

The little girl peeks out from behind the woman's hip, with fabric covering half her face, thinking that she is hidden. The woman doesn't acknowledge Mollie's presence, so Mollie speaks to the little girl. "Hello, I'm Mollie. Is your momma OK? What is your name, my dear?"

The shy little girl pulls more fabric over her head and begins to speak from underneath it. "My name is Lillian, and she's not my momma. Ruth is my sister. I'm hungry." Mollie hears her cries, even though they are buried in all that fabric.

"Ruth, I'm Mollie. I'm going to take you home with me, where you'll be safe, and we'll get you something to eat. Come climb in the carriage, Ruth. Lillian, will you help your big sissy? Come on out, and let me see your pretty little face."

The ride home piques Mollie's interest. Ruth only mumbles to God, while Mollie wraps her arms around her shoulders and tries to make her feel loved.

Once the ice is broken, Lillian is a chatterbox and spills her version of what happened earlier in the day. "Everybody says White

Daddy went crazy. I saw him pull Ruth to the ground in the barn and lay on her. Then after that, he poured kerosene on the house and set it on fire with all of us in it. We screamed. Everybody's killed but us two. I don't know anybody except you. Will we eat when we get to your house? Everybody calls me Lily. Only my momma called me Lillian. Preacher man said we go to heaven, and it's better than here. Do you think Momma is happy in heaven without me?" the little girl asks as she crawls onto Mollie's lap and falls asleep.

Mollie arrives back home, and the cook prepares her favorite meal—chicken and dumplings, cornbread, fresh hot peppers, and green onions. Ruth eats as though food will take away her pain and returns for seconds. Later that evening, when the two new arrivals are sound asleep, Mollie tells Sissy, "For some reason, I had to go back and pick them up on that lonely road. Herman says he heard that the fire is still burning over off Meridian Pike, at the big farm near the Lowry house.

"Keep them here while I'm gone and make them feel safe. You can teach Ruth to care for my momma. That'll be a big help to you. Keep them away from the business. They don't need to see all of that. I love you, Sissy, and I will miss you terribly.

"We'll leave for the train depot very early as it'll take extra time to load the carriage. Stay up with your studies, and make sure that you're going to be as smart as you think I am. Don't forget to drop off the letter to the Russian." Mollie holds her embrace with Sissy extra long.

Mollie dresses the same dull way for the train ride, and when Laura Ann arrives, she's a bit surprised that Herman and carriage will travel with them on the train as well. Then she thinks better of it and says to herself, *that's Mollie.*

CHAPTER 37

THEN I'LL HAVE SISSY

Sissy looks up Dixie Place toward Monte Sano Mountain and sees it disappear into the fog. The first glimpse of sunshine breaks through as Sissy quietly closes the front door. She holds her dress up as she walks across the dew-covered grass and then hesitates when a man walks toward her on the street. It's the Russian. *Well, good,* Sissy thinks. *Saves me the trouble of going to the hotel, and I can get on with my day.* She walks over to meet him and delivers Mollie's letter. She then points to the pasture and stables where his horse is kept.

Devastated, John barely gets his words out. "She's gone? Really gone?"

Sissy nods her head. "She left a couple of hours ago. I will miss her terribly. I wish you had never come here. Now we all lose her."

"May I read the letter under your porch light?" John asks, his big shoulders and head drooped. Sissy agrees and uncomfortably stays there on the porch while he finishes. His brow furrows with disappointment. "No, she can't mean these things," he tells Sissy, looking deeply into her eyes. He quickly turns and looks up, pretending that he doesn't want Sissy to see his fake reaction.

Sissy feels sorry for the Russian and reaches out to pat him on the back, comforting the distraught man. His hand reaches up and touches hers. She feels like she's been struck by lightning. At that exact moment, he knows that he now has Mollie's sister to use as revenge. How dare Mollie reject him.

He looks up at her, playing on her sympathy. "I'll never be worthy of love. I feel like I want to die, Sissy. Why go on? Nobody will ever want me." He covers his face with the palms of his hands. Sissy pulls in closer as she has never seen such a handsome man, and she can't let him think of ending his life.

"What is your real name, besides 'the Russian'?"

He sobs a few more times and removes his hands one at a time from his face, deliberately locking eyes with hers. "John. My name is John Turchin. I feel all alone, Sissy."

She reaches over and touches his hands, "It's going to be all right, John, and you're not alone. I'm here with you. Do you hear me? You're not alone."

"Do you promise?" he asks. For the next hour, John turns on his charm and convinces Sissy that she is the real beauty. And he bemoans, "If only I could be worthy of someone as pretty as you, life would be worth living."

Poor Sissy has never had a man sweet-talk her before, and she forgets all of her common sense. She never once thinks of Mollie— only the gorgeous man who gazes into her eyes. He says things she has always longed to hear. Sissy feels intoxicated.

All self-control for Sissy is over when John draws close into her face, almost touches her lips with his, and says, "Could you love someone like me, Sissy, and never leave me?"

"Yes," Sissy says immediately. He pulls her in close to his big, strong chest and begins to kiss Sissy, while pressing hard against her breast. He takes his hand to the back of her head and runs his fingers through her hair and softly touches her neck.

"Shall we go somewhere to continue this further, Sissy? Is it wrong of me to want you so badly? I'm pushing my luck. I should go. I'm sorry. I'll leave."

Sissy pulls John in for another kiss; she wants more too, and she tells him, "I want you too. Take me, John. My room is upstairs." John doesn't hesitate. He picks Sissy up in his arms and carries her inside the door and up the stairs.

Bedridden and very sick, Mary hears the entire seduction from her open bedroom window and is totally furious. She attempts to crawl out of bed to get her gun and shoot the man who murdered her husband and then hurt her only child and is now taking advantage of sweet Sissy.

Her feet make it to the floor, but she realizes she is too weak to stand, so she lowers herself to her hands and knees and keeps her balance with one hand on the bedpost. Her rage seems to help her scoot across the floor to the chest to get the gun, and she continues on to reach the door. She must stop this man. She reaches up to turn the knob and pulls the door open to see the Russian as he carries Sissy up the stairs in his arms. Weakness overcomes her, and Mary collapses against the door.

Later, the Russian leaves a sleeping Sissy without saying a word. He goes to the pasture for Belyy and decides to leave him as a constant reminder of himself to Mollie.

Lily awakens and explores around the house to look for anyone. She finds Mary on the floor. Quickly, she brings Ruth to Mary, and together they get her back into the bed. The cook comes in with breakfast, and Ruth still isn't talking, but her appetite is good as she eats biscuits and gravy, eggs and bacon.

CHAPTER 38

THE CONVENT

The trip to the gulf is long, but it gives Mollie and Laura Ann time to talk more about men. Laura Ann asks to talk about CC Taylor first and then the Russian. They talk for hours about CC and men in general as the train clicks down the tracks, until Laura Ann wants to know about the Russian. Mollie spares Laura Ann from the different sexual details and positions. Rather, she mostly admits her stupidity for falling for such an awful man. "I did learn from him," Mollie admits, and commences to tell Laura Ann the analogy of "boxes" and how it explains the totally different ways that men and women think. By the end of the trip, Laura Ann thinks that for Mollie to benefit the most, she should stay at the convent with her, not in a rented room.

"Merry Perry," Laura Ann Hobbs, and Herman Deeley all arrive safely at the Mobile train depot. But Mollie doesn't take Laura Ann up on the invitation to sleep at the convent and arranges for rooms at a nearby boardinghouse for herself and Herman. Then she takes Laura Ann to the boardinghouse at the convent. Mollie loves the serenity of the grounds of the school and church. Yes, she made the right decision. She needs this time to stop everything for a while. She must spend some time for herself, just resting and relaxing.

Tending to the sick is not relaxing, but it allows Mollie to nurture, through God's eyes, on levels that she has never thought about before. Each morning Mollie is the first to arrive to mass. She loves the calmness and order to the church. The entire scene is so far removed from her life that she seldom thinks of home. On her second week, one of the sisters asks "Merry Perry," "How do you like this simple life here? Will you be returning again next year with Laura Ann?"

Mollie doesn't have to think about it for long since she feels better here than at any other time in her life. "Of course, Sister," she replies. "This has been a place for me to heal. I want to come back every year. Reading is one of my favorite things to do. It brings me great pleasure to read to the patients who have poor sight and haven't read a book in years. Many can't read, and they listen so intently."

The sister then invites "Merry" to a special retreat the next weekend. "We are taking a ferryboat to the Gulf beaches for a picnic and fun in the water. Only women allowed, of course. You and Laura Ann are invited."

"Thank you," Mollie replies. "I love the water, and I'm sure Laura Ann will go as well."

The beaches at Gulf Shores, Alabama, are sugar white with emerald-green water and are as beautiful as anything Mollie has ever seen. The women set out blankets and baskets full of food. Laura Ann puts up her easel to paint under the shade of a palm tree that grows sideways, looking like a large bench that floats in the air.

Mollie gets her to put off her painting until after they walk on the beach, saying, "We are far enough away from the other ladies that they can't see us. Let's take off our clothes and go for a swim!"

Laura Ann's mouth drops open. "Do you mean nude?" she asks. "I can't be naked, Mollie. What are you thinking? Someone will see us. God will see us! That's a crazy idea."

"God made us naked, and I believe that he likes how we look. I'm going in by myself. If something happens, you'll have to save me and get your clothes all wet anyway," Mollie teases as she takes off her clothes.

Laura Ann watches and takes notice of how seductive Mollie is with even the simplest moves. "No wonder men love you, Mollie. You look like a goddess."

Mollie smiles and gestures her hands toward Laura Ann. "Look at you. You're beautiful too!" Mollie dives into a wave, jumps high out of the water, and shouts over the sound of the waves crashing around her, "I feel so good and refreshed, Laura Ann. You simply have to come in with me. The only ones who'll see you naked are me and God, and he already knows what you look like, sweetie." She laughs as she jumps and frolics in the waves.

Laura Ann gives in to the fun and begins to remove her clothes and join in the fun with Mollie. She modestly holds her arms across her chest as she slowly walks in, jumping over the next wave and saying, "I don't know how to swim in water that moves, Mollie, so you'll need to teach me. I've only swam in ponds and lakes, never an ocean."

"I've never been in the Gulf before either. Besides Mobile, the only time I've seen an ocean was in Savannah at Tybee Island. It was cold the day we went, and we just watched the large boats come into the port. I'm so glad you got in. Let's go further out to the sandbar and just float on our backs and watch the funny faces in the clouds," Mollie says as she looks happier than Laura Ann has ever seen before.

"You know, when you and CC get married, you have to name your first son, Percy. That's the alias name we used for CC during the war, when he saved our lives so many times."

Laura Ann clears her throat and talks with her hands in the air. "Married? Why do you talk such craziness? First son, Percy? Is that a biblical Christian name? We only met that one time."

Mollie responds, "I told you. I saw the look on his face, and he'll be there for you when we arrive home. You'll see. If he takes too long, I'll tell him what you look like naked."

"You will not!" Laura Ann snaps back.

Mollie laughs as they jump over waves, returning to the shore. "Let me show you how to dance for him—a wedding dance," Mollie says. As she and Laura Ann dry in the sun and wind, the dance lesson begins.

Herman has done as Mollie asked. He spends his days at the Mobile racetrack, making new friends and spreading the word about the Huntsville track. The new carriage is complete in time for their trip home, and its color matches Mollie's shiny black horses.

Later, on the ferry ride back, Laura Ann shares with Mollie, "I will always remember today as the happiest day of my life. You look happier than I have ever seen you, Mollie. You make everything special and fun. What a beautiful place too. I hope we can come back here someday."

Mollie's eyes water up, and she hugs her friend. "I love you too, Laura Ann. If it weren't for you, I'd never have seen this place. Thank you."

"Mollie, when we get back home, I want to frame your painting and give it to you. Then, if it's not asking too much, I'd like to do another."

Mollie is very appreciative of Laura Ann's talent and desire to paint her as a friend, but she says, "I am uncomfortable of the way that portraits and pictures portray how I feel. I had a photo taken of me once, and it made me look happy...I wasn't happy. Laura Ann, I don't need any more paintings. How about if I pay you to paint Sissy? She is beautiful, and I love her too.

"I'll pick up the painting on the way home. I already have the perfect frame. I will hang it proudly as a reminder of how a special friend sees me through her eyes."

"Mollie, I think that I understand. I would love to paint Sissy, but I got your aura right," Laura Ann says with confidence.

CHAPTER 39

MEANWHILE BACK IN HUNTSVILLE

All three passengers sleep soundly on the train ride back to Huntsville and are well rested upon their arrival. Herman tends to the horses and carriage. Mollie and Laura Ann depart from the train to look around. They immediately find that waiting for them with a huge arrangement of flowers is clean-shaven CC Taylor, with a fresh haircut, a big grin, and twinkling green eyes. "Hello, ladies."

Mollie jokes, "Hi, CC! You really shouldn't have brought me flowers," as she winks at Laura Ann.

CC doesn't hear Mollie. He has one thing on his mind. "Laura Ann Hobbs, I know we've only met once, but you are like a lightning bolt to my heart. All I have done is think about you since y'all left town. I know it seems sudden, and yes, I've already talked to your daddy and finally convinced him that I'm the right man for you." CC goes on one knee. "Will you marry me?"

"I told you. I'm right. I saw the look," Mollie whispers in Laura Ann's ear.

Completely surprised, Laura Ann says, "Can we take this a little slower?"

"Slower?" CC says. "I wrote you three letters while you were gone, and you wrote me back."

"Laura Ann, Laura Ann...you never once mentioned letters to me," Mollie says, grinning ear to ear. "You keep little secrets too."

Her father and mother step up to her side, and her father says, "Laura Ann, we were sort of under the impression that you and CC had known one another a little longer from the way CC went on about you. Why don't you two have a short engagement period? But you don't have time to take things too slow. You'll be twenty years old soon, and I didn't raise a beautiful daughter to be an old maid. If you want my advice, CC is a good man. I've gotten to know him. Heck, he has come over almost every evening since you two left. CC Taylor will make a good husband and provide well for you. And he's a Confederate hero to boot."

"CC Taylor, you are something else, you know. I don't know if I should be mad at you or what. It appears that you've taken the time to get to know my parents. Now give me that much time to know you, and you need to know me as well."

"You've made me the happiest man alive!" yells CC. "You're going to love the house I want to build for you. It will be plenty big for a family. Your mother said that you want lots of children. If you don't want to wait, Mr. Gunn wants to sell me his house. It's a big two-story with porches on both levels, with one thousand acres of land. It's also close to your parents." CC continues to ramble on as he stares into Laura Ann's eyes, "I'm going to make you the happiest woman on the Tennessee River."

Delighted with the good news, Mollie and Herman say their goodbyes, and she reminds Laura Ann that she'll stop by the general store to pick up the portrait.

Herman tends to the new carriage, and Mollie goes inside the general store while the clerk loads the week's supplies. She goes upstairs to the window and is in disbelief as she pulls the cover off the easel...the painting is gone.

253

"What happened to the painting?" Mollie shouts as she comes out the front door. The store owner looks down. "I'm sorry, Miss Mollie. I couldn't stop him. He said name whatever price you want, and he'll pay it."

"Who would steal it? It stays covered up!" Mollie demands an answer. Herman tries to calm Mollie and implores her to sit in the carriage. The store owner answers, "The rich guy—the one who owns all the land in and around Huntsville, Mr. Hall."

"Why on God's green earth would he want the painting? I've never even met him." Mollie says in confusion.

"He wants to meet you, and he told me to send word when you got back. Funny, he doesn't seem like the kind to call on you though. Real big Christian type, helping to build churches and doing things for other charity groups."

As he continues to load heavy bags of flour and sugar, Mollie, very irritated, says, "Send him word to meet me up in the window this Sunday when everyone is in church. That way nobody will see him with me—and he better have my painting with him."

"Let's go, Herman. I'm anxious to see Sissy and Momma. We need to share the good news about CC's proposal. I hope the cook makes fried chicken with mashed potatoes, green beans, and biscuits. Are you as tired of fish as I am?"

Herman chuckles. "You know me, Mollie—I like to eat anything, and a lot of it. For some funny reason, I feel good about the painting thief."

Mollie smiles as they arrive home to see Ruth and Lily snapping green beans on the front porch. Lily jumps up, hugs Mollie, and says, "You are real—I thought I dreamed you up, and you weren't real."

Mollie responds, "I'm real, sweetie," as she hugs her back. Mollie sees Ruth's smile, not crying now, and asks, "How are you, Ruth?"

Lily answers, "She still doesn't talk much, and she mostly eats—all of the time actually. Look, she's already eaten half this bowl of uncooked green beans just since we sat here. She looks better now that she's put on weight and gotten her smile back again.

"Ruth, Mama has gone to heaven. Can I call you Big Mama?" Lily asks her sister as she turns her little head sideways. Ruth nods her head that it's OK to be Lily's Big Mama.

Mollie leans over and hugs Ruth, saying, "Well, that's settled. I'll call you Big Mama too, and honey, you eat all the food you want if that makes you feel better. I have plenty of money to buy all the food we need."

Mollie is surprised that Sissy hasn't yet heard them and come out to welcome her home. "Sissy cries all the time in her room. Ruth and I've been looking after your momma, but she sleeps more and more every day. And guess what, Big Mama? She's going to have us a baby. It's White Daddy's. Too bad he died too," Lily says.

Mollie congratulates Big Mama but is instantly concerned about Sissy and goes inside. She looks in on her sleeping mother first. Then she goes straight up to see Sissy. She knocks on the door but gets no answer, so she goes in anyway. Sissy's shoulders are slumped forward, and she's looking down with sadness on her face as she sits on the side of the bed next to a suitcase. Mollie sits down and wraps her arms around Sissy. "What is it, Sissy? I've missed you so much. I had a really nice trip. I needed the time away to get my head back on straight. Why are you not happy to see me? I want to go again next year, and you should go with us."

Sissy doesn't look at Mollie and says in a low voice, "I finally went to meet my father, Judge Greenleaf. He wants me to live with him. I'm packed, and I've just waited for you to get home to say goodbye."

"Judge Greenleaf is your father? I thought I saw the resemblance. How did you find out?" Mollie asks.

"He found me. He has been looking for years since my mother ran away with me, telling me my father was no good. Mollie, I'm confused. I don't know what to believe, but I need to go live with him for a while and get to know him."

Mollie is upset with this news. "What? No. I don't want you to leave. You don't have to do any of the business. I traveled through a war to get to you. I'm not about to let you go, Sissy—you're all that I have. We are in this together. You, Sissy, are my family. You can get to know him and still live here with me," Mollie says, in shock at Sissy's demeanor.

"What happened? Lily says that you've cried all the time. We are in this life together, Sissy. You can tell me anything. Don't leave me," Mollie begs.

Sissy stands and picks up her bag. Too ashamed to look at Mollie, she barely speaks, "I don't deserve your love...to be your sister or your best friend." Then she walks out the door.

Mollie's heart breaks as she follows behind to the front door and then steps in front of Sissy to block her exit. "Stop! You can't leave. You're breaking my heart. You're my reason to live. I'm supposed to take care of you."

Determined, Sissy goes out the door and down the steps. Mollie screams from the front porch, "No! Please don't go," as she watches Sissy walk away. Mollie panics and wonders how she can go on. Sissy is half her life, and she promised God that she would always take care of her.

Lily's little bitty hand slips inside of Mollie's. "It'll be OK, Miss Mollie. Don't cry. I'll be your friend." Mollie smiles at precious Lily. Her previous hunger vanishes while she goes to bed and cries her heart out.

Mollie goes to Judge Greenleaf's home and is turned away daily. Herman checks around with the neighbors to see if they know what happened while they were away. One nosy neighbor lady says, "It's not much, but I saw the small lady on the porch for a long time with a big man the morning you left town. Never seen him before or since." Herman thinks it could be anyone as most customers know this is a private residence where Mollie takes care of her mother and that the working houses are down the street.

Mollie's and Laura Ann's usual Saturday afternoon session is now regularly followed up as a date night for CC to come over to the Hobbs house and court her.

Mollie goes to Saturday night mass in disguise. She places a bag of coins in the priest's hands and smiles.

CHAPTER 40
POETIC JUSTICE

It's Sunday morning. Mollie relaxes in the library with an article about the economic future of the South's manufacturing and forgets about her appointment with the portrait thief. She's surprised when Lily tells her that there's a man at the door. Mollie opens the front door to a well-dressed older man, the only one in town who owns a carriage as nice as hers. "May I help you?" Mollie asks.

He steps up, shakes her hand, and introduces himself, "My name is Mr. Hall, and we had an appointment set up at the window above the store. You failed to show up, so I came here to look for you."

Mollie is embarrassed about her absentmindedness and changes her tone. "Mr. Hall, I'm so sorry. I just forgot. Let's see—you're the painting thief. Did you bring it with you? Are you sure you want to be seen on my front porch? You're welcome to come in."

Mr. Hall accepts her offer and says, "I'll come inside if you like. To hell with what everybody else thinks." She opens the door wide for him to enter, and he speaks up immediately. "Months ago I was devastated by news from my wife. She informed me that she was leaving me for another man in Nashville. I sat there at the

Big Spring and just wanted to die, but that's when I saw you and another lady in the big window at the general store. Your youth and beauty made me smile.

"I came to the park every Saturday afternoon in hopes to see you two again. Sometimes I got brave and would get closer by walking near several times.

"Then, all of a sudden, you both were gone. I asked the owner about you. At first he was reluctant to say anything. Can you imagine my surprise when I found out that you were the dreadful Mollie Teal? You're the one that all the women at church talk about. I now can certainly understand why. They are all jealous of your beauty.

"I have something to show you. Will you come with me? It's not too far away."

She politely asks, "Will this lead to my painting?"

He says, "Yes," and then takes her by the arm to escort her to his waiting carriage. "Have you seen a large home under construction on Gallatin at a new street named Saint Clair?"

"Why, yes, it's a Victorian-styled house, unusual to this area, with so many Greek Revival homes in Huntsville." Mollie speaks with great familiarity of the different architecture styles, which Mr. Hall finds fascinating.

"The new street is named after my wife, Clair...ironic that I chose the word *saint* isn't it? It sits on fifteen acres, and there is a slave cemetery on the property. I built it for her, to look like her home in Great Britain.

"There are seventeen rooms, indoor kitchen, indoor plumbing with hot and cold running water, a ventilation system, and the entire inside is fully decorated from our travels abroad. I spared no expense and used only the finest craftsmen. Will you accompany me?"

A short while later they arrive at the nearby location and ride through the surrounding stone walls, with cast iron gates, that surround the entire property. Mollie is impressed as they draw closer, and she sees the wrap-around porches, lots of windows, and the landscaping of an English garden. Everything is perfect. "It's a nice house. Why are you showing it to me?"

Instead of answering, Mr. Hall opens the stained glass front door with the knocker and doorknob in the middle and invites her inside to the marble foyer, which includes an enormous crystal chandelier. Mollie walks in and looks around at the interiors. She notices the finest of everything and is very impressed until her eyes lock on the elaborately framed portrait of her displayed in the ballroom. "Why is that on your wall? Surely you do not intend to keep it!" Mollie says with some irritation in her voice. "Let's get to the real reason you have me here, Mr. Hall."

Mr. Hall looks around the beautiful home and smiles, saying, "Poetic justice, Mollie. I'm not judging you. I don't know the circumstances that brought you here, but you are what you are, Mollie. You are a prostitute, and you seem to be OK with that. I am too. However, my wife is not a prostitute but acts like one. So I say it's poetic justice that the house goes to Huntsville's young, beautiful, successful Madam Mollie Teal. Do you like it? I don't want it. I've spent over thirty thousand dollars on construction and furnishing. I'll sell it to you for fifteen thousand. What do you think?"

Mollie can read men like no other, and she knows he wants to get it out of his hair at any cost. "How about you pay me five thousand for the portrait and for me to not press charges against you for stealing my priceless painting? You know that I have a witness, and everybody knows the sheriff and I are close. So, that brings us to ten thousand. If I sold all my other properties and investments, which I don't want to do, the most I could put down would be five thousand. The bank won't loan women money—even if I have collateral. So, we're in a pickle, Mr. Hall. I'll just take five thousand for the portrait and leave. Good luck getting rid of your 'poetic justice.'"

Mr. Hall didn't anticipate this and needs to think for a moment. He can't wait to unload the house, because it's not about the money as he has plenty. It's a horrible reminder of Clair, so he negotiates further, "How much can you put down if you don't sell your properties?"

Mollie looks around with a neutral look on her face and replies, "Twenty-five hundred."

Mr. Hall shakes his head up and down, smiles, and thinks, *She's good, real good, at negotiations.* Then he says, "You have more money to put down than most men in town. You're a successful businesswoman, and you're absolutely right...the bank won't loan you anything. But I will. I can finance the house for you. You put twenty-five hundred down and make monthly payments until it's paid for or I die. How about that for a deal?"

Mollie can't believe her good fortune; she has seen plenty of nice houses, but never dreamed of owning one herself. Still, she has to ask, "Who gets the painting?"

"You do, Mollie. It was my ploy to get you here and now my gift. Do we have a deal? Twenty-five hundred down, and I finance seventy-five hundred?" He puts his hand out to shake hers.

Mollie wants to jump and shout for joy, but instead she turns around smiling and shakes his hand. "Yes, Mr. Hall, we have a deal. I'll get my lawyer, Septimus Cabaniss, to draw up the papers. Maybe even as soon as today. Mr. Hall, I have never made a deal this good without it involving sex. Do you want to show me the master bedroom? You know, to celebrate our deal?" she asks, knowing that he is going to decline her offer.

"Um, no, ma'am. Um, that's not the kind of man I am. I prefer a monogamous marriage relationship, but thank you. It's funny that you mention Septimus as your lawyer. His wife and her crew made all of these grandiose draperies and bedding. Matter of fact, she still has to come by to finish the bay window and sitting area over here. Then everything will be one hundred percent complete. Shall I show you the house?" Mollie lets him take her arm like a lady, and he escorts her through her new home.

Mollie and Mr. Hall agree that he will arrange the papers with both lawyers and meet up at three o'clock. She wants to stay and asks him to stop by her carriage house and send her driver to pick her up for the meeting.

Meanwhile, Mollie explores each room again. Everything is new. Nobody has lived here before, and it's all hers. She runs her fingers on the imported furniture, marble mantels, ten-foot-tall gold mirrors, hand-carved wood rails, and drapes made with threads of gold in the fabric. She touches the silver, crystal, and china on the table set for twelve. The bar area is all wood and smooth leather and is stocked with exotic liquors. All eleven of the bedrooms are finished with the finest of silk and other luxurious fabrics.

Mollie thinks she hears a woman's voice downstairs and goes to the top of the rail to listen. Then she says, "Hello? Who's here?" Of course she is thinking that it might be the drapery lady.

The answer comes in a very heavy southern accent. "Yoo-hoo, I'm Mrs. Cabaniss. Who might you be?"

"Oh, hello! Mr. Hall just sold me the house." Mollie says as she descends down the grand staircase. "At three o'clock today, I will be the new owner."

Mrs. Cabaniss gasps out loud, "Oh, mercy no! He is such a private man, and he put so much into every detail to please his wife. He would never, and I do mean never, sell this house. It means too much to him."

"Never say never," Mollie replies. "Why are you here on Sunday?"

"I usually don't come on Sundays, but my husband had unexpected businessmen at our home and asked me to leave for their privacy. I want to measure something here anyway."

Mollie holds up the key and points to the portrait. Mrs. Cabaniss doesn't mind being a tad bit nosy and asks, "Would you mind telling me why he sold it? I have been working with him for quite some time and have seen this house transform into a grand palace. I feel like I'm part of this house, too. I looked forward to seeing his wife's face the first time she comes in the door."

Mollie scrunches up her shoulders and shakes her head side to side and answers as little as possible. "Mr. Hall came to me, and I don't know his entire situation either. Mrs. Cabaniss, I have been to your dress shop, and I think you know me. You seem to be a real nice lady. Maybe you should speak with him."

"Perhaps, but, Miss Teal—pardon me for asking, but you seem to be very young. Buying any dress you want is one thing, but how can you afford such extravagance?"

Mollie has patience with this snoop and her four-syllable words as she twists her mouth from side to side while deciding on what to say next. "Mrs. Cabaniss, please call me Mollie, and you're welcome to come with me to your husband's office today to sign the papers, since he's my lawyer."

Mrs. Cabaniss's face becomes all red. She knows that her husband, inappropriately, has only has one female client...Mollie Teal. "Don't worry, Mrs. Cabaniss. I won't own it until three o'clock, so you don't need to be embarrassed that you're in the 'bad' house of a madam," Mollie says to tease the nosy lady. "Will you be able to finish the bay window before you leave today? Mr. Hall said that it's all you have to do before you're finished here."

Curiosity takes over Mrs. Cabaniss. She is actually in the soon-to-be home of the young madam whom many of her female acquaintances have heard about but never seen up close. In this setting she realizes Mollie is even more beautiful than she had imagined in the dress shop.

Mrs. Cabaniss decides to be nice now and secretly desires to use Mollie as a tool to learn more about sex and men. "Mollie, please call me Virginia, and forgive my manners. It took me by surprise about the house. Welcome to your new home. I did all of the upholstery, drapes, and bedding, since I am the only grandchild of an upholstery master, and he wasn't about to die without his trade being passed down in his family…even if it's to a girl. I'm a female businesswoman married to an attorney. Odd, I know. I'm sorry if I come across as pushy, Mollie, but I'm a mother of five boys and a demanding husband. As the only woman in the house, I have to come across as strong."

Knowing the answer, all Mollie can say is, "Does that work?"

Virginia sighs, "No, not at all. Let me show you some of the special aspects of this house, including a secret staircase behind a sliding wall in the master bedroom that leads straight outside.

"I want you to see the newest leather we used in the bar and billiards room. My eldest son did the entire room, and I'm quite proud of his talent." Virginia chats on from room to room and finally gets to the point. Like so many women before her, she thinks she can ask a prostitute questions about her sex life and yet scorn her on the streets.

"Mollie, how do you know what to do with men? I love my husband, and I want to keep him interested in me and happy. Yes, I have children, but I don't think things are all that exciting for him in the bedroom."

Mollie's dress distracts her as it doesn't have a tailored fit, and without permission Virginia begins to tuck and pull at the seams, saying, "First and foremost, I'm the best seamstress in Huntsville and probably in all of Alabama. You need to let me alter your clothes…actually make your clothes. You're beautiful, and you need better-fitting dresses. I could come here to measure and design what works best for your body shape. See, you're large breasted, so we should accentuate them." Mollie does see the difference, and she also notices Virginia's own beautiful dress. "You need a better seamstress, someone to make you shine, and I can do that for you."

Mollie questions, "Is this a sales call? You know that if I come into your shop, your business could be ruined. My girls are not allowed at any public counter. We have to enter from the alley to attend the Elks Theater and then sit in a special section. So what is your offer? What are you really getting at here today?"

Virginia informs Mollie, "While they built that big front wall and entrance gate, I've been arriving through the back private gates, behind the carriage house and stables for months. Nobody ever notices me. As I just said, I can come here any time without being noticed. I could make fancy evening dresses for all your ladies. It could be a lot of fun. I already have a sewing room here."

Mollie is a bit suspicious, for some reason, that clothes are not the only thing in Virginia's thoughts today, "OK, Virginia. I completely agree. If I'm going to live in such a big, fancy house, I'll need fancier clothes. Now, won't I? Besides the clothing business, what are you getting at? What else is it on your mind?"

"I'll ask you this privately in hope that you can help solve my problem."

Mollie gives her a nod of reassurance and says, "I won't stay in this business running my mouth. Yes, of course what we say is private."

"Mollie, my extremely uptight parents raised me in a puritan religious manner that I can't seem to shake. I will never be comfortable exhibiting myself in the nude to my husband. We have fairly enjoyable sexual relations with all my clothing on. However, I want him to have more, and it's something I can't provide...you know, visual arousal. The reason I tell you this..." she stops and looks around the room and whispers, "I want to hire you to help stimulate my husband to a boiling point and then send him home for me to take care of him...presex, if you will.

"Since he's your attorney, have him use the private entrance. I'll pay you a night's salary. He is a devoted husband, and I love him. I want to trust you, Mollie, to give him an erotic bath experience in your private quarters—wash his hair, shave him, give him a shoulder and chest rub and then a foot rub—all while your beautiful body is naked. Keep him aroused for no more than one hour, then send him home, and I'll be ready."

With a huge smile on her face, Mollie asks, "Have you spoken with him about this arrangement, Virginia?"

She replies, "I'm giving him this gift, and I know it'll help add some spice to our marriage. Do you honestly think he'll turn down this gift? He did mention you once and said you were every man's dream and smarter than most educated businessmen he's known."

The two women agree to begin the arrangement starting in one week…Monday evenings at Mollie's will be the weekly schedule. Mollie thinks it's fantastic…two business deals in one day, and neither of them involving intercourse.

Mollie adds, "Virginia, let's talk about you becoming a full-time seamstress. I have many different-sized girls that I want to always be looking more elegant than anyone else in town."

Herman arrives and rings the bell. He can't believe the house is really Mollie's. Finally, Mollie says, "It's time for me to buy a house, Mrs. Cabaniss. I'd love for you to go along with me and let your hubby know that we're secret friends. Herman, you're going to love the carriage house here. It's much larger and nicer than where you are now."

The two ladies arrive separately at the house closing. Mollie greets her lawyer, Septimus Cabaniss, and his wife in his private office. There he says, "Mollie, you constantly amaze me in the variety of people that you draw into your life. When Mr. Hall and his lawyer showed up at my house on a relaxing Sunday afternoon, I had no idea that you knew him. He and his brother are the richest men in town. They own more land in and around Huntsville than anyone else. You negotiated—no, almost stole—that house from him. I don't even want to ask—well, yes, I do, but I won't."

Mollie explains, "He stole something from me. I agreed to not press charges. That's all anyone needs to know, but no sex was involved. Not even close, and I tried."

Septimus smiles and says, "More importantly, my wife informs me that you two have worked out an arrangement, and we can't wait until next week." The attorney and his wife smile at Mollie and then into each other's eyes.

"You really do love me," he says as he kisses his wife. Mollie looks down in a bashful way and shoots the two a big, wide smile, saying, "It's a win for everyone today."

The paperwork goes smoothly, with Mr. Hall having one quirky request, "Mollie, if you ever name the place, would you ever consider naming it…?"

Mollie interrupts, "Poetic Justice? Yes, sir. As we arranged in the paperwork, I will look forward to seeing you at my house on the first of every month for a payment."

CHAPTER 41

SISSY

Herman is driving back to Dixie Place when Mollie suddenly screams, "Oh, my God! He did something to Sissy. Herman, I'll kill him this time if he touched her. We're going to Judge Greenleaf's now. Let's hurry."

Mollie doesn't take no for an answer this time and barges past the servant and runs as fast as she can up the stairs, taking two steps at a time, yelling, "Sissy, I know you're in one of these rooms. Sissy, answer me," as she flings open every door, peering inside and on to the next room.

Finally, there she is, like a steely-eyed doll under the blanket. Mollie runs to her bedside. "Sissy, it's me, Mollie. Snap out of it. I'm so sorry. I finally figured it out, and I should have never left you here with that monster in town. I should have known he would go after you. Baby sister, I'm so sorry. Please, please forgive me."

Mollie plops her face on the pillow next to Sissy's face and begs, "Please," as she painfully sobs in Sissy's ear.

Sissy reaches over to touch Mollie and comfort her. "It's not your fault, Mollie. It's completely my fault. I'm not sure what happened, but I know I didn't think of you one time. How could you ever forgive me for that? You have done nothing but love me, and I betrayed you. It's unforgivable."

Mollie snaps back, "He's a seditious monster is what happened. He knew how much I love you, Sissy, and that I was willing to risk my life to get to you. He knew that and used it against me by going after you. He's nothing but an evil, devious, lying pig. Please tell me he didn't hurt you."

"No," Sissy replies as she looks down with the saddest face.

"I forgive you," Mollie says. "God forgives you. I promised from the bottom of my heart to take care of you to the day I die. Sissy, there's nothing you could say to make me feel otherwise."

Head still held down, Sissy says, "I'm pregnant."

The new house is now home to Mollie and pregnant Sissy. They use bedrooms on the third floor. The apartment off the kitchen is now home to Big Mama, who's pregnant with White Daddy's baby, and Lily. Herman has the luxury apartment above the carriage house. Sadly, Mary only enjoys her daughter's new home for a month before she passes.

Sissy and Mollie are thick as thieves, even as Sissy's pregnancy progresses. They always laugh as they finish each other's sentences. As they brush each other's hair, like when they were little girls, Sissy says, "Mollie, I'm not sure I want this baby. It'll only be a bad reminder to both of us. Do we want that? I'm afraid it'll turn out to be a bad seed like him—then what?"

"Don't worry, Sissy. We can have a priest run the evil out of the baby at his baptism—then we'll get a voodoo doctor to chase any other evil out of the baby. You're going to make a wonderful mother, Sissy. If it's a girl, as sisters we'll spoil her rotten and give her the life we never had. If it's a boy, together we will raise him to be a good respectable man—nothing like his daddy. I'm going to be the best aunt to your baby, no matter the sex. I'm glad you agree to not tell the daddy about the baby. He would make both of our lives a miserable hell, and I know he's not capable of caring about the baby."

"You're right, Mollie. I shouldn't worry," Sissy says.

Mollie reminds her, "I'm going back again today to the headstone maker's place and see if I can get my name spelled right on Momma's tombstone. I know they'll probably keep giving me the runaround and never change it."

Sissy has a horrible childbirth and thinks it's because she betrayed Mollie with the Russian. In fact it is because she is a tiny woman giving birth to a giant baby. Hours and hours of labor, and the doctor, with Big Mama assisting, finally cuts the cord to a huge baby boy with bright-red hair. As hard as everyone tries to love the baby, she just can't. Even after the baptism and an exorcism, he just feels evil.

Sissy is the first to say, "I think I should give him up for adoption. The priest told me there is a barren Christian family in New Market that desperately wants a baby." She looks around the table, and no one disagrees. Mollie has Septimus draw up the legal papers for Sissy the next day.

＝＋ ＋＝

Later that month, Mollie is delighted to attend the marriage ceremony of Christopher Columbus Taylor to Laura Ann Hobbs. She dresses in her disguise as Merry Perry. She thinks Mr. Hobbs knows, but he does not say anything about her identity.

Mollie is most impressed that CC has combined his property and the marriage gift property from her father to present to his bride. "Laura Ann Taylor, my beautiful wife," he says, "as a wedding gift, I present to you the soon-to-be incorporated town of Taylorsville."

Mollie's gift is small in comparison…just a one-mile stretch of wasteland where she and Laura Ann went skinny-dipping at the beach.

＝＋ ＋＝

Nine months later, another baby, Percy Taylor, is born at Mollie's house. The baby flourishes because Big Mama, while not having had time to mourn the recent loss of her own baby by White Daddy, breastfeeds him while Laura Ann is unable. Mollie has Big Mama and Lily move to Taylorsville to care for Laura Ann and the baby—but mostly to protect them from her business.

CHAPTER 42

THE ATTORNEY'S WIFE

Both Septimus and his wife, Virginia, are very grateful to Mollie for the enhancement in their sex life. The three become close enough that Virginia invites Mollie over to her home, when no one is expected to be there until the next day. She intends to surprise her husband with a Mollie visit.

High up on a hill that overlooks downtown, Mollie walks up on the porch through the massive columns and rings the bell. With great expectations, Virginia is behind the butler as he opens the door. "Oh, Mollie, come on in. Welcome. Septimus has been delayed, which gives me time to show you around and tell you the history of our family home. It may not be as grand as Poplar Grove, but we love it."

Just as they finish their tour of the home, Septimus arrives home to a pleasant surprise. Over the past few months, Mollie has given Virginia a few marital tips, and now she is at least able to let her husband see her in a slip or nightgown, but tonight she is going to push her limits and plans to be completely nude under the sheets, with Mollie's help.

Much to Mollie's delight, Virginia has become incredibly skilled at sewing French lingerie for her. Tonight she has a white sheer-and-lace top and bottom with cover-up for Mollie.

Virginia nervously undresses, slips under the soft, silky sheets into the big oversize bed and places a row of pillows between her and where Septimus will be. Mollie calms her by making her a glass of milk with vodka and coffee liqueur and tells her, "This is a good café au lait. Drink it up fast, and it'll make you feel more relaxed. See, I'm having one, too."

Mollie instructs Septimus to get undressed and into bed under the comfortable covers. Septimus is well aware of the soft sheets tingling his smooth nakedness as he sinks further into the fluffy mattress. The room is dimly lit with the orange, soft glow of candles and a warm fire as Mollie makes her grand entrance. Slowly and seductively, she begins to dance and twirl.

The seductive dance arouses Virginia, and she tries to cover her eyes a couple of times but ends up peeping through her slightly open fingers. She doesn't know if she is excited by Mollie or by the naughtiness and expectations of the whole situation unfolding before her. The seductive, erotic dance continues as Mollie spins her head, with her long hair following in a big wide circle. Soon, all the lingerie has slipped off, and Virginia gets nervous and tries to grab up more of the sheet to wrap around the top of her ample breasts.

Mollie saunters ever so slowly to her bedside, looks into her eyes, and says, "You can't do that. We're not done." She takes Virginia's hand and places it on her belly button, "Touch me like this," Mollie says as she slowly begins to move Virginia's hand onto her breast and squeezes her hand for her. "Pinch my nipples, Virginia, and enjoy how hard and stiff they get." Mollie's fingers glide over Virginia's bare shoulders and then move to gently touch both of her breasts. Pulling back the soft sheet, and with both hands around Virginia's tiny waist, Mollie pulls her up off the bed close to her own bare-naked body.

Mollie can't help but see that Septimus's prominent erection has lifted the sheet, making a noticeable tent. The plan is working extremely well. Mollie encourages Virginia to fondle and explore her body, and Mollie also does the same in return to Virginia, keeping an eye on Septimus's growing enthusiasm.

Next, Mollie leads a naked Virginia to the candlelight where she danced earlier. From behind, Mollie pushes her sumptuous breasts up against Virginia's back. Then Mollie wraps her arms around Virginia's waist and begins to press her hips against her buttocks together as they both move and sway in rhythm.

As both women dance for Septimus, Mollie senses the strong sexual attraction that Virginia has is actually not for her husband but for her. Mollie, though not attracted to women, is unbothered by the revelation. She's in the business of pleasing her clients, no matter their particular preferences. Dancing over to the window, the bright moonlight covers their bodies with a warm glow as Virginia's breathing deepens.

Mollie removes Virginia's hands from her covered chest and tenderly shows her how to cup and lift her breasts. While pressing her body against Virginia, Mollie turns to her with both of their hands, now lifting Virginia's breasts for her husband to see.

Still swaying, Mollie leans in from behind and kisses her on the neck, saying, "See the excitement on his face for you, Virginia?"

Her head nods slowly, and she whispers, "I think I got it from here, Mollie." As her hips keep moving and dancing, Mollie quietly collects her clothes and gently closes the door behind her. Still naked, she leans back against the door, hearing the soft moans of the two lovers lost in an ocean of lust.

The next day, Septimus gives his wife privileged information about a possible land deal for Mollie to invest in. Septimus's friend Judge Walker is also a circuit judge who holds a part-time prostitution court in Huntsville.

As Virginia continues her weekly visits with Mollie, she hears of many of Mollie's competitors and gives the names to her husband, so Mollie's friends, the sheriff and police chief, can make an arrest from time to time. Then the judge convicts and fines them, making all three look like good servants to the community.

CHAPTER 43

TEA AND LAND NEGOTIATIONS

"Mr. Hall, please come in for tea. I do look forward to our talks together every Saturday now. You've taught me so much about business and industry." Mollie knows some men are turned on more by intellect than sex, and Mr. Hall is one of those men.

He says, "Thank you, Mollie. I'd love some tea. I enjoy our conversations as well. It's incredible the amount of knowledge you have on so many varying subjects. It truly is a pleasure to talk with you. I apologize for taking up your whole day on our last visit."

"Don't you dare apologize, Mr. Hall. I've planned our entire day together, including cooking you dinner. It's a nice dish I learned in Savannah—shrimp and grits.

"I hope you noticed that the new sign is completed over the entrance gate—'Poetic Justice.' It's just for you."

He smiles in appreciation and says, "Yes, I noticed. Thank you. That chapter is officially closed."

Mollie chuckles and knows he means that box is closed, and she continues on about their day, saying, "For now we are going to have tea and pick up our conversation about strategically buying property. I've done my homework like you suggested, and based on my research, I've determined some possibilities." She shows him on a map where future rail lines might be located. She also explains why she thinks certain areas might be developed for manufacturing cotton products one day due to the rail lines' location and a close water source. She goes further as to why certain residential areas should be planned for the future workers, as the population of Huntsville will grow in the process.

"Bravo! Bravo, Mollie. Once again, not only do you impress me with your elegance and beauty, but your mind is exceptional. I've never met a prodigy like you before.

"As promised, I'll sell you the land that you proposed as your potential future sites. I like your vision, Mollie. I may not live long enough to see the new machines invented that you say that could make the business of manufacturing cotton products explode. You're young, Mollie, and you'll live to see these things happen. Are you sure you want these cotton fields all the way to the river? That's fourteen miles to Wallace Mountain."

She smiles at the man she has come to respect so much as he agrees to the sell her the river property, some northeast Huntsville property, and the tract west of Pinhook Creek. "Yes, I'll just keep leasing it out to the same farmers that you use. They don't need to know a woman owns it, and they can make payments directly to the bank, under an account number only. I'd like to make a fair offer on all of this land for two thousand dollars. That's if you'll finance it like you have the house. Don't forget, I've been paying you triple payments so far. You want me to win, right?"

"You're robbing me blind in the daylight, Mollie." He chuckles. "You're right. I do want to see you succeed. You're smart, and you deserve it."

"I want to come boast to you one day that I turned all that cotton land over to some fat cat with the railroad for twenty thousand dollars," Mollie brags, and gives him that certain look with her eyes. The special information about land she gets from Virginia will be her little secret.

⇌ ⇌

A few months later, Mollie anxiously waits for Mr. Hall to arrive. Their relationship has become deeply significant to Mollie because he's so smart and takes the time to teach her about the business world of men. Today she is excited about sharing her news regarding a meeting that she had with the railroad executives—not to mention the large amount of money she is about to make when she flips the property. They also liked the idea of joining together with Mollie's other out-of-town investors, such as Michael O'Shaugnessey, a wealthy businessman from Nashville who has financial interest in developing Huntsville's cotton manufacturing industry. Mollie knows how proud Mr. Hall will be of this latest accomplishment.

Mr. Hall decides to go see his lawyer before his meeting with Mollie. "You heard me right. I might be thirty years older than her, but I'm asking Mollie to marry me. Today, as a matter of fact," he tells his lawyer as he pulls a huge diamond engagement ring out of his jacket. "She is perfect for me as a partner. I've never met anyone that is so brilliant. We've never run out of things to discuss. It's incredible, actually. I want to name her as the heir to everything I own, and I want to put all that I own in her name immediately. I'm confident she'll double my fortune after I'm gone, and she will be one of the wealthiest ladies in the South. She deserves it.

"Have you ever heard the legend of the White Dove? It's an amazing story that her driver, Herman, broke a secret and told me about her. I'll tell you the story someday, but take my word, she is special. Besides, I only have one brother, and he's as wealthy as I am. He doesn't need anything from me."

His lawyer replies, "I think you're crazy. Is your health OK, Mr. Hall? Let me get you something to drink."

The lawyer goes into the hall and tells his wife the news. He's a high church official, and now they're both desperate to stop Mr. Hall. They think this will bring scandal to the church and to his law practice. His wife says, "Honey, don't worry about anything. I'll go to the apothecary on Clinton Avenue to get something to calm him down right away."

When the lawyer's wife arrives at the apothecary, she tells the pharmacist she needs a mix of morphine and cocaine to calm her sister's nerves again due to hysteria. He concurs as he gives her the usual two-dose mixture and asks, "Does she have any health problems or allergic reactions or other problems?"

"No," says the lawyer's wife as she pays and goes out the door.

⊨ ⊨

After having some tea at his lawyer's office, Mr. Hall arrives at Mollie's house. Mollie overwhelms him at the front door with information and details about her good business news. He patiently listens. "Well, you haven't said a word. What do you think? Did I make you proud, Mr. Hall?"

He says, "I've never been as proud of someone in my whole life as I am of you, Mollie. Now, may I ask you a question?" She nods her head and waits for his question. "When the railroad deal goes through, which sounds pretty certain given all that you've told me, will you have to 'celebrate' with this business partner? No, that didn't come out right at all. What I'm trying to say is, what if you didn't have to?"

Mollie replies, "Mr. Hall, I never have to. It's my choice. But it does pay to be close to those in power, such as yourself. Remember when you sold me the house? It's part of who I am, Mr. Hall. I'm detached and indifferent on the inside, although no man I've ever been with would know that. I give everyone lots of love. Why do you ask?"

"Well, Mollie, I have another question. Will you marry me? I think we make great intellectual partners. I love every minute I spend with you. I think you enjoy my company as well." He picks up her left hand and places the beautiful ring on her finger. "I want to bequeath to you all that I own and to watch you double our wealth while you control everything during the time that I still live. I have already signed papers to transfer everything to you now. I really have that much confidence in you, Mollie. We can build you another house even bigger than this one. I'm serious."

"Mr. Hall, you really surprise me. I did not see this coming. I absolutely love our time together. I've never had a relationship as truly special as ours. You are the most kind and generous gentleman that I have ever encountered. I would be crazy not to take your offer, but you know what I am. Your friends and relatives will disown you."

"I'm a bit parched. Will you send for something cool to drink?" As Mr. Hall sinks down on the sofa in the parlor, Mollie rings the bell for a server.

⇒⊹ ⊹⇐

Mr. Hall's funeral is three days later, and Mollie is prohibited from entering the church for the service. Mr. Hall's lawyer comes by her house later in the day, and Mollie says, "Mr. Hall and I were engaged when he fell ill. Why was I banned from his funeral? He told me that he had a discussion with you about me before he came here that day, and you knew how he felt."

The lawyer says, "What a whore…after a dead man's money like that. Good grief, Mollie, it's illegal to forge a man's signature like this." He hands her the real document that Mr. Hall had signed. "However, I'll tear it up so you won't get in any trouble. Better yet, I'll throw it in the fire."

Mollie reads through the papers and is confused and says, "I've never seen these papers. I don't know why he would put all that he owns in my name."

He snatches the papers and tosses them in the fire. "You robbed the senile old man blind while he was alive. Everybody knows he wanted the church to have his money. Nope, all you get is this house that you've paid off and the other property you legally stole from him. Nothing else. You and your lawyer just try and go after the church's money. We'll shut you down and run your trashy women out of town once and for all."

Mollie calmly walks him to the door and says, "I don't need or want the money. That's not at all what we meant to one another."

Mollie is devastated by the loss of the only man who wanted to build her up and asked nothing in return.

CHAPTER 44

LESSONS FOR VIRGINIA'S FRIENDS

A few years have passed when Virginia arrives at her usual time for sewing and asks Mollie, "Can we talk privately? My friends won't let up. None of them have satisfying sex lives, and they want to know what you taught me. They don't know that it's you, of course. They think I went to a secret doctor for ladies only. There are ten of them from my women's league whose husbands will gladly pay three dollars once a week for a morning of learning. A very surprised Mollie spews out her tea and laughs out loud to such a hilarious request.

"Please don't laugh, Mollie. You have made such a big difference in our bedroom, and you know it. You don't have to tell them that I invite you in my bed to play around for Septimus to watch. I just don't think they will understand. You are smart, Mollie, about everything, but especially about sex. There is nothing for women to read about sex, but you know what they need to learn.

"Remember how I acted when we first met? Well, just think, if you turn just ten more uptight women into satisfied women, the ripple effect will benefit most of the population of Huntsville as they in turn teach others."

Mollie thinks for a minute and says, "You know, you're right, Virginia. We're taught that those of us who are given plenty should give back in return. Besides, the church always needs donations to help the needy."

Virginia jumps up and throws her arms around Mollie's neck, "Oh, thank you, Mollie. Just don't tell about Septimus and me. Would right now be too soon? I've talked with Herman, and he can darken out the lower windows of your carriage. That way, you can pick all us up at my back door and then come through your back entrance, using your private gate. I've already made them swear on the Bible not to tell who you are once they meet you."

Mollie laughs as she thinks of ten horny women waiting around at Virginia's house for their scout to return. Mollie says, "Virginia, you bring your sweet self and your lady friends back here in one hour. I'll get things ready."

"Oh, one more thing, Mollie, Septimus and I are having another gala on the second Saturday next month. As usual we want you there. We both absolutely love the looks on our guests' faces when you make your grand entrance, and Septimus and I are the first to receive you. You may outshine every woman in this town, and I'm so glad to know you."

Mollie goes to change into something more elegant and, yes, more revealing yet still refined. She adds jewelry, makeup, and perfume. After all, she has a thirty-three-dollar client who will expect such things. They want a show. Mollie laughs and says, "I'll give them a show they will remember."

When the ladies arrive at Mollie's, Herman, in an all-white tuxedo, opens the carriage door for them to a bubbling marble fountain in the center of the circular drive. They gaze around at the most beautiful lawn and gardens they've ever seen in Huntsville. One lady giggles and says, "This is so much fun—having a secret day, at a secret place, to learn secret things."

"I thought we were being sneaked in through the back door, Virginia," says another. "This is the back door, and remember that you ladies all swore on the Bible." As Virginia leads the way, they are met by a full staff dressed in formal attire on the elaborate wood-carved portico.

The guests are seated in the formal dining room, with an over-the-top place setting for coffee, as they wait for their host to arrive.

Mollie walks down the hall and hears her guests chatting about the opulence of the decor. A server rings a small bell to announce Mollie's arrival. The ladies felt like they were about to have tea with the queen of England.

Mollie enjoys the surprised facial expressions when their perceived "queen of the dark side" is introduced by the head sever with a strong British accent, "Ladies, may I introduce you today to Madam Mollie Teal."

You could hear a pin hit the floor as the women are stunned to realize that they are in the presence of a prostitute—and a very lovely radiant beauty at that. Mollie lets them stare, but only briefly, before she speaks, "Ladies, welcome to Poetic Justice. Later today, it will sink in how ironic the name truly is.

"Judging by the looks on your faces, I am the last person you expected to see today. Well, to tell you the truth, this is all new to me, too. I didn't get up this morning thinking today was going to be a 'lesson' day. That's what I call it when I get a fresh group of girls into my business.

"I'll bet most of you are uptight or stressed right now, and you all need to loosen up before we can begin talking about sex and the fun you can have with your husbands." She nods for the server to begin.

"Since it's still only nine o'clock in the morning, we are being served coffee, with Grand Marnier, an orange liqueur." The cups are small, and the liqueur is served in a warm cognac snifter. This is part of the lesson, so enjoy it, ladies. None of you have to be home until after lunch, and you all swore on the Bible to keep this secret. Right? Jesus drank wine, so don't let the preacher tell you that because you're a woman you can't enjoy a little dessert drink."

Mollie's guests look around at one another. Soon Virginia begins to taste her drink, and the rest follow. At first some of them gasp, but each keeps trying it, and eventually they all like it. A few have a second glass.

The fancy table is cleared. They spend a few short minutes introducing themselves to Mollie, who afterward recites each person's name perfectly.

Mollie begins, "I'll explain a few things about men, like why they are so focused during sex. Unlike women, they're singularly minded. They focus on one thing at a time, and I don't mean the children and ironing." The women give a big chuckle.

"Next, men like to be touched and aroused by you. I normally have a male volunteer for my pupils on this part, but today, for the sake of secrecy, we are going to use vegetables instead. Select a cucumber that best reflects your husband." Some of them are squeamish about the whole idea, but they all go along eventually. She has the servers go around the table with big baskets, but she notices that the women all went after the big ones to protect their men's pride. However, in all of Mollie's years, she has seen very few as large as the cucumbers these ladies chose. Perhaps in some cases it was from wishful thinking or misguided imaginations.

Each person is given a small dish with warm butter, two different jellies, maple syrup, and two small tomatoes. Mollie shows them the proper way to hold their husband for the most pleasure—never too hard but firm and steady pressure. She laughs to herself at the sight of eleven of Huntsville's most prestigious families represented at her table this morning.

"OK—next we're on to the sensitive tomatoes. Caress them, but remember that they're delicate. Here's the part your man will love. Pick your favorite flavor on the dish and wipe it on your man. Now let him see you enjoy it, like dessert, licking with your tongue and sucking with your mouth." Mollie seductively demonstrates, tilting her head back and stretching her neck long, with chin projected outward. Then she inserts her cucumber slowly in and out.

Mollie is encouraged at how eager these women are to learn to please their men and at the same time to not get pregnant again. She continues on different topics for an hour or so.

Mollie wants to conclude with the art of pleasing oneself before lunch. "Ladies, I bet many of you don't or haven't ever realized that your body is made to arrive at a climax just like a man does. Pleasure...I know, preachers don't want women to know about that either. I want each of you to spread your legs a little and put your hand down there." Mollie demonstrates. "Touch yourself, through the fabric. You're not really doing anything but touching yourself like you would your nose when it itches. Feel how cushioned you are, and don't worry...you're under the table. I just want you to touch and feel how warm it is, even through thin fabric. Feels good, doesn't it? And at home alone or in front of your man, you can continue to caress yourself as long as it feels good, and you may experience a very special reward.

"The best part is that you can feel this good any time you choose. Sometimes it is a great way to just take the edge off the day." She laughs as she sees their very large pupils and knows the ladies are all turned on by just a simple touch to themselves in a different way for the first time. Perhaps the old taboos are beginning to fall away.

"We will stop here for today," Mollie says, "Your homework is to practice what we learned today with fruit and vegetables. Don't get caught, or you'll look a bit silly.

"I want each one of you to feel confident to go to your husband in the middle of the day and turn his head away from anyone else. Cup your hand to his ear, whispering loud enough for him to understand clearly, and breathe heavy so that he feels your warm breath. Then say, "The doctor for ladies taught me new things to do with my tongue that I think you will like. I can't wait to show you tonight." At that point, gently touch his ear with your tongue for three 'Mississippi's'—then pull back and stare into his eyes with the same lustful look you all have on your faces right now, and slowly walk away.

"Your man will think about you all day long. Show him what a good pupil you are. That's why you're all here, right? Eventually I'll lead you to pleasuring his 'vegetable' while he's enjoying your fruit. During our lessons, we are going to learn multiple ways to enjoy sex, and you'll be in control of not getting pregnant while you have your own pleasures."

Mollie concludes, "Thank you all for your donations. Father Patrick will be here after lunch to pick up the money to send to the Convent of Visitation in Mobile, since their windows were blown out in a recent storm.

"Oh, by the way, I know all of you are from wealthy families, so in order to further help the sisters at the convent, weekly dues will temporarily be four dollars for the next four classes. The windows will cost at least three hundred dollars, and I'll match your contribution."

"Excuse me now while I freshen up. You're welcome to view the artwork or peek into the library. Lunch will be served in thirty minutes."

Mollie glides down the staircase in a beautifully tailored conservative dress for lunch. She has the table set with more plates, stemware, and utensils than necessary to show off a bit but really to see who of the bunch holds a torch to her in etiquette.

The ladies wait for Mollie to make all the first moves: prayer, napkin placement, when to start the meal, which spoon to eat the fresh crab soup with, and how to use it properly. Two small stuffed tomatoes are served on a bed of fresh greens—one with creamy pimento cheese containing pieces of bacon and the other with chicken salad sprinkled with almonds. Again, no one knows which fork, so they wait and watch Mollie.

Lunch ends with very little chatter, and no one knows what questions to ask. Mollie realizes that next week will be different after they have had time to think about the lesson and to try new things with their husbands.

She briefly thinks about the Russian and hates when he pops in her head out of nowhere. She wonders how he would feel to know that his lessons are being taught to wealthy housewives.

"Ladies, this concludes our first lesson. Be prepared over the next few sessions as we're going to speed things up. Also, our behavior on the streets must not change. You will look at me with your usual disdain and make your husbands look away. The reason I mention this is that I have a secret of my own.

Remember, you swore not to talk about what goes on here or what you see or hear." They all nodded, "I'm personally inviting you to the Fourth of July parade this Saturday. It starts on Clinton Avenue—then Jefferson over to the square. There's going to be a surprise. I hope you all can be there."

The bell rings, and it's Father Patrick, right on time. Mollie excuses herself and meets him in the parlor, which isn't far enough away with his loud Irish voice. "Mollie, dear, may God have mercy on your soul for your earthly sins. As always, you're the most generous of all Madison County citizens."

Mollie hushes him and points to the ladies leaving the dining room down the hall as she places a bag of coins in his hands. "This is supposed to stay quiet, remember? I'll see you next week at the same time."

Herman returns and laughs as he asks, "Mollie, do I even want to know what went on here today with all of Huntsville's fancy ladies? You constantly keep me entertained."

Mollie chuckles too, saying, "They came to me. Well, they didn't know it was me, exactly. Virginia refers to me as a sex doctor for ladies. Today was like a lesson day for new hires, only milder.

"Changing the subject, Romeo, Sissy tells me you have another one of our beautiful mulatto girls falling for you. You know, she'll try and get pregnant. You've often said, 'No one woman and no children.' Herman, you know women don't have boxes. Be gentle with her and switch up, or you'll soon be a daddy, and I'll be out a trained girl."

Herman smiles. "You're right, and I agree."

That Saturday, Laura Ann, CC, Percy, and new baby Chase stay with Mollie for the Fourth of July festivities. Laura Ann has to be reassured, with her children there in the house, that strangers don't just show up at the door. "Laura Ann, the house is not open to the public. I have only five clients, and I've known them for years. They don't show up here uninvited, and yes, I have held a few wild parties and all-night poker games…I always won by the way, but only with trusted friends. You know I always lock both gates. Herman has one of the stable guys stay awake and alert around the clock.

"More important than all that, Mr. Hall built this big house in the middle of the poor neighborhood, thinking no one else would build a big house next door to block his view of Huntsville or the beautiful Monte Sano Mountain. My neighbors are my eyes and ears, and they love me—sometimes I think more than white people do. I built an outdoor shelter by the cemetery for them to worship, and there's nothing prettier than hearing them sing to Jesus on Sunday mornings.

"Most churches ban my type, but I walk right in on them anytime, and they welcome me with open arms. We are in a safe neighborhood with good families." Mollie fails to mention that she brings in loads of crops from her different sharecroppers and donates the food for the women to sell on Saturdays at the worship shelter.

Mollie informs the Taylors to go early to the parade to get a good spot high up on the stairs at the National Bank on the square for a good view.

Laura Ann tells Mollie, "Why you need to have your carriage in the parade, Mollie, is beyond me. Aren't you just asking for trouble?"

"Oh, Laura Ann, when did you become such a worrywart? I'm just as much an American as anyone in that parade. I'm only putting a few red, white, and blue buntings and two flags around the carriage…that's all—nothing overboard."

Mollie quietly sits in her carriage as Herman, dressed in his favorite all-white tux, sits up straight and tall. He proudly drives up to the parade line pulled by four shiny black horses. A couple of minutes after the parade starts, Herman releases the only remaining latch on the collapsible cover, and with a cord he slowly lets it down, revealing Mollie and her twelve beautiful ladies. The ladies are all different colors and sizes, wearing makeup, dressed in Virginia's latest shiny blue or red revealing dresses. Mollie wears an all-white dress showcasing her large breasts. She sits perched on the back, like a queen, waving and smiling at all the customers, while sitting beside her are two ladies holding large American flags.

Mollie's ladies wave their little flags with one hand and throw out hundreds of daisies with their address tied to them with the other hand. Single men howl, whistle, and shout some of their names.

Her pupils don't disappoint her as they sneer and cover their husbands' eyes at such a lewd sight, just as they promised, while secretly looking forward to Monday's lesson. Mollie pokes her tongue out at a couple of them who are sitting together. Some men ask their wives how they recognize Mollie Teal since no one sees her publicly very much.

Sadly, Mollie doesn't win the prize for the parade that day, but she does break all records at her five very busy houses that night. Mollie, Sissy, Herman, and the entire Taylor crew (including Big Mama with her newlywed, ailing husband, Hank Freeman, and their son, Hugh, Percy's best friend) are there. Lily is there too, along with all of Mollie's staff, their families, and several neighbors. All cook and have a picnic outdoors that night at the gazebo in Mollie's backyard. Later, the men shoot off fireworks over the pond, and the group sings more patriotic songs and eats fresh ice cream.

CHAPTER 45

FRANK JAMES TRIAL, 1884

It's a very warm Saturday night as Mollie arrives at Poplar Grove mansion for another of Judge and Mrs. Walker's never-ending private parties and galas. The dress is always formal. Mollie knows some of the men attending tonight are the judge's wealthy out-of-town clients.

Mollie knocks and enters through the open massive front door, as she has many times before, but for some odd reason her hair is standing on the back of her neck tonight. She'll stay on alert for anything strange and have no wine or other liquor to be safe.

Mrs. Walker, with Virginia at her side, greets Mollie alone as someone in the middle of a circle of men has the judge's attention over in the corner of the ballroom. When Mollie catches Septimus's eye, he waves the three ladies over.

To Mollie's surprise, the judge's client is no other than Frank James, the famous outlaw, on trial at the Huntsville federal courthouse for holding up an army paymaster near Muscle Shoals. Mollie reads the paper and is aware that Frank is being treated as a former Confederate celebrity. After his arrest, he was greeted at the Huntsville train depot by a cheering crowd. He's allowed to stay with local trustworthy families instead of being kept in the city jail, and he is invited to numerous private dinner parties held by the local elite and his lawyer.

The judge seems proud to be representing an outlaw and introduces him to Mollie. "Mollie, so lovely to see you, dear, and you look lovely as always. Please meet our honored guest this evening, Mr. Frank James."

"The pleasure is all mine, Mollie," Frank says. "Judge, where have you been hiding this beauty queen all evening? No offense, Mrs. Walker or Mrs. Cabaniss, but you'll have to agree, Mollie's type of beauty is rare. She has that something that attracts men and women."

Mollie thanks him for the compliment and is eager to get away before there is any mention of Jesse James, whom she met on the traveling circuit in Memphis before she went to Savannah. She knew Jesse was bad way back then—the type that wanted only Mollie, and she refused him. He wouldn't let up on the pressure and was relentless in his tactics at trying to get Mollie to travel with him. He was nonstop in bothering the other girls to get at her. Finally the group moved on to Birmingham, and that was the only way for Mollie to get away from him.

Mrs. Walker realizes that Mollie is uncomfortable and says, "Mollie, I know this is not your first time at Poplar Grove, but I have never given you the tour. May I show you around?" The ladies excuse themselves as Mrs. Walker begins, "In 1814, Poplar Grove was the first brick mansion in Huntsville, built by the judge's grandfather, who is referred to as Leroy 'Father of Huntsville' Pope. He was the founder of the town and a pretty important fellow, because at one lawn gathering he hosted the most prominent men in the country, General Jackson, who became president, five future Alabama governors, and six men that our surrounding counties were named after. They were all out there in this beautiful back yard," Mrs. Walker says as they both look through the massive windows into the back lawn.

At the end of the tour, Mrs. Walker says, "You know they give credit, or blame, depending on who you talk to around here, to the judge, who was the first secretary of war for the Confederate States, for reportedly ordering the firing on Fort Sumter that started the Civil War. You'll have to ask him about that sometime when you're alone."

Later, during dinner, Mollie is unusually quiet, especially when Frank's minister, who has come to Huntsville in support of Frank, stares at her, trying to get her to look at him.

The meal seems to never end, with Frank telling stories and all the guests hanging on every word, asking for more. Mollie is able to get Mrs. Walker's attention to indicate that they have been seated long enough and that they might enjoy the evening air on the back porch. As everyone pours another drink for the porch, Mollie makes her exit when no one notices. "Herman, let's get out of here before trouble happens."

Herman says, "It's too late, Miss Mollie. You have the preacher as your passenger, and he's not getting out until he talks to you."

Mollie steps in. "I smelled trouble when I got out of the carriage tonight. Who are you? What do you want? 'Happy Fingers' has a revolver aimed at your skull, and I have one under my dress, pointing at your chest, so start talking."

The laugher starts off slow and then becomes howls of laughter. Mollie takes no chance that this is a ruse and steps back outside. "Get out. I decided not to shoot you in my carriage. It'll make a mess, but I'll get every man in this house to yank you out and beat the bloody stew out of you in the front yard."

The laughing stops as the stranger takes off his preacher disguise and says, "Mollie, get in. It's me, Jesse."

"What in the name of the devil are you doing here? You're supposed to be dead, and if not, you're a wanted man. I knew you faked your death—there's no way one of your own killed you. I don't want to be involved with you or your brother," Mollie insists.

"No, I'm not dead yet, and I'm not getting out until you get in," crooned Jesse.

Mollie speaks to Herman privately. She locks and closes the carriage door and begins to walk home. Herman quickly drives in the opposite direction, with Jesse raising cane on the inside. As the carriage takes a slow curve, Jesse opens the door and jumps out and runs in the direction of Mollie's house.

It's fairly quiet as she walks west on Eustis Avenue past the Schiffman building, but Mollie is on guard anyway, with her hand on the pistol in her bag. She hears the clop of horses' hoofs approaching and darts into a doorway in front of the building until she sees it pass by. To Mollie's surprise, Herman speeds past in her carriage. She waits a minute or two and then steps out and crosses East Side Square past the courthouse, across West Side Square to the National Bank of Huntsville and continues toward home, intending to go south down Madison Street.

Jesse runs up from behind, pleading, "Five minutes, Mollie... just give me five minutes." He leads her behind the bank toward the Big Spring bluff and pulls her to him, attempting to kiss her neck. Mollie steps back...finger still on the trigger. "Ah, come on, Mollie. I knew back when I was a boy that I'd be with you one day. We're meant to be. Can you just imagine my surprise when I opened the *Daily Mercury* and there's your Fourth of July carriage loaded down with beautiful women? On the front page was the title 'Huntsville Madam Mollie Teal Disgraces Parade.'"

Mollie laughs to herself as she had staged the picture with a photographer and paid him to give it to the newspaper. "Funny, I couldn't see your face, but I knew it was you when I saw your hair in the picture. I've waited a long time to have you, Mollie," he says as he runs his hands through her hair and tries to kiss her neck again. Mollie stomps his foot with all her might so that she can break away.

"Stop!" she shouts. "You're a pest. I'm not yours to paw at, Jesse. That was twenty years ago, and you haven't changed one bit. I thought when I first read about the robberies in the papers, that it had to be you. You turned out bad, Jesse—robbing banks, stagecoaches, trains, killing people—and you're wanted all over the country. I don't want to be seen with you and get shot because someone wants the reward. No, thank you. Please leave me alone."

He doesn't hear a word, as she expects. Jesse presses on, "I've been all around this country and have seen lots of pretty women, but tonight when I saw your face, I became a believer...a believer of love, Mollie. Heaven brought you and me together at last.

"Besides, Mollie, you know that all the money I robbed comes from Yankee Republicans that supported the Union Army that destroyed the South. Do you know that they killed my eight-year-old brother and blew my mother's arm off in a raid at her house? You've got to know this much. I have shared money more than any other man alive. I take care of my people all over Missouri.

"You can come back with me after Frank's trial. I have plenty of money hidden away for us to grow old together. Maybe I'll even become a real preacher like my daddy. What do you say, Mollie?"

"Jesse, I read in the papers that you're married to your cousin."

"Well, what about it? I could trust her. She gave me a couple of kids—but you, Mollie, you're my real love. I will love you, Mollie, until my last breath." He then tries to impress Mollie by climbing across the bluff above the spring to flex his muscles. The rocks beneath him suddenly give way and cause him to fall about twenty feet to the water below, with loose boulders landing all around him.

Mollie takes some steps down to the spring, but she still doesn't see Jesse emerge. With a few rocks still falling, she finally hears him say, "I can't swim."

"Stand up, you fool. The water's not that deep," she yells back.

"Can't stand up. I think my leg is broke. That's the reason I can't swim," he replies.

Mollie starts to wade into the cold spring water, saying, "I should have known that a little fall wouldn't be your demise. God, why do this to me? Can't you just die in a bank robbery shoot-out or something?" The water is getting deeper than she thought as she finally reaches out and takes his hand. Not so gently, she pulls him to shore with him screaming about his leg between saying, "I love you, Mollie...I love you Mollie Teal."

Mollie hears a carriage nearby and gives the hoot owl signal. Herman returns the call. They have no choice but to take Jessie by Dr. Lowry's house to see about his badly broken leg on their way home.

Ten long days of Jesse is enough to rattle anyone's feathers. The entire house is glad to see him leave. From his recovery bed, he gives speeches to anyone in hearing distance about how Mollie brought him from the dead and helped him find his way back to God. He is giving up crime and intends to become a preacher.

Frank James is acquitted and walks out of the courthouse still under arrest for alleged crimes in Missouri. Before leaving Huntsville, he meets Mollie so that she can turn over his brother to him. When they are reunited, he says to Jesse, "Hey, brother, look at you all banged up. What's this story about how you were climbing out the bank window with a sack full of gold when the bluff gave way beneath you? Bad luck, but where is the gold?"

Mollie says, "What gold? Who starts these rumors?"

Jesse turns to Mollie, saying, "Mollie, I guess that I sometimes don't know how to act...especially around you. For that, I'm sorry. Please forgive me, but God brought me to you for a reason, and I'll never forget that. I'm going home to preach his word. I'll be there when you need me." A very humble Jesse is assisted onto the train headed west, one car back from Frank.

CHAPTER 46

TAYLOR BEACH

Laura Ann, Sissy, and Mollie celebrate another anniversary of their time at the convent together. Over the years, CC always travels with them and builds something new on the beach. During the first year, he mistakenly used the local beach driftwood to build a big pole shed without walls. He learned over time what damages tidal surges are capable of doing to such flimsy structures. Yet only two constructions over the years were destroyed by hurricanes.

This year, with young Percy underfoot, he has brought in help along with fresh-cut cypress wood and enough concrete mix to build a castle, all to make a platform up on stilts that will last many seasons. He will add columns and a roof next year. He finishes the rails on the stairs just in time for the convent's "women-only" beach day.

Herman arrives with Mollie and the convent ladies. He brings more supplies on the ferry and is impressed at CC's endeavor. He and CC are assigned to the men's camp down the beach for the day. Each year CC adds on to make it more like a house on the inside. He eventually adds strong doors and windows that are designed usually for lighthouses along the coast.

Merry, Sissy, and Laura Ann all share in their love of the convent and school as well as the many years of history they've shared there together. On this trip, Mollie is caring for a man who has been brought over from the local hospital. A nun tells her, "He's a ship's captain, and his crew says they were in a storm. His daughter washed overboard, and his head was injured while they were looking for her. He is unconscious, and the hospital is giving up on him. They sent him over here to die. His wife passed away, and he has one brother who is on a long visit in Europe, and no one knows how to reach him."

For nearly a week, Mollie, still under the alias of Merry Perry, gladly takes care of and comforts the new patient, Captain Palmer Graham. He has transitioned during the week into a semiconscious state. Sometimes she reads to him all day, thinking he can hear her. Three times a day, she moves his arms and legs through exercises and stretches. She bathes him and rubs oil on his dry skin. She shaves his beard and combs his hair daily. Laura Ann says, "Mollie, you are so attentive to Captain Graham—you remind me of a child and her doll. It's really sweet how you read the Bible to him every morning and evening...and all the other books you share with him."

Mollie admits, "Laura Ann, it is strange, but he's like the perfect man—very handsome, strong build, pretty teeth, beautiful blue eyes, long black hair. I share everything with him...my faith, dreams, hopes, and even my fears. He never talks back or tells me I'm a bad person." She smiles as she massages his hands and forearms with floral-scented oil.

"How do you know his eyes are blue? You didn't lift his lids, did you? And his teeth?"

Mollie confesses, "Yes, I open them and talk to him. One day he'll hear me. I wipe his mouth out when I wash his face. They said, while propped up, he could only take small sips of fluids if you rub his throat for a swallow reflex, but I've been feeding him ice cream the last couple days, and today I'll mash up a banana—like you do for a baby. He's got to have food before he'll get better."

Laura Ann tells her, "I'm concerned that you've become so close. What if he doesn't make it?"

Mollie scorns, "Don't say such words in front of him. He needs hope. After it rained the other night, I went outside, and the sky was clear. As I looked at the millions of stars twinkling above, I knew that he's going to be all right. I feel like he will be significant to someone in my life. It's just a feeling. Sissy says she's at peace around him too.

"The ship's crew said he became grief-stricken about losing his daughter and acted like a mad man outside in the storm, and that's how he got hurt. We need to help him heal and find forgiveness in himself."

"Laura Ann, will it be OK with you and CC if I bring him to the beach? No one here will take care of him like I do. That's if they'll let me take him. I haven't asked yet, thinking that I would talk to you and CC first."

"Mollie, I'm surprised you would want that responsibility. Are you sure?" Laura Ann asks.

Mollie responds quickly, "Yes, we have plenty of help to move him on a stretcher from the house to the beach where CC built the palm-leaf hut for shade right on the water. I think fresh air, sunshine, and salt water will cure anything. It's worth a try."

"CC thinks it's going to be a surprise, but when we get to the beach, the new house will be ready. You can keep Prince Charming in the old house. Maybe this year you'll let me paint your portrait on the beach, and I'll hang it in the new beach house. Nobody will see it but my own family."

All Mollie says is, "We'll see."

The new beach house is completed, and CC explains how he reinforced the structure of the house with enough metal rebar and concrete to build a bridge. "Laura Ann, this one will withstand any storm. Let's celebrate and let the summer vacation begin." The adults cheer, and the little ones jump up and down, giddy at being so close to the water.

CC turns to Mollie. "You haven't changed one bit, always taking care of stray dogs, like me and Herman." He laughs and elbows Herman.

Sissy joins in the conversation, saying, "CC, don't go making fun of Mollie for seeing the good in all of us misfits. All three of you came through great difficulty to save this stray dog in Nashville, and I'll never forget that as long as I live."

Laura Ann adds her two cents' worth, saying, "I'll admit I was a bit of a loner and outsider before you took me into your life, Mollie. I was rebellious and a little unhappy, but that has all changed so much now.

"You even plucked Big Mama and Lily out of the sky one day. I can't imagine my life or the children's life without them and Hugh. Because of you, Mollie. Look all around. You are the reason for this big, loving family."

"This one is as special to me as all of you. I don't know why though. God will explain it in his own time. Sissy and I are staying in the old house and will take care of him there. The convent says that if he's not awake by the time we leave, he goes back to them. That's the deal. I think if we all pray for him, God will hear us."

That afternoon, Mollie has two of the big construction workers carry Palmer to the water, where she has built a wedge in the sand for him to lean back against. She begins to softly rub sand on his feet and legs, whispering, "Palmer, I'm going to wash all the sick and sadness off of you. You've been in the bed too long.

"I thought since you are a ship captain that you would feel better here with the salt air in your hair. I'm hoping it's going to make you want to get better. I'm so glad you were able to drink small sips of the fresh orange juice again today.

"Oh, there's something I need to tell you while we're here. My real name is Mollie, not Merry. If you go back to the convent, it'll be Merry again. I know, confusing, but that's the way it has to be for Laura Ann's family.

"Palmer, whether you know it or not, God has a plan for me to love you back to life, but you have to work with me, all right?" She continues massaging up his arm and shoulder as the small waves roll in onto the two of them.

Every day Mollie makes sure that she gets Palmer to the water and sunshine, and his skin begins to look more bright and sun-tanned. She continues to mash any kind of food that she can make him swallow.

At many of the family events, Mollie props Palmer upright with pillows in a chair in the middle of the activities in the house or on the beach and encourages everyone to speak to him, especially the children.

What everyone doesn't know is that Mollie and Palmer sleep together in the same bed every night. She knows it's only a fantasy to think about him as her prince, to fall in love and live happily ever after. But she continues because she loves to sleep snuggled under his arm with her head on his chest and to pretend.

She sleeps more soundly and wakes up more rested than at any time in her life. Every night after she reads the Bible to him, she tells him about their fantasy life together, along with her deepest dark secrets and innermost sexual desires before falling asleep in his arms.

On the eve of their departure in the bedroom, Mollie begins shouting at him, "Wake up! Feel my love for you, Palmer. Wake up, and be my man. Be my lover forever. I need your touch. These are the things I want you to do for me..."

Sadly, everyone's luggage is stacked high as they wait on the ferry boat to pick them up to start the long journey back to Huntsville.

Palmer, although heavier and more radiant than ever, has not regained total consciousness, and it's tearing Mollie's soul apart. She knows she has grown close to a man who is a stranger. Maybe that's because it's safe, or so she thinks.

The first night Palmer is alone again at the convent, he has a nightmare and screams out so loudly that he wakes the attending nun. The nun jumps with delight that he is starting to thrash about and move on his own. She also feels his sorrow as he cries out for his daughter. She sees this as a sign of healing and pats his hands. "It's going to be OK."

He says in a low mumble, "Mollie," before falling asleep again.

❈

A month after they get back to Huntsville, Mollie is still sad about having to leave Palmer at the convent. She has tried everything, including upping her charitable donations, but they have absolutely refused to let her bring him home to Huntsville. She mails her second letter of the week to inquire about his health and condition...again, no response. Laura Ann tells her, "It's the convent's privacy policy. They don't tell who they help, volunteers, contributors and donors, names of students or adoptions...total privacy."

❈

Palmer wakes over a few days, always asking, "Where is Mollie?"

The nuns, thinking that he's asking about his daughter, always answer, "She's in heaven, with God. She's been called home."

His brother arrives from Europe and takes him back to New Orleans to recover and rebuild his strength. He writes the convent daily, asking about who took care of him. Who is she, and where is she? He knows there is an angel out there who brought him out of his grief and back to life.

Two months after Mollie left Palmer with the nuns, she returns to the convent looking for him. As much as they love Merry and her large donations, they have a privacy clause that forbids them from giving out any information.

Mollie is able to pressure one of the younger sisters into telling her something. "He did wake up and kept asking about his daughter. Her spirit is the one, we think, who brought him back to life." Mollie's heart sinks. She thinks Palmer doesn't remember anything about her. The nun continues, "His brother came to take him home, but I don't know where.

"He did mention leaving Captain Graham's ship in Mobile Bay for the time being. I remember because Captain Graham kept saying it's his angel that saved him, and guess what? That's the name of his boat, *Angel.* I'm surprised it isn't named *Mollie* after his daughter. He cried out in his sleep for her almost every night until his brother picked him up."

Mollie's heart skips a beat, knowing that it's she that he cries for at night, and he misses sleeping with her.

Mollie goes straight to the port and inquiries about a transient ship, *Angel,* that is adorned at the bow with a woman with white angel wings on both sides of the ship.

Before long, she speaks to a small crew caring for the out-of-service ship. She learns that Mollie is not the name of the deceased daughter or wife. She inquires further about where his brother took him. No one could answer for sure; they only worked with him out of Mobile, and he didn't share much about his brother.

Mollie tells them she is staying at the Grand Hotel in Point Clear for the next week and to please forward to her any information.

Seven days come and go. Mollie is greatly saddened that there is no word from the crew or Palmer. She retreats to the Taylor beach compound indefinitely.

⇒⊹⇐

Palmer is at the busy New Orleans train depot. He leans over and tells his brother, "I know this sounds a little nuts since I've never met Mollie, but I think that she may be the one…the one who can steal me from my first love, the sea.

"Thank you for believing in me, brother. I know she's real, and all the memories with her friends and family are real too. I heard her. She loves me. It's not a head injury like the doctors say. She's real."

Palmer's brother responds with, "You know, even if you found her, you can't bring her back here. Every woman in Storyville will rat you out if they see you on the street with her. You're their money source, and they don't want to lose you to some straight and pure woman like you're talking about.

"Remember, you're the money bags for Josie Arlington's new bordello. How will you handle that? I hate being the older brother and pointing out the obvious, but you have too much to hide here. Live in Mobile. If you find her, build her a big house on the bay and watch your ships bring in fortunes from far away. You've had enough life on the sea. Time to be a land lover."

Palmer replies, "No retirement for me, I'll always have the sea in my life. Besides, it makes me a ton of money."

Palmer receives the same treatment as Mollie at the convent: no cooperation whatsoever, except from the same young nun who helped Mollie. "Her name is Merry Perry. She went to the port to look for your ship. Sir, I'm so sorry about your daughter."

Captain Graham sees the *Angel* for the first time since the accident, but he doesn't have time for that now. He's on a mission to find Mollie and is ecstatic to learn the woman in his dreams is real when the crew tell him that the most beautiful woman on the earth had been there looking for him. They forgot to get her name but do remember that she was staying at the Grand Hotel. Captain Graham asks the first mate, "How long will it take to supply the ship and get the rest of the crew together? We're going to go find her…today."

The *Angel* and crew arrive at the Grand Hotel pier just before sunset. Captain Graham has high hopes that she will still be there waiting on him. The desk clerk remembers her and tells him she left a week earlier. He remembers because she hired a ferry and loaded up supplies at the pier.

"Do you know where she was going?" pleads the captain. "Yes, it's the only big house on the beach, but your draft is too deep for the inlet waterways like the ferry takes, and its thirty miles by sea."

It's a clear night, the stars are bright, and Captain Graham thinks, *I've come this far. I can't lose her now.*

They begin the journey offshore. A few of the deckhands are able to bring in several red snappers and two huge groupers for dinner. After traveling over thirty miles by sea, the captain is able to find the houses, about twelve miles east of where he started. He decides to anchor out for the night and take a dinghy to shore at sunrise.

Mollie has been up reading since before sunrise. Now that the first rays of the sun are peeking over the horizon, she sees a ship just offshore and a dinghy is on the beach.

She feels chills up her spine and then hears *tap-tap-tap* coming from the glass door in the living room and a muffled man's voice. "Is anyone home? I saw your light on and thought that I'd take a chance that you were up. Hello."

Mollie's heart is racing as she walks into the living room. It's him in the early morning light, which is causing a beautiful glow around his face and tan wet chest. She walks, slowly staring as she unlocks the door. She notices he's much taller than she thought as she opens the door to her imaginary lover.

"Mollie?" He touches her face. "You're not a dream, you're real."

Her breath is swept away as she looks into his sky-blue eyes, saying, "You're standing! I never imagined what you would look like standing. I'm sorry. Please come in. You're all wet. I'll get something for you to dry with."

He interrupts, "I'm sorry about being wet, but I was swimming for strength when I saw your light on. I began to swim as fast as I could to the shore, then ran all the way here and up all those steps just to do this..." He pulls her close to him and touches his mouth to hers like a perfect fit. He kisses her with his soul, breathing in her essence, and they don't stop until they're both dizzy.

Mollie is surprised that she lets him break rule number one... don't ever kiss a man as it involves emotions. She not only lets him kiss her but devour her in his kisses alone. He stops only to say, "I remember everything—the beach, your loving touch, you mashing food, then placing it in my mouth, and you'd rub my throat until I'd swallow, every kind of fruit you could squeeze, you rubbing me softly all over with the sand, your family gatherings, and the books. You read more books than anyone I've ever met, and I remember you sleeping with me every night, and I remember all your kind deeds—your secrets and all of your desires. I want to be the man you begged me to be that last night."

She swore she would never fall in love because she isn't lovable, but this time was different, and she fell in love with a dream. Now the dream is alive and standing in front of her.

Palmer begins to kiss Mollie again. "You're alive—you're real and more beautiful than I could have imagined." He almost weeps and then resumes hungrily pressing his lips to hers as he wraps his arms around her back and pulls her body tightly in to his.

"I was awake the first night you took me back to the convent. I could feel your absence, but they were not about to tell me anything about my caretaker, and they kept saying to me that there is no Mollie and that my mind is just grieving for my daughter.

"I remember your touch, your smell, and your beautiful voice as you read to me about politics, literature, history, and fiction. Your voice sounded like an angel from the heavens as you read the Bible."

Mollie is swept away by her emotions. Rule number two to never break. Emotions. They mess up the box. She needs air and says, "Let's sit for a moment, and let me look at you. You're alive. I'm so happy you lived. I didn't know since the convent also kept me in the dark after I left.

"One of the nuns secretly told me the name of your ship. I met your crew and checked registration of the boat, and everything leads to Mobile. Where are you from? Do you believe in God? Do you believe in love? Don't you want to know about me? Looks can be deceiving, you know."

"Whoa," the captain says. "You're always so funny, Mollie. I wish you could have known how you made me laugh inside. I'm in the shipping business, originally San Francisco and now New Orleans for a few years.

"I believe God showed me a love in you that I have never seen before. You were the reason I got out of bed. The nightmares stopped about my daughter, and I got better to find you and your love, Mollie. I believe I know you better than you know yourself. You frequently told me things you wouldn't tell a best friend. I think I know you."

Mollie is almost embarrassed as she starts to remember all of the things she said out loud, thinking no one was listening or remembering.

Palmer continues, "I've had a lot of time to think about everything you said. I know you own a lot of property and that you were here with your family to celebrate making a lot of money off of an upcoming land sale. I have a lot of money as well. You don't want a husband as much as you need a best friend and incredible lover. These are things you confessed to me."

Mollie smiles in a bashful way. "Well, Mr. Palmer Graham, since you know everything about me, tell me more about yourself, your dreams, desires, and life on the sea."

"I'll feel better showing you, tonight at dusk. I will show you all of my desires." He kneels before Mollie and kisses her hand as though it's the most loved and delicate in the world.

And just like that, her Prince Charming has come in and filled Mollie's empty heart. "I have a lot to do to prepare for tonight. Thank you, Mollie. Your love saved my life, and tonight you'll know just how I feel about you." He pulls the wind-caught door to a close and waves at her through the glass. Mollie watches as he crosses the sand to the dinghy and rows back to the ship.

She has to wonder, is all of this happening? Is it too fast, and does she really love a man she doesn't know? She has spent the last twentysomething years believing the Russian's pronouncement that no one would really ever love her. Now she is thirty-nine years old and can let her guard down to love whoever she wants. Tonight she will do just that.

In the late afternoon, Mollie takes a refreshing outdoor shower with collected rainwater and rubs rose-scented oil all over her body while her hair dries in the wind.

Just before sunset, Palmer arrives at the door, without a shirt again, per Mollie's fantasy. She knows every inch of his body, and tonight he is going to explore and learn every nuance of Mollie's.

Her beach dress, crafted by Virginia, is a thin, flowy fabric, sleeveless, and it stops at the knee. He escorts her to the beach and takes her to where he has built a large bonfire. Only the top rim of the sun hangs over the horizon, leaving the sky full of orange and pink hues and shimmering streaks of light across the waves.

Palmer confidently looks into Mollie's eyes and tells her, "I'm going to recite something to you, Mollie." He unfolds a piece of paper with handwriting. "Actually, I wrote it down from memorization. I was afraid time would cause me to forget."

He takes a deep breath and begins. "'Wake up. Feel my love for you, Palmer. Wake up and be my man. Be my lover forever. I need your touch. These are the things I want you to do to me. I want you to show up at my door with a bare chest and whisk me to our love den on the beach.

"'I want you to build a big bonfire, whisk me off my feet and carry me to a big, high bed made of sand nearby. You'll have covers and pillows to keep us off the sand and cover it with fragrant magnolia blossoms. You'll lay me on the bed and remove my dress, taking time to appreciate seeing me for the first time. You lean over and kiss my lips, like you were kissing an angel, as your tongue explores past my lips to dance with mine. Your kisses move down to my neck while chills run down my spine. Your hands explore my body, and your soft lip kisses continue to my stomach, teasing my belly button. You use your tongue to explore and push me to limits I've never known.

"'You stop and slowly undress yourself. I want you to love me. Slowly at first as you stare into my eyes, building a bond between us. Then I want you to let loose and take me until our souls unite and become one. I'll scream out loud in wild desire for you as the waves roll in at our feet and the flames dance behind our heads. I'll beg for more until you bring down to me the heaven and stars from above, and we unite into one. Wake up, Palmer. Make my wildest dreams come true.'"

Palmer is breathing intensely; he folds the paper and places it in his pocket without ever looking at it. "I am awake, Mollie. Do you think for one second that I forgot about your request? Not at all. I remember everything you said to me. You pulled me out of my nightmares. It's what made me get up and want to heal—to get stronger to find you. No woman has ever been so clear. I love that you know what you want, and I'm here to give you all that and more."

He picks Mollie up and takes her to the beach bed. He begins her fantasy by removing her dress and stands back to admire what he sees as she slowly turns around.

Palmer is intoxicated with passion and love by his eyes alone. He begins to kiss Mollie as they collapse on their beach bed and bring to each other—new experiences all throughout the night, only waking to the waves crashing upon their feet. The moonlight is bright enough to see the water slowly eroding their bed. They take the bedding up to the dry sand.

Mollie looks at Palmer. "The moon is so bright, and it's warm. Let's go skinny-dipping." He takes her hand, and they walk into the dark waves together. When the water is at chest level, she wraps her legs around Palmer's waist and holds her arms around his neck. The waves bob them up and down, but it doesn't seem to stop them from gazing into each other's eyes.

No nightmares for Palmer tonight. The two wake in Mollie's familiar big bed with their arms and legs intertwined so closely that they are truly one. "Who's happier this morning, me or you?" Mollie asks with a big smile on her face.

Palmer opens his big blue eyes to Mollie's face, inches away. "Me! I'm the happiest man on the planet. Let me show you." He begins to kiss her lips softly at first and then sucks on her lower lip as his desire for her rises again.

Afterward, Palmer wakes Mollie again with a plate full of fluffy pancakes, including caramel butter syrup and thick slices of bacon. "Wow, Palmer, how did you know I'm starving? You cook, I see," she says as she takes a bite of the best pancakes she has ever eaten. "Oh my goodness, these are so delicious, and you found everything to make them there in the kitchen?"

"You're in for a real treat tonight. I'll make you flaming cherries jubilee, and yes, your kitchen is very well stocked. My next-door neighbor in New Orleans is a chef. He owns Antoine's restaurant, specializing in French Creole–type food. He lets me come over and help him cook in his kitchen until the wee hours of the morning."

For the next two weeks, Mollie and Palmer spend an enormous amount of time in bed while enjoying incredible sex, eating like kings, and talking about their future together. He prefers they live near a port since the sea is his business and in his blood.

Mollie decides she has plenty of money and will let Sissy live in the house and run the business for herself if Sissy wants to stay in the business. However, she really hopes Sissy will leave Huntsville and move with her since Palmer takes long trips at sea. Hopefully Herman will join her as well. She can visit with Laura Ann and CC when they return to the convent and beach.

Neither of them ever thought that they would be getting married. Mollie is quite happy to know that she is lovable. She can finally put the Russian behind her now.

Mollie wakes to the smell of French toast on her nightstand. She sits up, sleepy-eyed, looking for Palmer. He pops up from under the covers and kisses her bare shoulders and neck. "I love you, Mollie."

"I love you, Palmer. You spoil me with your fancy cooking. Let's see what surprise you have made me this morning. Mm...mm,

Palmer. Covered with fresh peaches. You are going to get yourself a big girl if you keep feeding me like this every day. Do you ever sleep?" Mollie asks. "You're always up so much earlier than I am, happy and cooking."

He says, "That's what I like about being around you. You make me happy, Mollie, and I want to do things to please you."

"Then why are you not sleeping? I thought we were happy, but isn't something bothering you?"

Palmer takes Mollie's hands in his to comfort her and says, "Appears that not only did you save me, but also you can read my mind. I have been hesitant lately to talk about me getting back to work."

Mollie's rapturous thoughts fly away as she suddenly realizes that, just like the Russian, Palmer doesn't know anything about her real life. She never mentioned being a prostitute while he was in and out of consciousness. Not wanting to delay the inevitable, she blurts out, "Palmer, what do you think about prostitutes?" The look on his face says all she needs to know. She swallows hard as her heart stops beating.

Palmer is caught off guard. He thinks to himself, *She'll hate me if she knew that I went to Josie's as a frequent customer.* So he says what he thinks a good Southern Christian woman wants to hear, "Whores and whorehouses are a blight on society. I think they should all be closed down." Bless his heart. The clueless man smiles broadly, thinking that he has made a clever response.

Mollie forces herself into the nonemotional part of her box and responds, "Oh, OK. When do you think you'll leave for a trip, and for how long?"

Palmer admits, "Soon, and that's why I haven't slept well lately. I didn't want to tell you. I'm going to Panama and will be gone about three months. Are you going back home? I'll send for you when I get back."

Mollie carefully crafts a letter explaining that she has thought long and hard and has decided to go to the convent permanently to work for God. She believes God has plans to heal people through her the same way he did for him. She apologizes that her worldly lust got in the way of God's plan. Contacting her will only make things more difficult. She places the letter in his bag on the morning of his departure.

Mollie waves as his ship pulls up anchor and says out loud to the wind, "What in the world drove me to fall in love with a sleeping man that I knew nothing about? A man of such strong morals could never love me!" Mollie never knew that Palmer went back to the convent for years to always be turned away.

≕ ⊹≔

Mollie is back home in Huntsville, sitting on her front porch with Sissy and Laura Ann, who then says, "Sissy, don't laugh at me when I ask Mollie this question, but, Mollie, how did you get pregnant? I mean I know how, but I thought you two had a way to make things like that not happen."

Mollie chuckles and replies, "I broke all the rules that I preach to my girls daily. I know better. In the first place, you never kiss a man on the mouth in this business. It involves emotions, which lead to passion and lust that we think is love. Then we get careless. Sex should always stay in a box by itself. Right, Sissy?"

"Right, Mollie," Sissy replies. "But I think a little Mollie around the house will be fun."

"Yes, it will be an adventure. I think I'll call her Molly, spelled M-O-L-L-Y after you and me. What do you think?" Mollie replies. "And how did you get pregnant?" Mollie laughs as she turns to the dog and rubs the Dalmatian's huge belly. "Lady, how did you get pregnant? Did you kiss a boy dog? I bet you have a dozen pups, judging by your size."

Sissy laughs, "Mollie, you're so right. I didn't stay in the non-emotional part of my box. Haven't kissed a man since. Don't forget, we've been summoned for our monthly dinner—Wednesday with my father...you, too, Laura Ann."

Mollie reminds her, "He's a pleasant man, Sissy. He just forgets to leave his 'Judge Greenleaf' hat on the bench sometimes. Knowing him keeps us out of the prostitute court. You're going to have to forgive him one day. He's getting old. Besides, it was your mother and grandparents that took you and ran off to Nashville, never to be heard from again. It was a complete fluke that we showed up back in Huntsville one day. In fact, we would've never met if not for your mother running away with you when you were just a baby."

"You're right, Mollie, but I just keep thinking of all that I went through and that I would have been safe here under his care if he had only come looking for me."

Laura Ann jumps in, "OK, you two—let's get back on topic and talk about Palmer. We've had your daddy conversation so many times, and you're never going to move forward until you forgive him, Sissy. Period."

Mollie then replies, "Sadly, Captain Graham was a mistake. I'll only remember the good, kind, and loving things about him. He's at sea where he's happiest. He has a very low opinion of my profession. I never even told him about it, and that's why he doesn't need to know about our baby. I'm completely finished with having any clients from this point on."

Laura Ann can't hold it any longer and happily shares her news to break the sadness. "You're going to have a baby, and guess what? I'm pregnant again, too. I had a dream we are both going to have a baby girl and they will grow up together and be best friends for life. Won't that be fun? I couldn't believe it when I first saw that you were pregnant, just like in my dream."

"Laura Ann, you've had so many miscarriages that almost took your life. I'm worried about you caring for a child again," Sissy says with her eyes furrowed at the brow and a sad smile.

"Don't you two worry about me this time," Laura Ann says with great certainty. "This one's God's child. She's in his hands and is going to be a healthy baby girl. I will name her Grace."

CHAPTER 47
1892, TOWN OF TAYLORSVILLE

As Mollie gets ready for the grand opening of the train depot at Taylorsville, Sissy reports to Mollie about a fire at one of her working houses on Dixie Place. "The fire did very little damage, thanks to the volunteer fire department showing up so quickly. Several of them stuck around to have a celebration of their heroism with the ladies.

"All the houses were closed, as the police chief had suggested, so that he could have a token raid and appease the concerned citizens of Huntsville about the health of the working ladies. How were we to know that he would raid the place when the firemen were there?

"The cute firemen were given freebees and were in the middle of a good party when the police showed up, and all the firemen were hauled off to jail. They're threatening to quit the fire department if they're not let out of jail immediately. I bet something will work out, and they don't spend the night. This one will make the papers, Mollie. Oh, well, it's free publicity reminding customers where we're located."

"Oh, the chief will handle that little slipup," Mollie says. "Right now, I'm concentrating on closing the land sale with the railroad tomorrow morning. It will seal the deal with the investors of Dallas

Mills Manufacturing Company for tomorrow afternoon's meeting. This is their one caveat before they will allow me to be a woman owner. The railroad tracks must come right to the property, and tomorrow I will deliver more to the table than all the men put together. Sissy, the added bonus is twenty thousand dollars in our bank account. Mr. Hall would be so proud. I miss him. I wish he were still here to see this and the Taylors getting a train depot and post office in their town.

"We will be going to the convent in Mobile soon after the opening of the Taylorsville depot. Then we will be staying at the beach for a long, well-deserved vacation."

⊷⊶

Opening day at the new train depot in Taylorsville brings widespread interest in the little community. Laura Ann Taylor, the small town's spiritual mother, has been heavily involved in preparing for the events of the day. Her request to CC was simply to make the landscape identical to her own front yard.

CC proudly shows his handy work of blooming azalea, rhododendron, hydrangea, and gardenia bushes, along with other little extras like hanging flower pots on their porch, as he tells Laura Ann, "Mollie, Sissy, Herman, and baby Molly will arrive on the inaugural train from Huntsville.

"We'll have the grand opening of the Taylorsville depot, and then Big Mama, Lily, Hugh, Percy, Chase, and baby Grace will join them to enjoy the remainder of the train's journey by steamship to Gunter's Landing. It'll take four hours to go up the river. Once there, the train will be unloaded off the barges and placed back on the tracks to Gadsden. Big Mama says that she made fried chicken and biscuits." CC grins and rubs his stomach.

The inbound train from Huntsville arrives to a waiting crowd. CC, the town's founder, is enthusiastic about the unveiling of the new depot and pulls the cover off the new sign.

Mollie is surprised at Laura Ann as she shouts to CC, "It's wrong, CC! All wrong. The railroad maps show the depot as 'Taylorsville,'" as they stand and stare with everyone else at an eight-foot-long wooden sign, painted white, with black trim, the raised black letters reading "HOBBS ISLAND."

CC looks around and says, "We're still going to call it Taylorsville. Now, y'all come inside and help us celebrate with Big Mama's fried chicken and biscuits and the best sweet tea in Alabama." Percy barely makes it back in time from his favorite place in the world, his tree house.

⇥ ⇤

Other than the train and steamship's loud bells and whistles terrifying the two small girls, Molly and Grace, the loading to the steamship goes smoothly. Mollie hands Herman her daddy's beat-up saxophone case. "You know how she loves to hear you play," she tells him as she kisses the cheeks of her baby girl and braids her long dark hair.

"I can't say no to those beautiful blue eyes," Herman baby-talks as he puts the instrument close to the baby for her to clamp her little fingers on. Then she begins to squeal, waving her arms, as she bounces up and down on Mollie's leg.

Now under way, Laura Ann finally calms down about the sign and puts a blanket down. Mollie places baby Molly down next to Grace, and she begins to dance as Herman plays. Baby Molly pulls Grace up to dance with her as they pass the banks of the river with the music man playing the saxophone.

The music works in tiring the two as each get a bottle and then are put down for a nap. "Thank you, Herman. I can barely remember my daddy playing, but I'm sure he would approve. CC and Laura Ann...congratulations! You two have established a bustling little town, and now it's official, with a train depot and a post office. At least they got the post office name correct."

Lily shares with everyone her latest dessert creation, "Lily's doughnuts." Percy, Hugh, and Chase arrive back from exploring just in time for dessert. Percy declares, "Big Mama, for my birthday, I want these doughnuts, not cake," as he eats a half dozen more than anyone else.

The next spring, the three ladies return to the convent with their two babies in tow. The nuns cherish having the little girls around, if only for a month, and they entertain the two girls as their mothers work.

The familiar beach house has been spared any storm damage again this year. By the time they arrive, CC, Herman, and the boys have extended the deck out another twelve feet. Laura Ann unpacks her paints and drawing supplies.

Later in the afternoon, Mollie has the two three-year-olds playing at the water's edge while Laura Ann sketches on her pad. "OK, girls—now we're going to exfoliate dead skin and increase our circulation," Mollie says. She then gently rubs sand on the bottoms of their little feet, as well as on their knees and elbows. Mollie continues, "Wearing shoes makes our feet ugly. This will fix that too."

Laura Ann watches and listens to the joyful giggles and laughter. "Mollie, I've been taking art classes from Miss Maria Howard Weeden. She has an incredible gift of capturing emotions on people's faces. You won't believe her paintings of colored people. She paints them in their real light, not a typical 'picking-cotton' scene. She sold some of her artwork to repair her home after the Yankees left it in shambles during the occupation of Huntsville. I hope to paint as well as she does someday. That's what I'm trying to capture now, the girls' emotions. Don't worry. I'm only using profiles. It's hard to believe that they are already three."

Mollie explains to Laura Ann, "Your boys are getting older. Perhaps I should stay away from family time with you before they start figuring things out and asking questions. You really don't want Grace growing up with the daughter of a madam as her best friend either. We could limit our visits to my house only."

"I think I get a say in the matter, Mollie. You alone don't get to decide the conditions of our friendship. I don't like the fact that my husband is in the horse race gambling business either, but he has provided us a very good life. Because of you, we have made a lot of money from land deals too. Haven't we all made enough money? Can't we just live a straight life devoted to God?"

"Laura Ann—CC, Herman, and I have always appreciated your pure heart. Spiritually you've saved us all. However none of us are as hands-on in our businesses as we once were."

"I know," Laura Ann replies. "But why not get out of the brothel and racetrack business altogether?"

"Laura Ann, we provide jobs for a lot of people to run that beautiful racetrack. I can't begin to tell you how many women and their families that I provide a safe, clean environment for them to work.

"As for the brothel, keep in mind that my women make more money than most of the men in Huntsville. The demand is always going to be here, Laura Ann. If it's not me, then someone else will take my place. Will they take all of the women and their children to Dr. Lowry's office for a health checkup once a week while providing security and child care? I genuinely care for these women. I understand, and I feel what they feel. None of us woke up one morning and decided to be a prostitute, but we survived it, learned to accept it, and it is our way of life."

"I guess I see your point...it's not all about us," Laura Ann replies.

"You know, since Molly was born, I have no clients...zero. Her safety is above all else." A big, white, foamy wave comes over the girls' heads as Mollie snatches them up in the air by the backs of their swimsuits—one in each hand.

Molly squeals, "We're flying, Grace."

Put your drawing down, Laura Ann," Mollie says. "We're flying." The two close friends play in the surf together as their mothers lift them by their arms above the crashing waves.

It's the end of summer. The sun is breaking first light as trunks and supplies are piled high at the dock, waiting for the ferry. As this chapter at the beach closes, Mollie has a strange feeling that she'll never be back again.

CHAPTER 48

HIDE, BABY MOLLY

Huntsville in the fall is beautiful, with many different colors of red, orange, and yellow leaves that have changed due to the cooler evenings. Mollie looks around her elaborate home with many dedicated workers, including security, all vowing to protect Molly. She finds it hard to believe her baby is now a little girl and getting so big. Now never leaving the estate, the mother and daughter create imaginative children's stories on the sprawling grounds.

Just then she receives a message from one of the workers that the next-door neighbors and security at the gate have reported that two police officers, twin brothers, are attempting to get past the guards at the gate. The same two officers were spotted by several others earlier in the morning as they tried to get over the fence, only to be stopped by a barking pack of Dalmatian dogs. They claim to be looking for a missing person, their very own sister, Anne Overton. They know that she works as a nursery teacher for Mollie.

Mollie is hiding Anne from her own brothers. She fled to Mollie's house after repeated sexual assaults in her home and hasn't been seen since. Mollie loves how tender and loving Anne is with her daughter and has vowed to protect her from her abusive brothers—uniforms or not.

Mollie pays the current chief of police well, but she has no relationship with, and therefore less protection from, rogue officers who raid and arrest her employees who are operating other houses in the "bad" part of town.

Anne, after nearly one year of employment with Mollie, is now engaged to Ivan Teal, Mollie's cousin from Virginia, who has been employed by Mollie for about five years. In fact it was Ivan who introduced Anne to Mollie. They want to get married but don't believe they've saved enough money.

Mollie knows that they both love music and has decided to pay their way to attend Belmont in Nashville to study music and set them up in a little house close to the school. It's to be a surprise.

The next Saturday, Sissy, Herman, Anne, and Ivan accompany Mollie and her daughter to the Hermitage Hotel in Nashville. Along the way, she breaks the surprise to them. "The only relative of mine that I trust...and let me clarify that. None of the people that claim to be my relatives are actually related to me. In any case, the only relative I trust is you, Ivan. You have worked for me for five years now and have never asked for anything extra during all of that time. You introduced me to Anne, and we know how much Molly loves Anne. A little birdy told me that you two don't have enough money to get married. That's why we are going to Nashville—to have a wedding...and to enroll you both in Belmont to study music!" Ivan and Anne are completely surprised, and both quickly hug Mollie's neck while thanking her.

It was a beautiful wedding arranged by the hotel. The next morning, before heading back to Huntsville, Mollie drops them off at the little cottage she has rented close to the school and gives them their first month's allowance, telling them that they can expect the same amount every month.

The very next night back in Huntsville, the scariest and final blow comes when Mollie catches a stranger in her bedroom trying to kidnap Molly out of her bed. Mollie puts a knife in his back and takes wailing Molly out of his arms before he falls out the window to the hard ground three floors below. "Hush, hush, ba-a-by, don't cry..." Mollie sings in a shaking voice as she bounces her daughter up and down, patting her back to help her breathe.

Sissy and a security guard run into the room and are shocked that someone scaled the wall up to Mollie's window. "Look, Momma hit the bad guy. Momma told me he's not coming back," little Molly says.

Mollie leaves her little girl with a trusted staff member as she, Sissy, and Herman take care of the body in the black cemetery that night.

Fortunately gravediggers are already there working at night to avoid the daytime heat. Mollie gives them money to dig the current hole about three feet deeper and leave for an hour. Herman takes the two arms while Mollie and Sissy each take a leg and carry the corpse out of the bushes over to the grave. Before they toss him into the deep hole, Mollie pulls her knife out of his back and wipes it on his shirt.

"Stupid asshole! Don't ever mess with my child. May you end up in hell for trying." She rolls her eyes to the grave. "Now I'm ready." They toss him down, hearing the thud as he hits the bottom. Each takes a shovel and begins to cover the body with three feet of dirt. "*Double grave* has a whole new meaning," Mollie says as they laugh to relieve the tension.

Mollie learns that there may be an organized effort to kidnap little Molly for ransom or as a bargaining chip to get her to tell where Anne is. Knowing that she has to do something, Mollie asks Herman and Sissy to plan to get up before dawn and quietly take little Molly by carriage up to stay a few weeks with Ivan and Anne. She tells Herman and Sissy of her plans to take three or four months off to travel and that she would like for them to join her. Tell Anne that we'll be up in a few weeks to pick up Molly."

When they pick Molly up, it is difficult for Mollie to hear her daughter refer to Anne as her mother, but that is what she was instructed to do for safety reasons. For the next four months, Mollie spends her time traveling with Molly, Sissy, and Herman.

Some of the places they travel are very memorable, such as the first lighting of a Christmas tree at the White House with the new Thomas Edison string of light bulbs and to New York City for shopping and plays.

Mollie wants to see the site of the 1893 World's Fair in Chicago. That's what she tells everyone, but in Chicago she looks up the Russian and goes to see him at an institution. She is so sad when she learns that he's now penniless and has dementia attributed to a heat stroke that caused him to resign from the army. He is as handsome as he ever was. His nurse says, "No one will miss him when he passes. He plays a gramophone every day with the same song, 'Dixie,' while he stares at that worn-out photo…it looks like you! You're the woman in the picture! See if you can get through to him."

John looks up at Mollie with an empty gaze to only return to staring at the photo. "No," Mollie replies. "It's the girl in the picture he's fixated on, and that's not me."

Just an emotional box, thinks Mollie as she leaves John's side. Maybe now she will be able to totally close a very lengthy chapter in her life.

 ⇒+⇐

Meanwhile, back in Huntsville, the Overton twins finally get a judge to sign a search warrant for Mollie's house. Per Mollie's direction, the staff quickly fill the house with the employees from all over the property and with friends from the neighborhood to prevent any ransacking by the two dirty policemen.

They try to mess things up, but there are too many people to do much damage. "She sure lives nice to be a whore," says Clyde Overton as his fingers slowly tip a crystal vase to the floor. "Funny thing is, she turns me down like my money is not good enough for her public snatch. She tells people she's not doing it anymore. David, I'm telling you now, I'll have her one day."

David says, "Calm down, Clyde. You can have her one day, I promise. We can't have the town whore disrespecting my brother."

CHAPTER 49

THE LAST DANCE

After months of traveling, Mollie is back in Huntsville. At Anne's insistence, she drops Molly off for a short stay in Nashville and tells Anne she will be back in two weeks to pick her up.

To Mollie's surprise, Laura Ann unexpectedly visits for advice about Percy just as the grocery store delivery wagon is leaving, with a pack of Dalmatians barking and snapping and at the wheels. "He's a handsome young man, and he has all the wrong young ladies chasing after him. I'm afraid the one I want to have my grandbabies is going to lose out to loose women. You are so wise about men, Mollie. How can we help Percy recognize that Linda Gail is the right one?"

Mollie thinks really hard for a few minutes. "Oh, Laura Ann, before I forget. You know the painting of the girls and me at the beach that you have in your dining room at your new house on Adams Street? I want you to put it in the attic for now. I'm afraid someone will figure it out and come after Molly again. You put the painting away for me, and I'll help you with your future daughter-in-law." Laura Ann nods in agreement.

"Now, how to make sure Linda Gail wins Percy? I'll invite you to the biggest poker game in town tonight. Bring Linda Gail, and you two can hide over here behind these slatted doors to the butler's pantry. As you know, I have been celibate since Molly came into my life. I'm completely out of the sex business. Sissy runs everything. But for you, I'll do a rare performance. Be here by seven o'clock, stay quiet, and take notes. Ask me questions later."

Mollie makes the time to visit on the porch with Herman. "I need your help pulling off a lesson for Laura Ann tonight. I didn't ask if CC knows about it, so I'm keeping my mouth shut. I'm coming out of retirement for a quick wedding dance to show the woman that Laura Ann has chosen to have her grandchildren how to catch Percy's eye. Who knew she is such a meddler?" Mollie laughs. "Anyway, will you play my daddy's saxophone with a pianist and singer tonight, about ten minutes after eight tonight?"

Herman smiles. "Mollie, how many years have we worked together? Too many to remember, I suppose, but I will say this about you: no matter the situation, you always have a smile and find something to be happy about. That's really nice. Your life is an adventure. Maybe you should write a book about yourself." Mollie's laughter is so loud that it becomes contagious, and each time she tries to talk, she gets tickled even more. Herman is not sure why Mollie is laughing but gets to chuckling so hard he has to walk away into the grass to catch his breath. He finally catches his breath to say, "But I still don't get it...why is that so funny to you?"

"Thank you for the kinds words, Herman, but no one will buy a book about a madam."

"Oh, yes, they will...especially if your picture is on the cover, and you tell of your time as the White Dove. Do you want me to play the song that makes you smile the most?"

Her grin says it all. "You know me so well. I wonder if all those folks would still love the White Dove if they knew I was a prostitute. One last dance, and we'll retire it and me for good."

⤙⟊ ⟊⤚

325

Laura Ann and her guests arrive through the back entrance with an extra person. The three ladies emerge out of the carriage almost dressed in disguise, with large hats and scarves covering their faces. Mollie is tickled as they come through the back door. "Who's the extra person under here?" she asks as she pulls the scarf off the stranger.

"Hi, I'm Kelly Garth, Linda Gail's sister. When she told me about coming here, I insisted on coming too. This is probably the most exciting thing I will ever see in my lifetime, I don't want to miss your performance. I'm married to the greatest man ever, but his family is super uptight and strict. They act like the Bible police. They'll surely send me to hell for being in your home." Kelly laughs and looks around. "What a beautiful house—much more glamorous than I expected."

Mollie politely replies, "The problem is that Laura Ann and I have had an understanding since the first day we met—nothing here gets repeated or gossiped about. I have to have your word that no one will ever know that you were here tonight. You cannot tell anyone who you see here tonight. You too, Linda Gail. Laura Ann, do you trust these two?"

Laura Ann says, "I know one thing. We are here tonight to get me the daughter-in-law that I trust to have my grandbabies. So, yes, I trust these two with that and also with all of your secrets, Mollie."

"OK—watch the men's faces as much as you watch me, Linda Gail. Tonight you're going to learn how to show Percy your package without giving it away.

⚊⊹⊹⚊

Five of Huntsville's wealthiest men, including the former mayor, probate judge, sheriff, and two other very successful businessmen, all arrive before eight and proudly walk through Mollie Teal's front door for their monthly poker night. Mollie has a new card table with luxury leather chairs, that is conveniently located in the bar. The bartender pours generously and takes care of everyone's needs before the cards are touched.

Jerry deals the cards and says, "Opening bet to our lovely hostess, Mollie."

Mollie smiles and begins her opening remarks. "Thank you, Jerry and gentlemen, for coming tonight. Michael O'Shaugnessey's presence will be missed again this evening. As a reminder, let's keep praying God doesn't take his sight completely. Poor man—I tried to tell him not to build the Kildare mansion on that site because a Cherokee chief cursed the land after losing his best warrior in a fight with the Chickasaw. I had Big Mama Ruth tell him about White Daddy going crazy and setting the house on fire the day I found her and Lily. Michael wouldn't listen, and now he can't live in that giant house." The men nod in unison.

Mollie then changes the mood at the table. "Let's make this exciting, shall we?" Each man at the table thinks she is looking only at him with her lustful eyes.

With the high card showing and without looking at her cards, Mollie says, "Opening bet, twenty dollars." No one flinches as he places money in the ante pile.

Johnny says, "I like higher stakes. I'll raise your bid ten more, Mollie." No one flinches again.

To ripen the pot, they're playing seven-card stud, and the last card is down. Two pair on the table bids ten dollars. Mollie locks eyes with Murry, almost daring him to raise it higher. And he says. "I'll see your bid, Johnny, and raise you twenty." Mollie proudly smiles at her table full of men and the pile of cash in the middle.

Behind the slatted door, Kelly has to cover her mouth while she shakes her head as she sees her grandfather and his best church buddy, Oscar. Laura Ann gives her that mother stare to calm her down. Linda Gail's eyes are big and wide with anticipation of the unknown as she is amazed at how comfortable Mollie is with a table full of men.

"Gentlemen, this is where I want to make tonight exciting," Mollie seductively tells them as she slowly pushes her chair from the table. All five gentlemen stand, and the bartender pulls her chair out to assist her. That is the signal for the piano to slowly begin. Mollie makes eye contact with each man. As she passes by, she tenderly touches each man's shoulders, and she begins to sway with the tunes. "You know, gentlemen, that I'm no longer in the sex business, but tonight I give you my final performance as an entertainer in closing one chapter in my life and opening new chapters for others."

The music picks up, and Mollie skips and twirls around the table to the joyful sounds of a slow "Dixie." The singer and the pianist both pause to let Herman play a long, seductive solo as only he can do. Mollie steps on the small stage in front of the fire with her back to the men. With one hand, she lifts her hair off of her back, pulling it forward to her front. With the other hand, she pulls the tie of the halter dress at her neck, and it drops to the floor, exactly the way Virginia designed it to fall many years ago. You can hear the sighs of the men over the music as they get their first look at the beautiful, totally nude body of Madam Mollie Teal from behind.

Over in the pantry, Linda Gail whispers to Laura Ann, "Mollie still has the body of a twenty-year-old, with long lean legs, a plump round bottom, and perky breasts."

Laura Ann quietly says, "Shush. You're going to get us caught. We can talk later."

Mollie begins to sway this way and that way. She moves her hands down her sides and her hips. Then she takes her long light-blond hair and lets it flow down her back. All the while, her hands are moving to the silhouette of her body. As the music changes, she begins to turn her front side to the men. Then her hips start to move forward and at the same time from side to side. Mollie's hands move as if to show them where to look, and they really do look. She uses her hands again, and they circle around both breasts without touching them. One hand goes straight up into her hair, pulling it high and then letting it fall over her nipples. Her hips never stop moving in the shape of two circles...more like the shape of the number eight.

All of a sudden, she turns her bottom back to the men and stands on the tips of her heels, and she begins shifting her weight back and forth, faster and faster. Her entire body begins to shake and shimmy. The men are all afraid to blink for fear that they might miss something. The music gets faster, and so does Mollie. She can feel the desires of the men who want to grab handfuls of her beautiful bottom. She turns her bare chest to the men, gets closer, and begins to spin in a circle with her blond hair chasing behind. Mollie knows this is too much for any man.

The bartender replaces the empty drinks as she turns back around in her high heels and dances from her heart. After the solo, the other musicians join back in as Mollie twirls in circles around the room, with her long hair swirling around her.

As the music stops, Mollie takes a couple bows, which are as sensuous as her dance, as the men hoot and clap. She steps back into her dress and asks Johnny to tie the dress for her. He nervously ties it while enjoying her earthy, sweet smell and watching her chest move up and down from breathing hard.

Mollie walks over to the table, sits down, takes a sip of her drink, and is ready to pick back up on the poker game as if nothing just happened. She is still not looking at her cards. "What's the bid?" she asks.

"Let's see," the dealer says, trying to get his composure back. "Bid was ten. Johnny raised it twenty, and Paul raised it twenty more, so that's fifty to you, Mollie." Mollie matches the fifty. "Pot's right," dealer says. "Last card down." Mollie has showing a nine, ten, jack, and queen—all hearts. She glances at her hold cards. With a pleasant but unreadable smile, she raises it fifty more.

With the eight and king of hearts not showing on the table, one by one each man folds, except Johnny. "I want to up it to a marriage proposal. What do you say, Mollie? Are you going to turn me down again? You make every man here want you, and now you want to play poker. Say yes, Mollie."

"Johnny, tonight's dance isn't just for your pleasure. It's for the children," Mollie says with a pouty smile.

"OK. You win, Mollie. I fold. But I'm never going to stop asking," Johnny says, undeterred by her turning him down once again.

"We know. You've been asking for years, Johnny," Jerry speaks up as he turns to Mollie. "We are honored that you shared your amazing talents with us tonight, Mollie. I will never forget your glow. I assume that well-deserved pile of cash goes where all the rest of our money goes, to the convent's orphanage in Mobile. How many children do we have there now?"

"Seventy. We provide food, clothing, and shelter for all of them in a safe, loving Christian environment. Thank you all," Mollie proudly states as she scoops the pile of cash. "You know all the orphan children from Huntsville get in first. We provide their transportation as well. I'm ready for another hand, so who's in?" The card games end at ten o'clock with a total win of over $2,000, the highest ever in one night. The men don't particularly mind losing to beautiful Mollie. However, they sometimes wondered how she won so often.

Paul is the last out the door. "Mollie, I believe you're a lucky charm. It's always a pleasure, and tonight is the most unforgettable." He places something in her palm. She secures the big door with chains and locks. Sissy is staying with her aging father tonight.

Mollie goes straight to the kitchen to see the ladies. She shows them an exquisite diamond in her hand, and then she lets them see the secret drawer in her library with a pile of proposal rings she has received. Boy, did they have questions for the next hour, with Kelly writing everything down word for word in her secret diary.

Laura Ann is the last out the back door. She says, "Mollie, you are truly a beautiful woman. Your body looks the same as it did the first day we played on the beach together. But what I find the most impressive is how you handle yourself so comfortably and confidently around a table full of men. You're amazing, I finally figured out why God put you in this business."

They hug and say their goodbyes. Mollie double-locks and chains the back door. Then, like always, she checks the locks on the windows before heading upstairs to bed—a habit she has kept since Molly was almost kidnapped.

She smiles to herself, thinking about her little girl and their upcoming trip to California.

Mollie climbs into bed and doesn't notice the rope on the bedpost. She has a hard time falling asleep. With her eyes closed, she replays the day's activities in her head. The convent will be thrilled with her donation. Her eyes pop wide open as she remembers that there was only one person in the delivery wagon when it left today, but there were two men bringing in the groceries.

Too late! By the time she sits up, a man in the dark has grabbed her wrist. He quickly ties her to the bedpost after he shoves a cloth into her mouth to keep her from screaming. He turns the lamp back up so that she can see him. "Now I'm going to teach you a lesson, you little whore. Never turn me down again." he says as he turns her head to let her see his knife collection. "I'm going to use every one of these on you, slowly slicing you up, you whore. No one will care or believe you over me."

He begins to cut her nightgown at the neck and straight to the bottom and opens it up to Mollie's bare body. "I saw your slut performance tonight, teasing all those horny men and taking all their money. I'll take that money tonight before I leave, too, along with all your hair. First, you're going show me a good time."

Mollie is terrified as he hastily unbuttons his pants as she sees his sores from syphilis. While he assaults her, he says, "I'm going to find your daughter next. Did you know that? I'm going to make her into my very own little whore."

Mollie couldn't fight until this point, but now her blood is boiling with rage. She uses her hip to thrust against his body, hard enough to throw him off. She then lands her knee directly between his legs, and he falls off the side of the bed, pulling her with him. The weight of the both of them snaps the bedpost and Mollie's wrist. He clamps his large hand around her throat and chokes her. Barely breathing, and with her hands still tied to the broken post, she grabs the broken piece of the bedpost with her good hand and begins slamming his head over and over until he stops moving. Finally, she collapses on top of him.

⋙⋘

Sissy, the early bird, arrives at the back door before sunrise and notices that the light is on in Mollie's bedroom upstairs. She knows that it's odd for Mollie to be up this early. She places the key in the first lock and then the next, but the chain stops her from getting through the door. She finds the same situation at the front door and decides to ring the bell. No answer. She rings the bell and knocks. She knows something is wrong and starts running to the carriage house. There she screams, "Herman! Herman! Wake up! It's Mollie! Something's wrong, Herman." She reaches the door and starts pounding and screaming as loud as she can, waking up all the house staff.

Herman hears her, throws on his pants, picks up his gun, and heads up to the main house with frantic Sissy while telling her, "Sissy, calm down! I watched all the poker players leave, and then Laura Ann and two others left out the back. Mollie locked all the doors and windows, and I rechecked them from the outside. Maybe she doesn't hear the door. That's all it can be, Sissy," Herman says as he tries to act calm himself.

"Herman, I hope I'm wrong, but bust down the hidden door anyhow. Now! I don't feel her in my heart. Something is really wrong!"

They quickly run up the secret stairs and slide the wall open. Nothing in the world could prepare the two for what they see in Mollie's bedroom. Sissy opens her mouth and lets out the most high-pitched, bloodcurdling scream as she sees two slumped bodies on the blood-soaked rug. They gently lift Mollie's body onto the bed. She is alive, but the man is dead from a crushed skull. Sissy orders one of the staff to go fetch Dr. Lowry immediately as she tries to clean Mollie as best as she can.

Herman recognizes the man and says, "What a sick psycho." Herman tosses the knives and bloody bedding on top of the body and rolls it up in the rug. "Society will never believe Mollie over him. I'll bury him in the slave cemetery before the sun comes up."

Mollie's longtime friend the sheriff spends all day and night scouring through the grounds looking for evidence of the attacker. Dr. Lowry spends all day tending to Mollie. He resets her broken nose, puts both wrists in splints, and tightly wraps her rib cage in bandages as he tries to keep her comfortable with high doses of morphine and ice on her swollen face, chest, and arms.

As Mollie struggles to wake up, the doctor speaks to her gently, "Baby, I need you to stay still. A monster hurt you really bad, and I'm trying to fix it."

Again she attempts to say something as she yelps in pain at her broken ribs. "The monster is going to take my baby. Go find her, Sissy."

She drifts back out. "I'm here," Sissy says as she holds ice on Mollie's face. "He won't be taking anybody's baby. You took care of that. He's dead. Little Molly is OK. Mollie, wake up. Do I need to go to Nashville and get her for you? Will that make you feel better?"

Mollie opens her eyes and mumbles, "Thanks, but I can't let Molly see me like this."

The next morning, Sissy and Herman check on Mollie. Mollie is only slightly better but manages to talk a little before they leave her room, Mollie whispers to them in an almost inaudible voice, "I need to talk to my attorney."

"What? What did you say?" Sissy asks. "You want to talk with Septimus? Honey, you're in no condition to talk much with anybody. Let's wait a few days."

"Tomorrow. Tomorrow morning," Mollie demands with all her strength, and then slips back to sleep." Septimus comes every morning for the next three days, hoping to find Mollie awake. On the third morning, she is up in her bed, somewhat alert, and waiting for him.

"Septimus, thank you for coming," she says.

"Mollie, I would do anything for you. They say you are getting better," Septimus tells her as he thinks, *How could anyone do this to such a kind, loving woman?*

Mollie asks one of the maids to go get Sissy and Herman. Being just outside the door, they both step into the room before the maid can turn around. "We're here, Mollie," they tell her.

"Thank you. Septimus, I need for you to draw up adoption papers for Ivan and Anne to adopt my daughter, Molly."

"Are you sure, Mollie?" he asks.

"Yes, I've been thinking about it since I woke up from this nightmare. I saw the syphilis sores on him, and I know chances are I will get it…What do I have, seven years or so? I won't see her tenth birthday. She needs a mother.

"Besides, I don't want my Molly to grow to be in or around this business. My life has been an adventure, and I wouldn't change anything, but I want my daughter to have a normal life, a family with kids and grandchildren. I can't let little Grace, Percy, and Chase be exposed to this business. I know she would disapprove of what I'm doing, but it wouldn't be fair to Laura Ann."

"I need for everyone who knows of Molly to keep this secret. That includes you, Dr. Lowry," she says, seeing that he is now in the room.

He looks sad and, with a forced smile, says, "What daughter?"

"I will provide a monthly allowance. I ask that Ivan comes to Huntsville or anyplace we agree and pick up the monthly allowance and bring me a picture of Molly and bring me up to date on her life. I may visit from time to time under the guise that I'm traveling, but Anne will be her mother."

Septimus agrees to have the agreement by the following afternoon, and Herman and Sissy will deliver it to Ivan and Anne the next day and explain the situation to them. Mollie knows that Anne loves Molly and is sure they will adopt her.

Ivan and Anne are sorry to hear about Mollie's assault but excited when they learn of the adoption. They explain to little Molly that Grandmother will be coming back soon and she sends all her love. As a three-year-old, little Molly thinks her world is normal.

Mollie is getting better, and for a while she is optimistic that she just may have a full recovery. Then Dr. Lowry walks in with more devastating news. "Mollie, I was concerned about the swelling in your neck and armpits. Upon my examination of you this morning, my diagnosis is syphilis. It normally is fatal within seven years or less. I'll begin your treatment with mercury right away. Regular use of Cuticura soap may help your skin to feel better when the sores appear, but that's about all I can offer. I wish I could do more for you, but there is nothing that we have that is effective now." Mollie doesn't respond. She is worried about her beautiful daughter, Molly.

Dr. Lowry continues to treat Mollie the best that he knows how to do. Mollie turns the business over to Sissy and maintains a low profile while reading and traveling...under the guise of traveling that always ends up in Nashville, where she plays the role of Grandmother.

Mollie appears on the surface to have recovered. She is happy and enjoys the monthly visits from Ivan to bring her up to date on

Molly. She gladly hands him the monthly allowance each time he leaves.

One month Ivan doesn't show up. Mollie is worried that something is wrong. She is not feeling good anyway because the syphilis is starting to take hold, and she asks Herman to take the carriage and hurry to Nashville. "Take Sissy with you," she says.

When Herman and Sissy arrive at the rented cottage in Nashville, the landlord is there feeding a starving dog. "I got a visit from the tenant next door to report this dog barking nonstop. I know the lady's husband suddenly died a couple weeks ago. So I knock. After no one answers, I go in. It's like she and the little girl just vanished. Food is on the stove, the table is set for breakfast, and nothing is packed. It's not like her to disappear and not tell anyone." Sissy looks around and says, "No pictures or paintings of the family anywhere. All gone."

Upon immediately knocking door to door, the two learn that a neighbor had seen two men. She remembered that one had yelled, "You're crazy, little sister, and I have the papers here to commit you." It was the only lead they had, but it paid off. After checking a few insane asylums, Herman and Sissy find that Anne Overton Teal was recently a patient at Cedar Craft Sanatorium, and the staff there is angry that her brother came with a court order signed by Judge W. T. Lawler, of Huntsville, Alabama, to take her, and he didn't even pay the bill. No word about where he took her. The two look for a couple of weeks, checking insane hospitals in Tennessee and North Alabama, to come up with nothing.

When they return to Huntsville, Sissy gives Molly the heartbreaking news about Molly missing and no sign of Anne anywhere. She also tells her that it appears her cousin Ivan is dead.

As soon as Mollie is able to think clearly, she hires the sheriff to privately look into David Overton's whereabouts. She learns that he has taken leave from the police department and is traveling overseas indefinitely.

Mollie's at a desperate point and decides no one will look for her daughter harder or longer than her beloved Palmer. She writes a heartfelt letter and apologizes for assuming he would not accept and forgive her of her past but that she really needs his help finding their daughter before she dies. "Sissy, please take this letter to the post office. Palmer will find her. He won't stop until he finds the daughter he doesn't know exists."

Sissy takes the letter right away to the downtown post office. Fourteen-year-old Suzette Miller is helping her aunt and uncle at the post office and takes the letter and drops it in the out-of-town mailbag. When Sissy leaves, nosy Suzette takes the letter out of the bag, opens it, and reads it because it's from Huntsville's notorious Mollie Teal. Instead of putting the letter back in the bag, she puts it in her pocket to read again later.

The letter is never sent. Neither are any of the other letters Mollie sends to Captain Palmer Graham. Finally, Mollie stops writing Palmer, concluding he wants nothing to do with an illegitimate daughter by a prostitute. He was not the man she thought he was about his child.

Mollie's will to stay alive is driven by the need to find her daughter. However, her disease has something else in mind. It's April 1899, and Mollie sees Dr. Lowry every day now for her mercury treatments.

He likes for Mollie to be his last patient of the day so that they can continue their long-term friendship. He enjoys her intellect and her strong passion for others. Except for her still-missing daughter, despite what life has brought her way, Mollie has an extraordinary attitude of happiness at which the doctor marvels.

They discuss how difficult it is for him and other doctors when they have more than one trauma patient at once. His aging parents live in his home, and his office is too small to adequately treat the many ills of Huntsville's citizens. He says, "Huntsville is large enough to support a hospital to take better care of patients such as yourself."

Mollie says, "That reminds me—I need to make a will before my brain becomes affected."

To Mollie's surprise, the doctor blurts out, "Mollie, I'm going to miss you. I don't know if you know this, but over the years…" He pauses. "You need to know that you have my heart. I think I'm in love. Funny, I know, and we have never even kissed. Now it's too late. You're at the very contagious stage of syphilis."

Mollie smiles and says, "I've always enjoyed our time together. I feel like you and I do have something special. You may have a small crush. You're a man, but rules are rules, and you're not allowed to fall in love with someone such as myself. Besides, you know this disease is horrible to watch the physical appearance change so drastically in the final stages. I know. I watched it with my mother—probably the reason she chose to get addicted to morphine and let that kill her instead."

"Mollie, you should know that when it comes to matters of the heart, you don't get a lot of choice. The heart wants what it wants. I propose that for the time we have together, you allow me to love you until your death. I know we will never be able to intimately touch, but it's your heart and mind that I have fallen for anyway," the doctor says as he gazes deeply into her still-beautiful blue eyes.

CHAPTER 50

MOLLIE'S WILL

Laura Ann practically lives at Mollie's house and approves of the doctor's attention and affection. This is the very first year since she's been a volunteer at the convent that she has not gone. With Laura Ann's assistance, Mollie puts on the new smaller-sized dress that Virginia has made for her. She insists on going to Dr. Lowry's office every day for her treatment.

Laura Ann, CC, and Herman are grateful for Mollie's generosity in selling her ownership of all their mutual business partnerships for one dollar plus taxes and closing costs. Mollie also donates her shares of Dallas Mills stock to the Saint Mary of the Visitation Catholic Church, the only church that didn't run her out.

The bulk of her cash she gives to Sissy and the convent in Mobile. Dr. Lowry receives a generous amount for the health care of her girls and others in need as does Mollie's protector, the sheriff, for continuing the search for Molly. Mollie's girls and the house and grounds staff all receive a considerable amount as well.

Mollie insists on having a farewell dinner with Dr. Lowry, Sissy, Herman, Laura Ann, CC, and the sheriff before her face begins to deteriorate. At dinner, without saying anything, Mollie places her daddy's saxophone in front of Herman and smiles in her special way. Then she picks up the old jar with all the original betrayal money from the night her mother sold her and gives it to Sissy, saying, "Sissy, it is just a token amount, but as I have forgiven my mother, the money is not tainted anymore. It just represents a path that God for some reason wanted me to take—and looking across the table at all of you...he was right. Use it to help someone."

She has the table arranged so there is an obvious distance between her and the guests. "Sheriff...Oscar, I'm so glad you could join my family for dinner this evening. As I mentioned earlier, I want your very creditable name as author of my will so that it won't be contested by one of my many illegitimate so-called family members. For added insurance, I've named the mayor and probate judge as my executors so nothing will go wrong.

"Family and friends, thank you for joining me this evening. As all of you know, I'm giving away my fortune before my death. I've had too many lawyers steal and double-cross me over the years, and I'm not about to let it happen to all of you after my death. I'm only leaving enough money in my account to take care of any unpaid affairs. The lawyers will squander most of it anyway." She pulls open a hidden drawer and pours the contents in the middle of the table. "All of these engagement rings and jewelry were given to me by silly men who didn't know any better. Some are from army officers that lived here after the war and are most likely stolen."

Mollie picks up one of the rings and clutches it in her hand. "This one is not the largest, but it has been with me on a long journey...a sweet, loving gay man gave it to me."

Mollie comes out of her reflection. "Laura Ann, you're being very quiet. Will you divide them up among you? One last thing to share with you—it's the house. My will..." She holds up the papers in her white-gloved hands, "I'm leaving my house to the city of Huntsville to be used as a hospital. Our city desperately needs it, and Dr. Lowry will make a fine leader of such an endeavor.

"Sissy will have the right of survivorship, to live here until her death, with enough money and gold to take care of my daughter when she is found. Please, all of you never stop praying and looking for Molly. I'm dying of a broken heart, not just syphilis."

Mollie needs three witnesses. The bashful plumber knocks on the wall as he enters the room. "Madam, it is my pleasure as always to work at your house. You're the only residential home in Huntsville that has indoor plumbing."

Rather than let the intrusion irritate her, Mollie welcomes him into the room. "Thank you for your excellent work. It's so nice having a plumber as a neighbor. Will you stay for just a minute and be a witness to me signing my last Will and Testament? I just need to get two others." She walks into the hall and waves for two of her hardest-working ladies to come toward her. "Thank you, ladies, for visiting and bringing me vegetables from your garden. Can I get you two to witness me signing my last will?"

"Oh, Mollie, this is too hard to believe. I'm going to miss you. You have always been so good to me and my children. Yes, we'll both sign as a witness."

Mollie signs the document "Mollie Teal" and then the plumber signs "Terrance O'Reilly," and the two prostitutes sign "Flora Barker" and "Eva Gray."

Mollie thanks the three out on the porch. As she leaves, she hears Eva say, "Hey, young fella, want to have some fun with the two of us?"

Mollie returns to the table and thanks the sheriff for drawing up the will. Sissy says, "What did I ever do to deserve you in my life, Mollie? You are so generous—to all of us."

Mollie shakes her head and smiles at Dr. Lowry. "No, you're wrong, Sissy. I'm the lucky one to have a table full of people who love me."

—◁+ +▷—

Sissy slowly comes out of her trancelike state and looks out over the court. The gavel does not strike this time. There is not a dry eye in the courtroom. The judge takes off his glasses, pretending that he has something in his eye. "Miss Sissy, thank you for your testimony, and I would have overruled any objection," the judge says to the applause in the courtroom. "Let's break early and thank the Lord at an on-time supper tonight." The judge calls for the court to reconvene the next morning.

Sissy walks out of the courthouse. At the top of the steps, a spectator who was in the courtroom audience runs up to her, saying, "It was Clyde Overton, wasn't it? You know, that Mollie killed?"

"Clyde Overton?" Sissy replies. "Last thing I heard about him was that he had gone to Dallas." Sissy smiles, knowing exactly where Clyde Overton is...he is buried facedown in the black cemetery on the south side of town.

CHAPTER 51

THE FUNERAL

On September 24, 1899, Madam Mollie Teal passes at the age of forty-seven—or is it forty-nine? Although Mollie has donated to every religious denomination in Huntsville, especially the Catholic Church, none of them will officiate the funeral.

Not all is lost as Reverend James McCoy of Birmingham Methodist comes to Huntsville and has the funeral for a small group of Mollie's friends at her house and those who worked for her. No politician, judge, law enforcement officer, business owner, or any clients attend, except the sheriff.

If Mollie can hear all the secret confessions of love that day, it will make her happy, but even she must be surprised at the confession from the preacher, who whispers to her, "Mollie, it's me, Jesse. Do you like how I use James in my fake name? I told you I wanted to go straight, so I went to God for answers, and he led me to be a preacher, just like my daddy.

"My faked murder was the best thing I could have ever done. I've already dug up the guy, so when it's my turn to go, my place is ready. Mollie, I told you I would love you until the day you die, and here I am weeping over your bones. My beauty, may God bring us together again in heaven."

At the grave site, Mollie has already had Baker and Conway Monuments make her tombstone, minus the death date. CC and all watch as Herman soulfully plays "Dixie" on her daddy's saxophone for the last time.

CHAPTER 52

ALABAMA SUPREME COURT, 1903

Four years after Mollie dies, Sissy walks up the steps of the Alabama State Capitol in Montgomery, Alabama. It's a Greek Revival style with Beaux-Arts influences. The front facade is 350 feet wide and 119 feet tall from the ground level to the top of the dome.

Today the five justices will announce the verdict of the appealed case of the last Will and Testament of Madam Mollie Teal and Celia Hall, the woman claiming to be next of kin. Sissy walks in early to an already crowded courtroom, smoking a cigarette and coughing as usual. She wonders about Molly, who would be thirteen years old now if she's still alive.

Ceiling fans pull the heavy smoke up, over the low roar of the crowded courtroom. The Alabama Supreme Court justices are scheduled to deliver the verdict today, the tenth day of July 1903, for the case of *Mayor and Alderman of the City of Huntsville, Alabama v. Celia Hall*, regarding the estate of Madam Mollie Teal. In the past few days, with the adamant objections of all parties involved, the justices have had two witnesses before the court in chambers—the plumber and the resident of the house in question.

Finally the fifth justice votes, leading to the case being passed back to the Chancery Court in Morgan County, where the final decision is made. The will stands as written. Those there will recall, "It was over after the plumber testified."

Chancery Court rules that Celia Hall, as Mollie's aunt, is to inherit any personal property not named as going to the city in the residence. That personal property includes the remaining cash plus some gold and diamonds of unspecified value.

Most believe that, if alive, Mollie would have denied she had an Aunt Celia. In fact, Ms. Hall started out in court saying she was Mollie's cousin and during court proceedings changed the relationship to aunt. Many speculate the court turned its eye to this blatant flip because many of the others making claims as being a relative of Mollie were "undesirable" characters taken advantage of by unscrupulous lawyers.

Was Mollie's claim of having no relatives in Tennessee correct? No one will ever know. The very day the court rules for Celia Hall to get everything except that which was clearly willed to the City of Huntsville and Sissy Greenleaf, she mysteriously dies...and her attorney gets it all. Fortunately, Mollie didn't totally trust attorneys and gave away most of her estate before she died.

No one will ever know how rich Mollie actually was. None of the many people claiming her as family associated with her in her life, but they sure had their hands out after she died. These are strange times in Alabama...one might say Alabama life and politics are wild, somewhat lawless and corrupt. Perhaps there is a simple explanation...poetic justice.

⇒┼⇐

Months later, on a bitterly cold winter night, Sissy walks into Mollie's favorite room, the library, now barren, lights another cigarette, and the horrible coughing starts up again. The room seems to represent how she feels inside. All of Mollie's books were donated to the public schools to be used in their libraries. She's glad she invited the sheriff over earlier that day to give him all of Mollie's gold to give her daughter, Molly one day.

Later in the evening, she is sitting on a pillow in her rocking chair in front of a roaring fire, with Mollie's portrait above her head. She opens the jar of betrayal money. The stench makes her feel Mollie's pain from thirty-nine years ago. She puts the money in an envelope and addresses it to the convent in Mobile. A smile comes to her face as she thinks, *Mollie keeps on giving long after she's gone.*

That night, she reads the diary of Madam Mollie Teal for the last time and stares at the Civil War–era photo of Mollie. Then, as she promised Mollie she would, she drops the picture in the fire and watches the edges start to burn and smoke. Gradually she sees Mollie's face fade away. Then she carefully places the diary in the flames too. It smokes and pops as slowly the flames engulf the words and memories of Madam Mollie Teal.

Sissy lays her head back and goes to sleep for the last time, not knowing that little Molly is just blocks away at 420 Echols Hill in Huntsville, Alabama, at the home of Loretta and David Overton.

Fate has a funny and unexplainable way of repeating itself sometimes. Fortunately, God does not give us more than what he knows we can take, and little Molly is a survivor, just like her mother.

CHAPTER 53
HUNTSVILLE HOSPITAL, 1904

I t's a steaming-hot July day, and after months of renovations, a ribbon-cutting celebration is held at the new Huntsville Hospital. Mollie's loved ones, Laura Ann, CC, Herman, Dr. Lowry, and the sheriff, are so proud to witness her final wishes become reality. The sheriff says, "We all just wanted Mollie's last wishes to come true, and now they have. That's all that matters."

Herman turns to CC and says, "We did as God directed us. We protected Mollie to our best ability. What do we do now that she's gone?"

CC smiles and replies, "We go on just as God and Mollie would want. We live life while trying to help others, as Mollie did."

"Yeah," Herman says, almost ready to cry, "CC, I miss her so much!"

"We all do, Herman. We all do," is all CC can say.

The new facility contains seven patient rooms, two rooms for nurses, a modern kitchen, and more bathrooms. A fee is charged to those who can pay, but the hospital treats the sick of the community, regardless of their financial circumstances.

During a very successful first year, 112 patients are treated, and a profit of $1,820 is made, making it possible to add on more patient rooms, an operating room, a sterilizing room, a physician's office, a private examination room, and a physician dressing room. The hospital serves the community for the next twenty-two years until a new larger facility is built on the property.

Huntsville Hospital today is a renowned medical complex serving Huntsville, North Alabama, and the southeastern region. It is apparent that Huntsville's health care community owes at least some of its initial success to a madam—Madam Mollie Teal.

THE END

ACKNOWLEDGMENTS

God helps me "Keep the Faith" on my life's journey, by believing in a higher power, which helped me find my purpose. As in my first novel, *The Doughnut Tree*, John Rankin, author and local Alabama historian, gave me the guidance and encouragement to write a second book. His in-depth knowledge and passion for Alabama history helped me sift through the vast amount of information found in the Madison County Records Center, old court records and newspapers was paramount in my historical, fictional romance novel. Next on my grateful list is Forest, my husband, who, after two novels, is still my best friend, and editing coordinator. Although my computer skills have drastically improved, he props me up, and is my number one cheerleader and encourager as I operate out of one box. Then there's Rich Ortiz, ONEUNITY Media who handles all my public communications, social media promotions and overall media support and was responsible for the book cover. Special thanks goes out to Donna Rovere, for allowing me to use her fabulous Straight Egyptian Arabian horse, Deevine Intervention, for the cover shot. I fell in love with this beautiful creature. Many thanks to all my friends that continue to give me support and encouragement... you know who you are. Of course, I still have Sugar...eighty-seven pounds of unconditional love under my feet as I write. Cheers.

Made in the USA
Columbia, SC
04 February 2020

87500522R00219